POWER,
SEDUCTION
& SCANDAL

Also by Angela Winters

View Park series

View Park
Never Enough
No More Good
A Price to Pay
Gone Too Far

D.C. series

Back on Top
Almost Doesn't Count
Nothing to Lose

Published by Dafina Books

POWER, SEDUCTION & SCANDAL

ANGELA WINTERS

Dafina
BOOKS

KENSINGTON PUBLISHING CORP.
www.kensingtonbooks.com

DAFINA BOOKS are published by

Kensington Publishing Corp.
119 West 40th Street
New York, NY 10018

All Kensington titles, imprints, and distributed lines are available at special quantity discounts for bulk purchases for sales promotion, premiums, fundraising, and educational or institutional use.

Special book excerpts or customized printings can also be created to fit specific needs. For details, write or phone the office of the Kensington Special Sales Manager: Kensington Publishing Corp., 119 West 40th Street, New York, NY 10018. Attn. Special Sales Department. Phone: 1-800-221-2647.

Dafina and the Dafina logo Reg. U.S. Pat. & TM Off.

ISBN-13: 978-0-7582-8659-8
ISBN-10: 0-7582-8659-7
First Kensington Trade Paperback Printing: December 2014

eISBN-13: 978-0-7582-8661-1
eISBN-10: 0-7582-8661-9
First Kensington Electronic Edition: December 2014

10 9 8 7 6 5 4 3 2 1

Printed in the United States of America

POWER,
SEDUCTION
& SCANDAL

1

Sherise Robinson took a look around and had to smile. At thirty, she was sitting on luxurious leather seats in the back of a driven car on her way to a meeting where she was going to be named one of the most powerful, influential people in the country. Not bad for a girl from the mean streets of Southeast D.C. who no one believed would ever amount to anything.

She checked her makeup mirror even though she didn't have to. She looked flawless. Her golden caramel skin was glowing against her silky dark brown hair that she'd recently cut to a few inches below her shoulders, adding more sophistication. She had perfect high cheekbones and full, sultry lips, but the highlight of her face was her piercing green eyes.

Her face and those dangerous curves framing her fit body created an image of beauty that Sherise used to her advantage. She wasn't afraid to admit that. She could make a man give her anything she wanted and make a woman concede defeat just at the sight of her.

But looks alone could never have gotten her where she was today; about to be named the press secretary to the next president of the United States of America. She'd worked her ass off for that.

Yes, she played dirty at times to get what she wanted, and to keep it. That was just the game of power and politics in D.C. She'd learned to play it as a teenager when she'd gotten her first internship at the Department of Agriculture. She was just making copies, but she made sure to leave an impression by being faster, more organized, and more presentable than anyone else. Sherise knew what most sixteen-year-olds didn't: in D.C., presentation mattered more than substance. She parlayed that into a college scholarship and several jobs on Capitol Hill.

Meeting and marrying an up-and-coming lobbyist didn't hurt at all, but Sherise put in the work and made a name for herself as one of the best message people in D.C. Her position in the communications department of the White House led to a job for popular Maryland Governor Jerry Northman's campaign as the Democratic candidate for president. He won the primaries and finally, two weeks ago, with Sherise running his communications, he won the highest office in the land.

And to think, just a year ago, it almost all fell apart. Everything was on the brink of being lost . . . everything.

She closed the mirror and placed it in her Furla purse. She had to always look perfect now that she was constantly in front of the camera, her face on newspapers and websites. She made sure her staff, now totalling five full-time and two interns, always looked perfect as well.

Her staff wouldn't be at this meeting she was on her way to at the campaign headquarters for Jerry. She'd gotten the message this morning when LaKeisha Wilson, Jerry's campaign manager, texted her and only other core team members to come in for an announcement. It was just a formality. Everyone knew that Sherise would be named PS for the new administration, but she couldn't help but be excited.

The phone rang with that familiar ring tone reserved for the one person who made Sherise's heart light up. It was her husband, Justin, the father of her two children and the love of her life. She didn't even want to think that, a year ago, their marriage was barely holding on by a string after it was revealed that they had both been unfaithful and their oldest child might not be his. That Cady turned out to be his helped make their attempt to reconcile go a lot smoother than it would have otherwise. They'd weathered some horrible storms, but got through them.

Now their marriage was stronger than it had ever been. Sherise never hid from the fact that, although she loved Justin, she married him for the advantages he gave her. Over time, she'd lost sight of how good a husband he was and made some terrible mistakes. One of those mistakes came back to haunt her in the worst way, and Justin strayed. She'd gotten him back. She knew she would. Sherise refused to give up anything that mattered.

Now marrying for advantages was out the window. She loved the hell out of that man and appreciated him for everything he was. Her career had always been her priority, but she would give it up, even a position as powerful as PS to the president, for her husband and her two babies.

"What you doing, hot stuff?" he asked in a playful tone.

Sherise smiled. "On my way to the meeting. You know that. You saw me leave."

"I know where you're going, smartass," he responded. "I want to know what you're doing."

"Just checking out how hot I look in my mirror," she answered. "Why? Did you want me to say I was thinking about you and touching myself?"

"Considering how well I took care of things this morning," his voice shifted from playful to serious in a split second, "I expected you to still be trying to cool yourself down."

"Oh my God, the ego on you, boy." She laughed. "You start your own business and now you think you're cock of the walk."

It was true that he'd been great in bed this morning, and the night before. Their sex life was better than ever. Justin had a new confidence now that he'd left the lobbying firm he worked at and started his own. A false claim of sexual harassment against him turned the firm that he'd made millions for against him. After the truth came out, they were all apologies, but Justin had made up his mind.

Only three of his clients followed him, but in the last eight months, he'd gotten five more. He had an assistant and an intern and was about to hire a new lobbyist to join him. He was doing well and future prospects were all positive. With a new baby on the way, it was a risk, but it paid off. His confidence was through the roof and Sherise was reaping the benefits in their bank account and their bedroom.

Justin laughed in the self-assured tone of a thirty-three-year-old man who knew he made well with his life. "So we're celebrating tonight?"

"I know what you mean by celebrate," she said. "You trying to get me pregnant again?"

"God forbid." He laughed. "I think you've made it clear that the baby factory is closed after Aiden."

Aiden, their six-month-old son, was perfect in every way. He was starting to develop his unique personality traits and Sherise couldn't love him more. Their older child, Cady, was almost three now and as stubborn and difficult as ever, just like her mama. They had a perfect family now, made only more precious considering it had all almost fallen apart.

"We both barely have enough time for the kids we have now," Sherise said. "You know how guilty I feel with two babies and working nonstop?"

"You've been on a presidential campaign," Justin said. "You couldn't pass up this chance of a lifetime. We made it work."

"It's not changing any time soon," she regretfully admitted. "Ugh, how did we get on this topic? You wanted to celebrate?"

"Sorry," he said. "Jeniah is at home with the kids and she

said she can stay until about nine tonight. I'll try and knock off early and we can just have a quick dinner somewhere nearby."

Jeniah was the nanny they'd hired just before Sherise gave birth. With her working on the campaign and Justin working overtime at the new business, there was no other choice but to bring someone in the house. Taking the kids to a daycare or a sitter was no longer feasible.

"You knocking off early? The tide is turning?" she asked.

"The calm before the storm," he said. "All the new elections. Everyone has decompressed and it's about to get crazy, so we better take it while we can."

"I don't know how long I'll be, but you've got a date." She felt the car stop. "Oh, I think we're here. I've gotta go, baby. I love you."

"I love you more," he answered back before hanging up.

Sherise smiled and took a heavy sigh. She waited for the driver to come around and open the door for her. As she stepped out in front of headquarters, everyone on the sidewalk stopped to take a look. Maybe one or two of them might have recognized her, but most were just staring at the beautiful young woman in the sharply tailored heather gray suit who looked like she'd been stepping out of driven cars her entire life.

If they only knew.

Billie Carter leaned her petite frame over the balcony overlooking the Atlanta skyline as the day was coming to life. It was only her third day in the city, but she was starting to fall in love with it. This was mostly attributed to the personal guide she'd had since arriving. That same guide came up behind her, wrapped his arms around her, and placed his head on her shoulder.

She turned her head slightly to the right and his lips met hers with a tender morning kiss that warmed her chocolate body underneath the silk bathrobe she was wearing. She turned around to face him, their lips still touching as she wrapped her arms around his neck and gently caressed the back of his head.

"I'm mad at you," Michael said slowly as their lips parted. "I don't like waking up with you not next to me."

Michael Johnson was the man of Billie's dreams and she'd almost lost him. They'd had a chance encounter on a train in D.C. and all she could see was a six-foot Adonis with cocoa skin, deep black eyes, thick dark eyebrows, and a smile that made her lose her balance. But when her stop came, she got off and thought she'd never see him again.

When she'd formally met the thirty-six-year-old executive headhunter just a few days later, it wasn't under the best circumstances. She was just trying to get her career as an attorney, which had derailed, back on track with a new job at Agencis. Agencis was one of Michael's clients, and he'd wanted someone else to have the job she'd gotten.

They got off to a bad start, but Michael was determined to break the ice that Billie had formed around her heart after having it broken by a cheating ex-husband and a lover who turned out to be a secret drug dealer. Her inability to get past the awful ex-husband almost cost her Michael's love, but she fought for him in the end, the way he'd fought for her in the beginning, and they made it through.

A year later, they were going strong and head over heels in love. Billie had never thought she'd experience this again. She was convinced her chance had passed. Yet here she was in the arms of this handsome devil.

She pouted and kissed his nose. "Poor baby. I'm sorry."

"Don't apologize," he said. "Just come back."

He took her hand and tried to lead her back into the bedroom of their luxury hotel suite, but she hesitated. He looked back at her, taking in the small features of her face, framed by her curly natural hair, cut close to her head. She wore her emotions on her sleeve and Michael seemed to notice.

"What's wrong?" he asked.

"I'm worried about lunch," she said. "I want things to go . . . better than before."

By before, she meant the night they'd arrived in Atlanta. It was the second time she'd met Michael's family. As his father had passed years ago, his mother, Dee Dee, and sister, Aisha, were all the family Michael had. They'd all had dinner at Michael's childhood home on the eastern side of the city.

The night had gone about as well as the first time she'd met Dee Dee and Aisha, when they came to visit Michael in D.C. four months ago. And by well, she meant not well at all. While Billie had bent over backward to be gracious to her new boyfriend's family, it was not returned. From the beginning, Dee Dee grilled her with question after question about her previous marriage. Apparently, Dee Dee still lived in the 1950s and believed that a divorced woman had to be to blame for not holding on to a man. It had gotten bad enough that a small argument had started, which Michael interrupted.

Aisha, on the other hand, had followed in Michael's activist roots. One of the things that Billie loved about Michael was that no matter how successful he'd gotten, he never forgot where he came from. He was active in the community in D.C., especially working with young black men in dire need of a role model. Billie related to him, as she spent most of her volunteering doing pro bono work, which stemmed from her past. Her father had been railroaded by the legal system and sent to jail for a crime he didn't commit. He'd died there and it had changed her forever.

But while Michael remained active helping the less fortunate, Aisha had taken it a step further. She was pretty militant and immediately pegged Billie, and her lifestyle, too bougie to be authentically black.

"Don't worry." Michael gently cupped her chin and lifted her face to meet his.

She was tiny and he was tall, always looking down at her in a way that made her feel protected . . . loved.

"Trust me," he assured her, "they will warm up. It's just how they are. How they've always been."

"I can't seem to say anything—"

The phone that suddenly rang was Michael's, which sat at the edge of the bed only ten feet away. They both looked at it and looked at each other.

"Go ahead and answer it," Billie said, knowing that Michael was seeking her okay.

"I don't have to," he said. "It can . . ."

"It could be your mother," Billie said. "If you didn't answer, she'd find a way to blame it on me."

"That's just silly." He quickly touched his finger to her nose before kissing her forehead and turning toward the phone.

It might be, she thought, but wasn't particularly far-fetched. The second meeting wasn't much different than the first. When Billie arrived in Atlanta three days ago, Dee Dee's first words were to ask Billie if she was planning to yell at her again. Billie hadn't been the first to yell in their initial argument, but apparently Dee Dee forgot that. She laughed it off, but Billie knew it was intended to insult. Aisha called her a princess twice, pretending to be friendly teasing, but the bite to her tone made it clear to Billie that she still thought she was a snob.

At thirty-one years old, Billie knew the best approach was to put on a brave face and remain as gracious as possible. She was in the woman's home, after all. But today, they were supposed to be eating lunch with them and Billie had been racking her brain trying to figure out how to make things better.

"Can you believe that?" Michael said to her as soon as she entered the bedroom. He tossed the cell phone back on the bed. "This is the third work call in as many days. Nobody respects vacation."

"Clients don't care about vacation." She fell back on the bed, loving the feel of the thick down bedding.

"That wasn't a client," Michael said. "That was my office. I need to fire someone."

Billie eyed him to see if he was serious, and it looked like he was. "That's a bit harsh. We all get called on vacation. It's not right, but it happens."

"It doesn't happen here," he said, pointing to the floor. "In Atlanta, people respect your vacation. Just another difference that makes Atlanta better than D.C."

"Don't knock D.C.," she admonished. "D.C. helped you build your agency. Most importantly, D.C. gave you this."

He watched with a wicked smile as she undid the top of her bathrobe, revealing her perfectly round, perky small breasts and flat stomach.

"I can't argue with that." He walked over and leaned on top of her on the bed.

He straddled her, leaning down so she could grab him by the collar of his robe and pull him closer.

"For all its faults," he said, "it gave me the woman I love."

Her heart leapt at his words. She would never ever get tired of hearing them and was warmed to her core at the ease with which he said them. There was no fear or hesitation.

"I love you so much," she professed, her hands coming gently to his face as she looked up at him.

"Show me," he whispered, before lowering his mouth to hers.

She closed her eyes as she tasted his lips and felt her body respond with a tingling sensation throughout. His mouth moved down to the place where her neck met her chest and she felt his tongue gently taste her soft skin. She let out as a moan as his lips kissed her again, this time lower. Then lower.

"Michael," she said, her voice already getting breathless. "The aquarium, remember? We're supposed to be going there this morning. If we start on this . . . Well, you know how long we can go."

He looked up at her, his mind already made up. "Do you want to play with fish or play with me?"

There was no need to answer. There wasn't anything she wanted more than his hands on her. And as he leaned back to remove the rest of her bathrobe, Billie had already forgotten the question.

When Erica Kent knocked on the door to her boss's office, she knew he wasn't going to be happy. She was late and the last thing she wanted was for him to think she took this job for granted. She had been arguing with her landlord over the phone because the toilet hadn't been fixed all week, and time got past her.

Still, that was no excuse and she wouldn't make any.

"Come in," he said.

She opened the door to the office of the CEO of Robinson & Associates, Justin Robinson, the husband of her best friend, Sherise, who had practically saved her life when he hired her eight months ago.

Erica was not in a good place in her life a year ago. She'd allowed herself to be suckered into working for Jonah Nolan's vice presidential campaign, believing that somehow she could have an actual relationship with the man she'd learned was her father at the age of twenty-five. He'd had a brief affair with her mother and the two parted ways with Erica's mother, who died when Erica was nineteen, choosing to keep her father's identity a secret.

He wanted to keep her a secret for the sake of his career. At the time, he was one of the highest-ranking people with the Defense Department and on the short list for the White House. Being selected as the Republican candidate for vice president in the last election was all part of the plan.

Erica wasn't part of the plan. She was often reminded of

how lucky she was. Jonah was an awful person who wielded immense power and used it to hurt anyone who crossed him. He used people, innocent people, and thought nothing of it. Jonah's complete failure as a human being was made undeniably clear to her in the worst way. She'd found out that he was also the father of Alex Gonzales, a man whose mother was a maid of Jonah's sister.

The worst part of it was that Erica and Alex had started falling for each other before finding out the truth. They'd even kissed. When the truth came out, there were no words to describe how devastated they both were. Their lives were ruined—Alex's more than Erica's because while she was still kept a secret, Alex's relationship, or the lack of one, with Jonah was declared to the world.

Erica quit her job on Jonah's campaign. Things were rough, especially with her younger brother, Nate, deciding to get a place of his own. Struggling with money had always been a part of Erica's life, but she was down to her last penny when, eight months ago, Justin came to her and offered her the job of his assistant at the new lobbying firm he was starting up. She knew this was more of a favor than a genuine request, but she made a vow to make it the best choice Justin could make for his company.

"I'm so so sorry," she said as she rushed over to his desk.

Justin looked up from his computer and reached out to get the report she'd completed. "You're lucky that the client is late for the meeting. Otherwise, I'd be in deep shit."

"I know," Erica said. "I just . . . I'm sorry. It won't happen again."

He placed the report on the desk and looked at her with an analyzing expression. "Are you okay, Erica?"

"Um . . . well, yes." Erica wondered what she looked like. "Is something wrong with me?"

The twenty-eight-year old was still the same vivacious, curvy girl she'd been since puberty. Her fair skin and light eyes high-lighted a pretty, full face. She had a girl-next-door look about her, but was now showing a little more sophistication in the way she carried herself.

"You look stressed," he said. "I need to know if this is too much for—"

"No," she insisted quickly. "This job is not too much for me. You know I've been doing admin jobs for the longest, Justin."

"This job is more than that," he said. "I know I require a lot of you, and if you think it's outside of your area . . ."

"I may not have gone to college . . ." Erica stopped herself, noticing that her tone sounded a bit defensive. Always being around people with college degrees, sometimes more than one, and not having any can make a girl that way. "I can handle it. Sorry I was late."

"Seems like everyone is late today." He glanced at his watch. "This meeting was supposed to start a half hour ago. Hopefully, it'll be quick."

"Would you like me to call them?"

"I think . . ." Just then the Skype ring came up on Justin's computer and he sighed. "Finally. It's them. It's fine, Erica. That'll be all."

"Let me know if you need anything," she said before leaving and closing the door behind her.

She needed this job. She had to make sure not to slip up. Money was extremely tight. She was paying for everything her-self. Before, it was her, her brother Nate, and her fiancé Terrell sharing the rent of a two-bedroom apartment. Then it was down to just her and Nate. Then it was just her.

It didn't seem fair, Erica thought. While her friends Sherise and Billie were able to go off to college on scholarship, Erica couldn't afford it. Nate was only twelve when their mother died and Erica had to take care of him. Neither had she found a lobbyist or lawyer to marry. The girls had loaned her money in the past, but Erica hated that. She hated being reminded that she was always the broke one.

This job paid decent enough and now that Justin was doing much better, she was promised a raise. She needed it desperately, so now was not the time to start messing up.

As she turned to enter her office just a few steps away from Justin's she heard the office doorbell. Their office, located on K Street in downtown Washington, D.C., shared a receptionist with the consulting agency next door. When she was out, the front door was locked and visitors had to ring a doorbell for Erica to let them in.

She rushed to the front of the office, toward the glass doors. When she reached them, she was pleased with what she saw. A very good-looking brother, sort of a walnut brown color, a close fade, and a finely shaven goatee, in a dark blue suit that was tailored perfectly to show that he had a large, muscled body underneath, but not too tight to make it seem like that's what he wanted you to see. He was smiling at her and he had a dimple on his left cheek.

Erica had a thing for men with dimples, but she pulled herself together and approached the door as professionally as she could.

"Can I help you?" she asked as she opened the door.

"Yes." His voice was deep and confident. "I'm Corey James. I have an appointment with Justin Robinson."

Erica had a hard time looking away from those deep eyes of his, but after a few seconds, she glanced down at her watch. "Your interview isn't until eleven. It's . . ."

"Ten thirty," he said. "I know. I didn't expect it to be so easy to get here from the Hill."

The Hill was the word used to describe Capitol Hill with the U.S. Capitol as its centerpiece. It was where Congressional staff, which Erica assumed Corey was, worked.

"He's actually running kind of behind," Erica said. "It's not his fault. A client took too . . ."

Erica realized his brows centered in a frown. He was looking at her weird and she suddenly realized why. She hadn't let him in!

"Oh!" She jumped aside, holding the door open for him to enter. "Sorry about that."

He laughed as he entered. "I was starting to worry I'd have to conduct the interview in the hallway."

"Please sit down anywhere," she directed.

The front of the office was sharply designed with a minimalist look of green and blue. The centerpiece was the large-screen television against the wall behind the receptionist desk. It was always on C-SPAN, the public affairs channel that covered Congress and the White House.

"So you're here for the associate position?" she asked as he sat down.

"Yes, I am." He had a generous smile that didn't hold back. "Are you an associate? I can tell you're not the woman I spoke to on the phone because she had a Midwestern accent."

"Don't tell her that," Erica warned as she sat down in the chair next to him. "She's from Minneapolis and hates it when people ask her about her accent. She thinks it makes her sound like a hick."

"I know the feeling," he said. "Being from Waukegan, Illinois, I got a lot of weird looks when I first moved here."

"Isn't that near Chicago?" Erica asked.

"A little less than an hour away," he answered. "Where are you from?"

"Right here in D.C.," she said. "Southeast, as a matter of fact."

She eyed him closely to gauge his reaction. D.C. snobs were predictable. If you came from Southeast D.C. you were considered ghetto no matter who you actually were. The elitist culture in the district would shun you right away. Erica wondered if Corey was a part of that culture.

But he didn't seem to react at all. Maybe he was a good actor. After all, he worked on Capitol Hill.

"Nice," he said. "I'm gonna need your help."

"With what?"

"Well." He placed his briefcase in the chair next to him. "First, I'm gonna need your name."

She laughed girlishly and was immediately embarrassed by it. "I'm sorry. My name is Erica. Erica Kent."

He held out his hand to her. She accepted and shook it firmly. His grip was strong, but not strangling. She liked it.

"Second," he said. "I'm gonna need you to show me around Southeast."

Was he asking her out? Erica didn't know how to react to this. After having been with the same man for five years, her one attempt at getting back in the saddle was with someone who turned out to be her half brother. Other than that, her dating experiences were rare and awful.

"Show you around?" she asked, trying to act unfazed. "How can you work on Capitol Hill and not know Southeast? You're in Southeast."

He shook his head. "I'm in Capitol Hill Southeast. You know that. I'm used to the hot spots to go eat and the food markets, but I don't know the real Southeast. The neighborhood. In the two years I've lived here, I've never been able to really explore the real D.C."

Erica liked what she was hearing, a man who saw past all the pretty regentrification that Capitol Hill always raved about. He wanted to learn about the D.C. that was there before people decided to bring in all the cafés and candle shops.

"You know what I'm talking about," he said. "The family joints, the dives and mom-and-pop places that the transients don't know about."

"I'd actually . . . I guess I could." So was this a date? She didn't even know this guy.

"I don't want to put you on the spot," he said, reaching into his pocket. "Here is my card. Don't worry about it now, but think about it later."

She hesitated a second before taking the card. "I'll think about it, Corey. I'll let Justin know you're here. Like I said, he's running a little behind."

"I'm good," he said, holding up his smart phone.

She went to the receptionist desk and grabbed the remote to the TV behind the desk.

"If you want, you can watch something other than C-SPAN." She handed him the remote.

"Thanks." He accepted the remote, but frowned as he looked at the television. "What is this guy doing on? I thought he disappeared."

Erica turned to the screen and felt dread at the sight of Jonah. It was stock footage of him and his now ex-wife, Juliet, standing in front of their massive Virginia house waving to the media. It was taken after Jonah was named as the vice presidential candidate more than a year ago. The piece was just reflecting on all of the high and low points of the presidential campaign that had recently ended. Jonah's bit was obviously a low point.

Disappeared was a good word to describe Jonah these days. After the news of his affair with his sister's maid and his love child he'd kept a secret all these years hit, the once hero war veteran and future of politics was everything that was wrong with the world. The campaign dropped him from the ticket, choosing a female senator to replace him.

Erica had cut all ties with Jonah after that, even though he tried several times to contact her. She heard about him resigning from the Pentagon, his wife filing for divorce, and his general withdrawal from the powerful society scene. It was unavoidable, but she still tried to stay as far away from it as she could. It was too upsetting.

Unable to even stand the sight of Jonah, Erica snatched the remote away from Corey and quickly turned to a channel focused on the day's financial markets.

"Better?" she asked, smiling, handing it back to him.

"Much," he agreed with a nod.

A blank screen would be better than Jonah, Erica thought as she walked back toward Justin's office.

2

Sherise was usually good at hiding her emotions when she wanted to, but she wasn't really trying right now. She was pissed off and everyone in Jerry's private office at campaign headquarters knew this.

Jerry stopped talking and his eyes settled on her. Yes, she knew that the fifty-eight-year-old man before her, distinguished and handsome with gray temples highlighting his blond hair, was going to be the next president of the United States, but for right now, he was the man who had wasted her morning and he wasn't above knowing about it.

"What is it, Sherise?" he finally asked.

Everyone in the room, Jerry's top five advisors, including his campaign manager, LaKeisha, turned to her.

Sherise gently placed her hands on her knee atop her crossed legs. "I'm just . . . I thought we were here for something extremely important, but you just want us to assist in . . . party planning?"

"I know it sounds tedious." Jerry offered his hands out in the way he always did when he knew he was asking a lot of someone.

"Party planning is tedious," Sherise said.

"He isn't asking us to be event planners," LaKeisha, who was sitting in the chair next to her, explained. "He's asking us to invite certain people."

"These are our biggest and most important supporters and donors," Jerry said. "I don't want them to get a cold invite, no matter how intricate the design might be. You're my top five people, and a call from one of you will assure them that we know how exceptionally essential they were to our victory."

Sherise nodded, knowing that it made sense, but said nothing.

"This list of donors is massive." Jerry pointed to Alan Sharp, his funding manager, who held up a large stack of paper about four inches thick.

"We're working off paper?" Sherise asked.

"Yes," Alan responded curtly.

Alan looked younger than a man in his late thirties, with a textbook Washington D.C. staff look. Ivy League educated, glasses wearing, khaki dressed, and usually clinging to three communication devices. But today he had paper.

"We need to work from the same list to save time," Alan continued. "If you each had your own list, it would take forever to cut and paste. Besides, we need to agree on the list and which one of us will call whom."

"There are at least twenty people who we know already," LaKeisha said. "I can call them."

"So how many are we talking?" Sherise asked.

"That's the question," Jerry said. "You all need to figure out who we won't be inviting and how to handle that. It will certainly get back to them that there was another party."

By another party, Jerry was referring to the formal celebration party that happened last week. It was held at the Hotel Monaco and all the donors and supporters were there. This party would be held at Jerry's home, the governor's mansion, in Annapolis, Maryland.

"That's going to be a nightmare." LaKeisha rolled her eyes. "Everyone thinks they're the most important."

"That's why I've called you in," Jerry said. "This is going to be a lot more complicated than it seems. And it has to stay under a hundred."

"We're inviting a hundred people?" For some reason, Sherise assumed this would be no more than fifty. "For a party two nights away?"

"Yes," Jerry affirmed. "Which is why you need to get started right—"

He stopped speaking, as there was a knock on the door.

"Who is it?" LaKeisha asked, annoyed.

The door opened just slightly and Diana Boone, Jerry's life-long assistant, stuck her head through the door. She looked like a mild librarian in her sixties, but was a sharp woman with a hidden aggressiveness that made it clear why Jerry used her as his barrier to the world.

"I know you said no disturbances," she started, "but Mr. Blair is here."

Sherise turned to Jerry, who quickly glanced down at his watch. He frowned and said, "He's early."

"Just a second, Diana." LaKeisha stood up.

"Who is it?" Sherise asked. That name sounded familiar, but she couldn't quite place it.

"Look." Jerry stood up from his chair and came around his desk. "We're done with this for now. If you guys can focus on this list for now. I think between the group of you, you can come to a consensus as to the most important people."

Sherise could tell that Jerry's demeanor and attitude were sharply changed. Even his voice suddenly sounded different. He wanted them out of his office now.

"LaKeisha," he said, "you'll let me know how things are coming along after my meeting is over?"

LaKeisha looked a little surprised. "Am I not staying for the meeting?"

Jerry cleared his throat and shook his head. "No, not this time."

As they all made their way out of the office, Sherise suddenly caught the name. She wasn't sure why it hadn't rung a bell earlier, because she knew Maurice Blair well. Everyone in politics in D.C. did. Currently the president of the small, not highly regarded Democrat Governors Association, or DGA, he'd been a part of many successful Democratic campaigns and projects.

Except for Northman's. During the campaign, Sherise had run into Maurice at several events, but he wasn't involved in the campaign. There was too much going on at DGA. He had his hands full with Democratic governors who were in tight races during that campaign season.

So what was he doing here now?

"You're early," LaKeisha admonished as he approached.

Maurice Blair was a slender, tall man, sort of a mushroom brown, in his middle forties. He was handsome in a way, but not if you looked too long. He had a slickness to him that men liked, but women stayed as far away from as possible. Used to be known as a power broker in D.C., but that ended about ten years ago after a couple of failed campaigns. He wasn't really on the top of many lists in D.C.'s social scene.

"Nice to see you too, LaKeisha," he said with a smile, his voice as smooth and velvety as always.

He glanced in Sherise's direction, and like every other time he'd looked at her, his eyes went straight to her breasts and stayed for a couple of seconds. He did it to make her uncomfortable, because he was an asshole, but Sherise wouldn't give him the satisfaction.

"You look lovely, Sherise," he said. "You always do."

"Yes, I do," she answered back with a cold stare.

He smirked as if amused by her aloofness with him. Sherise did not like this man. He had a bad personal rep as a ladies' man and someone who played real dirty. Sherise, being someone who played dirty when she had to, knew that there were lines she wouldn't cross that Maurice was known for crossing on a daily basis. But he used to get results.

Sherise showed no further interest in him, and he quickly turned and headed into Jerry's office. After the door was closed behind him, she rushed after LaKeisha, who was already heading to her office.

"LaKeisha." She reached out and grabbed her by the arm, turning her around. "What is going on?"

"We'll meet in the conference room in ten minutes," she said loud enough for the others, who were following behind, to hear. "I have to make a call."

"Not that," Sherise objected. "With Maurice Blair. What's he doing here?"

"I don't know yet." LaKeisha looked genuinely annoyed with the situation. "He just showed up on the appointment list very early this morning. I asked Jerry and he said he'll talk about it later."

"Jerry didn't look very happy to see him," Sherise said.

"I think he's calling in favors," LaKeisha mused. "He's probably gonna claim some responsibility for this win and is already playing a conduit for other politicians. You know, Cabinet positions, all that."

"Then you should be in there," Sherise urged. "You're going to be his chief of staff."

"He said no." LaKeisha shrugged. "Honestly, I can't stand the guy, so I'd rather avoid him if I can. Trust me, I'm gonna find out what's going on before I leave today."

Sherise wasn't going to leave it up to LaKeisha. She was going to find out for herself what the hell was going on.

Thelma's Kitchen was a neighborhood restaurant on Auburn Avenue in the Old Fourth Ward neighborhood of Atlanta. They served old-fashioned soul food and BBQ ribs. Michael had been eager to bring Billie to the place he'd hung out at since he was a kid, but warned her it wasn't in the best neighborhood.

The people were good people and the food was great, he promised her. Billie didn't doubt him. She'd grown up going to the same type of places in D.C., which most people wouldn't dare go into but had the best food and the best hospitality. She wasn't at all worried about the neighborhood. What she was worried about was the two women waiting for them at a battered table in the corner when they showed up.

"You good?" Michael asked her as they headed over to his waving mother.

She swallowed hard. "Of course I am."

Dee Dee, Michael's mother, was in her late sixties, but looked a bit older, like a woman who had been making it on her own for a long time and it was taking its toll. She was a dark chocolate with a generous figure and a chestnut-colored weave that reached her bra strap. She didn't smile often, at least not as far as Billie had seen.

Next to Dee Dee was Aisha, a couple of years younger than Michael. She was right out of a stereotype book of activism. She wore her hair in an afro with no makeup at all. She was somewhat petite, like Billie, but her figure was undecipherable in the unisex clothing she wore, which usually included a T-shirt with words of political protests of some kind.

Any hope Billie had of a peaceful new beginning ended the moment they approached the table and said hello. Instead of greeting them back with a hello, Dee Dee huffed.

"You're late," she said, rolling her eyes.

"We're not late." Michael gestured for Billie to slide into the booth. "We're supposed to meet at noon. It's 12:06."

Billie reluctantly slid into the booth, wishing that Michael had sat down first. She felt trapped. What would she do if she needed to run for it? Jump over Michael? Well, if it came to that.

"Like I said," Dee Dee continued, her eyes never leaving Billie even though it was Michael who responded to her, "You're late."

"Sorry about that," was all Billie could say.

"I would expect as a lawyer, you'd have to be on time to everything." Dee Dee seemed to make sure her voice sounded extra judgmental whenever she addressed Billie.

"I'd think the opposite," Aisha interjected casually with her slightly hoarse voice, her eyes still on her menu. "Lawyers tend to think they're special and think everyone has to wait for them."

"That isn't true," Billie said, maintaining the most calm she could.

"What evidence would you have of that?" Michael asked Aisha sarcastically. "When have you ever interacted with a lawyer? Oh wait, that's right. You meet a new one every time you get arrested."

Aisha's lips pressed together in anger. "Thanks for bringing that up and, for your information, I recall that all those lawyers were late for our meetings."

"But they got the charges dropped every time, didn't they?" Michael asked. "So I would say that wait was worth it."

Aisha rolled her eyes and turned to Billie. "Before you get all judgmental, I was arrested for protesting against injustice. Last year it was a bank known for preying on minorities with insane interest rates. I'm not a criminal."

"Because a lawyer got the charges dropped," Michael added.

"I wasn't thinking you were a criminal," Billie said.

"You were probably thinking it." Aisha shook her head. "Probably."

Billie realized that she could be completely silent and still offend both these women, so she might as well speak up for herself.

"I wasn't," she insisted in a strong enough tone that Aisha seemed to catch on that it was best not to respond.

Billie was grateful for the moment the waitress approached and took their orders. For at least a few minutes, the tension wasn't sky high. But the second she left, Dee Dee started in again.

"I was reading the paper this morning," she said, "and what a coincidence, I happened to stumble on an article about your ex this morning," she said. "What's his name again? Parker or . . ."

"Porter," Billie corrected. Dee Dee knew exactly what her ex-husband's name was and her mentioning the article was no coincidence.

"He's very successful," Dee Dee said. "Just made partner at his firm. He was quite a catch."

"Mom, what the hell?" Michael asked.

She laughed it off. "Oh, of course nothing compared to you, Michael. It's just so curious as to why . . ."

"Why what?" Billie asked.

She looked suddenly uncomfortable. "Never mind, I just . . . he mentioned his devotion to his daughter, said it was important to give her his all, considering he was the only parent she had."

Billie hadn't been prepared for this. She was willing to take stabs at herself and their little jokes about her failed marriage, but if they were going to bring Tara, her former stepdaughter, into this, all bets were off. She loved Tara like she was her own daughter and her motherly instinct revved up at the very mention of her.

"So," Dee Dee continued, "you don't have any relationship with her now?"

"We have a very good relationship," Billie responded sharply. "We're very close."

It had been rough, of course. During their bitter divorce, Porter often used his daughter as a tool to keep Billie close to him. When she wouldn't do as Porter wanted, or tried to move on from him, he would forbid her from seeing Tara.

Billie had played dirty as well. She'd lowered herself to his level and threatened to harm his career if he didn't let her see Tara. Porter had even gone so far as to send Tara to his family in Michigan to keep her away from Billie. In the end, their fighting turned Tara against both of them, and it had been a long road for them both to get back in the teen's good graces and try to have something resembling normal.

"I guess she was your only chance," Dee Dee continued. "At being a mother. It makes sense you would want to hold on to her. You're getting at that age when it is a bit late to—"

"Hey," Michael said strongly. "What's the matter with you, Mom?" He ended his question in a whisper as the waitress came with their drinks.

Billie realized what Dee Dee was trying to say and it boiled her blood. She felt herself getting flushed. Was this woman insinuating that she was getting too old to give Michael children?

Aisha laughed, nervously. "Mom is just playing around, Michael. No big deal."

"Let's just play nice, okay?" he asked.

"I thought I was." Dee Dee flattened out the napkin on her lap in a huff. "You're not offended, Billie. Are you?"

"What?" Billie asked. "That you suggested I'm getting too old to have children? Who would be offended by that?"

Dee Dee rolled her eyes. "I guess you city women are a bit thin-skinned."

"My skin is sufficiently thick," Billie responded.

"It's the only thing that is thick," Aisha said. "You need to get a full slab of ribs, not just a half. You're too skinny. Michael is used to more curves, aren't you?"

"How would you know?" Michael asked. "You have no idea what I . . ."

"Darina was curvy."

Everyone sort of froze for a moment and looked at Aisha. She had said the name. Michael had warned Billie of this. Darina Wheeler was supposed to be the love of Michael's life. They met in college and fell in love. They were both very active in their community and committed to speaking out against inequity in the South and injustices around the world. They planned to get married one day, but always assumed there would be time for that later.

They grew apart as Michael began to be successful in his business, executive search, and Darina became more radical in her protests and actions. She was arrested often, her trips usually financed by Michael's earnings since her job as a community activist barely paid a living wage.

This dynamic created a lot of tension between them. Michael had given Darina an ultimatum: him or the activism. She made her choice and broke his heart. He decided to leave Atlanta and move to D.C., where the majority of his clients were based. In no time, his business became ten times the success he expected.

Michael had gotten over Darina a long time ago, but told Billie that his mother and sister loved her and wished they had stayed together. They spoke of her often and Billie might want to be prepared for that.

"Aisha," Dee Dee snapped at her daughter. "Don't."

This was curious. Billie would assume that Dee Dee would love to see Aisha bring up Darina in an obvious attempt to make her feel insecure. But she was clearly upset about it. Or at least she didn't want the topic brought up.

"I'm sorry," Aisha said coyly. "Did I say something wrong? I mean I'm not insulting you, Billie. It's just that down South, men like their women a bit thick."

"Actually," Michael said, "I like my women beautiful, strong, sexy, determined, ambitious, kind, caring, and funny. Billie is all of those things tenfold. No one I've ever dated even compares to her. Are we clear, Aisha?"

His sister stuttered through her response. "I was just . . ."

"You were just being rude," he argued. "And so are you, Mom. Billie has been nothing but nice to you and I'm pretty taken aback by the way you're acting. You've spent so many years teaching me manners, but seem to have lost yours."

Billie felt a sense of glee as she watched Dee Dee gasp, almost dropping the glass of water in her hand. She would have given anything to take a picture of her expression and send it to Sherise and Erica at home.

"All joking aside," Michael resumed, "Billie is not just my girlfriend. She's my everything. I love her more than I could explain to anyone, and I expect people who love me to love her too. At the least, I expect them to show her more respect than either of you two have."

Billie reached under the table and grabbed Michael's hand. Her heart was exploding with joy with every word he said. She loved him so completely for this, but she didn't want him to get too angry. She could feel the tension in his voice tightening. If he ended up yelling at his mother, Billie would end up getting the blame.

She squeezed his hand very briefly and he stopped. He turned to her and she smiled at him. He took a deep breath and she could see his body relax as he exhaled. He smiled at his mother.

"Billie is perfect the way she is," he said definitively. "Just perfect."

Aisha kept her head down, seeming too embarrassed to even acknowledge that Michael had scolded her too. Dee Dee on the other hand cleared her throat, took a sip of her water, and smiled.

"Of course she is," she said sweetly. "We tease because we love. Of course Billie understands that. Don't you, dear?"

Billie smiled flatly with a quaint nod. "I understand completely, Dee Dee."

The woman's fake smile faded for just a second, as she was suspicious of Billie's meaning, but quickly returned.

Very little was said for the rest of the lunch. Billie was grateful when it was over and, despite having made love to him all morning in the hotel, couldn't wait to get her hands on him and show him how much she appreciated him standing up for her.

Erica was dead tired and glad to be leaving the office. The lobbying industry was still new to her. She was a quick learner, and having worked at government agencies her entire career had given her an advantage. On her first day, Justin explained it plainly to her. He actively advocated on behalf of his clients to Capitol Hill and government agencies to affect legislation. After a short while she figured he was paid heavily to go on three-hour lunches followed by cocktail hour get-togethers and a lot of parties.

As she got more involved in his day-to-day business, as opposed to simple administrative tasks, she realized it was actually pretty complicated and worked hard to learn the game, or the hustle, as she referred to it. It was exhausting, and at the end of a busy day like today, she could only think of getting home and curling up in her bed with a large glass of red wine.

She made her way to the lobby and was surprised to see Corey, the handsome young man she'd met earlier that morning, sitting in the same spot he was sitting in when she'd left him. When he looked up at her, he smiled and it made her feel nervous . . . but in a good way.

"You've come back?" she asked.

"Come back?" He looked confused. "I've been sitting here ever since you left. I'm still waiting to see Justin."

Erica blinked, confused for a second, even though she knew that wasn't possible. "But I've . . . I've walked past here at least . . ."

She saw the coy smile form at his lips and realized he was joking with her. She smirked in response.

"So you're a lobbyist and a bad comedian," she said, placing her hands on her curvy hips.

"A bad one?" He laughed, standing up from the chair. "Ouch."

"But really," she continued, noting again how big he was. She wouldn't mind seeing the muscles hiding beneath that fitted suit. "How long have you been out here?"

"Only about fifteen minutes," he answered. "The receptionist let me in before she left. I'm waiting for Justin. We're going to dinner."

"That makes me think this morning's interview went well," she said.

He shrugged confidently. "What can I say? I'm pretty impressive."

She looked amazed.

"I'm just kidding," he assured her. "Please don't tell him I said that. It was a joke."

"I get it," she said. "Usually, my sense of humor is better. I'm just exhausted. Long day."

"Can't tell from looking at you," he said. "You look just as pretty and fresh as you did this morning."

She couldn't help but smile and wondered if her fair cheeks showed a blush. It had been a while since a guy had that effect on her.

"Thank you," was all she offered, not willing to give any more away. She was cautious by nature, to a fault.

There was a short moment of awkward silence as their eyes stayed on each other before Erica looked away. Should she go now? Should she stay and talk? She had no idea.

Erica hated how bad she was at dealing with the opposite

sex. She'd been with Terrell for over five years, and Alex Gonzales didn't count. They never dated and she didn't want to think of that anyway. Ever.

"So where are you going?" she asked, to get her mind going in a different direction from Alex.

"Elephant and Castle," he answered. "The game is on there and we're both from Chicago, so we can root for the Bears together."

"That's right," she said. "Where in Chicago again?"

"Waukegan. I'm not too far from where Justin grew up."

"So you have that in common," she said. "I'm sure that helped. Too bad your team is gonna lose to my Washington Redskins tonight."

"Lose." He made a smacking sound with his lips and waved his hand away. "You must be crazy. My Bears have won six straight and are at the top of their division."

"A division that is at the bottom of all the stats," she responded. "Lowest-scoring division in football, and you can't even make your field goals. Not to mention the injuries you suffered last week against the Lions."

"None of that matters." His eyes lit up, signifying that he loved talking football. "My grandmother could beat the Redskins on her own. How many points have you scored in the last two games? Thirteen total. And that game against the Cowboys last week? You guys shouldn't have even bothered to show up in Chicago."

"You're dreaming," she admonished. "Both Smith and Jenkins were out the last two games. They're back tonight. You guys are going down. I'm calling it. Twenty-four to seven, Redskins. Fact."

"Fact?" He leaned back with an amused smile on his face and looked her up and down. "While you are wrong, I am impressed with your football knowledge. You like fantasy?"

Her eyes widened as she swallowed hard, not sure she heard him right. "Do I like . . . what?"

"Fantasy?" he repeated. "Do you play fantasy football?"

A rush of relief came over Erica as she realized what he was talking about. Of course that was what he was talking about. Why would she have thought that he meant anything else?

"Absolutely," she said, almost in a sigh.

He seemed confused by her reaction, but only showed it for a second before getting back on track.

"I'll make you a bet, Erica. That is your name, right?"

She nodded. "I don't bet money on games."

"No money," he assured her. "Dinner."

"Dinner?" Her eyebrows arched in curiosity. He wasn't wasting any time and she immediately realized she didn't mind that at all. "What's the deal?"

"If the Bears win, you treat to me to dinner. If the pitiful Redskins win, I treat you to dinner."

She tilted her head to the side flirtatiously and pressed her lips together. "You see, I kind of have a problem with that bet. I mean, what if I don't want to have dinner with you whether I win or not?"

He frowned with a slight pout. "Revised deal."

"I'm listening," she said.

"Same terms," he continued, "but instead of me treating you to dinner or vice versa, let's say I go to dinner by myself and send you the bill. You can do the same."

"I have expensive tastes," she offered, even though that wasn't true. Erica was a neighborhood girl. She'd pick a local joint over a fancy restaurant any day, but she wanted to play this game.

He paused, his expression turning softer and more serious. His eyes held hers for a moment before he said, "As any beautiful woman should. Do we have a deal?"

She hesitated for a moment.

"If it makes it easier," he said, "my Bears are definitely winning, so go on ahead and factor my dinner into your budget right now."

"You're smug," she stated. "That overconfident look on your face is going to make the Redskins' win all the more wonderful. You got a deal."

She held out her hand and he took it, shaking it firmly. She liked his grip. It was strong, but not too forceful. Most of all, she liked the smile on his face. It was one of anticipation. Erica imagined that just like her, he wasn't the least bit concerned about who won tonight.

They were both just happy to have an excuse to speak again.

As Justin caressed her round, firm breasts and pressed his hot tongue against her neck, Sherise felt a moan of pleasure rise in her throat and leave her body. His lips lowered and replaced his hands, taking her right breast in his mouth. He was picking up the pace, his mouth taking possession of her left breast now, his hands lowered to her hips where her body was grinding against his.

It was exciting to get back in this groove of great sex again. Getting back into shape after the baby took a little longer the second time around, but not once had Justin made Sherise feel anything less than sexy. But now she wasn't just feeling really sexy. She was feeling like a sexual being again. She expressed that every time Justin touched her and it urged him on to be more aggressive, more exploratory. Their sex life was better than ever.

She felt his manhood getting harder and harder against her thighs and her body began to boil. She wanted to give in to the passion completely as she felt Justin begin to lose control, but she couldn't. Something was in her way. Despite wanting her husband very much, Sherise had something other than sex on her mind. There was another man in bed with them.

"Justin," she said as she took his hand just before it reached her center.

She slid away from him a few inches, but he moved back toward her, his hands reaching for her naked hips to bring her back to him.

"Justin," she repeated, louder this time. "I . . . I'm sorry, but no."

He looked up at her as if in disbelief, which quickly turned to disappointment. "No?"

She shook her head with an apologetic pout.

"What's wrong?" he asked, leaning up from her.

"It's that fucking Maurice Blair." She sat up against the soft cushioned headboard of the king-sized bed.

"Nice to know you're thinking of another man while I'm trying to make love to you." He smiled at her, but as soon as he realized she wasn't in the mood for jokes, his demeanor changed to serious. "I wish I could do more for you."

"You've done all you could." She reached out and rubbed his arm appreciatively.

Things were different between Sherise and Justin now. After they'd both had affairs, their marriage was a mess. Then, with a new baby on the way, the sexual harassment claim against Justin—which turned out to be a calculated hoax—threatened to put the final nail in the coffin.

Instead, Sherise and Justin grew closer than ever by working together. Usually, when Sherise had a problem she would go to her sources, her private investigator or other people who could help her do what she needed to do.

She'd keep it from her husband as much as possible. Justin was a stickler for playing by the rules and didn't approve of her tactics. That changed with the lawsuit. Realizing that he'd been the target of a nasty revenge scheme, threatening to destroy everything he'd worked for, he decided playing by the rules wasn't what it was cracked up to be.

Now Sherise told him everything and they always worked together. He was the first person she'd called when she left Maurice

Blair outside of Northman's office. As a connected lobbyist, he knew how to find out almost anything on people in the political game. He went straight to work.

"I wish I could find out more," Justin said. "Everyone knows he's fallen off his perch of late. He used to be one of the top PR guys in the game. Worked on some of the biggest congressional races, then off to head the Democrat Governors Association."

"I should talk to people at the DGA," Sherise said. "What is he up to?"

"Lately, nothing," Justin disclosed. "He's dropped off, but I guess he's still connected if he can get a private meeting with the future president. He's a slime ball, known sexist pig, and all-around jerk. But you know this business."

Sherise nodded. "That's not a detriment in politics. Sometimes, I swear the sexism gets worse."

Her entire career was filled with battling sexist pigs that claimed to be card-carrying progressives. Politics was a game to win for a lot of PR people, not at all about actual beliefs.

"It's like he showed up out of the blue," she said. "I know he's up to something."

"I'll bet money, it's about jobs." Justin reached over to the edge of the bed for his T-shirt. "He's got a lot of Democrats who want to be in the Cabinet of the new administration. They want to call in their favors for supporting Northman and campaigning with him. He's in charge of . . ."

"But why kick us out?" Sherise asked. "We're Northman's top staff. We're supposed to be making these transition choices. Blair should be coming to us and we take the requests to him. He even kicked LaKeisha out."

"I know that's the protocol, but maybe Blair does it differently."

"It's not for him to decide how things are done. Northman was elected. We decide how it's done. I'm telling you, Justin, something is up."

"Tomorrow night at the party," Justin said, "you'll make Northman tell you what's going on. You know you can get him to do whatever you want."

He was right. As with most men, Sherise could work Northman to her advantage if she needed to. He favored her and she knew it. He respected her also, which made her not want to manipulate him, but she would do whatever she had to in order to stay in control of the situation.

"This is the big stage," Sherise said.

"As big as it gets," Justin agreed. "And you made it there."

"So people are going to be gunning for me."

"What makes you think he has you in his sights?"

"I don't know," she said. "I just got a feeling from the look on his face, he's going to be a problem for me."

"Like he wants to get you back for all those times he hit on you and you rejected him?"

Sherise pulled the covers on the bed over her, feeling a sudden chill.

"I'm just one of thousands of women who have done that. He probably doesn't even remember it. No, I just got that vibe from him. Not the pervert vibe I usually get, but the trouble vibe. He had a look on his face."

"You keep saying that," Justin said. "What exactly is this look?"

She turned to him. "A look like he was about to start some shit."

"So what if he is?" Justin asked. "He's no match for you. You'll handle him just fine and he'll learn the hard way. Don't fuck with Sherise Robinson."

She smiled wickedly, loving the way it felt to really be one with her husband.

That chill she just felt thinking about Maurice Blair suddenly vanished and the heat returned. She reached out to Justin, grabbing at the T-shirt that he'd just put back on, and pulled him toward her. He obliged and his mouth met hers without hesitation.

Without a hiccup, they picked up right where they left off. Or so Sherise thought.

Just before she felt herself begin to fall into him and lose any sense of the rest of the world, she heard the sound of cooing. Usually, they remembered to turn off the baby monitor while having sex, but this time they'd forgotten. Hearing your baby coo in the other room was not the greatest aphrodisiac.

Justin sighed, lowering his head. "I'll get it."

He kissed her quickly before getting up from the bed. Only before he could get to the monitor on the dresser to turn it off, the cooing turned to crying. He paused and looked back at her, his hand just inches from the button.

Sherise moaned and reached for her nightgown at the edge of the bed.

"It's just crying," Justin said. "He'll be fine."

"No." Sherise slowly, reluctantly got up from the bed. "He's hungry."

Justin let out a big sigh.

"Hey," Sherise said. "It's getting better."

"True," he agreed. "He used to cock-block me like it was his job."

She laughed, walking over to him. She turned off the monitor and kissed Justin on the shoulder. "I won't be long. Can you keep warm while you wait?"

"I'm always warm for you, baby."

3

Sitting on the bed dressed in one of Michael's T-shirts and a pair of sweatpants, having just gotten out of the shower, Billie could hear a commotion in the living area of their hotel room even though the door to the bedroom was closed. Room service had arrived and she was starving, but had to deal with work.

"Okay," Lane Redmond said on the other end of the phone. "I'm in the file."

"Do you see the folder named Merlot?" she asked.

Lane Redmond was a fellow lawyer at Agencis, the financial services company she worked for. In fact, he was the person who had gotten her the job she had now as associate general counsel. Lane had basically saved her career.

Once an up and coming public defender, Billie saw her dream of spending a lifetime defending the powerless against the powerful come to an end with the financial debt her divorce had left her in. She'd joined the ranks of the highly paid, extremely overworked law firm associates and was doing well.

That was until she'd met Ricky Williams, a handsome, smooth-talking pro bono client who, despite running a home for political asylum seekers, was also running a drug operation in Southeast D.C. Billie would like to say Ricky seduced her, but she wasn't the victim. She'd been attracted to him from the start and ignored all her professional ethical obligations and started an affair with him.

It didn't cost her her license to practice law, but it did cost her the respect of her boss and she had to quit the firm. After consulting, she'd come in contact with Lane, whom she'd known since they worked together on the Criminal Law Review at Georgetown Law School. Lane, an associate general counsel at Agencis, had given her two legal consulting projects, which led to an offer to join the company permanently.

"You named the file after a wine?" Redmond asked.

She laughed. "You have your methods, I have mine. Look, don't judge me. Just tell me if you see it."

Lane was chuckling as he said, "I've found it. That's it?"

There was a knock on the door and Michael called Billie's name.

"Just a second," she yelled.

"Yes," she answered Lane. "That's it. Inside, you'll find the brief draft. You're looking for point three, reform objections."

After a few moments, Lane said, "I got it. I'm copying it now. Look, Billie. I'm really sorry about this. I know you're on vacay, but the client is just freaking out and . . ."

"I get it," she said calmly, even though it did annoy her. "Unlike my boyfriend, I get that technology means there is no such thing as a work-free vacation. Just try not to do it again."

"I'll do my best," he said. "I guess I'll see you next week."

"Bye, Lane."

As she hung up, she heard Michael call her name again and hopped up from the sofa.

The second she opened the door to the living area, she looked around. The living area of the luxury suite at the St. Regis was expansive and beautifully decorated in a French style with soft creamy colors and perfect moldings. White and glass French doors led to a large Juliet-style balcony. This was where Michael was standing, waving her over.

Michael had made plans at a fancy restaurant in Buckhead, but Billie begged him to order room service instead. She couldn't wait to get back from the lunch from hell to show Michael her appreciation for him standing up for her against his mother and sister. After making love all afternoon, she was too exhausted to get prettied up and go out.

"I'm starving," she said, as she stepped out onto the balcony.

"Steak and lobster with garlic roasted red potatoes and grilled asparagus," he said. "Just like you wanted."

He took her by the arm and they walked around the table where the food was covered with sterling dish toppers. Billie stopped at the chair, expecting him to pull it out for her. Instead, he led her to the edge of the balcony overlooking the city.

"We're not eating yet?" she asked.

"Let's have a relaxing drink first." He grabbed the two glasses of champagne he had already poured and offered her one.

"Champagne?" she asked. "We're celebrating?"

"We're celebrating our marathon lovemaking session." He took a sip. "I think that's the longest we've gone straight through."

She reached out and pressed her hand against his chest, feeling his strong muscles underneath the soft cotton shirt. "If you count this morning, I think we belong in the Guinness Book of World Records."

He took her by the waist and brought her to him. He kissed her tenderly on the lips. "If we didn't, we need to find out what the record is and take a shot at it."

"I'm game if you are," she offered. "Honestly, Michael, I wanted to apologize for lunch."

"That was an apology?" he asked. "Damn, I'm gonna have to demand apologies from you more often."

"No." She laughed, hitting him playfully on the chest. "That was a thank you. This, here, now is an apology."

"You've got nothing to apologize for," he said.

"But I do," she corrected. "I should have been more gracious with your mom and sis."

"You were gracious," he said. "They were the ones who were out of line, but I think I settled it."

"But I don't want that," Billie insisted. "I don't want you fighting with your mom over me."

"We weren't fighting. Look, baby, I love my mom to death, but she can be trifling at times. She knows it. We're cool."

"But I know how this works," Billie said. "Although it's deserved, you put her in check, but I'll get blamed for it. You don't need to stand up for me. I can . . ."

"I will always stand up for you." He lifted his hand to her chin and cupped it gently. He tilted her head up so that they were looking into each other's eyes. "No matter what, no matter who, you're my woman and I will stand up to anyone for you. I love you, Billie."

Her heart bloomed and she felt her knees get weak. It wasn't just his words, but the sound of sincerity in his voice. Hearing him say those three words sounded more beautiful than the greatest symphony.

"My God," she said, almost breathless. "I love you so much, Michael. I swear I will make it work with your family. I will do anything I have to."

"That's good to hear." He took a couple of steps back from her and reached into his pants pocket. "Especially with the new dynamic."

"What new dy—"

Billie gasped as Michael slowly lowered to one knee and looked up at her. Life slowed to a crawl as she watched him open the ring box he was holding in his hand and hold it up to her.

At first she was blank, amazed, and shaken to her core at the surprise. But as it really sank in, Billie's heart was filled with bottomless joy. She felt overwhelmed and breathless.

"Will you marry me, Billie?" he asked with a look of restless eagerness on his face. He was smiling with nervous anticipation.

Breaking from her frozen state, Billie finally screamed and jumped into the air. She'd forgotten she was holding a glass of champagne until that champagne flew out of the glass and all over Michael's face and shirt.

"Oh my God," she said. "Oh my . . . I'm so sorry. Michael!"

"Um . . ." Michael coughed a little as he started to stand.

"No," she said.

She pushed at his shoulders to make him stay down, but it actually made him stumble back a little.

"Don't fall!" she shouted.

"I'm trying not to." He was laughing although he seemed a little confused.

"Just stay there," she said, reaching to the left and grabbing a white cloth napkin from the table. She kept apologizing as she wiped his face and part of his shirt. "I can get it off, I promise. I just . . ."

Michael grabbed her hand as she went to pat his head. "Stop it, Billie. It's okay."

She let him remove her hand from his head and dropped the napkin to the floor. She looked down at him somberly.

"I ruined it," she said.

"The only way you could ruin this is if you say no," Michael assured her.

"Yes! Yes! Yes!" she screamed loud enough to be heard a mile away.

"Good." He laughed loudly. "Now, can I get up?"

"Yes, you can."

She was trying to hold back her tears as he took the ring out of the box and placed it on her finger, but she couldn't. She looked at the platinum band ring, lined with a stripe of diamonds that led to a large oval diamond shining brightly under the romantically lit balcony. It was the most glorious thing Billie had ever seen.

"It's beautiful, Michael," she exclaimed, her voice almost a sigh.

"You know this was supposed to be more romantic," he said. "I'd set it up with music in a private room at the restaurant. It was going to be a whole thing. I had to improvise when you wanted to stay in. It would have been perfect."

You're wrong," she said. "Nothing could have more perfect than this moment right here."

Returning home from Saturday-morning errands, Erica was almost giddy at the great news that Billie had just texted her and Sherise. Michael had proposed to her last night and she'd accepted. Erica knew it was coming. Over the last year, she'd watched Billie and Michael fall more and more in love and couldn't be happier for her best friend.

As she opened the door to her D.C. apartment, Erica was also a little giddy for herself. She'd watched the football game Thursday night with fervor, rooting for her Redskins. Sadly, they lost, but the pain of that loss was quickly tempered by a text she got less than five minutes after the game ended.

U owe me dinner—Corey.

She texted him back immediately demanding to know how he got her number, even though she wasn't at all upset about it. He responded that he'd informed Justin of their bet and Justin gave him her number.

Send me the bill, she texted, referring to their plan B agreement.

Curious to see his response, she laughed out loud when he called her a coward. They texted teasingly, flirtatiously back and forth for a while before she agreed, pretending it was reluctantly, to go out to dinner.

So they made plans for dinner later that night and Erica couldn't remember the last time she was this giddy about a first date. She was so distracted by the idea that she hadn't been paying attention after she entered her apartment and placed her grocery bags on her kitchen counter. Out of the corner of her left eye, she saw some movement.

She turned and jumped, realizing there was a large dark figure in her living room, sitting on her sofa. Erica screamed.

The intruder turned on the lamp on the end table next to the sofa where he was sitting.

"Calm down," he said. "Don't scream again. Someone will call the cops."

"I'm going to call the cops!" she yelled.

Jonah Nolan didn't seem fazed by his daughter's threat as he simply stared at her with that immovable, authoritarian stare she'd gotten so used to.

He was a very attractive man in his fifties, with a powerful presence that seemed to radiate far beyond him. He was tall and trim, but not thin. He had a warm pink hue to his skin and dark hair that was graying at the temples. He had a firm jawline and thin lips that made him look very serious all the time.

"What are you doing here?" she asked, trying to slow her rapid heartbeat. "And don't say you have a key. I just had my locks changed."

A look of concern came over his face. "Why? Did someone try to break in?"

"Yes," she said. "There have been a lot of break-ins in the neighborhood. A few weeks ago, I came home and saw my locks had been tampered with. Had to replace them. Was it you?"

"No," he said, seeming almost offended. "I don't try and

break into apartments, Erica. You need to move out of this shitty neighborhood."

"I can't afford anything . . . wait, what the fuck are you doing here?"

He looked at her sternly, letting her know he didn't appreciate her language. Erica swallowed a bit. That look always made her nervous.

Jonah was the kind of man who could make anyone nervous. Not just because he had that look of authority about him, which he'd developed after years in the military, but also because he carried himself like a man who knew how much power he wielded. Or at least, used to. He was supposed to be in the Oval Office one day. A man who once could make people disappear, change the directions of their lives, and mold events to fit his needs was now mostly reclusive.

After the scandal hit, his wife divorced him and took most of the millions, which was only fair since she had brought most of the money to the family. His kids, the ones he acknowledged, didn't want much to do with him. His kids he didn't acknowledge shunned him too. He'd quit his job and the various boards and committees he was on, saying he needed to take a break from public life for a year.

Erica guessed that year was over and Jonah was on his comeback. Was this visit a check off his list of people to bring back in his life? Well, he had another think coming if he meant to do that.

"I've offered to help you one million times," he said.

"And I've declined your charity one million times," she answered back, not moving from her spot behind the kitchen counter. "How did you get in here?"

"It doesn't matter."

"It does!" she yelled. "I don't want you in my apartment! Did you steal my keys and copy them? Did you pay the landlord? I'll call the cops on him for helping you."

"Enough with the threats," he said, sounding annoyed.

"I'll ask again," she explained. "What do you want?"

"I wanted to come by and see you," he said, simply. "It's been almost seven months since—"

"Since you last ambushed me," she interrupted. "I made it clear to you then that this little shameful secret was done."

"I'm not ashamed of you," he said. "I never have been."

"Don't give me the speech." Erica was disgusted that he still didn't understand how cruel it was to keep a child secret for your career ambitions.

She had always wished she'd had a father like Billie's. One who loved her, treated her mother with respect, and was devoted to her. She'd thought her brother Nate's father was her own until Jonah found her at twenty-five and told her the truth. When he'd told her he wanted to be in her life but keep her a secret because of his political ambitions, it was a stab in Erica's heart. Time and time again, she tried to reject him for making her his dirty little secret, but he would pull her back into her life. She let him.

Breaking her heart to maintain his ambitions was a perfectly legitimate excuse for him. But then again, Jonah believed everything he did was perfectly legitimate. No matter whose life was destroyed, as long as it wasn't his. Look at where that got him.

"I'm too tired to do that," he said.

She looked him over. He did look different than usual, more humbled and less like a bully. It was likely another ploy. He'd used this before to get him on her side. It was all a ploy.

Erica realized he wasn't going to leave until he wanted to, so she went ahead and started putting her groceries away.

"After what you did to Alex," she said, "I will never forgive you. It's worse than the threats you made to Terrell and Sherise if they ever told anyone you were my father. I forgave you for that."

"Did you?" Jonah asked sarcastically. "Because you seem to

still remind me of it all the time. Doesn't sound like forgiveness to me."

"But with Alex," she continued, ignoring him, "you destroyed his life."

"His mother destroyed his life." There was a hint of Jonah's anger in his usually controlled voice. "Alex would have had a perfect life had she not exposed me as his father."

"A perfect life?" She turned to him in disbelief. "You just don't get it, do you? A perfect life not knowing the truth about who you are or who your real father is? Have you even tried to reach out to him?"

"I know he's in Miami," Jonah said.

"He had to leave D.C. and his dream of a life in politics," she reminded him. "But you didn't answer my question."

"I'm sure he wants nothing to do with me."

"That's the excuse you tell yourself." She looked at him shamefully. "You probably resent him for even existing, don't you? You blame him for ruining your chance at the White House."

"His fucking mother—"

He stopped when Erica slammed her fist on the counter.

"Had to expose who you were because we all believed that you were going to kill Terrell! It was the only thing she could think of to save him. This is all your fault, Jonah. You still don't fucking get it."

"I get it more than you know," he said calmly.

"Well, you can just leave me off your comeback tour, Jonah. Even if it is in secret."

"Comeback tour?" He frowned before smiling. "That's not what this is. I'm here to agree with you. You were better off without me in your life and I agree that we need to go our separate ways."

Erica studied him intently, trying to figure out what this game was.

Jonah stood up from the sofa and walked over to the kitchen

counter. Standing on the opposite side, he looked into Erica's eyes. He sighed like a man with a heavy heart, but Erica was suspicious, often questioning that he even had a heart.

"I'm going to leave you alone," he said. "But I wanted to tell you that no matter what I've done, and I've done a lot, I've never lied to you about your mother."

"Don't," Erica warned as she felt herself choking up.

"I'm not trying to use her to soften you up," he said. "Like I've done in the past. I'm just telling you the truth. I cared about Achelle. She was . . . one of the best people I've ever met in my long, traveled life."

"I don't need you to tell me that my mother was a great person," Erica said.

"I'm telling you anyway." Jonah stuffed his hands in his pants pockets, the move of a much less confident man than Erica knew him to be.

"And she was right to never tell you about me, Erica. She knew that I wasn't going to be what you needed me to. I would love to believe that if she'd told me about you, I would have done the right thing; the good thing. But I don't know and she didn't want to put you through the pain of that choice."

Erica looked away from him, trying to get control over her emotions. She never questioned her mother's devotion and love, but she did wonder what her life could have been like if she'd known her real father.

Would it have been even more painful to deal with his social rejection as a small child? Maybe he would have provided for her and her life would not have been such a financial struggle? Who knew? Erica would not question her mother's choices. She knew her mother loved her and her brother Nate more than anything in the world.

"And that's that," he said as plainly as if he was ordering food at a restaurant.

"So you're leaving," she said as firmly as she could muster. "For good this time."

He nodded. "Don't look too choked up about it."

"Are you going to tell me how you go into my apartment?" she asked.

He shook his head.

She rolled her eyes. "Then, yeah, I guess that's that."

He looked disappointed in her reaction, but Erica could tell he knew he had no right to expect anything more.

"Good-bye, Erica."

"Good-bye, Jonah."

With that, he turned and walked to the door, opened it and stepped out, closing it behind him. Erica stared at the door for several minutes, not knowing what to do or what to feel. She couldn't deny that hint of longing that had existed inside her ever since she'd gotten over the shock of finding out Jonah was her father. She couldn't help but wish for more.

Ultimately, she knew the truth, and it was that this man had brought her nothing but pain and fear. He had tried to control her, rip her from relationships that she held dear, and threaten to hurt those she loved. She had done nothing to hurt him and had given him chance after chance.

She felt anger begin to swell inside her. Who was he to walk out on her? Who was he to say this was over after she'd told him several times? Was this his way of having the last word? Another power play? Did he think she would fall for his ploy and beg him to be in her life?

Well, she wouldn't. This was no game. She knew she was better off without him in her life.

"I'm better off with him dead," she said soundly to an empty apartment. "To hell with you, Jonah Nolan."

"There he is," Justin said as he pointed out Jerry Northman. Sherise turned to look where Justin was pointing. She saw him. Jerry had just entered the great room of the Maryland governor's mansion. She'd been looking for him since they arrived at the house for the party, determined to get a chance to talk to him and get some answers about Maurice Blair. She hadn't been able to find him yet and enlisted Justin's help to keep an eye out.

"God dammit," she said. "He's with him."

Standing only a foot from Jerry was Maurice Blair, looking dapper in a tailored blue suit. There were also three senators and the biggest tech billionaire on the East Coast. Maurice was cheesing it up with all of them, doing the thing he was known for, schmoozing.

"You might want to watch your expressions," Justin said. "You look like you want to bite his head off and stuff it up his ass."

"I do," she said, regaining her composure.

She watched as a couple more people approached Jerry, but Maurice played guard. He was setting it up so that they had to greet him first. He had no right to do that. He wasn't a gatekeeper!

"I'll bet you he's gonna try and keep Northman by his side all night," Justin said, accepting a glass of wine from the waiter that passed by.

He offered the glass to Sherise, but she shook her head.

"No," she said. "I want to keep a clear head tonight. I've got to get Jerry away from him. I can't grill him on Maurice if he's hanging around."

"Just tell him it's an urgent matter." Justin took a sip of the wine.

"No," she answered. "I don't want to say anything around Maurice. I don't want him knowing that I'm trying to get Jerry away from him. He'll know something is up."

"Hello, Sherise."

Sherise turned to see Stephen Northman standing next to her. Stephen was the youngest child of Jerry's three children and the only son. At twenty years old, he was a junior at Harvard

University who had taken off the current semester to support his father on the campaign.

He was average height, about six feet tall, and thin. He was good-looking, with sandy blond hair and bright blue eyes. He favored his mother more than his father and had perfect teeth when he smiled, although he rarely did. He spoke very well, but always had a tone of boredom with life in his voice.

Stephen always seemed fine, but he never seemed happy. At least that was what Sherise had decided from the time she had spent around him in the past year and a half. He was very secretive. She'd remembered several times when neither Northman nor his wife knew where he was or what he was doing.

This was supposed to be a formal event, but he was wearing a pair of khakis and an expensive blue sport jacket over a button-down shirt.

"Hey, Stephen," she said with a smile. "How are you doing?"

He shrugged. "You look amazing."

"Thank you." She placed her hand on Justin's arm. "You remember my husband, Justin. You've met before."

"Oh yeah." Stephen, almost reluctantly, held his hand out to shake Justin's, but quickly returned his attention to Sherise.

"You know I'm going back to school at the beginning of the year," he said. "I kind of think I'll miss this."

"It's exciting," she said, raising her tone to appeal to him. She had just figured out a way to get Jerry alone and needed Stephen's help. "You've been such a great part of the campaign."

"I'd like to stay," he said. "Work with you and the others. But Mom and Dad don't want me to."

"We're gonna miss your contribution," she said.

She titled her head to the side just a bit, so that the tendrils of her long hair fell to the side. She had his full attention. It was very easy. It wasn't just because she looked amazing in the purple strapless gown she wore. She already knew that Stephen had a bit of a crush on her.

"You helped me often," she continued.

He stood up a bit straighter with a proud smile. "I liked working with your team the most."

"You know what," she said as if almost surprised at the idea that just came to her. "You can help me now. As a matter of fact, I think this is something only you could do."

"Anything," he said eagerly.

She glanced briefly at her husband, who rolled his eyes and smiled in response.

Sherise checked her phone for the time. She had been in the mansion's library for five minutes alone, waiting. She was starting to doubt that Stephen could come through for her until she heard footsteps outside the door.

When Stephen opened the door, he stepped aside to let his father walk in first. Upon seeing Sherise, Jerry paused for a second in surprise, but continued inside.

"What are you doing in here?" he asked, before looking back at his son. "I thought you wanted to talk to me about something important."

"I just wanted to get you away from those people," Stephen said.

Jerry wasn't pleased. "Son, those are very important people. Tonight is not the night for your games."

"It's not a game," Sherise said. "I asked Stephen to get you away. I need to talk to you, Jerry."

Jerry frowned. "You need to use trickery? Why couldn't you just come up to me and talk to me?"

Sherise turned to Stephen. "Thanks, Stephen. That'll be all."

He gave an accomplished smile before leaving and closing the door behind him.

Sherise walked up to Jerry, facing his disapproval with concern. He seemed to be veiling something. He didn't want to be alone with her.

"What's going on here?" he asked.

"Jerry, I'm sorry about this, but please don't act like you're being swindled by a stranger. I need to talk to you."

"You've said that," Jerry said. "Now please hurry so I can get back to our guests."

"What are you doing with Maurice Blair?" she asked.

She watched his reaction. His entire body tightened and he looked away.

"Sherise, this is something we can discuss at the office."

"I don't think it is," she countered. "I think something's going on. His access to you is . . . unheard of. I know you know this game. I know you know who should and shouldn't have access to you now that you're president-elect. He can't—"

"Don't tell me what to do," he snapped.

He could see from Sherise's expression that she was offended and he immediately softened. With an expression of regret, he reached out and touched her shoulder.

"There's a process involved," Sherise said, speaking slowly. "An outsider can't just come in and . . ."

"He's not . . ." Jerry sighed and lowered his head for a moment. When he looked back up at Sherise, he smiled. "Sherise, I value you more than you can know. You've been great at your job even with all of your challenges."

"Challenges?" she asked, confused. Was he talking about the baby? Justin's harassment suit?

"What I mean," he continued, "is that I . . . I might as well tell you now. Marcus isn't an outsider anymore. He's joining my administration."

Sherise gasped. She had always suspected Marcus was trying to get jobs for others, not one for himself. She should have known better.

"Jerry, if you think I'm letting that slime ball work for me on . . ."

"He's not going to be working for you." Jerry's expression changed, almost to a cringe. "You're going to be working for him."

"What?" She must have heard him wrong.

Jerry removed his hand from her shoulder. He looked terribly ashamed and could barely make eye contact.

"Maurice Blair is going to be my press secretary, Sherise. I'm sorry."

Sherise was too shocked and stunned to say anything as Jerry turned and walked out of the library. Even though he was gone, she was making a huffing sound, trying to speak, trying to comprehend what she'd just heard. This was impossible. It couldn't be. That job was hers. How could he . . . how could this be happening?

4

City Tap House on I Street in Northwest D.C. was an unassuming, but nice restaurant. It was warm and casual with an upscale refurbished factory design. It served basic food such as pizza, salads, steaks, and lobster rolls, but was mostly known for its selection of sixty different beers, two of which Erica and Corey were sampling on their first date. A date that, in Erica's opinion, was going great just two hours in.

Corey had picked her up at her apartment earlier that evening. From the way he almost seemed to be speechless for several seconds after laying eyes on her, she knew she'd chosen well with a sexy red wrap dress and her hair up in a waterfall French braid. Asking advice from Billie, Erica picked the right tone between looking nice and keeping it causal to match the restaurant, a place that Corey selected based on recommendations from friends.

As he drove to the restaurant, Erica wondered if this would be awkward, as many first dates can be, but she had no reason to. Just like before, conversation between the two of them flowed naturally. He was cracking jokes and being just flirtatious enough to make her forget this was a first date.

Sitting at a table in the lounge, they shared an appetizer of blue crab mac and cheese with their beers, discussing the traditional things one talks about on their first date. He grew up near Chicago, raised by a single mother who was a high-ranking administrator with the city. He had a younger brother who was a freshman at Northwestern University. Corey's parents divorced when he was only ten and his father, a city worker, fell off the face of the map. Erica sympathized with his mostly fatherless childhood, but respected that he didn't complain. Corey didn't seem like one to feel sorry for himself.

Any short moments of silence were tempered by the basketball game on the large TVs that sat at the bar in the center of the room. Either Corey or Erica would briefly comment on the game before returning the conversation to each other.

Erica was impressed with his experimental nature. When she suggested they order the Honey Goat Cheese pizza with sliced red onion, pistachio, and rosemary, he didn't even blink. "Let's go for it," he said with an eager smile.

He was a good listener, asking her about herself and Nate. Erica was naturally guarded and regretted that she couldn't be as open as he was, but she told him all she could—at least for the time being.

As she ate her cherry crisp dessert with vanilla ice cream, she listened attentively to him talking about his life in D.C. after graduating from the School of Public Affairs at American University.

"So after a year as a legislative assistant on the House Financial Services Committee, I got a job as a senior legislative assistant to Senator Harding. I've been there for three years, but as you might know, he lost his reelection campaign earlier this month."

"You don't want to move on to another senator?" Erica asked. "I'm not an expert on this stuff. I've only been doing it for a few months, but it seems like congressional staff move around a lot."

He nodded. "Yeah, but I'm not interested in that. If Harding was planning on staying in politics, I would stay with him. I respect that man a lot. But he's retiring. I'm ready to move on. That's why I'm interviewing in the private sector."

"Why Justin's firm?" she asked, leaning back in her chair.

His brows centered, suspiciously. "Am I being interviewed again?"

She shrugged. "I got Justin's back. He's not just my boss. He's like . . . family to me. I want to make sure he's bringing on good people."

Corey pointed at her with a nod. "You know, he said the same thing about you. That's why he was reluctant at first to give me your number. He's protective of you."

She smiled. "Yes, he is. His wife is my . . . she's basically my sister, so he's kind of my brother-in-law. I love his kids like they were my own."

"That's why you're going over there for Thanksgiving?" he asked.

She nodded. "Me and my brother. What all did Justin tell you about me?"

He shook his head with a coy smile that made Erica's stomach flutter a bit. He knew he was good-looking. This boy was going to be a handful.

"Nah," he said. "I'm not giving it all away. I'm basing my entire strategy on that intel."

She grabbed her fork and pointed it at him playfully. "I want that intel or you can stick this fork in our date. It's done."

"Threats?" he asked. "You're dangerous. I kind of like that."

"Don't get freaky on me," she warned. "Spill it."

"He said you were real."

"Real?"

He nodded. "He said Erica is a real chick, so no games."

"But you just said you had a strategy."

"Strategy isn't a game." He jauntily cocked his head to one side. "Strategy is serious business. Besides, I'm a man. I don't play games. I leave games to the boys."

"That's good to hear," she affirmed. "Because I don't play games either."

"He also said that you are very guarded."

Erica frowned. "Really? What did he mean by . . . Well, I guess he's right."

"He said I'd have to be patient because . . ." Corey paused as if trying to find the right words to say. "Because you don't easily let people in."

Erica's expression grew still and serious. "He's right. I've been through a lot, Corey. I'm pretty guarded. If that's not something you can handle, we might have a problem."

"Man, you are guarded," he said. "Already trying to push me off and it's only our first date. What can I look forward to on the second?"

Her eyes were sharp and assessing as she grumbled at his presumptuousness.

"Who says there's gonna be a second date?" she asked.

"Please." He pressed his lips together and shrugged, playfully pointing at her and then back at himself. "This is happening, Ms. Kent."

"This?" She mocked him, pointing to herself and then to him. "What is this?"

"So you plan on making this hard on me, huh?" he asked.

She nodded. "Any woman worth having would have to, now wouldn't she?"

"Yes," he agreed. "Yes, she would. And I'm okay with that. I'm okay with earning my way to your trust. As long as I get a fair shot. Are you fair, Erica?"

"I'm fair," she said, hoping that was true. She wanted to give him a chance. "You'll get a fair shot and you're lucky for it."

"Damn," he said, leaning back. "I like a lady who knows what she's worth. Even though her taste in football teams is awful."

She rolled her eyes. "Don't start on that. Your Bears got lucky. You got lucky."

"No," he corrected her, sitting up straight. "You're not getting away with that. Let's go double or nothing."

"Double or nothing? The game is over. You won. I'm paying."

"Girl, there is no way I'm letting you pay for dinner. You didn't think I was serious, did you? If it ever got back to my mama that I made a girl pay for dinner . . ."

"I lost a bet fair and square," she said, pointing at him. "You didn't make me do anything. And if you try and pay this dinner bill, you're gonna have me to answer to."

His eyebrows furrowed and he frowned as if thinking something over.

"What?" she asked.

"I'm trying to decide who I'm more afraid of," he said. "You or my mama."

"Your mama ain't here," she reminded him swiftly.

He sighed as if defeated and turned away. He looked up at the television playing the basketball game and his expression lit up.

"This dinner bill on whether or not Michaels makes both free throws."

She glared at him. "This dinner bill bet is over."

"Fine." He bit his lower lip in frustration. "Then a kiss."

"A what?"

"You heard me," he insisted. "If Michaels makes both free throws, you gotta kiss me."

Despite her look of extreme skepticism, Erica was suddenly very excited. She wasn't going to actually let him kiss her on the first date; even before the first date was over. Was she?

"And if he doesn't? Because he sucks at free throws."

"What do you want?" Corey asked.

"No more bets," she said. "This is getting a little too frisky for me."

"Deal." He held out his hand for a shake. "Come on, girl. He's about to shoot."

She sighed and quickly stuck her hand out to shake his. Just as she did, she turned to the screen and Michaels made his first shot.

She let out a quick gasp as she felt her entire chest tighten and her teeth clench. She was supposed to want him to miss the second shot, wasn't she?

"Here it comes," Corey warned.

When the second shot landed, several people in the bar and the lounge area surrounding it let out a victorious yell, including Corey. When he looked at her, he had a mischievous, very satisfied smile on his face that was borderline arrogant. It made her angry.

"You just think you're something, don't you?" she asked.

He laughed. "What would you think if you just won two bets in a row?"

"I'm not going to kiss you," she said.

He looked surprised. "What do you mean? We made a bet."

"I was coerced." She sat back in her seat and crossed her arms over her chest. "My friend Billie calls it under duress. That's a legal term."

"I know what under duress means," he said, with an annoyed tone.

"Then you know that's what happened," she said. "Agreements made under duress are not enforceable."

"So you're punking out?" he asked.

She grumbled. "I don't punk out."

He shrugged. "Yet I haven't gotten my kiss. A kiss that I won fair and square."

"That's your problem," she said. "You can't win kisses."

He pointed to the TV screen. "I just did. Sounds like some-one punked out."

"Don't say that again," she warned.

He smiled a daring smile as he leaned over the table. "Are you a woman of your word or what?"

She knew the game he was playing, but he was going to get away with it. She wasn't going to punk out.

"One kiss," she said, putting her finger up to make a point. "And if you even dare open your mouth, I will make you regret it."

He smiled triumphantly like he'd just won the basketball game all by himself.

"And knock that smile off your face," she ordered.

He tried to get serious quickly, but it wasn't working. His smile turned to laughter and soon Erica couldn't hold back her laughter either. This was silly, but deep inside she was a little scared. She was about to kiss him. She wanted to kiss him, but she wasn't sure that she should.

She leaned into the center of the table and he met her halfway. She looked into his eyes and couldn't help but smile. He wasn't teasing anymore. He was softer now, waiting, and wanting. It made her certain that she wanted to kiss him.

When her lips touched his, she felt an immediate spark of excitement and anticipation. She knew immediately that she wanted more . . . much more.

Then, suddenly, Erica was jolted by the sound of several people gasping and one person almost yelling out in surprise. Both she and Corey looked around and noticed that everyone was watching the large TV. When Erica looked up she was shocked to see that the game wasn't on anymore, but a breaking news report was there instead.

"As we just stated," the young, pretty blond reporter said as she looked into the camera with a grim stare, "it has been con-firmed by the Virginia State Police Department that former secretary of defense and recent Republican vice presidential candidate Jonah Nolan is dead from what appears to be a suicide."

The shock hit Erica like a brick to her face. She couldn't breathe. As she felt the room begin to spin around her, she gripped the edges of the table. She could hear Corey say her name once, and then again, but she could only feel the room spinning around her and his voice seemed to get farther and farther away. What had she just heard? Jonah . . . was dead? Jonah . . . killed himself? That was impossible.

Erica saw Corey face's come to within a few inches of hers as he gripped her arms with his hands. She was trying to focus on him and could see that he had a look of extreme concern on his face.

"Breathe," he ordered her. "Breathe!"

"Cady." Sherise called out her three-year-old daughter's name with a stern tone. "You know the rules. If you want to stay in the kitchen, you have to sit at the table. You can't run around and get into everyone's way."

Little Cady Robinson stood in the middle of the kitchen of the family's Georgetown home in her pink sweatpants and Hello Kitty shirt, her natural curls falling in tendrils framing her adorable brown face. Looking at her mother, Billie, and Erica in the process of preparing Thanksgiving dinner, she folded her arms across her chest with an adorable pout on her face.

"She's got your pout down pat, Sherise," Billie said.

"I'm serious, young lady." Sherise stared her down.

Her little princess had inherited a lot more than just her pout from her mother. She was stubborn as hell and Sherise knew she had to stay firm.

"I want Daddy," Cady finally squeaked out.

"Daddy is in the den watching football with Michael and

Nate," Sherise explained. "Why don't you go run around him in circles for a while?"

"I will, so now," she said as if her words were intended to upset Sherise. With a huff, she turned and stormed out of the kitchen, headed for the den.

"She can drive him crazy for a while." Sherise returned to her mashed potatoes. "Can someone hand me that roasted garlic?"

Billie looked at Erica, who was closest to the plate of roasted garlic bulbs, but she didn't react. She continued to wrap the bacon around the asparagus as if in her own world.

With a sigh, Billie walked over to her and grabbed the plate of garlic, handing it to Sherise. She and Sherise looked at each other before both turned to Erica.

"Now that Cady's gone," Billie said, "Erica, we want to talk to you."

Erica, in her world, kept wrapping the bacon until Billie grabbed her by the arm.

"Erica!" she yelled.

Erica jolted to attention and turned to face them. She didn't like the way they were both looking at her, like they thought she was crazy.

"I'm sorry," she said. "I was zoning out. What is it?"

"You know what it is," Sherise said.

Erica rolled her eyes and made a smacking sound with her lips. "Please don't start this again."

"You have to talk about it," Billie said. "Your father is dead."

"Not just dead," Sherise added. "He blew his head off."

Billie turned to Sherise with a warning glare. "Can we be a little more sensitive in our word choice?"

Sherise shrugged. She wasn't in the most sensitive mood. Her world had been turned upside down, and while she was dealing with the shock of it all, Jonah Nolan died.

"I don't expect Sherise to act like she's upset," Erica said.

No, Sherise wasn't going to shed a single tear for Jonah. The man had the power to destroy her entire life. Although Sherise had sworn to herself to never be unfaithful to Justin again after her one-night stand with Ryan Hodgkins, she broke that promise when she met Jonah Nolan.

When she was working on the Domestic Policy Council for the White House, she was assigned to work on a project in partnership with the Department of Defense. Sparks flew the second she met Jonah. She couldn't resist the temptation, but the truth was, she hadn't really tried. Sherise was drawn to his alpha-male qualities and his unquestioned power and influence. Their affair was brief and disastrous, and ended with Jonah basically threatening Sherise's life when she found out that he was Erica's father.

When Justin found out about her affair with Ryan, Sherise never even once considered confessing about Jonah. After all, with Justin's affair, Ryan could be forgiven. It was an even sin. But Jonah, no. . . . Not only was that two affairs to one against Sherise, but a man like Justin would never be able to get over the idea of a powerful man like Jonah getting his wife in bed. It would have ruined her life and cost Sherise everything.

Billie and Erica knew about the affair, but they would never tell. Sherise never doubted either of them. They would all take each other's secrets to the grave. That was how deep their connection was and had been since they were little girls. But as long as Jonah was alive, he was a threat. Now that he was dead, Sherise felt comfortable that their affair had died with him. It was a huge load off her shoulders.

"I never pretended to care that he's dead," Sherise said. "I'm upset for you, though, Erica. We both are, and no matter what you say, you need to talk about it."

"I've got nothing to say," Erica said.

Billie wasn't giving up. "Maybe you want to take some time off and just . . . you know, deal with it."

"I don't have that luxury," Erica said. "I have to work, re-member? I'm the broke one here. I haven't earned vacation days yet."

Sherise found this silly. "I'm sure Justin would understand if you wanted to—"

"I don't need him to understand anything," Erica inter-rupted. "I'm fine. What do you two want from me? You want me to cry? I can't. I didn't love him."

"You cared about him," Billie said. "That's why you kept giving him chances in your life."

"Which I warned you against," Sherise added.

"I may have once," Erica admitted. "But that all died with what he did to Alex. I was done with him a year ago."

"Have you tried to talk to Alex?" Sherise asked. "I saw the news. They were trying to locate him. You know where he is, right?"

Erica nodded. "And I'm not telling anybody. He wants to be away from all this and I won't betray him. And no, I haven't called him yet. I've got nothing to say to him. I'm not interested in talking about it with him, you guys, or anyone."

Billie sighed. "Erica, he's still your—"

"Stop it!" Erica yelled so loud that both Billie and Sherise jumped. "Stop trying to make me hurt for that asshole! He caused me nothing but pain. For Christ's sake, he never caused anyone I know and care about anything but pain and fear."

"Okay." Billie gestured for her to calm down. "Take it easy. We don't want the guys running in here."

Sherise dropped the garlic in the pot and began pounding it into the potatoes with the masher. "You flying off the handle is proof that you still have issues."

"My issue is with you two trying to ruin the holiday talking about a dead man I don't care about and won't miss." Erica re-turned to her job wrapping bacon. "Can we talk about some-thing positive, please? It's Thanksgiving."

"What about Corey?" Billie asked. "You're going on a second date as soon as he gets back from Waukegan, right?"

Erica didn't really want to talk about Corey either. Yes, she was excited about the chance to see him again, but more grateful that he still wanted to see her. After her shock at the newscast about Jonah's death, she had to make up a lie about having sudden chest pains so Corey wouldn't connect her ridiculous reaction to Jonah.

He wanted to drive her to the hospital, but as soon as they got out of the restaurant, she suddenly, one would say miraculously, was feeling fine. She had to do a lot of convincing to still keep him from taking her. Instead, he drove her home and she said a quick good night.

He called her later that night to check on her and again in the morning. Both times she apologized and, although he seemed hesitant at first, he eventually told her he wanted to see her again.

"Yeah, well," Erica began, "let's just move on to someone else, like you, Billie. Didn't you say that Michael's family barely even registered when you told them you were engaged?"

"Not the smoothest deflection," Billie said as she went back to her task of slicing the cornbread. "But that's not exactly accurate. It did register. They weren't happy."

"Did they get really ugly about it?" Erica asked. "How rude."

They weren't exactly ugly, Billie thought. She and Michael had stopped by the house on their way to the airport and told Dee Dee the news. Aisha wasn't there. Dee Dee was in shock at first. When she finally spoke, all she could say was, "So soon?" They'd been dating for over a year.

"His mom just put on that pasted smile," Billie said. "You know, the one that tells you she wasn't happy, but you couldn't call her on it. Her congratulation was so limp, it needed Viagra to be believed."

Erica laughed. "She'll come around. Are you letting it get to you? I mean, I expected you to bring about fifteen bride magazines here with you tonight."

Billie wasn't about to let Dee Dee's reaction to the news get her down. She was flying on a cloud right now. "I have all the magazines, but I didn't want to bring them over in case it was insensitive to you."

"That was a mistake," Erica said.

"Besides," Billie turned to Sherise. "When I was talking to Sherise about it on the phone yesterday, she didn't sound enthused either."

"What's wrong with you, Sherise?" Erica asked. "Jealous?"

"What am I jealous of?" Sherise said. "I've already got my husband."

"But you know the bride gets all the attention," Erica said.

"Shut up," Sherise said, turning to Billie. "I'm happy for you."

"Then what's with the attitude?" Erica asked.

Sherise hesitated a moment, feeling a stab in the pit of her stomach just at the thought. She didn't want to do this. Not here, not now.

"Nothing," she said, turning her back to them. "Just get back to work. I want dinner on the table by four thirty."

Billie and Erica looked at each other. They both noticed the hesitation. Something was wrong.

"Here's the deal," Billie said. "We're not going to do one more lick of work until you tell us what's going on. We don't keep secrets, remember?"

She turned back to them. "I can't do this right now, girls. Just don't. . . . We need to get dinner on the table."

"Hey." Billie walked over to her and placed her hand on Sherise's arm, squeezing it gently. "Something is really wrong. I can tell it in your voice."

"Yeah," Erica said, walking over to both of them. "You sound . . . you sound like you do when you're in over your head."

Sherise pointed to her angrily. "I am *not* in over my head!"

"Whoa." Erica held her arms up in the air to gesture surrender.

"I'm sorry," Sherise said as she sighed and leaned against the granite counter. She dropped the masher in the pot.

Billie and Erica looked at each other again. Sherise just apologized. Something was definitely wrong.

"Spill it," Billie ordered.

As Sherise relayed the bomb that Jerry had dropped on her a few days ago, she had to take strong breaths to keep from yelling. She told them about how she felt so enraged after Jerry told her that she didn't even trust herself to stay at the party and not lose it and destroy what was left of her career. She grabbed Justin and they immediately left.

Ignoring all the texts from LaKeisha and others asking where she was, Sherise told Justin how Jerry had just told her that everything she had worked for was going to be handed to Maurice Blair on a platter. He held her while she cried, but being Sherise, that only lasted five minutes. She wasn't the crying type.

"Why are you just now telling us?" Erica asked.

Since they were kids, they told each other everything. No matter how hard, how embarrassing or humiliating, there were no secrets between them. They shared each other's pain, which made it all bearable.

They were all sitting at the kitchen table, their chairs practically on top of each other as Erica and Billie flanked Sherise, who was leaning on the table wringing her hands together.

"You both had so much going on," she said, her voice a little shaky. "The engagement and Jonah blowing his head off."

Erica rolled her eyes. "Please, Sherise. We both love you, but being considerate of others is not your strong point."

Billie managed a bit of a laugh. "Exactly. You're our sweetie, but it's not like you to not let it be all about you."

Sherise had to smile. They both knew her too well to pull one over on them.

"Okay, you got me," she said. "I was . . . embarrassed. It's humiliating getting . . . rejected."

"It's rough on all of us," Erica said. "Just rougher on you, because you're not used to it. Sherise always gets what she wants."

For some reason, those words lit a spark in Sherise and she lifted her head, sitting up straight. She looked at Erica and then Billie.

"You're right," Sherise said. "I always get what I want and there isn't anything I've wanted more than to be press secretary to the president of the United States. It's all . . . all I've been working for since, well, forever."

"I'm so sorry, honey." Billie rubbed her back.

"Don't be," Sherise said. "I was in shock for a few days. I just knew that this job was mine and I let my guard down. Maurice Blair slipped in and took it. But it's my job. I've earned it. I want it and I get what I want."

"What are you planning to do?" Erica asked.

"I'm going to do what I've been doing since I was a little girl. What I'm best at." Sherise swung her head, flipping her hair back, with a smile. "I'm gonna fight."

Erica sat back in her chair, completely confident in Sherise without needing to know what her plan was. "That Maurice Blair has no idea what's in store for him."

They all turned to the archway to the kitchen as they heard baby crying sounds come closer. It was Michael, carrying Sherise's baby in his arms. Six-month-old Aiden Robinson was an adorable, caramel-colored baby boy with curly hair, big dark eyes like his sister, and very kissable fat cheeks. He was generally happy and joyful, but right now he was anything but. The fact that Michael was holding him away, with his hands under Aiden's armpits as if he was toxic, probably didn't help.

"Why are you holding him like that?" Sherise got up and rushed over to him. "He's not poison."

"I don't know how to hold babies," Michael said, handing him to Sherise. "Justin made me bring him to you. He won't stop crying."

Aiden was already starting to calm in his mother's arms as she kissed him on his soft forehead.

"And Justin was too lazy to get up himself?" Sherise rolled her eyes. "What a surprise."

"Actually," Michael said. "He got a call from work. Can you believe that?"

"Is my little sweetie okay?" Billie asked as she made her way to Sherise.

She leaned in and kissed Aiden on his cheek. He reached out and grabbed her face with his tiny hands and smiled. She simply adored him.

"He always smiles at his auntie Billie." Sherise cradled him so he was facing outward. "I think he just needs some air. It's still warm out. I'll just take him for a quick walk in the backyard. That should . . ."

"Let me do it," Billie pleaded, although she was already taking the baby out of Sherise's arms.

She kissed him again before bringing him to her and enfolding him in her arms. She looked at Michael. "This is how you hold a baby."

Michael started to follow Billie as she headed to the sliding doors of the kitchen that led to the small backyard, but as she stepped outside, he stopped at the kitchen counter and reached for a slice of cornbread.

"What are you doing?" Sherise slapped his hand away. "It's not dinner yet."

"Just one piece?" he asked.

"You guys have snacks in the den," Erica said. "Or did Nate eat them all again? That boy has a hollow leg."

"That boy eats like a young man with a young metabolism," Michael said. "I used to be able to eat like that."

"One piece," Sherise allowed. "That's it."

"Thank you." He grabbed a piece and took a bite. "Can you believe that? Justin's client calling him on Thanksgiving? That's D.C. for you. A man can't even spend time with his family in peace on a holiday."

"Well," Erica said. "He was actually watching football, to be exact."

"D.C. is all work," Sherise said. "You know it. You've been here ten years. It's just something we have to deal with. It's a challenge. You'll face it too when you and Billie have kids."

"No way," Michael said. "My kids aren't going to be raised in D.C. Not a chance."

As he turned and headed out to the back to be with Billie, Erica and Sherise looked at each other, confused.

"Did he just say what I thought he said?" Erica asked.

"Does Billie know this?" Sherise asked. "Because I think it's pretty important that . . ."

Both she and Erica smelled it at the same time, sniffing in the air. Something was burning!

"Oh my God," Sherise yelled. "My turkey!"

5

Sherise drove up to the governor's mansion without a hitch. She was a familiar face there now and was allowed to drive up to the house with just a minimal search. The only issue she had was the second she reached the door, the security guard, one she didn't recognize, told her she wasn't on the Governor's schedule today.

"I don't need to be on his schedule," she admonished him. "I'm on his staff. I'm here to work, not have a meeting with—"

"Ma'am," he said, holding up his hand to silence her. "If you work for him, you know that access has been severely restricted and no one who isn't on the list—"

"I'm always on the list." Sherise's voice was raised now. "I made the fucking list."

He frowned at her, clearly offended by her tone, but Sherise didn't give a damn. No new guy was going to treat her like this.

"It's okay," came a voice from behind the large man.

Sherise recognized the voice and smiled the second Stephen Northman appeared in the doorway.

"She can always come in," he said to the guard.

The guard didn't want to give an inch. "She's not on the list, and the orders are that anyone, even staff, has to be pre—"

"She's on the list." Stephen needled himself between the

guard and the door, making room for Sherise to take his hand and enter the house. "She's always on the list."

Sherise smiled at Stephen and stepped inside, ignoring the guard. A few steps in, Stephen let go of her hand.

"Thanks, Stephen," Sherise said with a warm smile.

"No problem," he said. "Things are weird around here. Ever since he won, things . . ."

"We won," she corrected him. "We all won that election. You too."

He smiled as if trying to be polite, but not really wanting that compliment. "You here to see Dad?"

She nodded. "Where is he?"

"He's out back." Stephen gestured for her to follow him and she did. "Is this about the party?"

"What about the party?"

"Well, I saw my dad leave the library real soon after he got there and then you left a few minutes later and looked . . . you looked kind of out of it."

"It's complicated." Sherise didn't want to talk to Stephen about it. She was already anxious enough about her impending confrontation with Jerry.

"I asked you what was wrong," he continued, "but you walked right past me. You didn't even look at me. You said nothing."

Sherise didn't even remember seeing him. She didn't remember much except grabbing Justin and getting the hell out of there.

"I'm sorry, Stephen. I had a lot on my mind. I would never purposely ignore you."

He looked at her and smiled appreciatively. "I didn't think so. That's why I was worried. And ever since the party, Dad has been acting really weird. Or weirder than usual."

They reached the patio doors that led to the expansive deck. Past the deck, Sherise could see Jerry in the yard, playing with the family's two Alaskan huskies.

"He's under a lot of pressure," Sherise said. "We all are, but I don't want you getting involved."

"I just wanted to help." Stephen opened the door and stepped aside. "I haven't been of much help lately."

Sherise placed her hand on Stephen's arm. "You're sweet, Stephen. You never give yourself enough credit. But this is a professional issue between me and the governor. I can handle it myself."

Sherise was near the bottom step of the deck when Jerry turned to see her. She was looking right at him, needing to gauge his every reaction to give herself an advantage. He threw the ball in his hand away, sending the dogs off and running, and turned to her. He was clearly not expecting her and didn't seem all too happy. He knew what he was in for.

"Sherise," he said, as soon as she approached, "it's the day after Thanksgiving. Can we at least . . ."

"This can't wait and you know it," she said.

"I can't tell you what you want to hear," Jerry said, shaking his head in a regretful gesture. "Blair has the job and . . ."

"Do you want me to come into work Monday?" she asked.

His eyes widened. "Sherise, you can't quit. I need you."

"Then you need to give me an answer. A real answer."

Jerry was good at emotionally connecting with people. He always had been, but Sherise had taught him to be even better. She could tell that he was using the skills she'd taught him when he looked into her eyes. His entire expression changed. The demeanor of his body language became very sympathetic and genuine.

"Sherise, I value you very much." His tone was soft and sincere. "I'll do anything to keep you as my deputy press secretary. Or maybe another position. What do you want? I can pay you the very highest salary allowed."

"I want what I've earned," she demanded. "To be press secretary for the president of the United States."

His demeanor deflated a bit as his tone turned more regretful. "You know how this game is played, Sherise. You can't get to the White House without owing people. You've done a great job for me, but there are people who have spent millions, given me priceless endorsements and . . ."

"Maurice Blair isn't one of those people," Sherise said. "He's a PR flack on his way down. His best days are behind him and he's not a golden donor."

"But he brought several of them to me," Jerry said. "You know that. This race was hard as hell, Sherise. Once President Matthews selected a female vice presidential candidate to replace Jonah Nolan, we faced an uphill battle."

"I get favors," Sherise said. "But you don't cow to the first PR flack who tells you you owe him. You put him in charge, Jerry. That's a horrible precedent to set. You're supposed to be in charge, Jerry!"

"I know I'm in charge," he snapped at her. "Do you know I'm in charge?"

She paused a moment, noting his more aggressive manner. He felt his authority was being challenged, so Sherise tried to temper her approach.

"Blair has lost his touch," she said, speaking softer. "Everyone knows it. He's good at getting people to support candidates, but when it comes to the press, he's alienated them all. You don't want him to be your liaison. The press will take out their disdain for him on you in their coverage."

Jerry frowned as if he was just now thinking of this. He looked very apprehensive, but almost—if Sherise was reading it right—helpless.

"Let's look at it positively," he said. "Press secretaries never last too long. The press will be hard on him and he'll realize he's in over his head and get out of the game. Then the job is yours."

"You're okay with that?" she asked, surprised at his reasoning. He was usually a very reasonable man. This was odd. "You're okay with the first face of your administration to the press eventually fucking up?"

"This is the way it is, Sherise. I'm just trying to make the best of the situation as I see it. It's at least something, isn't it?"

"No, it isn't," she answered. "And I'm not the hopeful type. I'm the type that . . ."

Sherise couldn't take it anymore. He was practically moving away from her, taking a step back. It was as if he wanted to run away from her. This was not the man she knew. Jerry didn't back down from conflict, and certainly not with someone who worked for him.

"Tell me," she said, her voice trying to sound sympathetic even though she was still very angry. "Tell me, Jerry."

"Tell you what?" he asked. "I've been telling you. The decision is made."

"Something is wrong," she said. "I know it. I can see it in your eyes, the way you're carrying yourself, your voice. I can feel it. This isn't just about favors you owe the donors."

Jerry turned away from her and sighed loudly and heavily. He was silent for a full minute, the seconds stretching longer and longer.

"I've told you all I can," he said. "I owe some people a lot more than I'm willing to tell you. I would not be here without them. I know this is unfair to you, but I'm counting on your loyalty and understanding. Some rewards take longer than others."

"Sometimes they cease to be rewards when they take too long," she countered.

"We've accomplished so much together, Sherise. Please, don't turn your back on all of it because part of it didn't turn out the way you wanted; the way either of us wanted. Don't quit on me."

"I didn't quit on you," she said. "And I won't. I think you're making a huge mistake and, like you said, that mistake will be realized very soon. It may end up correcting itself, or it might end up having negative repercussions that we can't predict."

"I know I can count on you," he said, as if ignoring her final dire warning.

Yes, he could count on her, but Sherise knew at that moment that she could no longer count on him. As always, she could only count on herself when it came to her best interests. Something was up with Maurice and if she couldn't find out what it was, she was going to have to work around it.

Jerry was right. Press secretaries left the White House often. It was a stressful job and she knew that Maurice wasn't cut out for it. But that wasn't going to be enough for her. She didn't want sloppy seconds. She earned the right to be the first. She was going to have to convince Maurice that he wasn't cut out for it before the administration began on January 20. That was exactly what she intended to do.

When Billie entered her office Monday morning, she let out a big sigh. No, there weren't piles of folders and files on her desk. In this digital age, that never happened anymore. Still, she could just sense the massive amount of work waiting for her. She'd taken almost two weeks off around the holiday. She needed to use the time or she'd lose it. And no matter how much she planned ahead to be away, she knew there would be hell waiting for her when she got back.

"Vacation is definitely over, Billie," she said to herself as she went to her chair behind her desk and sat down.

She leaned down to place her purse in the bottom drawer when she heard a familiar young voice.

"You're back!"

Billie looked back up to see Tara Haas, her stepdaughter, or ex-stepdaughter, entering her office. The sixteen-year-old with glowing, beautiful dark brown skin, her father's piercing eyes, and tiny features came rushing into the room, all smiles. Billie felt the familiar warmth in her heart at the sight of the girl she loved so much who was growing up way too fast for her liking. She could have sworn the girl looked older than she had the last time Billie had seen her just a few weeks ago.

Billie suddenly realized she had her engagement ring on and panicked as Tara made her away around her desk. She quickly snatched the ring and threw it in her purse. She would have to tell Tara about this, but right now was not the best time. She hadn't exactly figured out how to approach it, especially suspecting that Tara would not take it well.

"What are you doing here so early?" Billie asked.

Tara was an intern at Agencis due to Billie's efforts. It was a way for Billie to have Tara in her life without ruffling Porter's feathers too much. After two years of fighting tooth and nail to keep Tara in her life and Porter using Tara to hurt or punish her, they called a truce. The damage had been done. Tara had hated them both and they agreed to work together to regain her trust.

Over the last year, Porter had brought Tara, now a junior in high school, back home from Michigan, and she and Billie had gotten close again. Convincing Agencis to hire her as an intern was just another way to spend time with her, and Billie cherished every moment. The private school that Tara attended had an internship partnership program that allowed juniors and seniors to spend two mornings a week with an approved company.

"Daddy dropped me off before going to work." Tara reached out for her.

Billie reached up to give her a hug and kissed her on the cheek. She was grateful Tara didn't complain. She usually didn't like getting kisses anymore. It was hard for Billie not to still see her as a little girl.

"He gets up so damn early."

"So you're cussing now?" Billie sent her a look of displeasure.

This relationship was still weird. Billie was the only real mother Tara had ever known, but she had no authority over her. Not to mention the fact that Porter had a fit every time Billie tried to tell Tara what to do now.

"*Damn* isn't a cuss," Tara said in that high-pitched flighty voice she used when she wasn't bothered. "Lane said *shit* in the meeting last week. I was sitting in the back of the room. No one even reacted."

"You're an intern," Billie admonished. "It's not okay for you to cuss at work at all. Get it?"

She sighed, annoyed, but then nodded. "You know this is my last week. 'Cuz then I have exams and holiday break and that's it."

Billie hadn't realized how fast time had gone by. "Well, we'll have to celebrate. You'll be here on Wednesday. That will be your last day, so we'll go to lunch, okay?"

This would work out well. Billie would wait until the internship was over to announce her engagement at work. That way, she could have all the time she needed to ease Tara into the new reality.

"Can Daddy join us?" Tara asked.

Billie cleared her throat as she turned her computer on. "I was hoping it could just be me and you. Or maybe just people from the office. Work-related, you know?"

"It would be okay," Tara whined. "He behaves now, right? You guys get along really well. Last time he came by here to take me to lunch, you two talked for like ten minutes. I counted."

She was right. Things were going well between Billie and Porter. It was kind of a miracle. She had finally let go of all her anger and feelings of resentment toward him and their failed marriage. This created an unexpected reaction from Porter. He let his anger subside too. More for Tara's sake than Billie's, but Billie was reaping the benefits, and they were actually civil with each other.

But Porter wasn't as well behaved as Tara thought. When she wasn't around, he continued to pry too much into Billie's relationship with Michael and take jabs at the man. He was still jealous and he didn't hide it well. But all in all, he was well behaved and the effect was a happier Tara, which was the best possible result.

"Let's just keep it work," Billie said. "I'm sure Daddy wants to do something special with just you and him anyway."

"He'd want you there," Tara said, her expression turning somber.

Billie was grateful when a knock came at the door and she turned to see Lane Redmond standing there. Looking like an Ivy League advert with bright blond hair and blue eyes the color of the ocean, he was wearing a suit that cost even more than his well-paid position would allow. He didn't hide that he came from money.

"Welcome back," he said. "Do you hate me for calling you twice while you were on vacay?"

"Sort of," she said with a smile. "But I'll definitely be calling you when you're on vacation, so it's all good."

He laughed nervously, not sure if she was serious or not. "Hey, Tara."

"This is my last week," Tara said, smiling wide at Lane.

Billie suspected Tara had a little crush on Lane.

"Aww," Lane said. "This place is going to fall apart without you."

Tara was beaming now. Billie had never seen her so proud.

"I'll visit, though," Tara said. "I promise."

"Hey." Lane stepped into the office. "Someone put donuts in the kitchen near my office. You might want to rush if you want to beat everyone to them."

"Donuts!" Tara was already heading out of the room. "See you later, Billie. Glad you're back!"

Billie laughed. "The only thing more exciting to her than you is donuts."

"I've been dumped for food before." Lane took a seat in one of the chairs on the other side of Billie's desk.

"You just come by to welcome me back?" she asked.

He shook his head. "Dylan Scott is coming in today."

"Already?" Billie asked.

Dylan Scott was a senior counsel at Agencis who had suffered a heart attack a couple of months ago. He was in his fifties but weighed at least 350 pounds, so it wasn't entirely unexpected. He was on medical leave currently.

"He's not coming back," Lane said. "Gil told me that he's coming in to offer his resignation to him."

Gil was general counsel at Agencis, the top lawyer and everyone's boss.

"Is he not getting better?" Billie asked.

Lane shrugged. "Gil says they talked on the phone last night and Dylan said that the only time he gets chest pains is when he thinks of coming back to work."

"Damn."

Lane nodded. "I know, right? Anyway, he's not coming back is basically the gist of it."

Billie hoped this was the right choice for Dylan, but she knew that Lane was telling her for more reasons than concern for a coworker.

"So what does this mean for you?" she asked.

Lane smiled. "Gil said I had a lot of reason to be hopeful that his position is mine. You know what that means for you?"

"Your ego will be even harder for me to deal with?"

"Very funny," he said. "No, it means you could be in for a promotion to senior associate general counsel. Happy?"

Billie would have to say an extra prayer tonight. A little over a year ago, her personal and professional life had fallen into a shambles. Today, she was head over heels in love and engaged to be married, she had a healthy loving relationship with Tara, and now she was possibly in line for a promotion at her job.

"Not happy," she said. "Blessed. Very blessed."

Corey James lived in Takoma Park, Maryland, a suburb less than ten minutes from D.C. His favorite place to hang out was the unassuming Cedar Crossing Tavern. This was where Erica met him for lunch, officially the second date that Erica didn't think would happen.

That he would still want to see her after she basically freaked out during their first kiss said something very good about Corey, and even though she was having a pretty ugly week, she was excited about the chance to see him again.

Erica knew there would be some awkwardness when she entered the very cozy fifty-seat restaurant. She spotted him right away in the typical Hill business-casual khaki pants and button-down striped shirt. He looked young and vibrant.

He was talking to a pretty young waitress with red hair and creamy skin who looked like she was a size zero with large breasts almost popping out of her tight black top. As Erica approached, she could tell that the waitress was flirting with Corey. Not just from the way she giggled and leaned forward to show cleavage, but from the way her demeanor completely changed the second Erica approached.

"Erica!" Corey smiled and stood up to greet her.

She smiled back and felt very hopeful when he leaned in to kiss her on the lips. It was a quick kiss, but was warm and sincere. Maybe this wouldn't be so bad.

"Am I late?" Erica asked, pointing to the glass of red wine on the table.

"No," he answered. "I'm early. Citra here just wanted me to try one of their new wines. On the house."

"How nice," Erica said as she looked at Citra, who politely smiled. What in the hell kind of name was Citra?

"I'll be back in a couple of minutes to take your order," she said with a Southern accent before walking off.

Erica sat down in her chair and waited until Jessica was out of earshot. "She certainly wasn't happy to see me."

"What do you mean?" Corey asked.

"You're joking, right?" Erica asked.

"Not so much joking as completely confused."

"That girl was flirting her ass off with you."

He laughed. "No way."

"Yes, she was." Erica didn't believe for a second Corey was that naïve.

"You were here for five seconds. How could you see that?" he asked.

"I only needed one second. A girl knows these things, Corey. That tip of her head, the giggling and the leaning forward. I messed up her game showing up."

"Nah, she didn't have any game," Corey assured her. "She's not my type."

Erica appreciated what Corey was trying to do, but she wasn't a fool. "She's every guy's type. Come on. All guys love the pretty, real skinny girls with big boobs. I've always wished I could be that small."

Corey's brows centered in a frown. "What the hell are you talking about?"

Erica was a little surprised by his words and the expression on his face. He was almost . . . offended.

"I'm just saying that she's . . ."

"You think she looks better than you?" he asked.

"I didn't say that," Erica said.

"You better not be," he stated. "Real skinny girls are only hot to other girls. Not to men. Not real men, at least. You're ten times hotter than she is."

She smiled, hoping her blushing wasn't obvious. "That may be true, but . . ."

"It is true," he said quickly. "You and those curves make a brother lose his train of thought."

She laughed. "You're embarrassing me. Stop."

"This could be a problem," he said.

"What?" she asked. "My curves?"

"All of it," he said, looking her up and down. "I mean outside the office, I can handle losing my train of thought, but at work . . ."

"Wait!" she exclaimed, her eyes widening. "Did Justin . . . Did you get a job offer?"

He nodded with a proud smile. "I'm joining the firm right after the new year."

"Congratulations." Erica felt both excited and nervous about the prospect of working alongside someone she was also dating. "Do you think Justin is okay with . . . us?"

"I asked him," Corey said. "He is a little worried and that's understandable. But he was willing to trust us."

She grabbed a menu and began looking at the choices. "We have to be professional at work, you know. No flirting or foolishness."

"All business," he said with a nod. "I know how to play this game."

"Is this a game?' she asked, looking up from the menu with a playfully raised brow.

"Everything is a game," he said. "Some more difficult than others."

"Why do I get the feeling you're pegging me as difficult?"

"Clearly."

She leaned back. "You hardly know me. We've been out once."

"And I'm still trying to figure that out," he said. "I backed off because you clearly didn't want to talk, but . . ."

Citra the waitress returned with a wide smile for Corey. "Can I take your order yet?"

Corey ordered a glass of the new wine for Erica. While she merely acknowledged Erica's order of a taco salad, Citra praised Corey's choice of jerk chicken wings as great and promised him he would be very pleased.

"I know you said you're guarded," Corey continued after Citra left, "but I was really worried. I wish you'd tell me more."

Erica knew this conversation was coming and she had nothing more to offer him, even though she wanted to. She hated this secret and she hated Jonah for placing the burden of it on her.

"What I can tell you," Erica said, in the most reassuring voice she could muster, "is that it wasn't about you. I was having a great time. And that kiss. It was nice."

"Nice?" he asked, looking a bit injured.

"Better than nice," she added. "It was just . . . other things."

"What other things?" he asked.

"We're not there yet," she said, even though Erica didn't think they'd ever be there.

"Here's what I'll say." Corey leaned forward on the table, looking into her eyes. "I like you a lot, Erica. I just want a chance. Whatever it is you think you can't trust me with, I just want a chance."

There was something about the look in his eyes as he said those words that made Erica want to defy everything she knew. She wanted to open up to him, to tell him all about Jonah. It wasn't even keeping Jonah's secret because he'd wanted her to anymore. Now the thought of telling anyone about Jonah was painful to Erica. She didn't want to open up about that. She didn't want to reveal anything to herself that she couldn't handle.

Thankfully, Citra returned with a glass of wine to break the tension. Just before Erica reached for it to taste, her phone rang. It was sitting on the top of her purse in the chair next to her and she could see the ID from where she sat. Her heart skipped a beat at the name she saw: J. N.

"What the . . ." Erica reached for the phone, turning to Corey. "I'm sorry, but I have to see who this is."

"Go ahead," Corey said, taking a sip of his wine. "I don't mind."

She doubted that was true, but Erica couldn't have resisted seeing who was calling her from Jonah's phone.

"Hello?" she asked tentatively as she answered.

"Is this Erica?" the woman's voice asked curtly.

"Who is this?" Erica asked.

"This is Juliet Nolan."

Erica felt a thud in her gut at the sound of that name. Jonah's ex-wife, the blond ice queen. The woman who hated Erica for existing and messing up her idea of what she thought was a perfect life. Although they had come face-to-face fewer times than one can count on a single hand, the two women had never been in the same room without something bad happening.

"Why are you calling me?" Erica asked.

"I don't want to." She was clearly annoyed. "I have to. You know what happened."

"Of course I do," Erica said. "What do you want, Juliet?"

"I could only find your number on his phone and I needed to talk to you."

"What is it?" Erica asked, impatiently.

"The funeral," Juliet said. "You can't come."

"What?" Erica said loud enough to catch Corey's attention.

"I'm telling you that you can't come," Juliet said. "If you were thinking of coming."

"I wasn't!" Erica yelled. She had done her research and knew that the funeral was Wednesday.

"Good," Juliet said, her voice sounding very satisfied. "Because you aren't welcome. This is for family."

"You're divorced," she said.

"I'm still his family and I have his kids," she said. "His real kids."

"Excuse me?" Erica asked. "I'm not real?"

"You know what I mean."

"I know damn well what you mean, Juliet. You have no right . . ."

"I have every right!" she yelled angrily. "You are not welcome. Don't show up. I will have security there and if they see you, they know to throw you out. Don't embarrass yourself and my family!"

With that, Juliet hung up and left Erica sitting there stewing in her anger.

"What is it?" Corey asked as he watched Erica stuff the phone back in her purse.

"Nothing!" Erica snapped. She felt her chest tightening and her teeth clenching against each other.

"It's not nothing," he said. "You look like you're about to explode. What is it?"

"How dare she!"

That bitch thought she could dismiss her like that? She didn't want to go to his damn funeral, but she wasn't going to be told by that cold shrew that she couldn't. She wasn't going to be told she wasn't real.

"Seriously, Erica. What's going on?"

Erica could see the look of impatience on Corey's face, but there was nothing she could do about it. She was too wound up. She was feeling anger and resentment take her over and she wasn't sure how long she could keep it under control. She had a right to be angry at Juliet's cruelty, but she was feeling enraged right now.

She wanted to do something. She needed to do something.

She needed to make Juliet sorry for trying to make her feel like she wasn't a real person. Making her feel like she had no father.

"I'm sorry, Corey." Erica grabbed her purse and stood up. "I have to go. I just . . . I just can't do this right now."

Erica heard him call her name once, maybe twice as she rushed out of the restaurant. She wasn't really listening as she rushed down the street. At first the tears were small, but within seconds, they were trailing down her cheeks like waterfalls.

"That bitch!" she yelled to the air. "I am his real daughter!"

6

When Sherise arrived at work Monday morning, she already had a plan in place, but the second she stepped inside her office and saw her assistant, Winnie, putting her things in a box, she was knocked off her game.

"What are you doing?" Sherise asked, alarmed.

Was she fired? What happened?

"I'm sorry." Winnie put the box down.

Winnie was a twenty-three-year-old beauty, half black, half Asian. She was petite and dressed in the hipster fashion that was consuming D.C. all the way down to the glasses with no prescription and ballet shoes.

"Maurice told me to do it," she said.

"Do what? Throw my things away?" Sherise walked over to her desk and threw her purse on her chair.

"Move you." Winnie was almost shaking in fear. "I swear to God, Sherise, I didn't want to do it, but he said that he's the boss now and I need to move you because your office is the biggest."

"He wants my office?" Sherise laughed while gritting her teeth. "That son of a bitch."

Sherise reached in the box and began pulling everything Winnie had put in right back out.

"Is this the only box?" Sherise asked.

Winnie nodded quickly. "What am I supposed to say if he gets mad at me?"

"Tell him to come see me," Sherise said. "Look, Winnie. Maurice is an idiot. He tries to hide that by being overly aggressive. He'll try to intimidate you so you're afraid to point out his mistakes. When he does, you come to me, okay?"

She nodded again. "Why is he even here? That job should be . . ."

"Don't." Sherise held her hand up to stop her. "This is Jerry's decision. Don't worry. It'll all work out the way it's supposed to."

"I hope so," Winnie said.

"Can you go get me a coffee?" Sherise asked.

"That," Winnie said, "I can do."

Winnie left as Sherise began replacing all of the items on her desk. She took a few deep breaths. She couldn't let things like this get to her. She had a plan, and her plans always worked when she stayed focused and didn't let little obstacles distract her from the big ones.

She didn't have much time that day, and the second she heard voices outside her office, an angry man's voice, she pulled herself together, tossed the box behind the sofa near the left wall, and sat calmly in her chair. By the time Maurice threw the door open, she was casually glancing down at her phone, looking as if she didn't have a care in the world.

"Why did you tell her to stop the move?" he asked, his voice grating.

He was giving her a menacing look, but Sherise refused to be intimidated by this fool. She looked up at him with a calm expression and a smooth tone to her voice.

"Good morning to you too, Maurice."

He made a grumbling sound as he tried to calm down only because her polite demeanor made him look bad.

"Sherise, I'm the press secretary now. You're aware of that, right?"

She nodded. "Jerry told me."

"Good." He nodded definitively. "Then you know that I get the biggest office on the team. That's this office."

"This is my office," Sherise said. "There is one two doors down that Phoebe Gills works in. It's almost as big as mine. I'm sure she'd move for you."

"I don't care if she'd move for me," Maurice ranted. "Sherise, I want my office."

"This is my office, Maurice." Sherise calmly placed her phone on the desk and sat back. "I'm not moving."

He shook his head, almost looking as if he felt sorry for her. "I know this is hard on you, Sherise. You did a fine job during the campaign."

"I did a great job," she corrected him.

"I don't know if I'd say that." He shrugged. "You were fine, but this is the big show now. Jerry needs someone with more experience. The PS job is mine, so you need to—"

"I know how you got this job," Sherise said. "So let's not pretend it was because Jerry actually wanted you."

His expression grew very still before he blinked quickly. Sherise knew that she'd cut a vein there. He had a horrible poker face. But this wasn't her game right now. She didn't know enough to go this route. Time to get back on focus.

"Kind of sad," she opined. "You need payoffs for the suck-ups to get a job now."

His discomfort quickly changed to resentment. "I don't need suck-ups to get me my job."

"Yes, you do," Sherise said. "You used to be good, Maurice. I'll give you that. But you're too old-school. You couldn't keep up. You don't know how to deal with women in the workplace. Your reputation has been ruined."

"I'm here, aren't I?" he asked, sarcastically.

"Like I said, people you helped when you were good called in favors to the president-elect who owes them for supporting his campaign. That's why you're here. It's the only reason you're here."

"Even if that was true," he said, walking over to her desk and staring down at her, "the result is, I'm here. I'm your boss."

Sherise stood up, placing her hands in fists on her desk. She eyed him intensely and said slowly, "And this is still my office."

His eyes tightened to slits as he huffed. "Fuck the office. It's just a symbol. I don't need those. You still work for me."

There was a knock on the door before Winnie peeked inside.

"Sherise?" she asked.

"Come in, Winnie," Sherise said.

"I got your coffee." Winnie quickly hurried to the desk, making a point to avoid being near Maurice. "Anything else?"

"I'm good for now," Sherise said.

"Wait a second, sweetheart," Maurice called out just as Winnie had almost made it to the door.

"Her name is Winnie," Sherise said firmly.

Maurice smiled. "Of course. Winnie, right?"

Winnie nodded. You could see that she didn't appreciate the sweetheart remark. Sherise imagined that Winnie, being as young as she was, might not be savvy enough to realize that he'd done it on purpose, to make her uncomfortable. She would have to sit down with Winnie and give her a talk about keeping a record of everything Maurice said and did in her presence. She had to know he had no right to call her sweetheart.

"I'm going to need a coffee as well," he said. "Black with cream. Please bring it to the main conference room."

"Certainly," she said. "Anything else?"

The slightly sarcastic tone in her voice made Sherise think she had underestimated Winnie. She was clearly not pleased.

"Yes, I need you to get me a hard copy of the PTEA before our training meeting in an hour."

"The PTEA?" she asked.

"The Presidential Transitions Effectiveness Act." His tone showed he was annoyed she didn't know. "You need to know these things, Wanda. We're an important part of the president's transition team."

"It's Winnie," she said, flatly.

"Whatever," he said. "Just get me a hard copy."

"Actually," Sherise smiled wide, unable to hide how easy Maurice was going to make her plan, "the PTEA is outdated. It was amended by the PTA, the Presidential Transition Act, in 2000."

Maurice pressed his lips together and stared Sherise down. She could tell he was trying to see if she was making this up to make him look foolish. Sherise didn't blink as she met his stare with her own. She never stopped smiling. He was wrong, she was right, and he knew it.

"I'm sure that's what you meant, though," Sherise finally said, her smile tilting to the side slyly.

He swung around to Winnie, who was standing in the doorway, trying hard to stifle a smile by biting her lower lip.

"Just do it!" he snapped at her.

Winnie rushed out of the office and Maurice turned back to Sherise.

"You think you're funny?" he asked.

"No," she answered. "I think I'm more knowledgeable of the transition than you, even though you're the boss."

"That's right," he said. "I am the boss. You better get with the program, Sherise, or you will be sorry."

"That sounds like a threat."

"I don't know what you mean." He smiled, backing away.

He looked at her for a few minutes more before turning and walking out, slamming her office door behind him.

Sherise sat back down in her chair with a very accomplished smile on her face.

This was her plan. She was going to make Maurice look like a fool. He was clearly going to make it easy for her. No one on Jerry's team would have confidence in him. She would make him appear incompetent, or even more incompetent than he already clearly was. She was going to bring it to a point where there were only two solutions. Jerry would have to fire him to restore order to his team or Maurice would be so frustrated, overwhelmed, and humiliated that he would quit, knowing he wasn't up for it.

When either result happened, Sherise would be there to save the day and take her rightful place as press secretary.

"I'll get with the program all right," she said to herself. "My program."

Billie was in the small legal library taking a break. Since she'd come back earlier that morning, everyone was stopping by her office. They needed this file, that folder, this research done, that call made. It was as if she was the only person who actually worked there. She needed a quick break from it all and when she got a call from Sherise, she took it. The library was always a safe bet. No one actually looked for books anymore. Everything was online.

"So what are you going to do?" Billie asked. "Tell everyone how you made a fool of him? Is that gonna work?"

"I'm not stupid," Sherise said. "Winnie's gonna do it. Trust me. That girl can't keep her mouth shut to save her life. That's why I never tell her anything. By the time we had our meeting an hour later, people were already talking about it."

"I don't know, Sherise." Billie sat down in one of the tightly wound leather chairs in the center of the room. "If this guy is the asshole you say he is, won't he catch on that you're up to something and just fire you?"

"He can't fire me," Sherise insisted. "Jerry won't let him."

"You don't know that." Billie worried about Sherise sometimes. She thought she was invincible.

"I don't know a lot about what's behind Jerry's decision on Maurice, but I know that he wants me to stick around. He wants me to have this job. I'm confident that he won't let Maurice fire me."

Billie didn't doubt Sherise's power over Northman. This girl had the future president of the United States crushing on her. "You have less than two months to get this done."

"I'll only need one," Sherise said. "At most."

"Well, since you seem to be so full of solutions, what are we going to do about Erica? You got her text?"

Billie had gotten a frantic text from Erica telling them that Juliet Nolan had called her to disinvite her from the funeral. She was pissed, but didn't respond when Billie asked her for more information.

"Just before I called you," Sherise responded. "I wanted to ask you what you wanted to do. Can't believe that bitch did that. What a shrew."

"Are you really in a position to call a woman whose husband you had an affair with a shrew?"

"Why the fuck are you mentioning that?" Sherise asked. "It didn't happen, do you understand me? It just didn't happen."

It did happen, but Billie was okay with pretending it didn't, considering how angry Sherise suddenly sounded. As a woman whose husband cheated on her, Billie had some very tense moments with Sherise when she'd found out about her affair with Nolan. They made their way through it, but Billie wasn't aware she wasn't allowed to mention it at all anymore.

"Sorry," Billie quickly offered. "But Juliet isn't our problem. Erica is."

"She wasn't planning to go anyway," Sherise said.

"That's not the point, Sherise. It's like a doctor telling a woman who wasn't planning on having kids that she can't have kids. It still hurts. Besides, I don't buy that bullshit about her not caring that he's dead."

"She definitely cares," Sherise agreed. "She's just faking it, but I really think we need to let her work it out. Erica isn't like you and me. She doesn't want us to help her work it out. She just wants us to listen and let her work it out for herself."

Billie moaned. "I guess you're right. I just get a bad feeling about this."

"Let me deal with her," Sherise said. "You have enough on your plate planning a wedding. How did your coworkers react to the news?"

"I haven't told them yet," Billie said.

"You are the only bitch I know that doesn't want to shout her engagement from the rooftops. Especially with that fat ring on your finger."

"I wore it in," Billie said. "But I quickly remembered and I took it off."

"Remembered what?"

"Tara is still here," Billie said. "I don't want her finding out that Michael and I are engaged. I'll wait until her internship is over to tell everyone. I think . . ."

Billie paused the second she heard a gasp. She had been facing the window, looking out at the busy streets, but swung around to face Tara, standing just inside the doorway to the library. She was less than fifteen feet away, but Billie hadn't heard her walk in at all.

"You're getting married?" she exclaimed, her face a mixture of shock and hurt.

"Tara." Billie quickly got up and walked toward her.

"You wanted to keep it from me?" Tara asked. "Why? Why wouldn't you want to tell me?"

"I gotta go," Billie quickly said into the phone before hanging up. "It's not that I didn't want to tell you."

"No," she argued. "I heard you. You don't want me finding out."

"Yet," Billie said. "Just because . . ."

"Why would you want to keep it from me? It's because of Dad. Because you don't want Dad to know, right?"

"I just want to do this the right way."

"Nothing about this is right." Tara's voice was harsh and she looked disgusted. "You can't marry Michael."

"I thought you liked Michael," Billie said.

"Yeah, but . . ." She threw her hands helplessly in the air. "What about Dad?"

"Oh, Tara." Billie sighed. "We've had this discussion. You know that your father and I aren't getting back together."

"I don't want to hear it!" Tara yelled. "This sucks. You're keeping secrets again and now you're gonna marry him. It'll all be over!"

"Tara!" Billie called after her.

Tara turned and ran out of the room in a very dramatic way any teenaged girl would when she finally had to face the fact that her parents weren't getting back together. When Billie got to the door of the library, Tara was already down the hallway.

This was going to be ugly. She'd known that Tara might not take it well, but she got along with Michael, so Billie had assumed it wouldn't be a disaster.

"Oh shit," Billie said. "She's gonna tell Porter."

Billie rushed down the hallway in search of her. Dealing with Erica was one thing. Dealing with Porter was another one altogether. If she could find Tara and calm her down, it might save her some time before she had to deal with Porter's ego.

★ ★ ★

Erica had just gotten home from a long day at work. It wasn't a good day. After getting Juliet's phone call, Erica went for a long walk, trying to calm herself down. The walk lasted a lot longer than expected and she was late getting back to work. Justin was upset because there was urgent business that had come up. Because of the recent elections, there had been a change in leadership on an essential Senate committee that could greatly impact two of his major clients. Things were frantic and so was Justin when she returned.

She'd finally been able to get out of there and made her way home. To an empty home for yet another day, and she was fed up with coming home to nothing. She was tired and still angry. All day, no matter what she was doing, all she could think of were Juliet's cruel words. Those seven words. *I have his kids. His real kids.* Erica couldn't even think of how that would have gone if Juliet had said that to her face.

Now that she was home, she wanted to eat something fried or fatty to make her feel better. But the second she opened the refrigerator door, she knew that wasn't going to happen.

"Dammit!" she yelled into the air.

There was nothing in there but a couple of bottles of water, a jar of pickles, and some orange juice. She had intended to go shopping this past weekend, but the news about Jonah's death had distracted her from everything. She hadn't thought to pick something up on the way home because she was just so focused on ending the day. Besides, she had to stop doing carryout. Now that all the bills were hers alone, things were too tight.

She slammed the refrigerator door to express her anger, but immediately regretted it as she pulled away and the handle came with her. She looked at the handle in her hand in disbelief at first.

"Are you fucking kidding me?" she asked.

This day couldn't get worse.

This place was already a dump and it was falling apart even more. She felt trapped. It was really all she could afford. The neighborhood used to be relatively safe despite the recent break-in attempt. If she went for something cheaper, it would be in a worse neighborhood, and living by herself now, Erica didn't feel that was an option. She couldn't afford anything better. Now she had to look forward to having to nag the landlord for weeks before he would do anything, as usual.

She reached for her phone to order pizza, feeling resentful that she was breaking her rule on spending money. She didn't give a damn. She was broke and the rent was due, but she was sick of thinking about it. She just wanted to stuff her face with something greasy.

Before she could dial her first number, the doorbell rang. Her radar went up. Since the attempted break-in, she was anxious whenever she heard an unexpected sound. She reached into the top kitchen drawer and pulled out the biggest knife she could find.

"Who is it?" she yelled out as she walked toward the door.

"Ms. Kent," the person on the other side of the door said.

She peeked into the peephole to match a face to the man's voice. She'd never seen him before. He was a young white man with brown hair cut short to his head and dark-rimmed glasses. He had a large nose and thin lips. He had on a tie and what looked like a black suit. He looked like an accountant.

"Who are you? What do you want?"

He cleared his throat. "My name is Tyler Vincent, Ms. Kent. I need a moment of your time."

"I don't want to buy anything," she said. "And I already found Jesus, so no thanks."

"This is a very important legal issue, Ms. Kent. Something that needs to be discussed in confidence."

Looking at him, Erica could see that the man already looked scared to death to be in this neighborhood. He seemed harmless, but she wasn't stupid.

"We're in the middle of dinner right now," she said.

Never let a stranger know you're a woman home alone.

"It's regarding Mr. Nolan," he said. "It's very urgent. I won't take up more than a few minutes."

That was enough to pique her curiosity. She opened the door just enough to stand in the doorway, but didn't let the man in.

"What is it?" she asked.

He seemed relieved to at least come face-to-face with her. "May I come in, Ms. Kent? It's very personal."

"He's dead," Erica said. "How personal can it be? And how do you know my name?"

He looked to his left and to his right in the empty hallway before leaning forward and whispering, "He's your father."

She groaned and stepped aside to let the man in. She closed the door behind her and turned to face him.

"You have a few minutes," she said. "That's all you said you'd need."

"Okay." He looked around as if waiting to be asked to take a seat, but after a few seconds of nothing, he continued. "As you've said, Mr. Nolan has passed away. I'm one of the lawyers in charge of his estate."

"He told you about me?"

"It's in the instructions attached to his will," Tyler said.

He reached into the briefcase he was holding and pulled out a dark folder.

"I can't reveal the entire will to you, but . . ."

"Does he acknowledge Alex Gonzales as his son?" Erica asked.

Tyler looked even more uncomfortable. "I can't reveal the entire will to you, but no, he doesn't mention Mr. Gonzales."

"Son of a bitch." Erica shook her head. "Your client was an asshole, Tyler. You know that."

"You might not think that when you hear what I have to say to you." He offered her the envelope.

Erica didn't take it. "What do you want to tell me? And if you tell me this is some restraining order preventing me from showing up at the funeral, be prepared to get your ass thrown out."

He cleared his throat. "Well, I guess I can imagine why you weren't going, but this is not that. What I'm offering is a part of Jonah's will. The part I'm allowed to share with you."

"I don't want anything from him," Erica said, finally taking the envelope.

"Not even one million dollars?" Tyler asked.

Erica's mouth opened, but nothing came out. What did he just say? What did she just hear?

"One what?" she asked.

"One million dollars," Tyler repeated with a smile proud enough to make one think that it was his money. "That's what your father left you, Ms. Kent."

"Don't call him that," she said quickly.

He blinked nervously. "Um . . . okay. That's what Mr. Nolan left you."

Erica felt her knees going a little weak, so she made her way to the nearby sofa and sat down. This man was still sending her for a loop from the grave, and he wasn't even in his grave yet.

"He was even lying then," she said.

"Excuse me?" Tyler asked.

"He sat here on this sofa and told me he was staying out of my life from now on." She laughed. "He was lying. He always lies."

"Well, I can assure you, Ms. Kent, this will is not a lie. It is a fully executed legal document."

It took her a second before she regained her composure and looked at Tyler.

"This is control, you know. This is his way of pulling the shots, even from the grave."

Tyler pointed to the envelope still in Erica's hand. "There are no stipulations in this will. You can spend this money however you want."

"I don't want anything from him," she finally said.

This time it was Tyler's turn to be speechless.

"I hated him," Erica said. "I'm not going to load it on you, but that man . . . You just wouldn't understand."

"It's not my place to ask," Tyler stated. "But how could you not want a million dollars?"

"Alex is just as much his son as I am his daughter," Erica informed him. "He left him nothing, right?"

"A person is only obligated to provide for minor children upon death. Once your children are adults, you can choose not to give them anything."

"Because he's an asshole," she said. "He picks and chooses which kids are worthy of his estate. And let me guess, worthiness depends on how embarrassed he was about you. I'll bet his two kids with Juliet got ten times more, right?"

"He's leaving you more than any of his children," Tyler said.

Erica didn't have any response for that. She was genuinely shocked and Tyler could tell.

He shook his head. "I shouldn't have told you that. It just . . . It seemed odd to me. I would have imagined that you were close and that's why he left you the most."

"What was he thinking?" she asked. "What kind of fucking game is he trying to play?"

"Well," Tyler walked over to the sofa, looking down at Erica, "that's the same question his ex-wife and children are asking."

"What do you mean?" she asked.

"The family is contesting the will. Actually, they're contesting just this part of the will."

Erica shot up from the sofa, feeling a rush of anger ignite inside her. "What are they saying?"

She could see that her reaction was making Tyler extremely uncomfortable, but she didn't care. She was too consumed with what he'd said. It wasn't about the money. She didn't give a damn about Jonah's money. But she gave a big damn about what his bitch wife and spoiled brats were saying about her.

"They want this part of the will completely struck," Tyler said. "They don't think you should get anything."

"Why not?" Erica asked, her tone so menacing that Tyler actually took a step back.

"They haven't explained exactly," he answered in a shaky voice. "They've hired lawyers and we're told that we can expect to hear something by the end of the week."

"Those bitches!"

Erica could just imagine them all sitting there. Entitled Juliet with her children, all draped in their privilege, pissed that they weren't getting every penny. After all, that was real money, and his real money should go to his real children.

And what sort of people started plotting over the will even before putting the person in the ground? A bunch of greedy bastards, that's what sort.

"I've changed my mind," she said. "I can fight this, can't I?"

"Of course," Tyler said. "I am here to advocate for Jonah. My firm will fight to make sure his will is honored as he wished. Once we find out what they want and why, we'll know what we're fighting for."

"They want me to get nothing because they hate me," Erica accused. "I'm their dirty little brown secret. I'm the one they blame for their perfect life, that façade of a perfect life, falling apart."

Tyler looked around the open apartment as if somewhere he could find the inspiration for a right response, but nothing came to him. He only looked at Erica with a nervous smile and shrugged.

"Well," she continued, "I want that damn money and I'm gonna get it."

"I'm certain we can—"

"And when I get it," she continued, pointing a finger at his face, "I'm gonna shove it down their throats!"

7

A silence fell on the room for the second time in the last hour. In the office where Jerry Northman sat with his top six, formerly five, staff members, everyone was a little uncomfortable. It was the second time Sherise had corrected Maurice's mistakes on the communications transition strategy. His true incompetence, coupled with his arrogance, was making this so easy.

Maurice had his fill of her and, even though he was trying his best to conceal it, the rage in his face was evident. His eyes bored into Sherise as she sat casually on the sofa against the wall next to LaKeisha, who seemed to be enjoying this as well.

Sherise was enjoying it immensely, but she made sure to only look concerned and focused. It was having the added effect. Maurice was looking unfit for his position to the other leaders in the group, and especially to Jerry.

"Blair, you gotta get this stuff right," Jerry ordered as he sat behind his desk. He was looking annoyed. "Or else I'll have to bring more consultants in. I wanted to keep this small."

"No need for that," Maurice said quickly. "I'm on top of this."

Sherise sighed loudly, looking down at her tablet, where she was taking notes. When she looked up, Maurice was sending her the evil eye again.

"Sherise keeps interrupting me," he said. "Why is she even here? I'm in charge of communications now. She can go."

Sherise smiled and looked at Jerry.

"I asked Sherise to be here," Jerry said. "She's here to help you since you're the newest member of our team."

She had kind of forced his hand by voicing her extreme concern. She was there to help Maurice out, which she presented as her offer to get with the program.

This made Maurice even angrier. Jerry was exclaiming to the entire leadership team that he didn't have complete faith in Maurice. No one else had their number two person there.

"Honestly, I don't need her," Maurice said.

"Clearly, you . . ." Sherise began.

"Look, honey," Maurice said as he held his hands up.

There were one or two gasps in the room, LaKeisha being one of them. Sherise just feigned insult to add heat to the fire.

"Honey?" Jerry asked. "Really, Blair?"

"What century are you in?" LaKeisha asked.

"What?" Blair asked, with a smile as if trying to play it off. "I'm just kidding."

"That kind of kidding causes lawsuits," said Thomas Hayes, the fifty-year-old head of the agency review team and longtime friend of Jerry's. "You seem to be doing a lot of kidding like that around here."

Sherise was so glad to hear word was getting around.

Just then, Jerry's cell phone rang and he looked down at it. "It's my wife," he said. "I've got to take this."

LaKeisha stood up. "We'll all leave you to . . ."

"No, you can all stay." Jerry stood up. He looked at Maurice with something resembling disgust. "I need a break from this."

Maurice sighed, realizing that he wasn't going to be able to joke this one away. He got up from his seat on the other side of Jerry's desk and looked at Sherise.

"Thanks a lot," he said.

"You're the one who put his foot in his mouth." Sherise smirked.

Choosing not to respond, he quickly stormed out of the room.

"Where is he going?" Thomas asked. "Doesn't he know how Jerry hates being disturbed when he's on the phone with his wife?"

"He's about to find out," LaKeisha said.

Sherise turned to LaKeisha. "You don't look too upset."

"Well, I am," LaKeisha said. "He's hitting on every woman in the office."

"He made Winnie very uncomfortable," Sherise stated.

Sherise had done her part to fan Winnie's flames over Maurice's behavior. She reminded her of how disrespectful his behavior was and how women who were openly harassed in the workplace ended up losing the respect of their coworkers and it hurt their advancement opportunities. By the time she was finished with her, Winnie wanted Maurice Blair to burn in hell.

She'd had her first convert.

"He's a sloppy mess," Thomas said.

Others in the room nodded in agreement. Sherise had to garner all the willpower she had in order to stop from smiling with glee.

"Jerry knows?" she asked.

"I just . . ." LaKeisha sighed, sounded defeated. "Jerry's under immense pressure right now. It's our job to keep stuff like that away from him."

"But is that wise?" Sherise asked. "I mean . . . of course I can't tell him. He'll think it's just me trying to get rid of Maurice."

"I've got to deal with all the people he wants me to put on as head of the agencies," Tom said. "He acts like it's a game. These people have to be approved by the Senate, after all."

"This is what I mean," Sherise directed. "These are not

small problems. Yes, I can console the odd assistant who whines about him slapping her on the butt, but his behavior is threatening the administration before it even begins."

"I'm not going to let him bully me," Tom exclaimed defiantly.

"He's not bullying you," Sherise said. "He's bullying Jerry."

LaKeisha shook her head. "I won't let that happen. Whatever the hell is going on with Blair, he isn't running this administration. I'm going to be chief of staff. I'll be running things."

"You can't even find out how he got this job," Sherise said. She noticed the glare LaKeisha was sending her. "Don't tell me it's just favors. Something is going on here. You know and you're not in on it."

LaKeisha looked away, appearing very bothered by the situation.

Sherise watched with interest as the woman worked things through in her mind. She wasn't always the brightest and she had made some mistakes during the campaign, but LaKeisha had given her life to Jerry. If Sherise could make her feel even half as threatened by Maurice as she felt, her plan could move twice as fast.

"It's time," LaKeisha said, with a definitive nod of her head. "I need to have a serious talk with Jerry about Maurice. He's not going to fuck everything up."

Convert number two.

When Billie walked into the condo she shared with Michael in the NoMa neighborhood of D.C., she immediately smelled garlic and realized how ravenous she was. It smelled amazing. She let the scents of garlic matched with, possibly, roasted chicken waft around her as she walked down the hallway.

When she entered the open space she looked to her left and saw the table in the dining space that separated the kitchen from the living area was already set with a bottle of wine in the middle.

"I love you," she said, as she tossed her purse on the sofa.

Michael was in the kitchen and looked up at her with a smile. He was dressed in a Redskins T-shirt and sweatpants. He was carving the roasted chicken with his electric knife. She loved how comfortable he was cooking. She wasn't the most domestic of women, although she tried her best. The truth was, they mostly ate out, so this was a treat to see.

"Before you give me too much credit," he said, "I picked it up after work. I just put it in the oven to keep it warm."

"What is it?" she asked.

She entered the kitchen, noting the mashed potatoes and corn sides, along with the cheddar garlic rolls. She could dip her hand in those potatoes right now.

Michael paused for a second to kiss her.

"Peruvian coal roasted," he said. "Your favorite."

"Special occasion?" she asked.

"No." He placed the knife farther down on the counter. "Want to grab the sides?"

She grabbed the potatoes and corn while Michael took hold of the chicken plate and the rolls. They both went around the counter and into the dining area, where they placed the food on the table.

"Just after hearing about your run-in with Tara, I thought you'd need something nice."

She rubbed his back, kissing his cheek. "You are the best boyfriend in the world."

"Ah ah ah." He waved a finger at her as he sat down.

"Fiancé," she corrected herself. "I have to get used to saying that."

"Then," he added, "you'll have to get used to saying *husband*."

"Can't wait." She took her seat and started placing food on both their plates. "But honestly, it was horrible. I was able to stop her before she got on the elevator and calm her down."

Michael poured the wine in their glasses. "Do you really think she was that convinced that you and Porter were getting back together?"

Billie nodded. "I knew she was happy we were getting along again, but I didn't believe she actually thought we would be together. She knows how much I love you. I've told her. She's seen it."

"Kids hear what they want sometimes," Michael said. "I like the kid. I feel bad for her, but I feel worse for you."

"I hope you still feel that way after I tell you what I've decided," Billie disclosed.

He looked at her cautiously, pausing before taking a sip of wine.

"Take that sip," she directed. "You might need it."

"What is it, Billie?"

"I'm having dinner with Porter Saturday night," she said.

She noticed his grimace.

Michael hated Porter. It wasn't just out of jealousy. Porter had given him a hard time from the beginning. He didn't want Billie with anyone, and Michael was no exception.

Although Billie and Porter had made their peace, Tara was still an issue that caused them to interact. Whenever Michael was involved, Porter was rude to him. When Tara was over, she would repeat disparaging remarks that Porter had said about Michael. Maybe it was his state college education or his partial Southern accent.

Despite his improved behavior, it was clear to Michael that Porter wished Billie was his again and he hated the idea of her being anywhere near him, without him being alongside her.

"Before you start," Billie said, "I have to tell him. I made a deal with Tara."

"But why dinner?" he asked.

"That's what he wanted," she explained. "I called him and

told him I had something important to talk to him about and he said that was the only time he had free."

Michael shook his head. "He just made a date with you, Billie. In his mind."

"It's not fancy," she said. "We're meeting at the hoagie shop near his house."

"I'm in the mood for a good hoagie," Michael said. "When we meeting?"

"You're not coming along," she told him, with a warning glare. "Don't mess with me on this one. I don't want to do anything that'll make this worse. It's already not gonna be easy."

"You want to break it to him easy?" Michael asked. "Why? Fuck him. You've been divorced over three years. Send him a fucking text."

Billie laughed. "That's cold as hell."

"You think he deserves better?"

"This isn't for Porter," she reminded him. "It's for Tara. I have no legal rights to her at all. Being respectful to Porter keeps Tara in my life. I don't want to risk that. She's almost graduating. She has prom, college, a lot of things going on that she'll need me for."

Michael looked frustrated. "Well, I mean . . ."

"What?" Billie asked.

"What if you're not here?" he asked. "I mean, not in D.C. How are you gonna handle that? Do you think Porter will let her fly out to see you?"

"Why wouldn't I be here?" she asked. "D.C. is my home."

"Atlanta is my home," Michael stated. "I was thinking we should move there after we're married. You know, to raise our family."

Billie almost choked on the chicken she was eating. She looked at Michael, astonished. "Are you serious? Where is this coming from?"

"Billie you know how I feel about D.C.'s fast lifestyle. It's great for young professionals, but when you start a family . . ."

"You move to the suburbs," she said. "That's what we discussed. Where is Atlanta coming from?"

"You know I can do what I do from any location," he explained. "Being home really made me think of going back. I feel so centered there. I feel . . . right."

Billie didn't know how to handle this, but she tried to stay calm. "So all of a sudden you want . . . Michael, my job is here. I'm up for promotion. My friends are here. Sherise and Erica. Tara."

Michael seemed disappointed with her response. "I get that career and friends are important, but family comes first."

"Sherise, Erica, and Tara are my family," she exclaimed.

"Do any of them come before a husband?" he asked.

She sat back. Of course she knew the answer to that was no, but this was too much to handle right now. She was already in knots over dealing with Tara and Porter, and now this. He wanted her to leave her girls, the women she loved and needed dearly, her career, which she had fought so hard to recover, and Tara, who she thought of as a daughter.

What was she going to do now?

Upon realizing that Sherise wasn't getting off the phone anytime soon, Billie walked over to the nearby bench and sat down. She placed her bag full of bridal magazines next to her. They were at small, upscale Mazza Gallerie, a mall on Wisconsin Ave in Washington, D.C., doing their Christmas shopping.

It was supposed to be the three of them, but Erica hadn't shown up and wasn't answering their calls or texts. Billie was worried about her, but Sherise was focused on other issues, as Billie could overhear when Sherise walked over to the bench. She didn't sit down, but put her two Neiman Marcus bags next to Billie's.

"I know he's a PR expert," Sherise expressed into the phone. "He's spent his life making people's secrets go away, but there has to be something you can get on him."

She looked down at Billie and rolled her eyes. For some reason, her private investigator, Beth Martin, was coming up with nothing after a few days. Being honest, that wasn't really the truth. She hadn't been able to come up with anything that already hadn't been swirling rumors about. Sherise needed something to make him sweat.

"I need it by next Monday, got it?" she asked. "Good. Talk to you then."

She hung up and stuffed the phone in her purse, looking down at Billie. "I'm sorry, but that was important."

"Spying on your new boss."

"Don't call him that," Sherise ordered. "And don't give me that judgmental look."

"I'm not judging you," Billie said. "But I thought the plan was to make him look stupid. Not blackmail him."

"It's all part of the same game." She sat down on the bench as Billie slid over for her.

"Can I just give you one warning?" Billie asked. "From one sister to another."

"No," Sherise said.

"I get that Maurice is the problem," Billie continued, ignoring Sherise's response. "But you don't want to become more of a problem than the problem over there."

Sherise looked at her in somewhat disbelief. "Have we met?"

"I'm telling you," Billie said, shaking her head. "You're getting that obsessed vibe and . . ."

"Bitch, I'm not a rookie," Sherise said. "I've been doing this shit since day one. Don't talk to me like I'm some newbie who wants to make some drama at work for her own amusement."

"Don't snap, you nut job," Billie warned. "Just stay under control."

"I got this," Sherise said.

"You got what?"

Both women turned around to see Erica approaching them from behind.

"Where in the hell have you been?" Sherise asked.

"Don't start with you me, either of you." Erica glanced down at the bags. "You seem to have been doing just fine without me."

"Is everything okay?" Billie asked.

Erica sighed. "Let's not start that shit again."

Sherise stood up. "If you don't want us fucking with you, then answer a bitch's text. Okay?"

"Really," Billie said. "It's been two hours. It's not like you to be so late. So with everything going on, you know we're worried."

"I'm here now," Erica said.

"And I almost have to go," Billie said.

"Go where?" Sherise asked. "I thought we'd all grab something to eat before I have to head back to mommy land."

"I told you about Porter." Billie heard her body groan as she stood up. If that wasn't telling about how she felt about meeting Porter, nothing else was.

"Oh yeah," Sherise said. "Well, let's go, then."

"You're not coming," Billie informed her. "Why doesn't anyone think I can do this on my own? First Michael, now you two."

"We won't sit at the table with you," Erica said. "We'll sit at the bar."

"No," Billie urged. "You're just adding to my stress."

"No reason for that," Sherise said. "Just tell him you're getting married to a real man this time and be done with it."

"Make him buy your drink first," Erica added.

Billie laughed. "You're both worse than Michael. He wanted me to text him."

"I like him more and more each day," Sherise said. "Me and Michael are gonna get along just fine."

"For as long as we're here," Billie added inadvertently.

"What does that mean?" Erica asked.

"That's what I meant by added stress," Billie explained. "Michael wants to move back to Atlanta after we're married. It just came out of nowhere this week."

"Nowhere?" Erica asked. "Are you sure?"

"Yeah." Billie was intrigued by the curious look on Erica's face. "Why?"

"Well," Sherise stated, "he mentioned it to me and Erica at Thanksgiving."

Billie shot up from the bench. "Why didn't you say anything to me?"

"We assumed you knew," Erica said. "He said something like . . . his kids weren't going to be raised in D.C."

Billie wasn't sure what to think. Had there been clues she'd ignored?

"But we talked about moving into the Maryland suburbs. Not leaving D.C. I can't leave D.C. I'm licensed to practice in D.C. I can't leave Tara. I can't leave you two."

Erica reached out and rubbed her back reassuringly. "Calm down. It's not set in stone yet. You have just as much say as he does."

"More so," Sherise added. "He's not doing you a favor by marrying you. He doesn't call all the shots. That man loves the hell out of you. If you say you're staying in D.C., then you're staying."

"What's he going to do?" Erica asked. "Call off the wedding?"

Billie didn't even want to think of that. "It's not that simple. I want him to be happy too. I want this marriage to work."

"It will," Sherise assured her. "It will work and you'll stay.

Now, on the topic of weddings, let's go show Erica what we saw for bridesmaids' dresses."

"You've already picked them out?" Erica asked. "Without me?"

"Show up on time, bitch." Sherise pointed to her. "Come on. They're in Neiman Marcus. It's a really gorgeous Alexander McQueen lavender one-shoulder open back."

"Alexander McQueen?" Emily asked.

"It's gorgeous," Sherise said. "Billie loved them."

"Yeah, but . . ." Billie held her hand up to halt Sherise. "The dress is $890. I told you that Erica can't afford that."

Erica frowned. "You were both discussing how poor I am behind my back."

"Again." Sherise stepped to Erica. "Get here on time and we'll discuss how poor you are to your face."

"Why don't I just smack you in your face?" Erica asked.

"Hold on." Billie got between them. "Take it easy, Erica. We'll help you buy the dress if you need—"

"More charity again?" Erica asked. "I'm not a charity case. I don't need either of you to buy me a $900 dress."

"Good," Sherise said. "Because I wasn't going to buy you shit after you threatened to smack me in the face."

"What do you mean?" Billie asked.

Erica looked at them both and simply said. "I'm about to come into a million dollars."

She explained Jonah's will to them both as they stood there with their mouths open to the floor. She explained he left Alex nothing and that Juliet and her children were fighting the will. She'd just found out that Jonah only left his two children with Juliet equal shares of his million-dollar life insurance policy, which the insurance company was already trying to contest paying out due to Jonah's suicide.

Erica added, "They think they can convince the court that

Jonah couldn't have been in his right mind if he left more to a stranger than his own . . . real children."

"Somebody needs to get that family a dictionary," Sherise said. "I don't think they understand what the word *real* means."

"Exactly," Erica said. "They have half his DNA and so do I. Bunch of assholes."

"I'm just surprised you're taking it," Billie said.

Erica couldn't hide the look of guilt on her face. "I wasn't going to."

"Of course you're taking it," Sherise said. "Money is money."

Erica shook her head. "His money is dirty."

"Bullshit," Sherise countered. "All money is dirty. All you ever talk about is how sick and tired you are of not having enough money."

That comment rubbed Erica the wrong way. "Because you two are always talking about how I never have enough money."

"That's not true," Billie said.

"It is true," Erica insisted. "Besides, I didn't want it until they wanted to take it away from me. I'm not going to let Juliet erase me from Jonah's life."

"A life you claimed not to want to be connected to," Billie reminded her. "One you were glad to be done with."

"I have my reasons." Erica's tone sounded as defensive as she felt. "They thought they could just dismiss me, and I'm going to show them they can't."

Billie frowned, not liking this side of Erica at all. "That sounds vindictive. You're not the vindictive type."

"Maybe it's time I am," Erica said. "Besides, if I get it . . ."

"You'll get it," Billie said. "Unless they have some proof of duress or mental incapacity, Jonah will get what he wants."

"What he wants is to still control me," Erica said. "From the grave."

"And if you take it," Billie said. "You let him."

Erica shook her head. "I'm gonna give it to Alex. It was wrong of Jonah to leave him out. Alex's life was ruined by Jonah's bullshit. He deserves it."

"So do you," Sherise said. "If you give it all to him, you're an idiot. And you'll still need $800 for a dress."

"Besides," Billie said. "Alex might not want it. Like you said, Jonah did sort of ruin his life."

"Have you told him?" Sherise asked.

Erica shook her head. "I'm not focused on him right now. I'm just going to fight Juliet."

"Use their embarrassment to your advantage," Sherise advised. "They want to keep you a secret to save what's left of the image they wanted to portray of their family. If they want to keep that, they need to fuck off."

"They want to punish me," Erica said. "Punish me for something I'm not responsible for. But they're about to get punished."

"Stop this," Billie demanded. "You're sounding like a vengeful witch, Erica."

"I love it," Sherise said.

"I've earned this," Erica said.

Billie recognized this behavior. It was what consumed her over a year ago. A chance to get back for the wrongs she believed had been done to her. It spiraled out of control and came back to bite her in the ass.

"You need to really think about this," Billie urged. "I think your heart is in the right place, but you're convinced that—"

"You don't know my heart!" Erica snapped.

"Who do you think you're talking to?" Billie asked. "Yes, I do know your heart. I've known it since you were ten years old. You're angry and you're hurt. You're gonna lash out and end up hurting no one but yourself."

Erica threw her hands in the air. "I don't need this! You know what? You don't get it. Neither of you do."

"I told you to get the money," Sherise said.

"But you want me to do it for the wrong reason," Erica said.

"And you think what you're doing is the right reason?" Billie asked her.

"I don't need this," Erica said. "There wasn't any reason for me to even come here. I'm out."

"Is she walking away?" Sherise asked in disbelief as she watched Erica turn and head right out of the mall.

"Erica!" Billie called after her.

Just then, she got a text alert on her phone. She pulled it out of her jacket and saw it was from Porter.

I'll be there in twenty.

"Dammit." Billie checked her watch. "I have to go meet Porter."

"What are we going to do about her?"

"You were the one who said leave her be," Billie reminded her.

Sherise gestured in the direction Erica left. "That was before I could see that she's fucked up inside over this."

Billie was shaking her head as she sighed. "We'll figure it out. I can only take one problem at a time. I've gotta go."

"Call me the second you're done breaking that asshole's heart," Sherise said with a smile.

Porter Haas wasn't happy. As he sat at the table across from his ex-wife looking like he'd just stepped out of a *GQ* cover model shoot, he had been silent for a long time. Billie was certain they wouldn't make it past appetizers, but went ahead and ordered anyway.

As she waited for him to take it all in, she drank a sip of her wine and admired his attractiveness. She hadn't forgotten that she once loved this man with his finely chiseled jawline, dark chocolate skin, and piercing dark eyes. Every detail about Porter was always perfect. Hair, nails, brows, clothes were never out of place or errant in any way.

There was a time when Billie could not resist Porter. They had an amazing sexual chemistry from the beginning. He had such a hold on her body that she even slept with him after she'd found out he cheated on her. Even after she'd filed for divorce. Even after he moved his mistress into the home they had once shared together.

Even after she was able, with the help of Sherise and Erica, to find the strength to break herself from him physically, he still held on to her emotionally. Much damage was caused before she was able to let him go emotionally as well. Now they had Tara in common, but nothing else. It was new, looking at this man she'd been married to and not feeling a connection to him. It had taken some getting used to, but Billie knew it was a good thing. Giving her heart to Michael completely made this possible.

"Tara knows," he said, although it was more of a question. "That's why she's been in a bad mood all week. She wouldn't tell me, even though I asked several times."

"It was an accident," Billie explained. "She overheard me talking to Sherise. She promised not to tell if I told you . . . nicely."

"Is there a nice way to tell your husband you're marrying someone else?"

"You're my ex-husband," she corrected him. "And we're playing nice, aren't we?"

He sighed and looked away as if he was remembering something. These moments were familiar to Billie; the moments when Porter actually reflected on his life, his choices. They were rare and deceptive. Porter, once a mostly thoughtful, hopeful young man, had turned into a mostly selfish and greedy one. These moments never lasted very long.

"What do you want me to say?" Porter asked.

"You don't have to say anything, Porter. I just wanted you to know and make sure that we're okay."

"Am I okay with this?" he asked. "No, I'm not okay with you getting married to someone else."

"I didn't want to make sure you're okay with me getting married," she specified. "I just wanted to make sure we're okay. To make sure we're clear and there are no problems. At least not any that anything can be done about."

"So you're not asking for my blessing, I take it."

She shook her head. "I'm asking for Tara's blessing, and that apparently includes you making peace with this."

"I'm not going to lie," Porter said.

"This is new," she responded back with a smile, but stopped when she realized he wasn't smiling back. "Sorry."

"I was hoping it wouldn't work out," Porter said. "I don't . . . I guess I thought we were getting along well enough that things would eventually work out between us. I mean, I knew we were nowhere near that right now, but eventually. These things take time."

"Oh, Porter."

"Was that so impossible?" he asked. "I mean down the road. None of my relationships have worked out because I want them to be what you were to me. No one is going to be, are they?"

"I can't answer that for you," Billie said.

She wanted to feel sorry for him, but she'd given him everything and he'd exchanged it for a roll in the hay with a twenty-three-year-old blonde. It wasn't that Billie didn't want him to find happiness with someone, it was just that she wasn't willing to invest her heart and time into helping him do it.

"Porter," she continued. "We've progressed beyond that. We've both agreed to move on."

"We agreed to move on," Porter agreed. "But it looks like you're the only one who can actually do it. I guess that's justice. I was the one who screwed it up."

"We're not looking back," Billie said. "Just forward. We agreed going forward was just about Tara. Not us."

"So I have to deal with it," Porter said. "But my little girl. I'm sure the reason she's so upset is she's afraid that you're going to start a new family and forget about her."

"She knows I love her more than that," Billie insisted.

"You're the only real mom she's ever known," he told her. "I promised her that you would always be there for her."

"I've promised her the same."

"Can you keep that promise?" Porter asked.

Billie opened her mouth to say, yes, but was halted by thoughts of what Michael said about moving to Atlanta.

"Billie?" Porter's brows centered as he leaned forward. He was clearly worried.

"No one can say exactly what the future holds," Billie said. "I'm marrying Michael and we're going to start a family. But nothing will change how I feel about her. I love her and I will always be there for her no matter what."

"I hope you mean that," Porter said.

So did she.

8

"Can I get everyone's attention?" Sherise asked as she stood in the center of the open area at headquarters.

Everyone who was working there and walking by stopped and turned to her. She could see some were on the fence, so she raised her voice.

"It's important, trust me." She gestured them to come closer to her.

Winnie, who had been sitting at another woman's desk, stood up and walked toward Sherise.

Once Sherise was satisfied she had enough attention, she began.

"Mrs. Northman and the kids will be here today. They'll be bringing treats and want to thank you all again for your work during the campaign."

She glanced toward Maurice's office. The door was still closed. How long could she drag this out? As long as she had to, she decided.

"I just want to remind you all of the rules," she continued. "No pictures of the family while they're here. Even when Mrs. Northman is speaking and the professional photog is taking pics. Is that clear?"

There were nods in the crowd, but most people had already lost interest in what she was saying.

"What treats?" said a young man with fire-red hair who Sherise had seen around several times but had no idea who he was.

"Treat treats," Sherise said with a shrug. "It's free food. What difference does it make?"

"I just want to know if I should bother buying my lunch if the food is going to be substantial or should . . ."

A few others in the crowd started laughing.

"You're such a cheapskate, Brian," Winnie, who was standing next to Sherise now, said.

Brian laughed, seeming okay with it. Sherise was just grateful that it bought her the time she needed. Everyone was still there when Maurice's office door down the hallway swung open.

"Sherise!" he yelled out loud, heading directly for her office.

Everyone turned to look at where the yelling was coming from.

Sherise watched as he approached her office and noticed via her open door that she wasn't there. He turned to look for her and his eyes set right on her. She tried to look completely surprised as to what he wanted, but she knew damn well what he was angry about.

And boy, was he angry.

He stormed over to her, his arms swinging with purpose at his sides. His eyes had turned to slits and his lips were pressed tightly together. When he reached her, he stopped only a foot away from her.

"Who the fuck do you think you are?" he asked her.

She could hear a couple of gasps in the crowd as everyone was fixed on the two of them.

"What . . ." She purposefully stuttered. "W-What are you talking about?"

"You stole my interview!" he yelled. "I was supposed to talk to Kevin Clatch at NBC. You know I get all the major network interviews."

She held up her hands with a calming gesture. "Now just hold on a minute, Maurice. I can exp—"

"I'm preparing all of my shit and finally call him." He raised the hand holding his cell phone in the air. "Only to find out that he just got off the phone with you!"

Sherise looks around before saying, "Let's go into your office and discuss this in a private—"

"What the fuck are you up to, Sherise?" He was yelling very loudly now.

"Hey," Winnie said, alarmed.

Sherise put up a hand to silence her. "If you insist on airing this here, then fine. The truth is, Kevin texted me this morning. He was upset that his interview had been switched from me to you. He's used to talking to me."

"I don't give a fuck what he's used to," Maurice proclaimed loudly. "I'm the PS! I get the major networks. He knows that."

"He mentioned that the last time he talked to you . . ." Sherise's expression made it appear as if she was very uncomfortable saying this, although she wasn't at all. "He said you weren't . . ."

"I wasn't what?" Maurice asked, too angry to realize that he was making this worse on himself.

"That you weren't professional." She cringed as she said the last word. She was a great actress. "He said he thought you were drunk."

There were some whispers in the crowd and Sherise could see that Maurice was finally aware of everyone around him. He'd been so angry before that he hadn't paid much attention. He looked at everyone, all of them looking at him. A few turned away, showing how embarrassed they were for him.

"That's bullshit," he said, turning back to Sherise. "You're making that up."

"She's not," Winnie interjected. "If you want to check her phone, the texts are still there. Show him your phone, Sherise."

"That's not necessary," Sherise said. "I think we can all—"

"That's defamation," Maurice said. "I can sue him."

"Not a good move for a PS to file suit against prominent members of the press," Sherise said. "You have to be more gracious than that."

"Don't tell me what I have to do!" he yelled. "I'm the boss."

"He's not the only one," Winnie said. "Petra Garron of CNN also wants to talk to Sherise instead. They've worked together for years."

"Petra?" Maurice looked genuinely hurt. "But she knows me."

"I can decline it," Sherise offered. "I didn't know you weren't aware of Petra or Kevin, for that matter."

"You better decline it!" Maurice snapped. "You interview with who I want you to. Do you understand me?"

"That isn't necessary." Sherise was doing everything she could to keep her temper civil.

She could see how amazed many of the team were by Maurice's behavior and knew if she raised her tone, it would take away from this. Graciousness in the light of rudeness was not her strong point, but she could fake anything like a pro.

"Oh, I think it is," Maurice retorted. "I think even more is necessary, Sherise. And you're going to find out if you keep trying to usurp me."

Another gasp from the crowd and a female voice saying, "Did he just threaten her?"

"No, I didn't," Maurice yelled out to no one in particular. "Why don't you all just mind your own business? Get back to work."

"These people don't work for you," Sherise reminded him. "We were actually having a quick—"

"I don't care!" Maurice looked fed up. "I prepped all morning for that fucking interview. You don't—"

"Maurice!"

Everyone's head swung around toward the other end of the hallway as LaKeisha, dressed in a sharp gray pantsuit, came into view. Seeing the fed-up look on her face, Sherise couldn't have been more pleased.

"I can hear you all the way down the hall!" LaKeisha said through gritted teeth. "You're yelling."

Sherise could tell that Maurice wanted to snap at her. In his mind, he thought all women were beneath him, but in reality, he knew that LaKeisha ranked above him, so he held his tongue.

"We were just discussing a mistake Sherise made," he said.

"Were you?" LaKeisha asked. "Because all we can hear down the hall is you yelling. Now I come out here to see you're doing it in front of the whole staff. You're disrupting the entire office with this."

"No," he protested. "They were already all—"

"Enough," LaKeisha said. "All of you get back to work. All of you. Mrs. Northman is coming by today, for Pete's sake."

LaKeisha turned and headed back the way she came as Maurice swung back to face Sherise. If looks could kill, she knew she'd have been dead five seconds ago.

"I talk to Petra," he exclaimed, this time in a lower, yet still-angry voice. "From now on, you clear everyone you talk to with me. Is that clear?"

"Of course," Sherise said with a cold stare, her lips barely forming into a smile.

He furiously stomped away from everyone back to his office.

Sherise's main goal was to make him look like a fool to everyone. This, plus the rumors already circulating, was all part of her plan. It was really in her best interest to play shocked, but with that last icy stare and wicked upturn at the edges of her lips, she let him know that she, like everyone else, knew he'd just really fucked himself.

She couldn't help it. After all, she was Sherise Robinson.

Located in historic Old Town Alexandria, Belle Haven Country Club was the pride and joy of those who treasured exclusivity and luxury in Northern Virginia. Since the 1920s, the rolling hills, fine dining, golf, and all the other amenities made Belle Haven the belle of private clubs in the area. Membership was by invitation only and of course, their standards were higher than most could meet.

Erica didn't have a hard time getting in. There was a lot of chaos at the club that day. They were having a few events at once. In addition to a Santa event, where many members were lined up with their little ones to sit on Santa's lap, there was a charity event and a holiday party that a member was throwing for his small tech company. This last party created an opportunity for Erica to enter the club without a member designating her their guest.

Walking up the tree-lined entry drive, she noticed a young couple struggling with their errant daughter who looked around five years old and quickly made her way to them. The father was holding the little girl as the mother carried two large presents. The girl was reaching out for her mother and kicking her legs.

As they reached the front porte cochere member's entrance that led to the large dark front doors, Erica swept in. She casually offered to hold the presents for the mother while she took her daughter. The mother quickly accepted. They all walked in together.

The men at the door didn't ask for a name, even though they had a checklist. There was no way someone like her would get through those doors without inspection, but she counted on the men at the door assuming that she was with this couple that clearly fit in. She laughed with a bit of disgust as she imagined they probably suspected Erica was the nanny.

Once inside, she handed the presents to the husband, who thanked her, and she quickly went on her way. Erica had a mission and she wanted to get to it before it was found out that she wasn't supposed to be there.

She'd heard from Tyler, Jonah's estate lawyer, earlier that day that Jonah's children had filed a formal contest to the will and a date was set for a hearing. Juliet, who had weak legal standing since she was no longer his legal spouse, wasn't mentioned in the will and their children were both adults. But they were represented by Juliet's lawyer and the filing is mostly her own claims of mental incapacity on Jonah's part.

During her conversations with Tyler, he mentioned it would be awkward if he ran into Juliet at Belle Haven, as they both belonged to the country club and he knew she would be there for a charity event. In the end, Tyler was glad this gave him an excuse not to go since he didn't want to in the first place.

This gave Erica the idea. She entered the ballroom the elegantly designed signs led her to. Once inside, she noticed the richly colored yellow walls with large white boxed windows framed by golden curtains. Elegant, draping chandeliers adorned the walls, shining the light on beautifully decorated circular cloth-covered tables with crystal and china and colorful flower settings in the middle.

No surprise that everyone looked her way when she walked in. No one else in there looked like her. At least, not anyone who wasn't wearing a server's uniform. She didn't care. She had eyes for only one table in the far right corner. There, Juliet sat with her daughter, Elizabeth, right next to her.

Elizabeth was almost a clone of her mother. Looking like they were dressed more for an Easter event than for something in late November, both women were blond and thin with small blue eyes. They had the same sharp features, high cheekbones, and tight lips. They were both wearing their hair back in tight buns. Juliet was in her fifties, but you had to get up close to her to see the signs of alcohol. She drank too much and you saw it in the lines around her eyes and mouth, and the slight redness of her nose.

Erica felt a pang of jealousy seeing Elizabeth sitting there so prim and proper, looking every bit the privileged and entitled woman that she was.

"What are you doing here?" Elizabeth demanded to know, after seeing her mother was too shocked to even say anything.

"Hey, sis!" Erica exclaimed jovially, just loud enough for the immediate table to hear.

Elizabeth was mortified. She stood up and came around to her mother's chair. "You don't belong here," she said, her voice almost snarling.

"She's right," Juliet finally found the strength to say. "Get out of here."

"You don't give me orders," Erica informed her sharply. "Don't worry. I won't be long."

"You've already been too long," Elizabeth said. "Get the hell out of here or else."

"Or else what?" Erica asked, taking two steps closer to her. She looked her dead in the eyes and repeated. "Or else what?"

"You're a thug," Elizabeth said. "Just like I imagined you'd be."

"I'm not the one pushing people around," Erica said.

"I'm calling security," Juliet said.

"Don't bother," Erica told her. "I just wanted to let you know that your attempt to contest the will isn't going to work."

"I won't discuss this with you," Juliet said, dismissively. "That's what lawyers are for."

"Not surprised you wouldn't know that," Elizabeth mumbled.

"I know what lawyers are for," Erica said, eyeing Elizabeth

intently. "They just won't be necessary. Jonah was of sound mind when he made that will."

Juliet huffed. "No, he wasn't. He couldn't have been."

"Why not?" Erica's voice got considerably louder. "I'm his daughter and he loved me. He loved my mother. Why wouldn't he want me to have his money?"

"Stop it." Juliet stood up this time, her eyes like daggers for Erica.

Elizabeth grabbed her mother's arms to control her. "Don't let this ghetto trash get to you, Mother."

Erica looked around the room, doing her best not to tear the girl's hair out for her insults.

"This room looks a little bored. Maybe they'd love to hear my story. One last chapter in the flawed life of Jonah Nolan."

"You wouldn't," Juliet said. "You know what happened to that boy when the truth about him came out. His life was ruined and he had to run away."

"That boy's name was Alex," Erica said. "Alex and I aren't the same. I don't give a shit. And for a million dollars, I'll take some press attention. What about you? How many of these wonderful little parties will you be attending when everyone is talking about yet another illegitimate brown child Jonah had?"

Suddenly, Erica felt someone come up behind her and she turned to see a large man dressed in a black suit. He had to be security. He was looking right at her.

"Get her out of here," Elizabeth demanded. "She's crashing this party and insulting the guests."

"And what about all the other women?" Erica asked Juliet, ignoring the man behind her. "You don't know about all his affairs. I know about some as well. I could even write a book."

"Ma'am," the guard said in a deep, authoritative voice.

"You decide to fight me," Erica said. "Well, you should know, this kind of fun is just the beginning."

"Don't you hear her?" Elizabeth asked the guard. "She's threatening my mother."

Erica kept her attention on Juliet, who was no longer amazed or shocked. Her face was stone, covering up disdain and resentment. Erica knew that nothing mattered more to Juliet than what she looked like to her peers. Jonah had done so much to damage that, but she was trying to salvage all she could. It was all she had left.

"You're trash," Elizabeth sneered to Erica. "You'll get nothing."

"No," Erica said, pointing to her face. "You're the one that's going to get nothing. You see, I know what he left you. Just half of his life insurance policy. That's barely half a million. So sad. I bet you thought he actually loved you."

Elizabeth let out a hateful growl before reaching back to the table. The second Erica saw her snatch a glass of wine, she jumped away. The guard, thinking she was trying to run away, turned to grab her. Just in time. When Elizabeth tossed the glass that she intended to hit Erica in the face with, all the wine hit the guard on the back of his jacket.

The whole room reacted to the scene as the guard let go of Erica and tried to see what damage had been done to his suit. He wasn't happy.

"You bitch!" Elizabeth yelled out to Erica.

"Lizzie!" Juliet snapped at her. "Quiet down. You're making a spectacle of yourself."

Erica smiled at both women before turning to the guard and politely saying, "I'm ready to be thrown out now."

"This one," Billie said as she showed Michael the page in the magazine.

Lying next to her on the bed of pillows they had made next to their toasty fireplace, Michael took the magazine and gazed at the picture. He read the message written in cursive below.

"The perfect location, the only location for the classic bride is the center of the world. The Hay-Adams Hotel, a registered Historic Hotel of America, is your place for the wedding of her dreams."

He looked at her with a sly eye. "Sounds a bit . . ."

"Bougie?" she asked. "I know, but it's such a beautiful hotel, Michael. I used to walk by it as a young girl and wish I could go inside, and every time I've been inside, I've been in awe."

"I've been there a few times," he said. "For a lunch or a charity or two. It's pretty amazing. You know the Obamas stayed there before moving into the White House."

"And it's haunted." Billie giggled. "Clover Adams, a family member of the presidential Adams."

"So you're telling me you're crazy." He handed the magazine back to her.

"I think it's romantic," she said. "It has the Elizabethan and Tudor motifs everywhere. All that beautiful architecture. Everything about it is perfect."

He pointed to a note, in less obvious writing, at the bottom. "Menus starting at $180 a plate. You know what that means? For $180 you get half a cold chicken thigh and two pieces of iceberg lettuce. A real menu is gonna be at least $100 more."

"We aren't inviting the universe," Billie said. "We already agreed just our close family and friends. We can do this."

"I'd pay for five hundred guests if that's what my baby wanted."

She turned her head to his and kissed him sweetly on the cheek. She scooted her body closer to him so that there was no space between them.

"We're both paying for this wedding," she insisted. "And you don't have to worry about five hundred. The place only seats three fifty."

He rolled over onto his side and wrapped his arms around her. "I'll make 'em knock down a wall if you need the room."

Billie felt her body tingling as his warm, strong arms wrapped around her. "So you agree? The Hay-Adams?"

He nodded. "But when?"

"We have to be flexible," she said. "They're in high demand. Unless we want to wait another year to—"

"No," Michael said. "I'm not waiting a whole year to make you my wife, Billie."

She felt indescribable happiness at hearing him say those words and knowing he meant it. She couldn't wait another year either.

"Then we might have to be flexible on the day," she said. "Like maybe not Saturday?"

"Who gets married on a Saturday anymore?" he asked, jokingly. "That's old-fashioned. We get married when we want. Tuesday at three a.m."

"So I'll call." Billie looked around the living room area, wondering where she'd left her phone.

"Not right now," Michael said. "I don't want you to get up. I'm enjoying this too much. We haven't snuggled in a while."

"I love that you love to snuggle." She rubbed her nose against his.

"You just better not tell anyone," he warned playfully. "I have my manhood to protect."

"Too late." She laughed. "I've already told Sherise and Erica you're a cuddler."

"You tell them everything," he said. "I should have guessed."

Billie didn't want to spoil the moment, but things were so good right now, she thought maybe it was the best time to bring this up again.

"I also told them about you thinking about Atlanta," she said. "But it seems like you'd already mentioned something to them?"

"When?"

"Thanksgiving. You said something about not wanting to raise your kids in D.C."

He shrugged. "I might have. I don't remember. Look, baby, I'm sorry for springing that on you. It's just . . . I've really been thinking about it. I miss Atlanta."

"I know you do." She brought her hand to his face and held his cheek. "Baby, I want you to be happy. Wherever you are is my home, but . . . leaving Tara and the girls just feels so painful to me. Can you understand that?"

He was looking tenderly in her eyes. "Of course I do. I want you to be happy too. This isn't an easy decision."

"We both have to keep our hearts and minds open about it," she said.

"I promise I will," he said. "We're getting married. We have to make these big decisions together, right?"

"We're getting married," she said in a giddy voice as she leaned forward and kissed him on the lips. "We're really getting married."

"At the Hay-Adams Hotel," he added. "Shit just got real, Billie. You ready for it?"

"Am I ready?" she laughed. "Baby, I been ready. I bought this magazine four months ago."

He squinted at her with a sweet smile before leaning down to kiss her on the lips. She met his lips with eagerness.

Within a second, their hands were all over each other frantically. Billie let out a quiet moan as she felt his hands, hot and commanding, reach up her loose blouse. She wasn't wearing a bra, so his hands went immediately to her small, firm breasts. Her body responded to his touch by moving into him.

Billie reached down and felt him getting hard in her hands. She aggressively caressed him, making him groan her name.

The sound of the doorbell ringing jolted them both from

their haze. Their eyes met, each wondering if the other had heard it. Then it rang again and they both rolled their eyes.

"Why now?" he asked.

"Who could it be at this hour?" she asked.

"I'll get it." Michael stood up and headed for the short hallway that lead to the front door.

"Who is it?" he asked loudly before reaching the door.

No response, just another ringing of the doorbell.

Billie was just tucking in her blouse when she heard Michael gasp. She rushed around the corner of the living room into the hallway just as Michael opened the door. She walked at a brisk pace down the hallway, waiting to hear Michael greet the person, but he didn't speak.

"Hello, Michael," said a woman in a sweet Southern drawl.

Billie finally reached the door and could see who was on the other side. The woman who was looking at Michael with a tender, but cautious smile turned to look at her. Their eyes met and Billie could see that the woman wasn't expecting to see her. She didn't seem unhappy to see her. Just surprised.

She was an attractive cinnamon-colored woman with gentle features on a makeup-free face that looked to be in its mid-thirties. She was medium height and had an earthy look to her, with soft black hair that fell in several twists just past her shoulders. Her form-fitted multicolored dress went just past her knees, covering the top of her sandy brown boots.

"Hello," Billie said to her.

The woman smiled in response.

Billie turned to Michael and could see from her side view of him that he was shocked. She nudged him in his side with her elbow. He turned to her and blinked before turning back to the woman.

"What are you . . . What are you doing here?" he asked.

Billie found that a curious greeting. She could see from the woman's expression that it wasn't surprising to her at all.

"I didn't mean to interrupt you and . . . Billie, right?" She turned to Billie.

Billie nodded. "Billie Carter."

"It's nice to meet you, Billie." The woman held her hand out underneath the arm that Michael still held against the archway of the door.

Billie accepted her hand and shook it firmly. What was going on?

"And you are?" Billie asked.

"Darina," the woman said, turning to Michael to finish. "Darina Wheeler."

Billie felt a thud in her gut. Darina Wheeler.

So this was her. The woman that Michael had once thought was the love of his life. He'd never shown Billie a picture. The woman everyone thought, and his family still hoped, he would marry. The woman who broke his heart when she chose activism over him. The woman he hadn't spoken to in over a decade. She was standing in his doorway, in their doorway.

"How did you even know where I live?" Michael asked.

"Dee Dee told me," Darina answered. "You know I've kept in touch with your mother. Well, not very well in touch, but she told me where I could find you."

"Uh . . ." Michael wasn't sure what to do, but seemed to be getting over his shock.

Billie watched with interest as he lowered his arm and stepped aside, opening the door wider. He looked at her and Billie wasn't sure what she saw in his eyes. He clearly had no idea she was coming.

"Would you like to come in?" he asked.

"I don't want to interrupt you tonight," she said. "I just . . ."

"It's okay," Michael said.

She took one step inside and Billie took a more in-depth look at her. Now that she knew who she was, Billie was looking at her in a whole new light.

Darina looked around and nodded. "Nice place."

Billie wondered if that was judgment or genuine. From everything Michael had told her, Darina didn't like displays of wealth, and their hallway was well decorated with an English Tudor oval table and two Harlem Renaissance paintings that cost a pretty penny.

"Thank you." Billie would decide she was being genuine until given a reason otherwise.

She looked at Michael and wondered if he was embarrassed for Darina to see his wealth.

"I guess congratulations are in order," Darina said, clutching tightly to her Navajo-style purse. "Dee Dee says you're engaged."

Billie was actually surprised that Dee Dee was sharing that news with anyone, considering she wasn't happy about it.

"Thank you," Billie and Michael both said at the same time.

They shared an awkward glance before turning their attention back to their guest.

"You said my mother told you where to find me," Michael said. "You're still in Atlanta?"

"No," Darina replied. "I've been living in Opelika, Alabama, for the last eight years."

So what was she doing here, Billie wanted to know.

"You came from Alabama to D.C. looking for Michael?" Billie asked.

The smile on her face faded as she grew serious. "I need to talk to you, Michael."

"I'm kind of at a loss for words," he said. "I haven't seen you in . . . eight years."

"Eight?" Billie asked. "You mean eleven, right? You came to D.C. eleven years ago."

"We broke up eleven years ago," Darina informed her. "But it's been eight years since we've seen each other."

Billie didn't like the sound of that. She could have sworn

Michael told her that he hadn't seen her since they broke up and he left Atlanta.

"That's kind of what I need to talk to you about." Darina's voice sounded a bit hesitant.

Darina looked nervously in Billie's direction before looking down at the floor. Billie knew what she wanted. She wanted Billie to leave them alone. *To hell with that.*

"Billie is my fiancée," Michael said. "She knows everything about me."

Not exactly, Billie thought.

"Whatever you want to say," he continued, "you can say in front of her."

Darina didn't seem too happy about that, but she nodded with a smile of acceptance before turning to Billie.

"Eight years ago, Michael came home to Atlanta and we met. We were both dating new people. It had been two years, so it was just a friendly lunch."

"Darina." Michael held up his hand. "What are you trying to get at?"

"You said I could talk in front of her," Darina said.

"What does us having lunch eight years ago have to do with why you're here now?"

She looked at him as if disappointed that he didn't get it. "Because that lunch turned into something more."

"Wait a second," Michael said, not a happy man.

"What's going on?" Billie asked. She knew exactly what Darina was alluding to, but she didn't want any more beating around the bush. "You're saying you hooked up? That was eight years ago. Why would I need to know that?"

"It was just once," Michael said, his eyes pleading for Billie's understanding. "Why are you bringing that up, Darina? Why are you here?"

"We never saw each other after that day," Darina said. "We never talked or emailed or anything."

He swallowed hard like a man who was nervous that his past was coming back to bite him in the ass. "We agreed that was a mistake and we didn't want to make it again."

"But it wasn't a mistake," Darina countered.

"Excuse me?" Billie asked.

Darina turned to Michael. "We didn't make a mistake. We made a miracle and his name is Duncan. And Duncan wants to meet his father."

9

As she walked down the hallway toward Jerry's office at headquarters, Sherise was feeling extremely proud of herself. If he had called her there for the reason she thought, it meant that she had beaten her own deadline for getting rid of Maurice.

It had only been a few days since Maurice's outburst, but everyone was still talking about it. Not only that, but it was starting to leak to the outside that there was discord within Jerry's transition staff.

Discussions about the outburst led to other discussions about his inappropriate behavior elsewhere. Just that morning, Winnie had told Sherise that one of Tom's assistants, a very young beautiful blonde named Shelly, had threatened to quit if Maurice hit on her one more time.

Maurice had made this easier on her than Sherise could have ever expected. She knew he wasn't competent enough for her job, but she didn't expect him to be this obvious, this sloppy. Even someone as lacking as him had to know the chance he'd been given was a once in a lifetime opportunity. It amazed her that he almost seemed eager to lose the job, but the second he felt it was threatened, he reacted fiercely.

Secret Service replaced Maryland State Police as Jerry's security once he became the Democratic nominee. They were always present, but it was easy to forget that they were there. Which was why Sherise was a little taken aback when the man with the standard black suit, stone face, and earpiece standing outside Jerry's office held up a hand to stop her from going in.

"I have an appointment with the president-elect," she assured him.

"I know Mrs. Robinson, but there's someone inside right now," the man said in a smooth, low voice.

"Dammit!" yelled a male voice from the other side of the door.

"Enough, Stephen!"

This came from Jerry, Sherise recognized. Stephen and Jerry were arguing.

"What's going on?" she asked.

"Just one moment," the man said. "The governor asked not to be disturbed yet."

Sherise looked around for Diana, Jerry's assistant, but she was nowhere in sight. She sighed as she struggled to hear the words that were fading in and out. She suspected that the men were moving toward and away from the door during their argument.

"It's not fair," Stephen yelled. "It's messed up. It's not right!"

"Enough, Stephen," Jerry ordered with hint of a plea.

"So you're not going to do anything?" Stephen asked.

"It's none of your business!"

It sounded to Sherise that Stephen was laughing now.

"I can't believe you just said that!"

"Stephen," Jerry said, "I want you to go home now. Just go home and . . . just do something with your life!"

"You want me to do something?" Stephen asked. "While you do nothing!"

"This conversation is over!" Jerry yelled.

"Go to hell!" Stephen yelled back.

Just a second later, the door to Jerry's office flew open and

Stephen came face-to-face with Sherise. The look of anguish on his face suddenly turned to surprise and then embarrassment.

"Sherise," he said. "I . . . Um . . . Hi."

"What's wrong?" she asked.

"He's an asshole." Stephen's voice was very shaky. "He doesn't understand anything. He's a coward."

"Why would you say that about your dad?" Sherise asked.

This was confusing. From everything she had witnessed, Stephen had a great relationship with his father. Even when they argued, it was always lighthearted.

"I don't want to talk about it. I'm sorry."

"You don't have to apologize to me," Sherise said. "I just think you might want to rethink running away from your problems with him. Things are very stressful for all of —"

"I know," he snapped. "I get it. He's under a lot of stress. Leave him alone! I've heard it a million times."

"I didn't mean that," she said.

Stephen sighed, looking away for a moment. He looked exhausted and frustrated.

"I didn't mean to snap at you," he said. "I like you, Sherise. I actually like you the most out of everyone here. They're all phonies and fakes."

"Your father isn't fake," Sherise said. "I know that. He's as genuine as they come."

Stephen looked confused. "I can't believe you still have faith in him after he gave your job to that asshole, Maurice Blair."

Sherise's antenna went up. "Is that what you were arguing about? Maurice Blair?"

Stephen shook his head. "I don't want to . . ."

Sherise suddenly remembered something. Stephen liked Shelly, Tom's assistant!

"Stephen, did Shelly tell you about Maurice hitting on her?"

He nodded. "He's been hitting on her nonstop. She didn't

want to tell me, but, she finally did this morning. He disgusts her. I told Dad and he won't do anything! He can't—"

"Stephen!" Jerry said his son's name with a sternness that alarmed both Stephen and Sherise. He stood in the doorway to his office, looking unusually haggard. "That's enough," Jerry said to his son. "Go home."

Stephen looked at him, as if he was debating whether or not to listen.

"Now," Jerry added with authority.

Stephen didn't acknowledge Sherise as he lowered his head and walked off.

"Come in, Sherise," Jerry said, in a calmer voice, as he turned and walked into his office.

She entered, closing the door behind her.

"He's very upset," Sherise said. "He likes Shelly a lot. You're honestly not going to do—"

"Stay out of it!" Jerry snapped. "You shouldn't have been snooping."

"I wasn't," she said, although that was sort of a lie. "I could clearly hear you well outside the door."

"That was between me and my son."

"I'm sorry," Sherise said. "It was just a shock to hear that. I thought you called me here to—"

"I love my son," Jerry attested. "I love him more than words can say. Nothing means more to me than my children. Don't ever question that, Sherise."

"I wasn't," she insisted.

"I know what you're doing." He turned to her, leaning against the front of his desk. "And it has to stop, Sherise."

"If you're somehow saying that I'm responsible for what's going on between Shelly and Maurice, I've got to say that's ridiculous."

He eyed her in a way that told her this was a serious moment and she wasn't going to be able to talk around him. It wasn't Jerry and Sherise talking honestly now. It was an employee talking to her very powerful and important boss. She had to straighten it up.

"Sir, I warned you about Maurice," she said.

"I can deal with Maurice," Jerry said. "But I need you to stop making the situation worse. You're setting him up."

"That's what he told you?" Sherise shook her head. "All of the damage he's done, he's done to himself. And it's all damage that anyone could have predicted, considering his very public past."

Jerry rolled his eyes, shaking his head as if he was tired of having this conversation. Sherise imagined several of his top advisors had been telling him the same things she was right now. Why wasn't it making a difference?

"And honestly," she continued, "would you really believe him over me?"

"I know you feel betrayed," Jerry said. "But I've told you that patience will work in your favor."

She leaned back, folding her arms across her chest. "Patience isn't my strong point. Especially when so much more than just what I want is in jeopardy."

Jerry slammed his fist on the desk and Sherise inhaled quickly. She couldn't remember ever seeing him this angry. Well, not with her at least.

"I won't tolerate any more of this!" he shouted. "I'm about to become the president of the United States. Not to mention transferring my gubernatorial duties over to my lieutenant governor."

"I know you're under immense pressure, sir."

"Much of it is your doing," he insisted.

"That's not true," she protested, even though that sort of was. "I'm doing what you would expect of someone who has the incoming administration's best interest at heart."

"You're supposed to be what I need you to be," he said. "Right now, I need a team player."

"I'm thinking of the team," she said. "I'm trying to keep everyone focused and not distracted with staff problems."

"Maurice fucks up a lot," Jerry admitted. "But I need you to help him. You cover for him. You don't let him flounder."

"I'm supposed to do his job and my own?" she asked.

"You do everyone's job if that's what I ask you!" he demanded.

"Maybe I can help him sound more competent to the press," she said, even though she had absolutely no intention of ever doing that. "But I can't make him keep his hands off young girls' asses."

"You can keep him busy enough that he doesn't have time for that shit," Jerry said. "You can keep him away from them."

"So now I'm his keeper too?" she asked. "His babysitter. His moral conscience?"

"You're whatever you need to be in order to make things go more smoothly in communications. You do your job. Just like everyone else."

"But Maurice," she corrected. "Just like everyone else but Maurice." She sighed, frustrated with the direction this was going and feeling unable to steer it another way.

"Do you actually think that this will get better?" she asked. "That he won't get worse later if he gets away with this now?"

"I said I can deal with Maurice."

"But a lot of other people here can't," she responded flatly.

They eyed each other for several seconds before Jerry's expression grew resolute.

"Sherise, I'm going to be president. If you want to be a part of that, you'll do what I say. You'll stop questioning me. You'll help Maurice. You'll play along."

"Jerry, I—"

"Or you're gone."

★ ★ ★

After wiping his mouth, Corey placed the napkin on the table and sat back in his chair. He sighed a heavy, satisfied sigh.

"Man," he said. "Erica, you did that up."

Erica smiled as she watched him, feeling complete inside at the sight of his satisfaction. She had done it up. She cooked up a storm when she was frustrated, and after her showdown with Juliet and Elizabeth a few days ago, her frustration had only grown stronger.

It confused her. When she'd walked out of that country club, Erica was elated. She had stuck it to both of them. Elizabeth's reaction alone, when she took a jab at her about the life insurance, made the trip a success. She'd embarrassed them and frightened them and made them acknowledge her. She was real. That confrontation made that abundantly clear.

Yet, just a few hours afterward, the satisfaction subsided and feelings of frustration and anger returned. In fact, Erica felt it even stronger. That, coupled with the complete lack of understanding and support from Sherise and Billie, left her feeling resentful.

So she cooked and cooked. Tonight, for dinner at her place with Corey, she'd broiled marinated chicken breast smothered in mozzarella cheese, olive oil, garlic, and cherry tomatoes with a side of broccoli sautéed in butter. It was a cheap meal that looked expensive. It was filling and delicious.

They were sitting on the small table against the window in her dining area. It wasn't very romantic. The window faced the brick building next door. It didn't matter. Being with Corey was the first time in days that Erica actually felt good. They had made out a little before eating and it made her forget her problems. It made her feel like a schoolgirl, and the only reason they stopped was because the oven timer went off. Erica briefly considered letting the food burn. It felt so good to escape it all.

He reached for his bottle of beer and pointed to her plate. "You better eat a little faster or I'm gonna steal what's left."

"Here." She picked up her plate and slid her chair closer to his under the table. "You can finish it. I'm full."

He ignored the plate. "Now that you're sitting this close to me, I'm really not thinking about food anymore."

He leaned forward to kiss her and she met him halfway. She felt a tingling sensation rush through her body at the taste of his full lips, his sexy, masculine scent arousing her senses.

Then the doorbell rang.

"Dammit," Erica said, rolling her eyes.

"Were you expecting someone?" Corey asked.

"No."

She turned toward the door, tempted to yell out for who it was, but knew that probably wasn't the lady like thing to do. So she got up and walked over to the door and took a look in the peephole. Expecting one of her nosy neighbors, she was surprised to see Tyler, Jonah's estate lawyer, on the other side.

She opened the door and said, "You really don't believe in calling ahead, do you?"

He shrugged with a smile. "I was on my way home."

"You expect me to believe you live around here?" she asked with a smirk.

"For your information, I live five blocks from you."

Erica imagined he lived in one of the regentrified parts of the neighborhood, an issue causing great contention with the people who had been living here for several decades. The new condos were kicking all of the longtime residents out, razing everything and building up new apartments, restaurants, and bars that only wealthy professionals could afford.

"Well, I'm kind of in the middle of something," she whispered to him, her head gesturing behind her.

"This will be brief," he said. "You'll want to hear this."

"It's not that simple," she told him. "Whatever business you have . . . is not something I want to get . . ."

"Who is it?" Corey asked loudly.

She turned around and saw him walking toward her with a curious look on his face. Of course he'd want to know what man was visiting her at her apartment at night while he was there.

"This is just work stuff," Erica told him.

Corey reached the door, studying Tyler.

"I'm sorry to interrupt you," Tyler said.

"I'm starting at Robinson Associates at the start of the year," Corey said. "Is there anything I can do?"

"Not that business," Erica said. "It's actually kind of . . . private."

"Oh," Corey said. He looked at Tyler a little suspicious, before turning to Erica. "I guess I'll just go to the bathroom or . . ."

"That would be fine," Erica said, nodding. "It's down at the end of the hallway. This will just be a moment."

Corey took his time turning and heading down the hallway, but when she felt he was at least out of earshot, Erica turned to Tyler.

"Is this about the country club?" she asked.

He nodded. "I guess you can say that."

"I knew it would get back to you." Erica hadn't much thought of the repercussions of her behavior and really didn't care. "I didn't do anything illegal, but can we just schedule an actual time to talk about this? I'm really in the middle of something."

"I didn't think you'd want to wait to hear this," he said.

"What?" she asked. "Are they suing me or something?"

"They caved," he said with a firm, wide smile. "Whatever you did, it did the trick. They aren't going to contest what Jonah left you in his will. They plan to contest some of his other bequeaths, such as leaving his war memorabilia collection to—"

"Are you serious?" she asked. "What . . . You mean, that's it?"

He nodded. "Whatever you said to them must have made them think twice about it."

Erica couldn't believe it. This was what she wanted, right?

She didn't want to fight. She just wanted them to know that it would be hell to try and cut her out of the will. They couldn't deny her right to Jonah anymore. They were giving up.

"Old Juliet got scared," Erica said. "I'll bet it was her idea. I'm sure Elizabeth would have still fought me. She had more to lose."

"Doesn't matter," Tyler said. "It's done."

"It does matter," Erica insisted. She noticed Tyler's surprised reaction to the urgency in her tone. "I mean . . . I guess it doesn't. It's just . . . I thought they would fight."

"They won't," Tucker said. "What he left you is not affected by his estate tax. It was in several financial accounts that will be closed and the full sum sent via wire transfer to your bank accounts, your financial advisors, or whatever you . . ."

"I don't have a financial advisor," Erica said. "I only have one bank account."

"Um . . . That's not going to work. Most banks are only FDIC insured for $250,000. You don't want more than that in one place."

"What about taxes?" she asked.

"Well, D.C. is under federal law, so there are no inheritance taxes for this amount. It's all yours. But you need to figure out your banking situation and get a financial advisor."

What he was saying was starting to sound like Chinese to Erica. She was still on needing more bank accounts. Why did she need a financial advisor? What was he talking about? But mostly . . . she'd just inherited one million dollars.

She wanted badly to discuss this, but as she heard the broken, creaky bathroom door open from down the hall, she knew now wasn't the time.

"Later," she said. "I have a week, right?"

He nodded. "Yes, but . . ."

"Let's talk tomorrow, okay? I have your number. Not here. Not tonight."

Just as Corey appeared back in the kitchen, walking toward the dining table, Erica was shutting the door on Tyler with a speedy good-bye.

When she turned and headed back to Corey, she could see that he was skeptical of the whole situation. What could she tell him? She could lie to him. Make something up that satisfied his curiosity, but she didn't want to. She was sick of secrets and lies.

"What was that about?" he asked. "Or am I not allowed to ask?"

She walked up to him and wrapped her arms around his waist. She pressed her chest against his and looked deeply into his enticing eyes.

"No questions right now," she said.

He rolled his eyes. "It's always no questions with you."

"I'm sorry that our evening got interrupted." She reached down and took his strong hands in hers and backed away. "But I don't want to talk about all that right now."

"All what?" he asked, letting her lead him away from the table and into the living room area.

"There are much better things for us to discuss," she said, feeling her excitement rising as she led him to the sofa.

"Can I at least ask one question?" he asked.

She turned him around and pushed him so he fell on the sofa.

"What?" She looked down on him with a seductive bite of her lower lip.

"Is everything okay?" he asked, his expression deadly serious.

She smiled as she lowered herself onto his lap. She took his face in her hands and lifted it up to hers.

"You're so sweet," she said. "And yes, everything is okay. As a matter of fact, it's more than okay."

"Is that right?" he asked.

She knelt down and slowly, seductively placed her lips on his. She let them linger teasingly on the surface until he pressed against hers. She responded by kissing him passionately, fully.

"Oh yes," she said. "Let me show you."

Their lips devoured each other, their passion growing more voracious by the second. Erica loved the feel of his large, strong hands on her body. She lifted up as they slid down her back and gripped her butt firmly. She straddled him, leaning in and wrapping her arms around him.

They rolled around on the sofa, quickly removing all their clothes. Erica felt no sense of self-consciousness revealing her curvaceous body next to Corey's muscled, large figure. The way he touched her, as if every touch made him ravenous for more, made her feel so sensual, so perfect.

The seduction intensified as Corey's possessive, hungry kisses trailed down her soft belly to her center. He teased the edges with his tongue before entering her. His forceful hands gripped her hips as he went deeper, making her go crazy. He was relentless and quickly brought Erica to orgasm. Her body melted like liquid as she felt him return to her, the weight of his body straddling hers, a feeling she had missed so desperately.

She looked up at him and saw the intensity in his eyes. He wanted her so badly, and she couldn't help herself.

"Your turn," she said.

Sherise was very educated on the natural progress of babies and determined that Aiden would excel just as his sister was. Cady was already a year above average for the toddler stage. Based on her understanding, Sherise felt Aiden was average for an infant, but he showed a great deal of promise. Despite her demanding career, all the drama she was dealing with at work and other distractions, Sherise's children were her priority and she didn't let a day go by without some quality interaction with them.

It was late and Justin was on his way home. Dinner was warming in the oven and the kids were supposed to have been put to bed, but Sherise was bad on consistent bedtimes. She knew she would regret it with Aiden just as she had with Cady. They sat in the living room with Cady learning about shapes and colors on her garden activity cube and Sherise teaching Aiden on the Einstein music table. It was a noisy toy. So noisy that she didn't even hear Justin until he was halfway through the door.

"Hey, Princess!" Justin said as he first set eyes on Cady.

Cady screamed and hopped off the sofa, almost falling on her back on the floor. She turned and ran to her daddy, her arms opened wide. Sherise smiled as he picked her up and gave her quick kisses all over her face. By the time he reached the sofa, just seconds later, she was already wiggling to get free.

"So much for that," he said, letting her go.

"She just wants her kisses and she's done," Sherise said.

Cady gave out a sweet laugh as she went back to her toy.

"Hey, little man." He knelt down to give Aiden a kiss on his forehead.

Aiden looked up and smiled, saying a few coos before returning his attention to the much more interesting loud music machine.

Justin leaned to the right and kissed Sherise on the lips.

"Dinner is ready whenever you are," she said.

He placed his briefcase on the floor and sat in the lounge chair next to the sofa. "I'm starving. You recovered?"

He was referring to Jerry's lashing of Sherise earlier that morning. She'd told him about it after she'd gotten over the shock of it all.

Sherise shook her head. "I can count on one hand how many times he's been that direct with me and still have a few fingers left over."

"So you know it's bad," Justin said.

"He won't even listen to his own son. And he loves that boy with all his heart. That, I am sure of."

"Well, I've asked around and I'm getting the same thing you're getting," Justin said. "He's got some powerful people who have his back. You know how this game is played."

"We all do," she stated. "But this goes beyond favors. He's wreaking havoc in the office. It's leaking to the press. The *Washington Post* is planning to run a story on transition drama, mostly focused on him."

"With some help from you, of course."

She smiled. "Well, I might be an anonymous source, but I'm not the only one. My inside guy says they have several sources. I know Jerry wouldn't let someone taint him like this. Not even for favors."

"It depends on the pressures backing those favors," Justin said. "Knowing Blair, he's not above blackmail. He's done it before."

Sherise didn't want to believe that. "Do you have proof of this?"

He shook his head. "No, just rumors like you, but you know it's true."

She sighed. "My P.I., Beth, is useless. All I'm getting are rumors too."

"Guys like Blair, they hold on to blackmail until they're at the end of their career and use it to stay in the game. If he's got something good on enough people, they've probably placed enormous pressure on Jerry."

Sherise thought about it. It was true. She herself had held on to information about coworkers or others in the past in order to have something to save for when it was most needed. She had several little gems in her back pocket she had collected over the years. Maurice wouldn't be the first guy to use info to keep or get a job. It just seemed ill-advised for someone to pressure the president-elect to his own detriment. Something at that level usually came back to bite you hard.

"I've got to find out who exactly has urged Jerry to hire and keep Maurice on. If I can, maybe I can partner with that person."

"And do what?" Justin asked.

"If I can neutralize the threat that Maurice poses, the pressure is off and I can get rid of him."

"I don't know," Justin said. "Whoever pressured Jerry had to be a major game player. Their secrets are usually hard to neutralize."

"I don't have a choice," Sherise responded. "Jerry isn't going to budge. I'm running out of time."

Just then, Sherise's phone rang. It was set on the coffee table and she reached forward to grab it, holding it up high enough so a reaching Aiden couldn't snatch it away. She read the message sent from Billie to her and Erica.

"Holy shit!"

Billie had had her fill of being the supportive fiancée. After Darina's surprise last night, she had been trying to help Michael cope with the possibility that he had an eight-year-old son out there he'd never met. But now, she needed some answers.

Upon hearing the news, Billie immediately became suspicious of Darina. Well, she'd been suspicious since she showed up, but especially so once she shared the news. The woman who had played nice and reluctant to invade their evening was suddenly dropping life-changing bombs, thinking a kind smile would make it all okay.

It wasn't okay. Michael was in shock at first as Billie was the one to ask all of the questions. Darina explained that once she found out she was pregnant, she wasn't sure she would keep the baby at first, knowing that things were over between her and Michael. Then, once she decided to have the baby, she felt it was best to move on.

This was when Michael finally got himself together enough to speak up. He was angry that she thought it was best to not let him know he had a child. She explained that their lives had taken different turns. Michael had chosen the capitalist path, as she described it. She didn't want her child involved in that. She added that starting a new business, she imagined Michael would not be able to commit to a child in any way it would need.

The arrogance of her presumptions hurt Michael, but infuriated Billie. She was angry that the woman could pull off such a deceit and then show up without any proof to support her claim and expect everyone to just take a deep breath and get on with it.

Darina apologized several times, stating that she knew she'd done the wrong thing and was trying to make it right. After realizing she was getting nowhere with Billie, Darina focused her pleas on Michael. She wanted him to meet Duncan, gave him a picture of a little adorable child that looked nothing like Michael, with her hotel room number on the back.

After she left, Michael just stared at the picture for a while. Billie rubbed his back and asked him to express his feelings. He couldn't. He just didn't believe this. Billie didn't believe it either, but her disbelief was more from skepticism than shock. She suggested that the timing was suspicious. They'd just announced their engagement to family and friends and suddenly Darina showed up with a long-lost child.

Billie wanted more answers from Darina and, after a sleepless night, she wanted more answers from Michael.

"You lied to me," she said as she approached the breakfast table where Michael was sitting, looking out the window.

The picture of the kid that was supposed to be Duncan was next to his coffee cup.

Michael looked at her, his red eyes denoting his lack of sleep. "What are you talking about? I didn't know . . ."

"Not the child," she said. "Darina. You told me you hadn't seen her since you broke up and moved to D.C."

Billie could tell from the change of expression on his face that he realized what she was talking about. He clearly didn't want to get into it.

"Really?" he asked. "That's what you want to talk about now? I just found out I have a son that didn't even know I existed for eight years."

Billie sat down in the chair next to him. "I realize on the scale of everything that's going on, this may not seem big, but it needs to be answered, Michael."

Michael reached for his cup of coffee and took a slow sip. "I was ashamed."

"Why?"

"It was a stupid mistake," he explained. "A one-night stand."

"There is no such thing as a one-night stand with the woman you were recently in love with." Billie knew this all too well. How many times had she said her post-separation trysts with Porter were just a one-night stand?

"I went home," he explained. "I was lonely and she was . . . familiar."

"You were lonely?" she asked. "But Darina said you were both in relationships at the time. That's why you thought it would just be a harmless dinner. Who did you cheat on?"

Michael looked at her angrily. "I'm not a cheater, Billie. I don't cheat."

Billie was trying to control her own emotions so she could hear what he was saying. It was hard. Infidelity was a sore subject for her for obvious reasons.

"I wasn't in a relationship," Michael confessed. "The truth was I hadn't been on more than two dates with anyone since we'd broken up. I lied to her so I wouldn't seem . . . pitiful."

"And you lied to me . ."

"For the same reason," he said. "I didn't want you thinking I was the type of guy who couldn't move on. I liked you very much. I wanted you to think highly of me."

"You know what I think highly of?" Billie reached across the table and placed her hand over his. "The truth. We've all been weak. We've all made bad choices. The truth sets us free."

Michael lowered his head. "I don't know exactly what I'm getting into, but I know I can't get through it without you. I need you."

"You have me." She squeezed his hand. "We'll get through it together."

"I want to meet him right away," Michael said.

"No," Billie stated definitively. "We need to sit down and talk to Darina more. We need to demand that she show us proof that he's yours."

He looked at her confused. "Proof? I mean . . . Darina wouldn't lie about that."

"Says who?" Billie asked. "The woman who kept you from the boy for eight years? She's been lying to you for eight years. There's a high probability that this kid is not yours."

"There's nothing to gain from lying to me about this," Michael said. "This is something that can easily be disproven."

"She has to give you proof," Billie urged. "Before you meet with the boy. If she's lying, you'll be hurt, but that kid will be—"

"Darina is a good woman," Michael insisted. He sat back in his char. "She's not a liar. She's a bit extreme when it comes to her politics, but she's honest. She wouldn't fuck over her own kid like that."

"She was in a relationship with a man at the time," Billie reminded him. "Which makes her a cheater."

"You can't judge her," Michael said. "You don't know what her relationship was like."

"I can judge her," Billie stated. "She's disrupting our lives with this bomb. I definitely am going to judge her and so should you."

"I don't care about that man," Michael said.

"You should," Billie said. "Who is he? She has to at least prove that the kid doesn't belong to him. When did you have sex? When was Duncan born? She could lie about anything. We need to see—"

"Can you stop being a lawyer for a second?" he asked.

"No," she answered. "I can't. This is a situation that is fraught with legal land mines. Women do this shit all the time. We need to look at her finances. If she's down on her luck, she could be looking for a payday."

"Darina doesn't care about money!"

Billie wasn't at all pleased at the urgency with which Michael defended this woman. Did he think she was a saint? Clearly she wasn't, or she wouldn't have kept this truth from him for eight years. If it was even the truth.

"Why are you so reluctant to see what's in front of your face?" she asked. "This is suspicious at best, Michael."

"She wouldn't lie to me about my own child," Michael said. "I know this woman. You don't."

"But I will," Billie proclaimed. "I'm gonna find out everything about what she's been doing since your one-night stand to see what she's up to."

"What if she isn't up to anything?" Michael asked. "You put all your effort into this shit and it turns out she was telling the truth?"

"I'll be so happy that I wasted my time," Billie said.

"You're being insecure," he accused. "I understand that you might feel threatened by this situation, but you shouldn't be."

"Bullshit," Billie said. "I'm not new to this game. Something is fishy here and I'm telling you, Michael. You need to hold off on letting this boy into your life until you have more proof."

"You want her to be lying," he said, angrily. "You want to demonize her because you don't want me to have a kid."

Billie was shocked. "Michael, are you really going to attack me? I'm just trying to make sense of this. We need to figure out what's going on."

"Seems like you've already figured it out." He stood up from the table and walked over to the window, looking down at the street.

"I didn't let a child keep me from marrying Porter," Billie said. "I loved Tara from the first second I met her. And if Duncan is yours, I'll love him the same. But there were no questions about Porter's paternity."

"I can't focus on that right now," Michael said. "I'm just going to meet him. I want to look at him. I want to see him. He needs to know I didn't know."

"I know what you're thinking," Billie said softly as she walked up behind him, wrapping her arms around him. "You're thinking of your absent father, how much you missed out on. How it hurt to know he just walked out of your life and acted like he didn't care."

"I won't be him," Michael said.

"You're not him. Once you find out Duncan is your boy, you'll be a great and present father. But the last thing you want to do is let a little boy get attached to you and have to let go."

Michael turned to her. "If he's mine, you're okay with me going all in."

"I wouldn't want to marry a man who didn't believe in going all in at fatherhood."

He placed his hands over hers as they lay across his chest. "You know if this is true, that makes the issue of moving back to Atlanta even more important. I mean, we'd have to go back. I'd have to be near my son."

Billie felt inevitability come over her at this realization. She didn't respond. She couldn't do that truthfully and she didn't want to upset Michael any more. He was probably right. He'd need to be near his son, but what about Billie needing to be near her daughter?

She had to stay focused. She knew that Michael's emotions were getting the best of him and she couldn't let this thing get out of control. She had to get proof and figure out if Darina was really a woman who was just trying to right a wrong or if she had more nefarious motives.

Either way, she wasn't going to let this get in the way of the happiness she'd found, a happiness Billie never thought she'd have again.

10

Even though she was in the living room and Corey was all the way down the hallway in the bedroom behind a closed door, Erica made sure to keep her voice low so he couldn't hear.

"It's been a while," said Alex Gonzales on the other end of the phone.

"I know," she responded. "I'm sorry. How long?"

"Almost seven months." His voice held a hint of his hesitation. "I was thinking of calling you when . . . well, you know."

"I was thinking the same." Erica curled her feet underneath her legs on the sofa. "But I assumed you didn't want to talk about him any more than I did."

"He doesn't exist to me," Alex said. "So in my opinion, no one I knew died."

"I feel the same." Erica felt envious of Alex's clarity.

"I thought you'd be more affected," he said. "You know. You were closer to him. You had an actual relationship with him."

"I wasn't close to him," she insisted. "I mean, I gave him more chances than I should have, but after what he did to you, he was dead to me."

"But he still tried to contact you," Alex said. "Never once even called me."

"When Jonah does something wrong to someone, he blames them for feeling wronged. In his fucked-up head, he probably thought you and your mother owed him an apology."

Alex laughed somberly. "I would tell him not to hold his breath, but I guess he's not."

Erica laughed. "God, you're really not upset at all, are you?"

"No," he said. "Honestly, my life here in Miami is great. I have a great job as a teaching assistant in the political science department of the university. I got my own place. I have a girlfriend."

"You have a girlfriend?" she asked. "What's she like?"

"She's nice," he said. "She's Cuban and she works in administration on campus."

A moment passed before Erica congratulated him. This was still a little awkward, but they both pushed through it. Erica had stopped having feelings for Alex the second she found out he was her half brother. She was sickened to the point of throwing up whenever she thought of the time they kissed.

There wasn't much chance to deal with it. Once the news hit, Alex left town and didn't look back. After a couple of months, they would text each other and then talk on the phone. Both of them knew this wasn't their fault, that they'd done nothing wrong. This was all Jonah's fault.

"I'd like you to meet her if you ever came to visit," Alex said after that short silence.

"That goes both ways," Erica said.

"No." His tone was less open now. "I'll never go back to D.C. Now that Mother has moved down here, there's nothing that can get me back in that city."

"I can understand that," she said. "So maybe I'll come down. It's starting to get cold up here anyway."

Erica wondered if he really wanted to see her. She wondered if she really wanted to see him. It seemed safe, these emails, texts, and infrequent phone conversations. They could be friends this way. While they might have both moved on from their little romance, they weren't ready to acknowledge being brother and sister. Maybe they'd have to do that if they ever came face-to-face again.

"I'm dating someone too," she said. "His name is Corey. He's a lobbyist."

"A lobbyist?" Alex asked. "I don't see you dating a lobbyist."

"He's really cool," she said. "Down-to-earth and all that."

"Does he know?"

"About Jonah?" she asked. "No, but I don't know how much longer I can keep it from him. I don't want to keep it from him at all."

"It's a huge secret to keep," Alex said. "Not sure how you could have a real relationship with someone without telling them. It's such a big part of who you are."

"No, it isn't!" Erica surprised herself at how adamant her tone was. "Nothing about Jonah defines me. My life is the same as it was before I ever met him. I'm the same person."

"Whoa," Alex said. "You don't have to bite my head off. Look, it doesn't matter. He's gone. It's done."

"I hate him." Erica was feeling suddenly very sad. "I hate him, Alex."

"There's no point in that," Alex said. "Not anymore. I don't hate him anymore."

"How can you not?" she asked. "He knew you were his from the beginning and said nothing. He was your father, but he barely showed you the attention that a distant friend of your parents would. And when it all came out, he didn't even try to make up for it."

"I'm not saying he doesn't deserve to be hated," Alex said. "I'm just saying, it's done."

"He didn't even leave you anything!" Erica blurted out.

She tried to catch herself, but it was too late. She hadn't intended on bringing up the topic like this.

"In his will?" Alex asked. "I didn't expect him to. I wouldn't have accepted it anyway."

Erica didn't understand that. "Don't you think he owes you?"

"There isn't anything he could give me to make up for what I missed out on, not having a father."

"No," she agreed. "But it's not fair. I mean you and I—"

"Erica?" Alex asked after some silence. "Did he leave you something?"

"I don't want it," she quickly said. "That's why I'm calling you. I want you to have it. I want to stick it to him for being an asshole."

"You can't stick it to a dead person," Alex said.

"It's one million dollars," she said.

There was a silence for at least five seconds.

"He left you one million dollars?"

"His bitch wife and kids tried to keep it away from me, but I got it. The check is in the mail, so to speak."

"You accepted it?" he asked.

"Well . . ." She was suddenly feeling defensive. "I mean, I didn't want to."

"But you did."

"For you," she insisted. "I wanted you to have something. You're the one whose life was turned upside down by his lies and deceit."

"No, Erica. I never wanted anything from him."

"But you deserve it!"

"I don't want it," Alex stated soundly. "I don't want anything from him. That money is . . . It would only bring him back into my life. I don't want that. I can't believe you do."

"I said I didn't!" she exclaimed, her tone harsh. "I couldn't let her do that."

"Who do what?" Alex asked.

"Juliet. She was trying to make me invisible like I didn't matter."

"Why do you care what she thinks? She's a WASP-y old hag."

Erica shot up from the sofa, feeling her blood start to boil. "But she wanted me to accept that I wasn't real. That I was less a daughter because I wasn't hers too."

"She's a bitch. You can't let her get to you like—"

"But I got to her," Erica said. "I found her weak spot and she decided not to fight the will. The whole family backed down. Even that bitch daughter of his. I proved to them that . . ."

"That what?" Alex asked.

Erica sighed impatiently. "Alex, it's a million bucks. You can't turn that down."

"I can," he said. "And I am. Keep the money, Erica. It means something to you, not me."

"What's that supposed to mean?" she asked.

"Obviously it's some sort of victory for you," he said. "So keep it."

"The victory was for both us," she explained. "Hey, why don't we share it? I'll give you half and—"

"I don't want any of it," Alex said.

"Well, what the fuck am I supposed to do with it?" Erica asked.

"If I were you," he said. "I'd get rid of it before it changes you."

"Why would it change me?" she asked. "I'm not some flaky person who lets money fuck them up."

"It will change you because it's from Jonah. Nothing good ever comes from him."

"It's money," Erica said. "It's not him. There are no strings attached."

"There aren't any answers either. All the money in the world won't explain the lies, the rejection, the shame, and the lost time."

"I don't care about that." Erica heard her own voice choking a bit. "I thought you knew me, Alex. How could you think I'd be so gullible as to let money make me forget all he's done?"

"I don't think you're gullible," he said. "But I think you have a lot of unresolved issues with him and you could easily let the money help you avoid dealing with them."

"You don't know me at all," she yelled. "Dammit, Alex. I was trying to help you."

"I don't need help. My life is going great."

"Well, mine isn't!" she shouted. "And your bullshit is just making it worse. I'll remember never to do a favor for you again!"

She hung up the phone and threw it farther down the sofa.

"What the hell is going on in here?"

She turned to see Corey come out of the hallway and into the living room, looking alarmed.

"I'm sorry," she said. "Did I disturb you?"

"You were yelling," he said.

As Corey walked over to her, Erica couldn't believe she had gotten that loud, but she was so angry right now, she wanted to yell some more.

"What's wrong?" Corey approached her cautiously.

"Don't," she said, as she noticed he was about to wrap his arms around her.

"Okay, that's it." Corey ran his hand over his head in frustration. "Erica, what the hell is going on with you? You look like you're about to cry."

"If he doesn't want it," she said, "I'll keep it. To hell with him!"

"Keep what?" Corey asked.

"I deserve it just as much as he does," she said. "Hell, I deserve it more after all I went through!"

He sighed, annoyed. "So you're just gonna have a conversation with yourself? Even though I'm standing right here?"

"You try and do something good for someone, they don't

appreciate it!" She began pacing the small space between the living room and dining area, her arms folded across her chest. "No one understands. Everyone just judges."

"I haven't judged you," Corey said. "And you haven't given me a chance to understand you."

She turned to him, feeling her body want to calm down at the sight of his calm, understanding demeanor. He was trying to reach out to her. Maybe he was right. Maybe he was the only one who could understand and wouldn't judge her. There was no history here, no baggage.

Erica rushed over to him and threw herself into his arms. She loved how he was big enough to make her feel small. She wrapped her arms around him and placed her head against his chest. She felt her body calm as his arms tightened around her.

"You have to talk to me, baby."

She lifted her head and looked up at him. "Baby?"

"You're my baby, right?" he asked, with a smile.

She leaned up and kissed him on the mouth. "I like the sound of that," she said.

"I like the sound of some truth," he said back. "How about I get some?"

She nodded, leaning away from him. "You're right. We need to talk. We're going to dinner still, right?"

"I thought we might check out that Ethiopian place you were talking about."

She shook her head. "No, we can do that another night. I want to go somewhere nice. Real nice."

"Like how nice?" he asked.

"Don't worry." She patted him on the chest. "Tonight, dinner is on me."

"Erica, you know how I feel about—"

"We're not on a date," she said. "Remember? I'm your baby and you're mine. That means I can pay sometimes. And I feel like spending a shitload of money right now."

"Do you have a shitload of money to spend?" he asked.

"Get dressed," she ordered. "You've asked enough questions tonight."

Sherise hung up the phone after talking to Beth, her P.I., feeling more confused than ever. Maybe she needed to hire a different investigator. A person's relationship with their P.I., especially one who had come through so many times, was a sacred one. But there wasn't anything on Maurice yet. At least not anything strong enough to use against him.

They'd spent the last half hour discussing the biggest donors to the Northman campaign that Sherise was aware of, using the list the staff had been given for party invites. Beth had done some quickie investigating and found the usual scandals. A mistress here, an illegitimate child there, and maybe a bank account or two in Switzerland.

It would seem odd to someone not in politics, but this was not a big deal. Certainly not enough to force someone to influence the incoming president to hire you. Sherise was frustrated and felt, for the first time since starting on this mission, that she might not succeed. She felt completely stunted.

She was broken from her concentration by a knock on her partially open door. When she looked up, LaKeisha stuck her head inside.

"Busy?"

"No." Sherise gestured for her to come in.

"Wanted you to hear the latest," LaKeisha said as she rushed inside and closed the door behind her. She made a beeline for the seat on the side of Sherise's desk.

"I know you get pissed at me when you hear something secondhand." LaKeisha sat down.

"What happened?" Sherise could only hope it was something bad about Maurice.

"Shelly just quit," she answered. "She told Tom she couldn't work in the same place as Maurice anymore."

"Did he do something else?" Sherise asked.

She shook her head. "But he's done enough. She just doesn't feel comfortable in the office around him."

"Has Tom told Jerry?" Sherise asked.

"He was really upset because Shelly is important to him. They're in a fury over agency appointments. He needed her. He told Jerry that, but . . ."

"Nothing," Sherise said with a sigh.

"He said he'd talk to Maurice, but that doesn't help Tom. Shelly is gone."

"I'm not surprised," Sherise said. "Don't tell him I told you, but Stephen even put in a word for Shelly. You know he likes her."

"Wow." LaKeisha shook her head in disbelief. "Jerry loves Stephen to death. I can't believe that didn't sway him."

"Who exactly was it that pressured Jerry the most on hiring Maurice?" Sherise asked. "I know all the powerful donors and the party leaders that supported us the most, but I've been making calls and I can't find out who is in Maurice's corner."

"You and me both," LaKeisha said. "I'm getting so frustrated. I'm supposed to know everything Jerry knows. I've talked to him about this and he won't say who pressured him into hiring Maurice. I've gone out on my own to the people I know he'd listen to. Not a one admitted to pushing Maurice forward."

Sherise found this bizarre. "Why wouldn't they?"

"Well, they don't want to give a clue that he's blackmailing them to do it, I guess." LaKeisha shrugged. "As far as the politicians, we know who is who. Where the private donors are concerned, we vet them if they're giving us a lot of money. Most have little to no connection to Maurice."

"What about the agency appointments?" Sherise asked. "Who is Maurice pushing for?"

LaKeisha nodded. "You think maybe it was a quid pro quo? You pressure the governor to hire me as PS and I'll make sure you get Head of Education."

"Tom said Maurice was pressuring him about appointments."

"So far, none of his suggestions have passed vetting," LaKeisha said. "Congressman James Cannon, Governor Ryan Wilson, and there are others, but so far Tom has nixed them all and Maurice hasn't put up much of a fight."

Sherise didn't think there was anything there. It was a thought. She was desperate. She had to look at every avenue.

"Funny thing," LaKeisha said. "The only job he seems to have secured is his own."

A light blinked on in Sherise's head as she sat up straight. Of course! It had to be. They had been on the wrong path all along. There was a reason they couldn't find a donor or politician who pressured Jerry into hiring Maurice. They weren't trying to cover up blackmail. Maurice wasn't blackmailing any of them to get the job. He was blackmailing Jerry to get the job!

It was the only real explanation, and Sherise felt stupid for not having figured it out already. She'd wasted so much time!

But that brought on many other questions. What was so horrible that he could blackmail Jerry, the man who was a few months from being the most powerful man in the world, into doing something he didn't want to? Not only was Jerry no pushover, he was an actual good guy. It took a while for Sherise to believe it herself, thinking it was all a façade and Jerry was just better at it than most politicians. But after getting to know him and learn of his past, she became a believer. There were no mistresses, no drug abuse, and no dirty backdoor business dealings in his past.

But Maurice had something on him, and Jerry was risking a

lot to make Maurice happy. Was Jerry not the clean-cut husband and father Sherise had known him to be? And how would Maurice know about that and not any of his closest staff? Did he know something that could ruin Jerry's presidency, and thus Sherise's aspirations, before it even began?

It was time to rework her strategy and Sherise knew that there was very little time left.

There were people all around them in the jewelry department of Bloomingdale's at the Shops at Wisconsin Place in Chevy Chase, Maryland, so Sherise tried to keep her voice low. It wasn't easy. She was angry.

"That was a stupid, stupid move, Billie."

"I told him he had to get the blood test results first," Billie said. "He didn't want to wait. They're leaving in a few days and he wanted to see the kid."

"You should have insisted," Erica said as she saw the piece that she'd seen here before. A red and gold Ferragamo buckle leather bracelet.

"I did," Billie explained. "He had it done yesterday. The results will be back within a week. They'll be back in Atlanta by then."

"So?" Sherise said.

"Well, I guess it's better he get to know him here," Billie surmised. "I don't want to have to go back to Atlanta so soon again."

Sherise was shaking her head. "No. It's best he wait no matter what. You don't know what this bitch is up to."

"I'm not stupid." Billie placed a pair of earrings back on the stand. "I watched her like a hawk when they met up last night. She was perfect or she's really good at playing perfect. She just seemed very happy to see Duncan and Michael together."

"How was Michael?" Erica asked.

"Emotional," Billie said. "He tried so hard to keep it all in. He wanted to make sure that things didn't get, you know, caught up at the first meeting. It was only an hour, but he had to fight to keep cool."

"Does the kid look like him?" Sherise asked.

"No," Billie said. "I tried to see it, but I couldn't. He looks like Darina."

"I'm pissed at you for not taking a picture of her," Sherise said. "I want to know what she looks like."

"I told you," Billie said. "I don't even care about her looks. I care about her motives. Michael is a mess. I'm worried about him."

"I'm worried about you," Sherise said. "What P.I. did you put on her?"

"What?" Billie looked at her. "I'm not hiring a P.I. on my own."

Sherise didn't believe that. "You have to."

"It's a good idea," Erica added as she placed the bracelet on her arm. She loved it now even more than when she first saw it. "You need to know who you're dealing with."

"I told Michael we should do that," Billie said. "I'm not going to do it behind his back. That's not who I am."

Sherise made a smacking sound with her mouth and rolled her eyes. "Michael isn't thinking straight right now. You can't wait for him to get his head together to know what you're heading into. When he does, it might be too late."

"Between this and Michael going on about moving to Atlanta, I have enough on my plate. I don't want anything else getting between us and this wedding."

"I thought you already told him moving to Atlanta is off the table," Sherise said.

"I'm trying to convince him," Billie stated. "He's trying to convince me otherwise."

Erica didn't like what she was hearing. "Billie, you can't

come between Michael and his son. The poor kid already went eight years without a father."

"He's had a father," Sherise corrected her.

"Not his real father," Erica said. "He needs that relationship. You have no right to interfere with that."

"I'm not trying to do that!" Billie was offended by the accusation. "Have you been listening to anything I said?"

Erica shrugged. "It's just shitty if you turn into the wife who tries to shut out kids that came before you."

"I'm not trying to shut him out, Erica! I'm just trying to make sure he's who Darina says he is and—"

"Just shut up, Erica," Sherise interjected. "You're projecting."

"I'm what?" Erica asked.

"Projecting your fucking baggage from Jonah on Billie," Sherise clarified. "She's not trying to keep him from the kid if the kid is his."

"Fuck you!" Erica shouted loud enough for people to hear. "Not everything is about Jonah. Why do you keep bringing him up?"

"Because it's obvious," Sherise said. "Jonah's shrew of a wife didn't want you in his life. But the fact is, if he wanted to openly be your father, he could have."

Shocked by what Sherise had just said, Billie knew this was about to go downhill fast.

"It's not important," Billie said. "Let's just . . ."

"You know what, Sherise?" Erica asked, "You're a fucking bitch! You always have been and you always will be."

She turned and headed to the other end of the jewelry counter where an employee was standing.

Sherise looked at Billie and said. "Tell me something I don't know."

"Don't mess with her," Billie said, even though she was angry at Erica for her insinuations. "She's extra touchy these days."

"These days?" Sherise asked. "As opposed to when?"

They walked over to Erica as she offered the lady her credit card.

"Who are you buying that for?" Billie asked.

"Myself," Erica answered, not looking at either of them.

"We're supposed to be Christmas shopping for others," Sherise said.

"What have you bought?" Erica asked, looking around Sherise to note that she had no gifts.

"That bracelet is over four hundred dollars," Billie said. "Erica?"

"I have the money now." Erica smiled as the two women looked surprised. "I told you it was coming."

"I thought you were giving it to Alex," Billie said.

"That jerk didn't want it," Erica said flippantly. "And after I thought about it, I deserve it more than he does anyway."

"How do you figure that?" Billie asked.

"None of your damn business," Erica responded before turning to sign her receipt.

"Well, have you gotten a financial manager?" Billie asked. "That's a lot of money. You can't just put it in the bank, Erica. You have to—"

"I'm not an idiot," Erica said. "You guys think I'm so stupid, don't you? Just because I don't have a college education, I don't know that I need someone to manage my money?"

"I wasn't calling you stupid," Billie said.

"Even educated people don't know all that stuff," Sherise added. "Don't be so fucking sensitive."

"I know what I need and I've got it." Erica took her credit card back from the salesperson. "I've got a financial manager and I have a real estate agent looking to buy me a house."

"Already?" Sherise asked. "You might need to slow your roll."

Billie was genuinely hurt. "Why would you do all of this without talking to us first?"

Erica placed both hands on her hips, feeling like she was about to explode. "You both think I'm a damn five-year-old or something. I don't know how to handle more than ten bucks and now, I can't even look for a home without your help."

Billie rolled her eyes. She was exhausted with this bullshit. "Erica, you know I would want you both in on buying a new house. It's a big deal. It's a stressful experience."

"Not when you're rich," Erica said haughtily.

"You're not rich," Sherise said. "You're showing your ghetto side, thinking that money makes you rich."

"Not to mention you're only twenty-nine," Billie said. "It's not a lot of money at all."

"You're just jealous!" Erica retorted. "You can't stand that I'm not the charity case of the group anymore. You think you can still convince me I need your help, your guidance with everything. You want to make sure I don't get too big for my britches!"

Sherise threw her hands in the air. "I can't deal with this shit."

"Then don't!" Erica told her. "I didn't ask you to and I don't need you to. I don't need anything from either of you."

"Erica, you do need us," Billie said. "We all need each other."

Erica accepted the bagged bracelet, thanking the woman, and turned to Billie.

"Well, maybe things change," she said. "Maybe you liked our situation when you both had your little Erica to look after and guide. I'm not that girl anymore. I don't need your guidance. It's insulting and condescending. I think I'm gonna finish my Christmas shopping on my own."

Erica turned and walked away, her head held high. She was asserting herself now and they just couldn't deal with it. They couldn't deal with her not needing them to show her the way anymore. All their education and money meant nothing to her anymore and they couldn't handle it. She didn't need to deal with it and wouldn't anymore.

11

As she watched from the sidelines, hating Maurice with every inch of her being, Sherise tried to keep her mind straight. She had to let go of the fact that it should be her sitting there, under the bright lights of the news studio on the number one Sunday-morning talk show. Instead, she was just offstage being the supportive minion that Jerry wanted her to be.

Everything was different now that she realized she'd been on the wrong path. She felt stupid for not seeing it. Although, in her defense, Sherise had been certain she knew absolutely everything about Jerry. The man was a political campaigner's dream, a politician with a boring personal life. Even his college years were bland.

Something had happened, and it was bad enough to frighten Jerry into doing the bidding of a man who could ruin his reputation. But what was it, and how did Maurice know about it and no one else? The two men hadn't shared any connection that would give them access into each other's lives.

The truth was, nothing Sherise had planned to do would make a difference. If Maurice had Jerry by the balls, her only chance was to find out what he was using for his grip and neutralize that grip.

Her first thought had been to go to Jerry and pretend as if she knew, but that was playing it too risky. He was already upset with her and if he called her bluff, she would fail and that would be it for her. She'd be fired and it would all be over. No, she had to get the information from the man who was walking toward her now.

"Did I look shiny?" Maurice asked as he approached. "I hate it when they make me look shiny. That stupid makeup chick overdid it."

"You looked fine." Sherise handed him his phone.

He started walking as he checked his phone and Sherise kept his stride.

"The car is downstairs to take you to your next interview," she said.

"Which one?" he asked.

She sighed. It was unbelievable that he couldn't keep track of this. "Charles Burke, Maurice."

Charles Burke was arguably the most powerful political journalist in D.C. It killed Sherise to think of how inept Maurice was going to look to him, but it angered her even more that Maurice didn't seem to give a damn.

Maurice stopped and looked at her with a displeased frown. "What was that?"

"What?" she asked.

"That sigh." He pointed at her, his finger only a foot from her face.

She wanted to slap him. "What sigh?"

"I don't need your attitude, Sherise. Not today."

"I have no attitude," she said.

"Just take a Midol or whatever you women take when you're on the rag and pull your shit together."

He started walking again, but Sherise didn't walk with him. A few feet away, he realized that she was still standing there and turned back to look at her. Her desire to please Jerry could only go so far and from the murderous look on her face, Maurice knew that.

"It was a joke," he said, walking back to her. "Come on, Sherise. You have to have a sense of humor if you're going to work for me."

"Sexist humor isn't really my thing," she remarked flatly.

"Everyone is so fucking sensitive." He shook his head in disappointment. "I know you're pissed about this situation, but don't you think it's time you got over it? All of your games haven't worked."

"You're making a lot of assumptions," Sherise told him. "But just because I don't laugh at your bad jokes doesn't mean I'm pissed. Say something funny and I'll laugh."

"I should give you some credit," he said. "You haven't tried to sabotage me the past two days."

She tilted her head to the side sarcastically with a smile. "You stay in your office and don't interact with any staff and voilà, there are no incidents. That has to be my doing, right?"

"I am who I am," he said with a shrug.

"And we're all so grateful for that," Sherise snarked. "Now can we just go to the next interview?"

"I'm trying to get along with you, Sherise." He seemed clearly angry she wasn't going along. "I'm trying to make this situation better for you."

She wanted to laugh, but she didn't. "Just do your job and you'll make it better for everyone."

"Bullshit," he said. "You don't want me to do my job. You've been doing everything you can to make me fail."

"I wanted you to fail at first," she admitted. "But I get it now. So all I want is for Jerry to look good going into his administration."

He looked her over as if he was trying to believe what she

had to say and finally, after a few seconds, shrugged as if it didn't matter.

"Fine," he said. "As long as you know your place."

"Your place," she answered slowly to control her emotions, "is in that car outside. We need to get going to—"

"I'll go to the Burke interview," he interrupted, looking at his watch. "You have to go to Market Lunch and meet my sister."

"At Eastern Market? To meet who?"

He rolled his eyes. "I'll speak slower, so you can understand. My little sister, Kimberly, is going to meet you at Market Lunch in a half hour."

"For what?" Sherise asked.

He waved for her to follow him to the elevator. "You need to talk to her and figure out how to get her a job at your husband's firm."

"Excuse me?"

"She's a legislative aide on the Hill and she wants to be a lobbyist. I told her she can go work for your husband."

"So you told her that, huh?" Sherise asked. "Too bad you're going to have to break it to her that he's not hiring."

"I promised her."

"I don't care what you promised her," Sherise said. "My husband and I don't fuck with each other's jobs, Maurice. Justin hires who he wants."

"And he'll want to hire her," Maurice said. "She's young and pretty. That's all a girl needs to be in order to make it in lobbying."

"In your world maybe." Sherise stepped into the elevator and pressed the button for the lobby. "But in the real world, where the rest of us live, you need actual talent."

"Which I'm sure she has." Maurice was busy scrolling on his phone. "She's my sister, after all."

"Poor girl."

"I'll ignore that." Maurice stepped out into the lobby. "I'm sure you can catch a cab out there."

"Are you serious?" Sherise asked. "You really expect me to do this? I'm not a headhunter, Maurice."

As soon as they reached the revolving door of the building, Maurice turned to her. "Sherise, I know you can convince any man of anything."

"Go fuck yourself," she said.

"Speaking of which," he answered back, unfazed by her insult, "with that body and what I suspect are your skills, I'm sure you'll figure out a way to get your husband to do whatever you want."

Without thinking, Sherise reached out and slapped him in the face. There were a few people in the lobby and everyone stopped what they were doing and looked at them.

Maurice barely blinked and recovered quickly with a wide smile on his face. "You are a fiery one, aren't you?"

"I'll turn a lot more than fiery if you ever talk to me like that again," Sherise warned. "I'm not some intimidated twenty-two-year-old assistant who feels ashamed when you pat her butt."

"I know you're not," he responded. "That's why I find you so sexy, Sherise. You're a firecracker and a nutcracker in one. That's as sexy as a woman gets."

He reached for the door and opened it. Before stepping out, he turned to her and added, "I look forward to getting slapped by you again."

Sherise's hands were clenched in fists as he walked along the sidewalk and got into the driven car. She prayed for a giant anvil to drop from the building and smash the car like in the cartoons she watched as a child. She didn't just want this man out of a job. She wanted him dead.

But there was one thing that made Sherise calm down. She needed the truth and she had a feeling that Maurice was the only way she was going to get it. He was a born fuckup and there wasn't any reason why he wouldn't be the same with whatever arrangement he'd made with Jerry.

Sherise had come so far in life that she had believed finally all she had to do was be great at her job to get things done. But Maurice changed that. He was forcing her to go back to her old ways. He was a pig and he was clearly attracted to her. The thought of it made her sick, but she would have to use that to her advantage to get what she needed from him

When Billie showed up at Asia54 on P Street, she walked in on a scene that didn't sit at all well with her. She was downright pissed. The waitress led her to a table across from the bar where she saw little Duncan sitting between Michael and Darina, both parents doting on him and all three laughing.

Like a cute little family.

Michael had asked her to meet him there for dinner. He never mentioned anyone else. Besides, Billie knew she was only about ten minutes late, but it looked like they'd been there for a long time. Had Michael given her the wrong time so he could spend time with Darina and Duncan without her? Why didn't he tell her?

Stop it, she told herself. She was being paranoid. She couldn't do that. Still, she couldn't help but be bothered by what she saw.

"Hi, everyone!" she said loudly, as it was clear not one of them noticed her walk up.

When Michael looked up, he smiled, getting out of his seat to greet her. When he reached her, he leaned forward and kissed her on her lips.

"Hey, baby," he said.

"What's going on?" Billie asked. "I thought it was going to be just you and me."

"I know," he explained, "but I invited the two of them.

They're leaving soon and I just wanted to spend some more time with him."

"You mean the two of them?" she asked.

"Well, I guess, yeah. She goes where he goes."

"I wish you'd told me," Billie said. "I brought some wedding prep stuff to go over."

"We have time for that," he said. "He's leaving soon, Billie. You understand."

She really didn't have much choice but to understand, did she?

"How long have you been here?" she asked, even though she hated herself for doing so.

"Just a few minutes before you," he answered. "Are you okay?"

"I'm fine," she lied with a sweet smile.

Billie turned to Darina and thought she caught a glimpse of a frown as the woman watched the two of them show affection.

"Hi, Darina," she said kindly.

"Hey, girl." Darina smiled widely. "You don't mind us joining you, do you?"

"Of course not." Billie walked over to the table and placed the bag of wedding magazines in the chair next to her purse. "Hey, Duncan."

The young boy greeted her with a sweet smile and a wave. He was really, very cute and Billie knew she'd have no problem coming to like him if things turned out to be as Michael suspected.

"You look nice," Darina said. "Doesn't she look . . . professional, Duncan?"

Duncan nodded and Billie smiled appreciatively, although she suspected there was a hidden dig there. Darina didn't respect the corporate life at all. Was this her game? To seem extra sweet with veiled insults?

"Have you ordered yet?" Billie asked.

"We did," Darina said. "It's my fault. I didn't expect you to be here this early. You corporate ladies are usually so busy with your jobs that it's hard for you to get anywhere on time and Duncan was hungry."

Billie looked at Michael, wondering if he noticed the not-so-thinly-veiled part of that insult, but he was focused on Duncan, not paying attention to either of them. This was going to be a long dinner.

"I need a drink," Billie said, before turning and heading to the bar.

"What can I get you?" the pretty, black-haired woman behind the counter asked.

"An apple martini," Billie said, but just as the woman reached for a metal shaker, she changed her mind. "You know what? Make that a Jack Daniel's on the rocks."

The bartender smiled and reached for the whiskey.

Billie barely had time to catch her breath before Darina slid up to her at the bar.

"We ordered a ton of sushi," Darina said. "There should be enough for you unless you want to order something for yourself."

"I'll be fine." Billie pretended to focus on getting cash out of her wallet to avoid eye contact.

"I noticed you had other plans for dinner tonight," Darina said.

Billie looked at her. "Excuse me?"

"I sneaked a peek in your bag." She feigned guilt. "I'm sorry. I'm usually not so nosy, but I noticed the bridal magazines."

The nerve of this woman. Looking through Billie's things and then trying to play it off so Billie looked like the bad guy for getting mad at her.

"No problem," Billie said, noting the surprise her careless tone evoked from Darina.

Did she actually think she was going to goad Billie into getting upset and making a fool of herself in front of Michael?

"We have plenty of time for wedding planning," Billie continued. "Duncan is what's important right now."

Truth be told, Billie thought, finding out the truth about paternity was what was most important now. If only that damn lab would speed things up.

"Look, Billie." Darina reached over and placed her hand over Billie's as it lay on the bar's counter.

Billie looked down at her hand, the gesture feeling extremely contrived and fake to her. Billie looked back and could see that Michael was looking at them. Of course, that was the only reason for the gesture. This woman was good.

"I know," Darina continued, "that this situation isn't easy for you. I can understand you feeling a little threatened."

Knowing that two can play that game, Billie reached over and placed her hand on top of Darina's, her mouth forming the sweetest smile she could muster.

"That's so kind of you to be worried about me," she said. "But you don't need to be. I'm not at all threatened. Michael loves me completely and has gone out of his way to assure me that nothing will come between us and our wedding."

"Has he?" Darina asked. "That's so good. Because, like I told you, I'm not here for Michael or his money. All I want is for Duncan to know his father."

"Now," Billie added.

"Now?"

"All you want now is for Duncan to know his father," Billie said. "After eight years. Darina, you have to understand how confusing this is for Michael. And me, for that matter."

"I think I've explained that." Darina's voice hinted at a slight irritation.

Billie removed her right hand from atop Darina's to take hold of her drink. "You said that you didn't want to bother Michael as he was starting his business and you had concerns about the influence of Michael's desire to join the capitalist world."

She took a sip as Darina studied her. She was calling bullshit on her and Darina had a choice to stick with her story or adjust. What was she going to do?

"You're right." Darina smiled softly, as if she wasn't interested in any resistance. "Those factors played a role, but a smaller role than I'd like to believe."

"What was the main reason?" Billie asked.

"I think you know the answer to that," Darina responded. "I was in a relationship at the time. I was happy with Marcus. He wanted to get married when we found out I was pregnant. He was a great father to Duncan while we were together. I wanted to keep things fluid. Simple is best for children."

"But simple doesn't always equal right."

Darina's pretense of kindness disappeared in an instant as she snapped, "I know that."

In a second, she caught herself and the façade returned. But it was too late. Billie had already seen the real Darina.

"I'm sure we'll be able to work it all out," Darina said. "After all, if you two will be moving to Atlanta, we might even be able to become friends."

"You're moving to Atlanta?" Billie asked. "I thought you . . ."

"I forgot to mention it?" Darina asked. "Part of all of this is not just to get Duncan to know his father, but Michael's whole family. We've already gotten an apartment there."

"It's not a done deal that Michael and I are moving to Atlanta," Billie said. "I'm sure he's told you that."

Darina nodded and looked down at her hand, which had stayed on top on Billie's left hand. She looked at the engagement ring on Billie's finger for a couple of seconds before looking back at Billie.

"Nothing is a done deal," she said, "until it's done."

She slowly turned and walked away, seeming satisfied that her message was received. Billie turned and watched her join Michael and Duncan, smiling and laughing like she hadn't just insinuated that Billie and Michael's wedding might never happen.

Michael looked up and waved for Billie to join them. She loved him dearly, but he was being a fool, and now that she knew what this bitch's game was, Billie was going to have to get Michael up to speed. Not tonight, of course. This wasn't the time. Tonight she could play Darina's game and smile, being sweet and friendly.

Tomorrow would be another story.

Erica had only been in her office for ten minutes when she felt the desire to do a little shopping. She'd seen a woman on the street on her way over here wearing a pair of Gucci glasses that she had to have. She took a picture of the woman without her noticing and was now looking for the pair online.

She thought she'd just found them at the Gucci website for $325 and was about to zoom in when her office door swung open and an angry Justin came inside.

"Where the hell have you been?" he asked.

"I'm sorry I was late," Erica said. "I just couldn't get things together this morning."

That wasn't exactly the truth. She'd spent last night in a fancy hotel room with Corey. After asking to meet him in the lobby bar for drinks, she surprised him with her hotel key card and they went upstairs. They made love for hours before ordering dinner and wine.

Like the last time Corey demanded some truth about her situation, she tried to distract him with sex. It didn't work last night. So she lied. She told him it was her Christmas bonus and stuffed his face with chocolate-covered strawberries.

She had a headache when she got up in the morning and, in all honesty, didn't want to get out of that warm, soft bed.

"I'm here now," Erica said. "I've got everything under control."

"That doesn't do me any good!" Justin yelled. "I had to do all my prep for this morning's meeting in the Hart Building!"

"That can't be right," Erica said. "I prepped all of that on Friday."

"You prepped it wrong." Justin came around her side of the desk and showed her his tablet. "Look at these notes. These are for the afternoon meeting in the Russell Building. You mixed them up."

"I did?" Erica asked even though it was clear from the notes on his screen that she had. "I'm sorry, I've had a lot—"

"Shopping?" he asked, looking at the sunglasses on her computer screen. "You come in late and the first thing you think of to do is shop?"

"I was just . . ." Erica quickly minimized the page.

"What is the matter with you, Erica? You're fucking up left and right just as this business is going nuts. I can't rely on you anymore."

"Justin, it was one mistake." She found his attitude annoying.

"It wasn't just one mistake," he told her. "You fucked up my notes. Not to mention, the notes you gave me had a ton of errors in them. Add to that you were late this morning. Last Friday, you left early without telling me. I was looking for you."

"Okay, okay," Erica said. "I get it. I messed up. I'm sorry."

"Don't be sorry," he snapped. "Just fix it. Now. I have to get on a conference call, but I want the afternoon notes put together, without errors, in an hour."

"Okay, I'll . . ." She looked at the time on her screen. "Oh wait, I can't."

"What do you mean you can't?"

"Corey is gonna be here in a few minutes. He's taking me to meet his friends at—"

"Fuck Corey," Justin yelled. "You think you can show up late and then turn around and leave?"

"I wasn't aware that I was this late. Time just got away from me."

"Well, get it back," Justin ordered. "Corey is canceled. Get to work and tighten your shit up, Erica."

"I'm not your minion," Erica stated as she shot up from her chair.

"What?" Justin asked.

"You can't talk down to me like that," she insisted. "You're so fucking condescending, Justin!"

"You know what I am?" Justin said. "I'm your boss and if you—"

"I'm not some factory worker in Venezuela," she argued. "I'm a professional and I deserve to be treated like one!"

"Professionals show up for work on time," Justin said. "They get their work done and you're not doing either, so I'm treating you exactly right from where I stand."

"On your damn high horse!" she yelled. "I'm sick of being treated like a house slave."

"A house slave?" Justin laughed out loud. "Are you fucking kidding me? I pay you a decent wage for—"

"Decent?" This time Erica laughed. "You pay yourself a decent wage, Justin. You pay me crap."

"Erica, you're acting like Cady. I don't have time for this. Do your job!"

"What job?" She reached into her drawer and grabbed her new Burberry purse. "I don't have a job here. I quit."

"What?" Justin asked as she walked past him.

"I quit, Justin." She headed out of the door. "I don't need this job or your bullshit!"

"Erica, stop!"

She could hear him following her, but she didn't stop because he told her to. She stopped because the second she en-

tered the lobby, she came face-to-face with Corey. The look on
his face was stark confusion.

"What is going on?" he asked. "I could hear you and Justin
yelling all the way from here."

"This is all bullshit," she said. "Bullshit, and I don't need it."

"What are you—" Justin halted at the sight of Corey.

"Let's go," Erica said to Corey, ignoring Justin behind her.

Corey looked from her to Justin, not sure what to do.

"Corey," Justin said. "She can't go to lunch with you and
your friends. She has work to do."

"Don't you get it?" Erica asked as she swung around to face
Justin. "I just quit. I'm not working for you. Fix your own
notes!"

"Erica, you can't do this!" Justin implored. "You can't just
bail on me because you don't like being called out for a fuckup."

"Do you see how he talks to me?" Erica asked Corey. "I
don't need this job."

"Yes, you do," Corey said. "Just calm down, Erica. Look, we
can do lunch another day."

Erica looked at him, stunned and disappointed. "Of course
you would take his side."

"I really feel like I'm taking your side," Corey said. "You
love this job. You said so yourself."

Erica laughed and shook her head. "You're right. We don't
need to go to lunch today, or ever. I'm out of here."

She shoved past him and rushed out of the door, leaving
both men standing stunned in the lobby. Nobody was going to
tell her what she had to do anymore.

Sherise was standing in the main conference room, clearly
visible from the glass windows that circled half the room. She
knew that Maurice was leaving soon and he'd have to walk by
the conference room to head out. She knew he would notice

her. She looked amazing in her red Akris Punto skirt suit. It fit all her curves perfectly, stopping just above her knee to expose long legs that led to sexy, black Birman suede heels.

The idea of using his attraction to her sent a shiver up and down her spine, but it was a means to an end. Besides, how hard was it going to be? The man wasn't the sharpest knife in the drawer.

She'd gotten a text a half hour ago from Tom, telling her he'd done his part. She asked him to invite Maurice into his office for drinks. Get him a little liquored up were her instructions. She had expected to have to explain, but Tom asked no questions. He was eager to get rid of Maurice and decided instructions were all he needed.

The text told her that Maurice had had a couple glasses of whiskey. Not too much. It would have to be good enough. She needed his guard down as much as possible.

When she heard his door slam shut, Sherise leapt into action. She rushed over to the mini-bar area, where beer and wine were stored for special occasions, and began pouring herself a glass of wine. She could see a figure out of the side of her left eye begin to walk by, but then stop. She smiled and slowly turned her head to face him.

He was standing outside of the room, staring at her with a pleased smile. He looked her up and down. She raised the bottle to him and gestured for him to come inside. There was a short look of hesitation on his part, but it didn't last long. That was the whiskey. Oh, and that red suit that she knew she had no business wearing in the office.

"What are you up to?" he asked as he entered, placing his briefcase on the conference table.

"Drowning my sorrows in a shitty day." She made sure to make her voice sound as if she'd already had a drink or two as she reached for another glass. "I get that the outgoing administration is upset that they lost, but for fuck's sake, why do they have to take it out on us?"

"They're being dicks," Maurice replied. "It's what losers do best. Who gave you a hard time today? I'll make sure to do something about it."

"That's nice of you," she said, "but I have to fight my own battles."

"Thanks." He accepted the drink. "Is anyone going to be joining us?"

"Whoever walks by," Sherise said. "Or nobody."

She noticed his eyes still held deep suspicion. He wasn't as stupid as she thought.

"What?" she asked. "I didn't force you to come in here."

"Like I could have resisted . . ." He looked at her figure. "This."

"I didn't wave you in here for that," she said. "I wanted to give you some good news."

"Good news? From you?" He leaned against the table and took a sip of wine. "I've gotta hear this."

"Your sister has a job if she wants it."

"Your husband okayed it?" he asked.

She nodded. Justin wasn't at all happy, but Sherise let him know that she needed Maurice to trust her if she was going to get any truth out of him. The fact that Erica quit earlier that morning made it easier on him.

"It's temporary for now," Sherise said.

"Temporary isn't what I asked for."

"You didn't ask for anything," Sherise reminded him. "You ordered and assumed."

"Still," he protested. "What the fuck is with this temporary shit, Sherise?"

"Congress has all gone home for the holiday break, so there isn't even much to do until the next session starts in January.

Once things are back in swing, if she turns out to have compe-
tence, he'll keep her. If not, she's gonna go."

"That's not acceptable," Maurice said.

"It's all I could get you," Sherise answered. "And it's more
than you deserve for being so self-assuming."

He was shaking his head, but then sighed as if he no longer
concerned himself with the issue. "It's at least good to know
you're facing reality."

"Don't push it," she warned. "I'm trying to deal with this.
It's hard enough without you throwing it in my face."

"I'm not throwing it in your face," he said. "It's just what it
is. You're the one who's made me have to keep pointing it out
to you."

"I just want things to work," she said. "We've all worked too
hard to get here. The press about the infighting, all of that, doesn't
make Jerry look good."

"Finally!" He finished his glass of wine and held it toward
Sherise, expecting her to pour more. "Finally, you get it."

Sherise poured the wine, wishing it was poison. "You don't
understand all the work I've done to protect Jerry and to make
sure things go well. Now he barely even talks to me. It's frus-
trating."

"Sherise, you're a beautiful, sexy woman. You know how to
get a man's attention."

"I used to have his ear because of the great job I did, Maurice. Not my ass."

"I'm pretty sure it's always been your ass." Maurice laughed
as he said this, as if he found it silly Sherise would even suggest
anything else.

"Well, I still have the same ass, but I don't have his ear anymore. How do you explain that?"

"I'm here now," Maurice answered. "That's how I explain it.
I have his ear."

"You'd better be careful," she warned. "You could lose it too."

"Oh hell no," he assured her. "I'll never lose his ear. He'll always listen to what I have to say. If he knows what's good for him."

"What the hell is that supposed to mean?" Sherise asked.

"Nothing," he answered. "It just means that I have his ear whenever I want it. I can prove it to you. Tell me something you want him to do and watch me make it happen."

"I want you fired," she said.

He laughed. "Anything but that, you little devil."

"You think you're special, Maurice, but you're not. Just like any of us, you could fall out of favor with him just as quickly as you appeared to have fallen in his favor."

"Not me," he said. "I have insurance."

"Insurance?" Sherise walked up to him, standing about a foot away. She eyed him suspiciously. "What are you not telling me?"

"Not anything that's any of your business." He was smiling now, liking the attention she was showing him.

"You know what I think?" she asked. "I think you want us to think you have something on him, but you can't possibly. You're bluffing. You're not that smart."

"Excuse me?" he asked, his offense showing. "I'm not that smart? Little girl, you don't know who you're talking to. I've lived a life in politics. I'm smart enough to know what you gotta do to get ahead."

"Oh, I know plenty," she said. "I know Jerry better than you, and he's clean. He can't be bought, especially not by you."

"You really underestimate me, girl." He shook his head. "I've bought plenty a politician, some smarter than Jerry."

"But not more powerful," she said. "He's going to be president in a little over a month. You don't have the firepower to buy the president off."

"I have all the firepower I need," he responded.

"So you did buy him?" she asked.

He shook his head. "You ask too many questions."

"And your evasiveness is telling." She pointed at him skeptically. "You didn't buy him, so then what?"

"We're done here." Maurice stood up straight, walked over to the mini-bar, and held up his half-full glass of wine. "Could I just put this down here? You'll clean up, right?"

"Running away, I see." She stared at him, her entire demeanor a challenge.

"I'm not running away," Maurice said. "I'm just not—"

"Chicken," she mumbled loud enough for him to hear. "Go ahead, put the drink down and run away."

"You know what!" His voice was tight and his expression angry.

Sherise knew he was a chauvinist at heart and being challenged like this by a woman would infuriate him. He had to give her something.

"You're just . . ." He was pointing at her wanting to call her some names, but thinking better of it. "You want to know what my power is?"

"What power?" she asked, laughing.

"This!" He pointed to his glass of wine on top of the mini-bar.

"Your power is cheap wine?" she asked, confused.

"No," he said. "Liquor. A lot of people say it's the root of all evil, but you know what I say? I say it's the root of opportunity."

"What opportunity?" Sherise asked.

Was he suggesting he knew what she was trying to do?

He walked over to the conference table and grabbed his suitcase.

"You see, I'm not like you, Sherise. I'm not like anyone else here. I see an opportunity and I take it. I'll never fall out of Jerry's favor because I never needed to be in it."

Sherise let him leave because she didn't need to ask him for more information. It was clear he was suggesting that liquor was the key to his hold on Jerry. But what did that mean? Jerry didn't drink. The man led the life of a Mormon. No alcohol, drugs, cigarettes, none of that.

Of course, that didn't mean that other members of the Northman family didn't drink.

12

"Hi, Billie."

Billie could tell from the sound of Michael's voice over the phone that he was still upset with her. It hurt her heart to not hear him greet her with his usual enthusiasm. She loved to hear the pep in his voice when she called.

"You're still mad," she said.

He sighed. "I don't really want to go over that again."

That was referring to the argument they'd had over Darina. Choosing to no longer stand on the sidelines and hope for the best as Michael was doing, Billie had decided to be proactive and tell Michael about her conversation with Darina last night at the bar.

She told him that she'd coaxed the truth out of Darina and made her admit that it was just a selfish desire to not rock her own boat that was the real reason she kept Duncan a secret from Michael. She made it clear that she suspected Darina's move to Atlanta already showed she intended to pressure him to move.

Billie felt like she had Michael somewhat on her side until she mentioned her interpretation of Darina's comments in connection to the ring on her finger. When she suggested that Darina meant to say that their wedding wasn't a done deal yet,

Michael started to believe this was more insecurity on Billie's part than a true plot of deceit by Darina.

This led to an ugly argument that had him sleeping on the sofa and her tossing and turning all night in the bed, alone. They'd both said their apologies in the morning, but it didn't set right with Billie.

"I'm just calling to apologize again," she said. "I don't want us to fight each other over this situation. We need to be united."

"I'm trying to," he said quietly. "I really am. Look, I'm sorry too, but I can't really talk about it right now."

"I know," she said. "You're busy and so am I. We're meeting with the wedding planner for dinner, we can sit down and—"

"I can't do that," Michael said. "I'm sorry, I forgot about the wedding planner."

"Michael, we can't cancel. She's in high demand. We need her to want to take us on, not the other way around."

"I'm rearranging my schedule so I can get off early and spend some time with Duncan."

Billie knew that what she was about to ask would sound evil, no matter what. "I thought he was leaving today."

"Nice, Billie." His voice sounded very disappointed.

"I didn't mean I wanted him gone today. I just meant . . ."

"His flight is tomorrow morning," Michael said. "Darina is going to visit with some friend she has at Georgetown and I'm taking Duncan to a movie and maybe get a bite to eat."

"Michael, I . . . I'm just worried about all this," she said. "The blood test results aren't even due until tomorrow and . . ."

"Would you stop bringing that up?" he asked impatiently. "We're past that."

"We can't be past what we don't know yet," she admonished.

"Let's just reschedule with the wedding planner for tomorrow," he said.

"I can't, Michael. Tomorrow I'm spending the day with Tara. You know that."

"That's right," he said. "And you wouldn't want to cancel that for a wedding planner. Now you understand how I feel."

"It's not the same thing."

"How is it different?"

"I already had plans with Tara."

"I didn't have that option, Billie. I'm doing the best I can without a lot of time to schedule."

"Fine." Billie knew she was being selfish, but after her last run-in with Darina, she felt that a little selfishness on her part was called for. Was she wrong?

"What do you want me to do?" she asked.

"Just pick another date for the wedding planner," he said. "How about Sunday?"

"That's just the thing, Michael. I don't know if we can get Sunday. She did us a favor by fitting us in before she gets into the Christmas weddings she is in charge of. We might not get an appointment with her until the first of the year."

"What's the harm in that?" he asked. "It's only a few weeks away. Let's just do that. Let's just push all that stuff back to the first of the year."

"That stuff?" she asked, offended by his dismissive tone. "That's what you're calling our wedding? That stuff?"

"You took that wrong," Michael said. "I just meant all the appointments."

"I didn't take it wrong. I know what you meant. It just bothers me that . . ."

Billie stopped when she heard the voice of a woman in the background. That voice she'd only heard a few times but had come to disdain.

"Is she . . . Is Darina there? In your office?"

"Yes," he answered. "But can we discuss this another time?"

"This woman came to your office at your company?" Billie was fuming. "Did she bring Duncan?"

"Of course she did." Michael's tone was attempting to give the impression he didn't see the issue.

"Do you know what that looks like?" Billie asked. "It looks like . . . they're, she's in your life."

"You're overreacting, Billie. It's just an office visit. I get them all the time. No one cares."

"Let me guess," Billie said, "She didn't call ahead or anything. She just showed up."

"Well, yes, but . . ."

"No, no, no." Billie was now up, pacing in her office. "This is another part of her plan, Michael. She doesn't just want Duncan to be a part of your life. She wants to be a part of your life."

"I can't do this right now."

"Why not?" Billie asked. "Because she's listening in? Of course she is. She knew I was speaking to you and that's why she spoke up. She wanted me to know she was there so I'd get angry. She wants us to fight."

"So let's not," he said.

"Fine." She took a deep breath. "But this isn't over."

"Clearly," he said. "I'll talk to you later, baby. I love—"

She hung up.

Billie was steaming mad. Under any other circumstance Darina's visit to his office would be a little thing, but not anymore. Not now that she knew Darina's sneaky ways. Everything this woman did was about something, for the purpose of something, and Billie wasn't buying that it was all for Duncan's good.

The one good side to this was that Darina wouldn't be spending the day with Michael and Duncan. And tomorrow morning, she'd be gone. But so would Duncan. It wasn't a win-win. Billie realized that Michael was already in love with Duncan and she couldn't come between that. Darina, on the other hand—she could and would come between that.

She wasn't going to be a bystander in her own love life again. When Billie found out that her ex, Porter, was cheating on her, she was knocked to the ground in shock. It seemed to come out of nowhere. Her entire life was sent hurling into space in seconds. But looking back, there were signs and flirtations that she noticed. She had chosen to ignore them, let them pass as nothing. After all, Porter loved her. He was her husband.

Then, bam! No, Billie wasn't going to let that happen again. She saw the warning signs that Darina was sending and she was about to respond with some warning signs of her own.

While waiting for her brother, Nate, in Cava Mezze restaurant, Erica looked down at her phone. There had been a dozen texts from Billie asking her to call her. There were at least twenty from Sherise, all cussing her out for quitting on Justin. Then there were the texts from Corey.

Erica wondered if it was time to change her number. If everyone would just get off her ass for five minutes, she wouldn't feel the need to.

When Nate showed up at the table, she placed the phone down and got up to greet him. They hugged and kissed before returning to their seats.

"You look good," she said, looking him over.

That motherly instinct she had for him was still strong. She'd been raising him herself since he was twelve and was still suffering from empty-nest syndrome.

Twenty-two-year-old Nate Kent was tall with an athletic build. He was a nut-brown color with thick black eyebrows that framed his handsome young face, made up of a distinctive nose and full lips. He was sticking with the completely shaved head look and was coming into it well.

"I look good?" He shook his head. "Look at you. You got your hair did. Look at that watch, girl. You gank that?"

Erica made a smacking sound with her lips. "I have never ganked anything in my life, you thug. You know how I got this."

"Oh yeah." He reached for his menu. "That's right. You're Miss Money Banks now. You got that Beyoncé money?"

"I'm about $150 million short of Beyoncé money, but I ain't complaining. How about you?"

"You know me," Nate said. "I'm working to pay my bills, like always."

"Still at that radio station in Rockville?"

"You mean since you asked me at Thanksgiving dinner?" He laughed. "Of course."

"Well, I don't know with you," she said. "You can be a little indecisive."

"Talking about work," he said, "I'm off right now. What are you doing hanging out in the middle of the day? You ain't dressed for work, that's for sure."

"I quit Justin's firm."

"And here you are questioning my job situation." He rolled his eyes. "Why did you quit? I thought you liked that job."

"I liked it until I didn't." She shrugged. "Justin was getting on my damn nerves."

"That's what bosses do, Erica. That's like their main job, to work your last nerve."

"Well, I don't have to put up with it." She looked at the menu. "Hey, get whatever you want. It's on me."

He smiled. "You don't have to tell me twice."

The waiter came to their table with water and they ordered quickly. As he left, the conversation returned to Nate's life.

"Yeah, but I got Aubrey now." He smiled wide at the mention of his girlfriend's name. "She's got me on the straight and narrow. No more job hopping for me."

Like any mother would be, Erica was suspicious of this new girl in Nate's life. "Why is it that I haven't met this girl? I need to know about her background. I need to make sure she's good enough for you."

"She's more than good enough for me. She's the best girl I've ever met." He grabbed the fork from the table and started examining it. "I wish she didn't have to go home to L.A. for the holidays again. You could meet her at Christmas."

"An L.A. girl?" Erica turned her nose up. "That's your type now?"

"She keeps it real," Nate insisted. "As a matter of fact, I'm planning to move in with her."

"So soon? You've been together a couple of months."

"What can I say?" He asked with a shrug. "When you know, you know."

Erica rolled her eyes. "Your track record of knowing ain't so good."

"Look at you! Terrell fucked up all the time, and Alex . . . That was fucked."

Erica reached out, pointing her finger at him in a threatening manner. "I told you to never talk about that!"

"Take it easy." He held his hands up in the air and sat back in his seat. "Don't kill me. I'm not saying. I'm just saying."

Nate was one of the few people who knew about Jonah being Erica's father, so when the news of Alex being his son came out, he'd known that Erica was close to Alex. Erica didn't want it ever mentioned again. It nauseated her just thinking that anyone knew. Being her brother, Nate felt it was his duty to tease her about what made her feel awful, but she'd made it clear to him that Alex was off-limits.

"I have Corey now," Erica said.

"So you two are legit together?" Nate asked.

She nodded, even though that wasn't entirely the truth. Since their last encounter in Justin's office, the lovemaking had only temporarily distracted him. As soon as it was over, he was back with the questions and pressuring her to apologize to Justin and get her job back. She didn't feel like dealing with it. He would have to be taught a lesson. If he wanted her to return his calls, he had to lay off about that shit.

"Where is he at?" Nate asked, looking around. "If he's so legit."

"He's at his damn job," she said.

"So he's employed," Nate said. He was joking around, but could see from Erica's glare she wasn't in the mood. "I'm just kidding. I'm happy for you. Can you be happy for me?"

"I am." She managed a smile. "Just moving in is a big deal."

"I love being with her and . . . well, she lives a lot closer to my job."

"So this is more of a convenience to you?" Erica asked.

"No," he protested. "The convenience is just the icing on the cake. I'm excited about living with her. I feel like a grown-ass man."

"It's about time," she said. "You've been a grown-ass man for a while."

He smirked. "Whatever. I just have to figure out how to get out of this damn lease."

"How many months do you have left?"

"Five," he said. "Maybe your friend Billie can give me some advice on how to get out of it."

"You don't need Billie. You have me, and you can't get out of it. But I can."

"You can?"

"That's what I wanted to talk to you about." She leaned forward, lowering her voice. "Let's get this straight. I'm not taking care of you. Like you said, you're a grown-ass man. But I can hook you up."

"Hook me up?"

"Let me pay off your lease," she said. "Five months isn't that much for that cheap little rat hole you live in anyway."

"Hey!" Nate looked as if he wanted to protest, but decided against it. "It's a shitty place, I admit it. It was cheap."

"So it won't be anything for me to pay it off. You won't even have to bother with the headache of subletting it."

"I didn't want to have to deal with that at all." He started nodding. "If you want to do that for me, then, yeah, I'm cool with that. Thanks."

"I'll just need the information."

"Wait a second." He leaned forward across the table. "What are the strings attached?"

Erica was offended. "When have I ever attached strings to a favor I've given you? You're my baby brother."

He leaned back, still a little wary. "Yeah, but money changes people. They start expecting shit from other people. They start thinking they have rights that others don't."

"How you gonna say something like that to me?" Erica asked, truly hurt by his words. "You know me. When have I ever been anything but real? Even when it hurt."

He nodded. "I was just thinking . . . I mean, you quit that job. Erica, that ain't like you to do that to a friend."

"Justin stopped being my friend the day he hired me. He turned into my boss and an asshole."

"But what about Sherise?" he asked. "She's your best friend. She has to be pissed at you for it. I wouldn't think you'd do that to her."

"I didn't do anything to her," Erica insisted. "That job has nothing to do with her."

"She got you that job."

"I got me that job! I don't need her to get a job. Besides, I don't really care much about what Sherise thinks these days. I've had enough of her stank-ass attitude."

Erica noticed the look on Nate's face was the familiar expression when he didn't believe what he was being told, and it upset her. Was he not on her side? She was offering to help him out of a big situation and all he could do was judge her?

"What?" she asked.

Nate rolled his eyes and turned his focus to looking at the dessert menu. The waiter came and placed their appetizers on the table and Erica could tell that he sensed the tension, because he practically dropped the food trying to get away from there so fast.

Just then, Erica's phone rang and Corey's I.D. came on the screen again. She rejected the call.

"You're just like him," she said.

"Who?"

"Corey, you, everyone. Now that I have some money, everyone is second-guessing everything I say or do. It's like you don't think I can handle money. Or maybe you don't think I deserve it."

"Don't put words in my mouth," Nate said. "It's just not like you to up and quit like that. Even if you have a little money in your pocket. That's a fact. I'm just pointing it out."

"Do you want my help with this lease?" she asked.

He nodded. "Of course I do."

"Then stop pointing shit like that out, okay?"

Sherise waited for the voicemail beep and spoke sharply into her phone.

"Erica, if you don't fucking call me, I'm coming over there. You can't avoid us forever. You go and quit on my husband without even an explanation and Billie is going through some serious shit with Michael right now. Do you even care? Call me! I mean it!"

She hung up and took a deep breath, looking around the empty private family dining room of the governor's mansion in Maryland. She had a lot on her mind and was resentful that she even had to deal with Erica's bullshit, but after hearing about Darina's latest exploits from Billie, she needed Erica to get her head on straight and help them figure out how to help Billie control her situation without jeopardizing her relationship with Michael.

But for now, she was focused on her own issue, and as she waited patiently, Sherise's focus turned to the large armoire against the wall. This thing was not made in a factory somewhere. It was beautifully handcrafted in dark cherrywood with large doors and lower cabinets, showcasing intricately designed handles.

Everything about it said old money and everlasting style. All the details distinctly matched, except for one. The most recent addition.

"Sherise?"

She turned around, her back to the armoire, and faced Stephen Northman. She could see the apprehension in his every step as he walked closer to her.

"Hello, Stephen." She smiled kindly to him, hoping to make him more comfortable. He couldn't have any idea why she was here, but he was still nervous.

"They said you wanted to see me?" he asked. "Not my dad?"

"No," she answered. "I came here to talk to you. How are you doing?"

He stuffed his hands in the pockets of his khakis and shrugged his big shoulders. "I'm fine, I guess. Getting ready for Christmas. You?"

"The same." She gestured to the chair at the head of the table. "Sit down, Stephen. I want to talk to you about something."

"I think I'll stand," he said. "You're making me nervous. What's up?"

"I was thinking about the last time we spoke," she explained. "I almost walked in on you arguing with your dad about Maurice hitting on Shelly. Do you remember that?"

"Of course I do. It was only a couple of weeks ago."

"We were talking about your dad giving my job to Maurice and how it wasn't fair. It wasn't fair that Maurice was able to keep working there even though he was harassing Shelly."

"Well, it's not fair," Stephen insisted. "But Tom got Shelly a really good job with Senator Goren. She's feeling a lot better now."

"That's great," Sherise said. "But I want to focus on Maurice and your dad."

Stephen lowered his head a bit. "I don't have much to say about that asshole."

"I don't believe you," Sherise said. "I think you have something to say, but you were told not to say it."

He looks up at her, realizing what she's getting at. "I really gotta go, Sherise. I'm sorry, but . . ."

"Don't you think I deserve better than that?" Sherise asked.

Stephen had turned to leave, but turned back to her.

"After everything that has been done to me," she said. "Everything I've worked my entire career for and this is what I get. I didn't do anything to make this happen."

"I can't talk to you," Stephen said. "I was told I can't talk to anyone."

"You're an adult, Stephen," she said, sharply. "You're not a kid anymore. You're free to do as you please, and that includes telling the truth to someone who deserves it. Or do you think I should keep getting lied to?"

"Of course not," he said, "But I'm not the one who—"

"Understand me, Stephen." She took several steps closer to him. "I'm not blaming you for anything. I'm not even blaming your father. This is Maurice's fault."

"It's not just . . ." Stephen sighed. His whole body sighed as if he just couldn't go on with this anymore.

Sherise could see that just a little more pushing and she could get what she needed out of him.

She went back to the room's centerpiece. "I was noticing this armoire. I remember asking your dad about it the first time I saw it. It's a family heirloom, right?"

Stephen shrugged.

"I love how it opens up and has all these hidden drawers and slots, and the glass in the back just makes it such a classic liquor cabinet, like in the old movies."

She reached for the large door handle and tugged at it, but it didn't open.

"Then a year ago, I come over here and I see this." She pointed to the golden padlock connecting the big door handles. "I asked your father why the padlock was on there. His response was that liquor is a poison for some. I didn't ask any more questions because it's none of my business. Then I forgot about it."

She walked over to the table and took a seat. She gestured to the same seat as she had before. "Sit down, Stephen."

This time he listened and slowly took a seat. His gaze switched from her to the armoire to the table. He was clearly getting upset.

"That yellow car in the driveway is your car," Sherise said. "It's a new car, right?"

"I got it for my birthday," he said.

"You were driving a red car during the campaign. Just five months ago. What happened to that car?"

"I think you know the answer to that," Stephen responded.

Sherise was pleased he wasn't being coy anymore. He knew what this was about.

"You crashed it," she said. "But I never heard about it. I was basically running Jerry's communications during the campaign and I didn't know about his son crashing his car. That usually makes news."

"So does the governor's son being in the hospital," Stephen said just above a whisper.

"How many times have you been in the hospital for drunk-driving-related accidents, Stephen? How many times in the last year?"

He wouldn't lift his head at all this time. "Three."

"How did Maurice know about that and none of us in the campaign knew?"

"He only knew about the last one," Stephen said. "The first two times, Mom and Dad took care of it on their own. They paid people to stay quiet and called in some favors. But the last time it happened . . . I hit someone."

Sherise gasped. "Oh my God, Stephen. Was the person okay?"

"They had a broken leg," he said. "But the thing was, after I hit them, I . . ."

"You drove away." Sherise couldn't believe this was the same young man she knew.

He nodded. "I tried to, but I rammed into a light pole. It was like three in the morning over in Southeast, I think."

"But I still never found out," Sherise said.

"They weren't going to let me off that time, but I got lucky. Or at least I thought I did. The night they booked me, Maurice was at the jail."

"What was he doing there?"

"He told me he was helping someone out." Stephen began wringing his hands together. "I was still kind of drunk. I was in handcuffs. They were about to put me in a cell when he came over to me. I don't even remember it, but I guess I told him everything. I was freaking out because I knew it was all over that time."

"Maurice went to your parents with this," she said. "He threatened to tell the press that you committed a hit-and-run."

Stephen nodded. "He said he wanted this position of PS in exchange for not telling people what I did and what dad did to cover it up. He offered my dad the opportunity to get rid of it all too."

"So it wasn't just blackmail," Sherise said. "He added some favors to it."

"My parents couldn't risk going to their contacts this time. I'd hit someone. People aren't willing to cover that up. Maurice said he could do it. He got someone high up at the police station and the hospital to get rid of the records."

"Who?"

"I don't remember exactly," Stephen said. "He told my dad. I guess it worked, 'cuz a couple of weeks after it happened, he got the job."

"I guess it did," Sherise added.

"Maurice said he could make sure they'd get rid of not just the hit-and-run, but the other two accidents and all my hospital stays. It will be like none of it ever happened."

"Your dad couldn't turn that down," Sherise said.

Stephen let out a pained sigh as he lowered his head into his hands. "It's all my fault, Sherise. I've just ruined everything!"

Sherise tried to set aside the anger she felt at having her life so disrupted by things that were completely out of her control. Sitting before her was a broken young man who had a serious problem.

"You have to get help, Stephen. You're going to end up killing somebody or yourself."

"I know," he said through tears. "You don't know how hard it is."

"I can imagine it's harder when you still have access to a car," she said.

He looked up at her. "I need a car to get around, Sherise."

"No, you don't," she said. "Your dad is going to be president. You don't ever need to drive again. And what about rehab? You should be in rehab."

"I go to AA meetings," he said, wiping his tears away.

"That's not enough!" Sherise said. "You almost killed someone!"

"Then people will know," Stephen said. "Mom and Dad don't want that."

"There is a way around that," Sherise said.

She had to say that she was very disappointed in Jerry. She didn't think he would try to cover up a crime, but then again, this was his son and she agreed that she would have probably done the same for her own kid. Using your power and influence to protect your child didn't make you a bad person.

But she couldn't bother with that part of it right now.

"Can you find it?" he asked. "A way around it? I want help. I don't ever want to hurt someone again, but the guilt I feel over all of this . . . it makes me want to drink."

Sherise sighed. "I have my own shit to handle, Stephen."

She could see the look of despair on his face.

"Fine," she said. "I'll figure out what we need to do for you, but I have to figure out how to get Maurice's hold off your dad first. Until then, you don't get in a car for anything! I mean anything!"

"I promise," he said. "I'll help you however I can."

Sherise knew she should have told him not to get more involved, but at this point, she was pretty sure she needed all the help she could get. She knew what the blackmail was about now, but that was only her first task. Her next, and seemingly impossible task was to somehow neutralize the power of Maurice's blackmail over Jerry so she could get rid of him and not risk him exposing Stephen's extreme fuckups and Jerry's attempts at covering them up..

Sherise left the mansion feeling overwhelmed. Usually, when faced with a challenge, she was already contemplating options for solutions before the challenge was even fully realized. Right now, she was drawing a blank, and that scared the hell out of her. How was she going to do this? Did she even have this in her? Had she finally met her match in Maurice Blair?

13

Billie needed today so badly. After the office visit disaster, she and Michael barely spoke. When she'd woken up today, her only consolation was that at least Darina had left D.C. She tried to get her mind off the whole situation and looked forward to today.

Today was her day with Tara, and the two of them had a ball. They'd gone shopping for new boots, and to Tara's extreme embarrassment, bought the exact same pair. It was followed by a trip to the National Zoo to look at the new baby panda and Sumatran tiger cubs. Although the zoo was her idea, Tara made Billie swear not to tell anyone they'd gone. That was until she saw four of her friends there with their parents.

They ended the afternoon with an early dinner at Medium Rare in the Cleveland Park neighborhood before Billie dropped Tara back at home. As she pulled up to the sidewalk in front of the condo that used to be her own home, she was sad to see the day end.

"You okay?" Tara asked as she looked at her.

Billie nodded. "I just hate it when you have to go."

"I know." Tara smiled. "But we're going to the Wizards game next month, right?"

"Can't wait." Tara reached out and gently touched Tara's cheek. "You okay? You know, with everything we talked about today?"

"You mean about you possibly moving to Atlanta?" Billie nodded. "I'm sorry you didn't hear it from me first."

Tara shrugged. "Whatever, I guess. I'm not worried."

"Not worried?" Billie asked. "I thought you'd be upset."

Billie had been a little concerned about Tara's reaction. Porter was the one who told her Billie might move to Atlanta when she was married and, according to Porter, Tara was extremely upset. However, when she and Tara discussed it today, adding the discovery of Duncan and what that might mean, Tara seemed calm. Billie wondered if it was just delayed reaction.

"If you're upset," Billie told her, "you can say so. Tell me how you feel."

"Like I said before, I guess we'll see."

"You know it means we won't be able to see each other as much as we do now."

"I doubt it." Tara casually took her sunglasses off and placed them on her head, looking not at all bothered.

Just as Billie suspected, Tara was in denial. "Honey, trust me, things will be different."

"If you go," Tara said. "But I don't think you will."

Billie sighed. "I don't know yet, Tara. With Duncan in the picture now, moving to Atlanta is even more of a possibility than it was when we got engaged."

"I think Michael is going to go to Atlanta, but I don't think you will."

Billie was shocked. "Tara, you know I love you, but I'm going to live with my husband no matter where he is."

"But Duncan changes everything," Tara said in a very nonchalant tone. "With his mom wanting to get back with Michael, I don't even think you'll probably get married."

"What are you talking about?" Billie asked. She hadn't told Tara anything about what she suspected about Darina.

"That woman," Tara explained. "She's using Duncan to get Michael back. I think she's gonna screw things up."

Billie was suddenly second-guessing everything she'd said earlier that day. Had she actually railed against Darina and not noticed? No, she would never say that to Tara.

"Where are you getting this from?" Billie asked.

"Don't get me wrong," Tara assured her. "I don't want you and Michael to break up. I know you love him and he makes you happy. And . . . I guess I know you and Daddy aren't getting back together."

"Tara answer me. Where did you get this idea that Darina is trying to break me and Michael up?"

"Daddy," Billie answered as she pointed toward the building.

As Billie turned to see Porter, dressed in a Georgetown Law T-shirt and sweatpants, walking out of his building toward them, Tara hopped out of the car.

"That's impossible," Billie said.

Billie hadn't said anything to Porter about Darina or Duncan. She hadn't even spoken to him since telling him that she was in engaged.

Despite being double-parked, Billie turned off her ignition and got out of the car. She followed Tara over to Porter, not sure if she should be angry or worried. She was both.

How did he know? Was he spying on her again? Porter had been getting information on Billie's private life, comings and goings for a long time after they were married. He even had a spy at the law firm she previously worked at relaying her work schedule to him.

"Hey!" Porter leaned down to kiss Tara. "Glad you're back. I was just gonna run down to the store and rent a DVD for us to watch. What did you buy?"

"Boots." Tara held the bag up. "Wanna see them?"

"Sure." He turned to Billie. "Hey, Billie."

"Tara," Billie said. "You can show Porter your boots after he returns from the store. Go inside now. I need to talk to Porter."

Tara's eyes widened as she looked at her confused father. "I didn't mean to get anyone in trouble."

"Who's in trouble?" Porter asked.

"Tara, please. I need to speak to Porter."

"Ugh." She sighed, annoyed by the entire situation, then turned and went inside the building as ordered.

"What did I do now?" Porter asked.

"Are you spying on me again?" She approached him closely, her tiny frame a stark contrast to his large, muscular body. "Porter, I thought we had gotten past that shit?"

"We have," he said. "Calm down, Billie. I'm not spying on you. What's wrong?"

"Tara is telling me she thinks my fiancé's baby mama is gonna keep me from getting married. She got that idea from you. How did that happen, since I never told you about Darina?"

Porter nodded in recognition. "I was going to get around to telling you about that."

"At your convenience, I guess." She placed her hands on her hips. "Spill it, Porter."

"She contacted me," he said. "Darina."

"How?"

"That's what I asked her," Porter said. "She didn't want to answer."

Billie felt a sense of dread in the pit of her gut. "Start from the beginning."

"She showed up at my firm claiming to be a close friend of yours who had information that I needed to know. When I came to the lobby to greet her, she told me that she was actually Michael's ex-girlfriend and the mother of his child."

"When did this happen?" Billie asked.

"About two days ago," he answered.

Billie slapped him on the arm. "And you're just now telling me this?"

"I'm a busy man, Billie. I'm sorry if I don't make your boyfriend's baby mama drama my priority."

She rolled her eyes. "Go on."

"It didn't last long," he said. "The second she told me that you were trying to keep Michael from being with his son, I knew she was full of shit. You'd never do something like that. Can I at least get credit for that?"

"Yes," she said impatiently. "Go on."

"She asked if I had any interest in making sure you and Michael don't get married. I said no. I warned her not to mess with you."

"Did she offer to work with you to break us up?"

"Not exactly, but I'm assuming that's what she meant. Why else would she ask me that? I shut her down and told her to leave. That was it."

Billie put her hand to her belly and shook her head in disbelief. This woman was diabolical.

"So," Porter added, "you're welcome."

"I can't believe this bitch," Billie said. "She's worse than I thought."

"I shouldn't have said anything to Tara," Porter said regretfully.

"You really shouldn't have," Billie said. "She doesn't need to hear that shit, Porter."

"I'm sorry," he said.

"How did she say she knew who you were?"

"Like I said," he stated, "She wouldn't answer that. She probably asked Michael about you and your past."

"He would have never told her about you. At least not without asking me if it was okay first."

"Then how else?" Porter asked.

"She did her research," Billie said. "This woman is calculating."

Without saying good-bye, Billie headed back to her car, already calling Michael on her cell phone. She was fuming when the call went straight to voicemail without ringing at all. That meant he'd turned his phone off. She had no choice but to leave a message.

"Michael, you have to call me. I'm coming home now. It's urgent. Darina has been checking up on me and she basically tried to recruit Porter to help break us up. You can't trust her at all. Call me!"

"Hold on a damn minute!" Erica yelled in response to the hard knocking on the door to her apartment.

When she reached the door in her bathrobe, she checked the peephole. It was Corey. She sighed, not wanting to deal with this, but knowing it was inevitable. She stood at the door, trying to get her head straight.

"I know you're there, Erica. Let me in!"

She took a deep breath and opened the door to see his handsome but very angry face.

She pointed a finger to make a point. "If you think you have it like that, so you can show up without warning, you don't, Corey."

"Stop trying to put me in my place." He barged in, brushing right past her. "That won't work with me."

"Hey!" she yelled. "I didn't invite you in."

He stood in the middle of her apartment, looking at her. His expression made it clear he wasn't there for games.

"No more bullshit," he demanded. "No more avoiding me. I swear to God, Erica, I want answers now or I'm out that door and never coming back."

"You're giving me ultimatums?" she asked, closing the door behind her. "Who do you think you are?"

He pointed to his chest. "I'm the guy who's been putting up with your mixed messages who deserves better!"

"I don't have to tell you—"

"I talked to Justin," he said. "You didn't get no damn bonus, Erica."

She was mad now. How dare he? "Why are you going to other people about me?"

"You haven't given me any choice," he answered. "You lied to me, girl. I can accept you not telling me everything. We haven't been dating that long, but lying to me is fucked up. I don't deserve that."

Erica was hit with the guilt that accompanied the truth of his words. "I know I've been avoiding you and I'm sorry for that. It's just that everyone has been giving me a hassle lately."

"I'm giving you a hassle?" he asked. "I'm trying to talk to you. I'm trying to understand you!"

"What makes you think I need understanding?" she asked. "I'm not some case for you to solve."

Corey threw his hands in the air. "Well, what the fuck am I supposed to do, Erica? You keep secrets. You tell lies."

"I warned you about me." She walked over to the living room sofa and sat down.

"Yeah, and the cuteness of that wore off a while ago. I want some answers and I want them now."

"You seem to think making demands is going to get you what you want," she said. "Good luck with that."

"I don't need luck, because I'm not leaving here without what I came for."

"And what is that?" she asked.

He looked around the apartment. "Let's start with all the shit you have in this apartment. All this expensive stuff that wasn't here the last time I was here. How about that hotel room that you paid for with your bonus, the bonus that Justin said he hadn't even given you yet and wasn't going to be enough to afford that room for an hour, let alone a whole night including room service."

"Oh, I get it," she said. "This is about your ego. It just kills you that I'm not letting you pay for everything."

"Where is the money coming from?" he asked. "Erica, I care about you, a lot. More than I even expected to this early in our relationship, but if you're doing something illegal, I—"

"Illegal?" She shot up from the sofa. "How dare you accuse me of . . . Do you really think I could be a drug dealer or something?"

"I don't know what the hell you could be," he answered. "My gut, my instinct says no. You're a woman of deep morality and principle. But the secrets, the lies and erratic behavior. Something is fucked up here."

"Then why did you come?" she asked, touched by his original assessment of her. "If you know something is fucked up, why come? Why not just run away?"

He walked over to her and looked her deeply in the eyes. Standing only inches from her, he grabbed her and pulled her to him. His lips came down on hers hard and his kiss was angry.

It sent Erica's head reeling. She was frozen in place as his mouth's possession took her over. Her mind told her he was trying to dominate her and she needed to fight it. But her body was instantly ablaze, telling her to give into it. She craved this intense connection.

Just before deciding to give into her body, Erica was jolted when he pushed her away. He looked at her with fierce intensity. She could tell from the look in his eyes, the set of his face, and the feeling of his hands gripping her arms that he was serious. And so was she, about him.

"Fine," she said, quietly. "I'll tell you the deal, but remember, you asked and it ain't pretty."

As Erica told him the truth about how she met Jonah and found out he was her father, Corey's reaction was subdued. She didn't tell him exactly everything. She briefly touched on her painful memories of his attempt to have a secretive relationship with her, his underhanded deeds to control her and those around her. However, she left out his affair with Sherise, and while she told him about Alex, she left out exactly how close their relationship had really been.

She skipped straight to his death and will, the one million dollars, and how she had to fight his family to get the money.

"So that's the ugly story of me," she finally said. "Can you understand why I don't want people knowing?"

"I won't tell anyone," Corey said.

They were both sitting on the sofa at this point and he reached over, placing his hand gently on her thigh.

"And you're wrong," he said. "This is not the ugly story of you. Even in the short time I've known you, I can tell there is much more to you than anything that has to do with him."

She smiled appreciatively. "So you understand me now?"

"I understand what you just told me," he said. "You found out you had a dad, who turned out to be an asshole, died and left you a bunch of money. That's easy."

"Easy?" she asked.

He nodded. "What I don't understand is why you're acting so defensive, so impulsive?"

She rolled her eyes and slid away from him on the sofa. "I don't think I am, but let me guess. You disagree and you want to tell me why."

"What I think is you told me the CliffsNotes and there's still some unresolved shit that's expressing itself in you buying a bunch of stuff, quitting your job, and pushing away anyone who is trying to help you."

Erica threw her hands in the air with a labored sigh. "Here we go again with someone trying to help poor little ghetto Erica. She's got no college education and she's never had money, so she needs to be told what to do. She can't handle having more than enough money to pay her bills and—"

"Enough." He held up his hand to stop her. "I don't know what conversations you're having with other people, but don't put their words in my mouth."

"Fine," she said. "Maybe not you, but everyone else is accusing me of going nuts, acting like I need to ask permission and approval before I do anything."

"What does that have to do with quitting your job?" he asked.

"I'm just tired of putting up with bullshit, and for the first time in my life, I don't have to."

"How long will that last?" he asked, looking around. "Because it looks to me like you're spending as if you're gonna need a job again real soon."

She looked around her place, noticing her new tobacco brown coffee and end tables. The leather ottoman and turquoise glass table lamps that had been in her wish list at one of her favorite websites for a very long time. Her eyes moved to the shiny sterling silver coffeemaker, deep fryer, and the $300 bright red Kitchen-Aid mixer on her counter. The beautiful stoneware on the new dining room table that had been delivered just the day before cost a few hundred dollars, but was likely not going to be used more than once a month. It was all just a drop in the bucket.

Nothing to be concerned about.

"You're shopping your emotions," Corey suggested.

"You might be right," she reluctantly agreed. "But there's nothing wrong with me. I just need to find another way to channel my emotions."

She slid back toward him with a wicked smile on her face.

Corey was immediately aroused by her actions, but there was still some caution on his face.

"I don't think we're done here, Erica."

"You know," she reached for the bottom of his polo shirt and tugged it ever so teasingly, "I like the way you came barging in here like that and pitching a fit."

"I wasn't pitching a fit."

"Most men would back down when I pushed them away," she continued, her hands now rubbing against his chest. "But not you. You didn't let me intimidate you at all. That way you grabbed me and took charge of the situation. You got what you wanted."

"Look, Erica," he protested. "I think we should—"

She pressed her finger against his mouth. "But now, I'm gonna take charge and you're gonna give me what I want."

She looked deeply in his eyes as she moved forward. His lips were ready and eager for her kiss, but she backed away with a coy grin on her face.

"So you gonna play games now?" he asked.

She stood up from the sofa and positioned herself against him, her legs touching his thighs as he looked up at her. She slowly took the belt to her new plush cashmere bathrobe and undid it. The robe slid off the sexy, generous curves of her body, which was still shiny and wet from having just stepped out of the shower only seconds before he'd come over.

She smiled powerfully as she watched Corey drink in her figure and lick his lips. She wanted him so badly right now she could barely contain herself. And as he reached for her, grabbed her, and pulled her down to him, she felt a rush of heat consume her in anticipation of what was going to happen.

He kissed her hard and demanding and she returned his kiss with greed and possession. No, this was not a game. This was Erica's new life. A life where she got what she wanted and when she wanted it. She was never going back to what it was before.

The condo appeared empty when Billie entered, calling out Michael's name. He had never returned her call or picked up her phone message in the few minutes it took her to get here from Porter's apartment. In that short time, her mind had gone in all kinds of directions trying to figure out what to do about Darina's master plan.

Why else would she recruit Porter unless she was hoping he would help place a wedge between Billie and Michael, giving Darina the space she needed to get what she wanted?

There were a lot of questions, especially how she knew about Porter in the first place. Michael had spent time with her when Billie wasn't around. Would he really have entrusted the story of his fiancée's ex-husband to her during that time? Billie was feeling herself consumed with anger not just at Darina. She wanted to strangle Darina, but she was also mad at Michael for confiding in her about Billie's past.

If, in fact, that was the case. She didn't know. All she knew was that Darina was a scheming, manipulative bitch and Michael had to know about this before taking one step further in negotiating his relationship with her for the purpose of staying in Duncan's life.

She called his name again, believing he had to be home.

She'd seen his car outside their building, and aside from going to retrieve the blood test results, he had no plans today but to stay at home and get some work done.

When Billie tossed her purse on the chair right at the end of their hallway entrance, she noticed something on the kitchen counter. A phone. It was Michael's phone, and as she reached it, she thought it was dead. But it wasn't. It was only turned off. She pressed the power button and the phone, almost fully charged, came on. He had deliberately turned his phone off. He never did that.

Billie turned to head toward the bedroom, but something bright and green caught her eye. She turned to her left and noted the object on their living room sofa. It was all too familiar and she was shocked at the sight of it. Darina's cheap Navajo-style purse with razzled frills at the edges was sitting right in the center of Billie's living room sofa.

How could that be? Darina and Duncan had an 8:00 a.m. flight out of D.C. that morning. Billie had checked three times with Michael to make sure. What in the hell was her purse doing there?

Billie suddenly heard a sound and it was coming from her bedroom, their bedroom. The closing of a drawer? A shoe on the hardwood floor? Her heart stopped and she felt adrenaline rush through her at the speed of light. All of her senses were screaming to her and things began to feel a little unreal. She refused to give in to her fear. It couldn't possibly be what her fear was whispering to her.

Billie rushed to the bedroom, grabbed the doorknob, and flung the door open. Her heart stopped as she witnessed the scene before her.

Michael was sitting on the edge of the right side of the bed. Shirtless and with bare legs, the fluffy white down comforter covering his midsection. Just as he turned to her, looking like a man awaking from a deep sleep, Billie turned to the left of the bed where Darina stood, in the last moments of wrapping the belt of her cinnamon brown wrap dress around her body.

Billie's gasp was more of a desolated groan, eliciting the shock and pain at what she was witnessing before her.

"Billie?" Michael called her name as if he wasn't sure that's what it was.

"How could you?" she yelled at him.

Her shock quickly turned to pure, white-hot anger. She was boiling inside, but felt almost scared as if she was in the middle of a disaster and not sure what would hit her next.

"How could you?" she repeated, walking toward him. She wanted to strangle him.

"Um . . ." Michael looked around the room, as if trying to find something that could answer his question.

"Answer me!" she demanded. "You fucking asshole! You can't even answer me!"

"Wait a second," Michael cautioned, holding up his hand to her. "Calm down. Let me think."

"Think?" Without thinking herself, Billie reached for the first thing she saw, a single shoe on the floor. She picked it up and threw it at him.

"Ouch!" he yelled as it hit him in the shoulder. "What are you doing? Calm down."

"Calm down?" Billie couldn't believe what was going on.

Was he really going to act like this? Like he didn't really get what she was so angry about? Who was this man? How could he do this to her? How could she be so wrong?

Billie noticed that Darina was trying to wipe something off the nightstand next to her. She wiped it into her hand and tossed it in the garbage. For the first time, Billie noticed the smell of marijuana in the air. They had been smoking weed and making love in her bed! In their bed!

"You fucking bitch!" Billie yelled as she rushed over to her. "Get out of my home! Get out now!"

Darina didn't smile. She frowned deeply, showing her true face, one of anger and resentment. "You better watch it, Billie. I'm not afraid of you."

"You should be, bitch. You fucked with the wrong woman!"

"I didn't make him do anything he didn't want to!" Darina insisted, slipping her feet into her shoes.

"Darina?" Michael was standing up now, fully naked, looking at both women. "Hold on a second, Billie."

"Hold on?" she yelled. "You want me to hold on? How dare you? Both of you!"

She was so full of rage, she wanted to set the room on fire. Her head was spinning and her anguish was consuming her.

She took a step closer to Darina, a woman about four inches taller than her. "I said get the fuck out of my house, you hoe!"

Darina didn't move and stared Billie down defiantly. "If you're thinking about slapping me, you better think twice!"

"Bitch, I don't slap!"

Billie clenched her fist and with a fast right cross, she connected with Darina's left cheek. Darina let out a pained scream as she stumbled backward against the wall.

"You bitch!" Darina yelled, holding her hand to her face as she tried to stand up straight again.

"You want more?" Billie asked, pushing her so she fell against the wall again. "I got more for you, you fucking slut!"

"Billie!" Michael was slowly coming up behind her, reaching out to her. "Stop."

"Fuck you!" Billie yelled at him before turning back to Darina.

She grabbed the larger woman by the arm as tight as she could. Darina let out a sharp yell as Billie, with all of her strength, threw the woman forward. When she let go, Darina stumbled again, this time falling to the ground on her knees in front of Michael.

Michael looked down at her. "Darina, what are you doing?"

"Don't try to blame this all on her!" Billie demanded. "I'm not falling for that shit!"

Darina reached for Michael to help her stand up, but he backed away. He stepped around her and started for Billie.

"Billie," he pleaded, "I can explain all of this."

He reached out to her, but she slapped his hand away and stepped away from him. She took two steps toward Darina, who had stood up now.

"You have two fucking seconds," she warned.

"Go to hell, bitch!" Darina yelled before turning and running out of the bedroom.

Billie hurriedly followed her out and watched as she grabbed her purse off the sofa and rushed out of the apartment, slamming the door behind her. It wasn't until that moment that Billie actually started crying. In a fraction of a second, her body began to feel the emotional pain and tears were streaming down her face. She was still angrier than hell, but was heartbroken.

"Billie, wait a second!" Michael, more aggressively than before, spoke as he stood in the doorway to the bedroom. "This isn't what you think. I promise you."

"Promise me?" She returned to face him.

He had grabbed the bed sheet and wrapped it around himself.

"You're a lying, cheating asshole!" she yelled. "How could you do this to me? After everything! I thought I could trust you! You're no different than Porter!"

"I'm not Porter!" he yelled. "I didn't cheat on you, Billie!"

"I saw it with my own eyes!" she spat back, using the back of her hands to wipe her eyes, clouded with tears. "Don't you

fucking try that with me. I've been through this shit before! I'm
not falling for it again!"

"This was Darina," he accused. "It was—"

"It was both of you!" She rushed over to him. "That bitch is
a whore, but you, Michael. I would have never thought you'd do
this! You've ruined everything! Everything!"

She clenched her hands in fists and hit him in his bare chest
several times, forcing him to back up into the bedroom.

Begging her to calm down, he grabbed her hands, using his
strength to stop her. She tried to pull her hands away from him,
but he held them tight.

"I didn't do this!" he said. "Billie, please."

"I hate you!" she yelled, her voice barely able to form full
words as her emotions had crossed a threshold. She was not in
control of her own body at this point.

"I hate you! I hate you!"

"Billie, please!"

"No!" she screamed and jerked her hands out of his grip.
With all of her might, she pushed against his chest.

The force was only enough to make him take a step back,
but it was all that was necessary. The bed sheet, which had been
hanging to the floor, had gotten under his feet and he tripped
over it. He fell backward, slamming against the ground, letting
out a pained groan.

Billie didn't waste another second. Unable to trust herself
not to get more violent, she knew she had to get away from
him. She wasn't in any condition to drive, but she had to get out
of there. She turned and rushed toward the door, grabbing her
purse on the way. She felt like she was choking. She needed
some air. She needed to breathe.

Once outside, she grabbed the railing that bordered the
stairs to her building and leaned against it to keep herself up.
Her knees felt weak and she wanted to throw up. She tried to

inhale, but through her crying and choked tears, all she could do was cough.

She imagined the second he got some clothes on, Michael was going to come looking for her, so she used that to muster the strength to keep going. She'd gotten halfway down the block before she saw a bus stop and sat down. She fumbled through her purse, searching for her phone. She needed her girls. They were the only ones who could save her from her own insanity.

14

"You know you can pay the lady at the store to do this," Justin said.

"It's not the same," Sherise responded. "Just find the scissors."

Wrapping Christmas presents was a tedious thing, Sherise would admit to that. But with her enormous task ahead of her, she needed something tedious to do. It wasn't so much a distraction because all she could talk about was her discovery of the real Stephen Northman and what she was going to do to get her job back and help him.

"Found them," Justin proclaimed after sifting through discarded wrapping mistakes strewn across the floor of their den and pulling out a pair of scissors.

"Thanks." She took them. "I'll cut the paper and wrap. You do the bows. You're wasting too much paper with your mistakes."

"I didn't want to do this at all," Justin reminded her. "You're the one who needs this tedious therapy. Both of the kids are sleeping. You know what I'd rather be doing."

She rolled her eyes in response to his suggestive grin.

"Not right now." She pointed to her head. "All of my energy is focused on one thing right now. I've gotta figure out what to do."

Shaken from her conversation with Stephen, Sherise had rushed home to tell Justin. Her anxiety and doubt had only gotten stronger since. She was racking her brain trying to figure out what she could do, but was coming up blank.

"I'm scared," she said. "It's just not like me to . . . not know what to do. To not have a plan."

Justin reached out and placed his hand on her thigh. "We'll figure something out, baby."

She looked at him with hope in her heart, but the look on his face told her what he really thought.

"You think it's over, don't you?" she asked.

He sighed, but shook his head, sending two separate messages. "I feel like it's a dead-end situation for anyone. That is, anyone except you."

She smiled, hoping he meant it. She needed his support. She needed his ideas. "I just feel like I'm cornered, like I'm trapped."

"You've been there before," he said. "We've been there before together and you've always saved yourself and us."

"I won't let Maurice do this to me or Jerry. None of us deserve this."

"I don't know," Justin said. "I don't think Stephen is suffering as much as he should."

"He's not the bad guy here," Sherise said.

"He kind of is. He could have killed someone. He needs to be in rehab."

"I know he does and I'll get him there, but . . ."

"That's not your job," Justin interjected. "Baby, I get that you care about the kid and you're grateful he told you the truth, but you don't owe him anything. If it wasn't for his criminal behavior, you wouldn't be in this situation."

"I know," she agreed, "but I sort of blame Jerry more for

that. He should have gotten Stephen help at the beginning instead of covering it up."

"He's an ambitious politician," Justin said. "That's what they do. They keep their own from dealing with the consequences that we all have to deal with every day."

"He did what he had to in order to protect his child." Sherise offered Justin the perfectly wrapped present. "We'd do the same for our little bits, wouldn't we?"

He nodded. "Good point."

Sherise stood up and walked a few steps over to the sofa, sitting down. "Everything I think of leads me to exposing what happened with Stephen in order to loosen Maurice's grip on Jerry."

"You can't do that," Justin told her. "He'd never forgive you for poisoning the beginning of his administration and for embarrassing his precious son."

"There's no way for me to do this without him eventually finding out what I know and why it's happening," she said. "At least I can't think of any way."

After placing the final ribbon on the present, Justin placed it down and got up, joining Sherise on the sofa. She leaned her head into his chest as he wrapped his arm around her shoulders.

"I know you don't want to hear this, baby, but I have to tell you how I feel."

Sherise knew what was coming and wasn't happy about it.

"Northman said it himself," Justin continued. "Maybe the best plan is to wait it out. Press secretaries never last very long. Maurice wants the prestige of being the first. Once . . ."

"I know, I know," she said. "Once the press starts hammering him with questions, making him do the actual job, he won't want it anymore."

"Then he'll move on to something else," Justin said. "You'll get what you want. Not in the perfect way you wanted, but I think we've learned that there are many ways to get to the promised land."

Sherise understood what he meant. He was referring to their marriage and the struggles and obstacles they'd faced. They had cheated on each other, lied to each other, and somehow found their way back to each other. They were happier, closer, and more in love than ever before. Sherise couldn't be happier with her personal life now, despite the messy road it took to get here.

"You know I'm too stubborn for that," she said. "If things had just happened the way that, you know, shit happens, maybe I could take sloppy seconds."

"The most prestigious sloppy seconds a communications professional could ever want."

"But sloppy seconds still." She listened to the sound of his heart beating against his chest, wishing she could just be happy with what she had and what could be coming to her soon.

"I am who I am," she said. "And Maurice isn't just shit that happens. He deliberately and joyfully stole the fruits of my labor from me. He won't get away with that."

"Which is why I won't push." Justin tightened his grip on her. "I know my girl and there's no telling you what to do. Just be careful, Sherise. This level you're at is as big as the game gets."

"I've been preparing for this level my entire career," she said. "I won't bow out and wait. I'm just not made of that."

Just then, Sherise's phone, sitting on the floor next to un-wrapped presents, rang. She slowly moved from the sofa to the ground and grabbed it after looking at the Caller I.D. and seeing it was Beth, her P.I.

"It's Beth," she said.

"Put her on speaker," Justin requested.

"Hey, Beth." Sherise placed the phone between herself and Justin. "I've got you on speaker. Justin is here with me."

"Oh," came across the other line. "Well, is . . ."

"It's okay, Beth." Sherise had to laugh. "Justin knows what you've been doing for me."

This had to be new to Beth. Sherise had been using her as her P.I. for years without letting Justin know. She'd helped her find out about Justin's affair a couple of years ago. She was unfamiliar with this newfound openness and honesty between Sherise and her husband.

"Okay," she responded in her usual, curt tone. "Hello, Justin."

"Hi, Beth," Justin responded.

"I was hoping to hear from you," Sherise said.

After she'd told Justin, the second person she told was Beth, and she had her see if there was any additional information she could get.

"I might have found something," Beth said. "I can't say exactly what it means, but I can say what I think."

Sherise looked up at Justin with a sparkle in her eyes. "Go on."

"Remember what Stephen told you about meeting Blair at the D.C. jail on D Street?" she asked. "He came across him when he was still in cuffs, about to be put in a cell."

"Yes," Sherise answered. "Maurice was there helping out a friend."

"That's just it," Beth said. "He couldn't have been. You see, the jail process is pretty precise, and when prisoners are cuffed and about to be put in cells, they aren't allowed near visitors, not even their lawyers. They aren't allowed to meet up with whoever bailed them out until they get into the pickup area and collect their belongings."

"Wait a second." Sherise realized what Beth was saying. "Maurice wasn't helping anyone out. He was in trouble."

"Exactly," Beth continued. "So I did a little checking. The guy has great connections, because he was never brought up on any charges, but I think he was so focused on Stephen, he didn't bother to get his own arrest removed."

"What was he arrested for?" Justin asked.

"Soliciting prostitution," Beth answered. "I wish it was juicier than that, but I did find one thing. He has a long history of soliciting prostitutes. I just came from H Street, where he was arrested. I found the hooker that the cops caught getting into his car, Diamond."

Justin laughed. "Of course her name is Diamond."

Sherise smiled and slapped Justin on the thigh. "Go on, Beth."

"Well, he's a regular around there. Has been for years. He picks them up and takes them to the District Hotel, room 204, every time. They do some drugs, usually coke or X and that's it."

"Is he into anything weird or kinky that we could use against him?" Justin asked.

Sherise looked at her husband, somewhat surprised by his question. Proud, but surprised.

"Not really," Beth answered. "I wish I had more, but I found it interesting at least. Do you think this would be enough to put something together?"

"No." Sherise was feeling all her switches lighting up. "But if we take it up a notch, it will."

"What do you mean?" Justin asked.

"Beth, I need your help in doing something pretty off-the-charts insane," Sherise said. "Are you up for it?"

"How many laws will I have to break?" she asked.

Sherise thought about it for a second. "Maybe one or two."

"I don't know about this," Justin interjected. "Sherise . . ."

"I'm in," Beth quickly offered over the phone.

"Okay," Sherise said. "None of this will get back to Jerry, but I'm still going to need his help."

The phone beeped to indicate another call was trying to get

through. Sherise looked down at the phone and noticed it was Billie. She pressed the Ignore button.

"Here's what I want to do," Sherise continued. "We get him to pick up a plant and take her to the District Hotel. Then . . ."

She was interrupted by another call from Billie and realized that if she decided to call again instead of leave a message, it was likely urgent. She had to take this call.

Stepping out onto the sidewalk in front of her apartment building in search of moving boxes, Erica heard her phone beep. She checked the text and saw it was from Sherise again. It was about Billie, and Erica felt a tug at her heart. It hurt her so much to hear that Michael had cheated on Billie. She wanted to be there for her, the way she'd been there for her when Porter broke her heart.

But she couldn't deal with the bullshit that was inevitable being around the girls. Things had changed permanently between all of them, and Erica couldn't be bothered right now with trying to make it right. She was dealing with her own life right now.

When they were ready to accept her as an equal, and not their little charity case, things could be good between them again. But as long as they insisted she was some child who needed scolding and couldn't make a decision without their direction, she was going to stay away.

She knew Billie wasn't going to be alone in this. She had Sherise and she would help her deal with it for now. Besides, with Sherise's anger over her quitting Justin's firm, Erica knew that a face-to-face with her would only result in more fighting. She was sick of it. She was sick of all of it.

Placing her phone back in her jeans pocket, Erica looked up to see a man, looking about in his thirties, with a little girl walking down the sidewalk. The little girl looked around five years old. He was laughing and looking down at her. She laughed back and stopped, throwing her hands up in the air.

He responded by leaning down and picking her up in his arms. She grabbed his face with her tiny hands and pressed her nose against his. He kissed her and she giggled. He secured her in his arms and continued walking down the street. As they passed Erica, she could hear them singing a song together. It sounded like a gospel song Erica remembered learning in church with her mother.

But not with her father and, as she watched the two of them continue down the street, Erica found herself feeling the opposite of what she should have felt. She was angry. She was angry at the look of pure joy and contentment in that little girl's face. Her tiny soul exuded a sense of confidence, of being, of importance in her father's arms.

"Fucking Jonah," she mumbled under her breath.

"Hey, Erica!"

Erica, still feeling anger, although trying to ignore it, turned to see her brother, Nate, rushing down the sidewalk toward her.

"Where you going?" he asked breathlessly, when he reached her.

"I'm going to the office supply place to pick up some moving boxes," she answered. "What are you doing here?"

"Damn, I almost missed you. I need to talk to you."

"You can always call ahead and—"

"This is sort of a face-to-face thing." He gestured toward her apartment. "Can we go inside?"

"Come on, Nate. I'm on my way out. What is it?"

He looked around as if he was concerned someone would hear him before taking a step closer to his sister. He looked at her apprehensively.

"Um . . ." He lifted his shoulders in a humble gesture. "I sort of need some . . . you know, money."

"I just gave you a ton of money a few days ago," she said. "Enough to pay off your landlord and a little extra for you. Did you lose the check?"

"No." He pressed his lips together, clearly reluctant to explain himself. "I sort of . . . well, I spent it."

"You spent it?" she asked. "You were supposed to give it to your landlord!"

"That's the thing." He ran his hand over his head. "I sort of fucked up."

Erica gasped and from the look on her face, Nate seemed to know what she was thinking.

"No," he said, quickly. "It's not drugs. I swear to God. It's not that at all."

"Then what?" she asked, after a sigh. "How in the hell did you spend all that money?"

"I intended to give it to the landlord with that letter to end the lease, but . . ." He shook his head as if even he was in disbelief over what he was about to say, "My buddy, Skip, came over and . . ."

"Skip?" Erica knew what that meant. "That fucking gambling addict? Did you go gambling with him?"

"We went down to the Maryland Live! Casino and, I swear, Erica, I don't really know what happened."

"You know damn well what happened!" she snapped. "How could you do that? You lost it all? All of it?"

He nodded, looking extremely ashamed of himself. "I'm so sorry, Erica. I . . ."

"You were drinking, weren't you?" she asked.

He held up his hand defensively. "Hold on a second. I'm not an addict. I don't do drugs anymore. I never had a problem with alcohol."

"It's all the same," she said.

"No, it isn't!" he insisted. "Look, the point is, my landlord is still waiting on that money. He doesn't believe me and thinks I'm going to skip without paying him. He's pissed."

She leaned back, placing her hands on her hips. "I don't know what you're looking at me for."

"Come on, Erica. Don't fuck around. I need the money."

"I gave you the money," she said. "This is how you show your appreciation, by gambling it off. That's not my fault."

"I know," he said. "I fucked up. Just give me some more so I can get this guy off my back."

"Do you think I'm a free money tree?" Erica was pissed at his attitude. "You act like you just know I'm going to give it to you. Like I owe it to you."

"You have the money," he said. "You know you have it. It's not a lot to you, so don't be stingy."

"Stingy? How dare you? I gave you—"

"I did this because of you," he said. "I told my landlord I was moving out and paying off the lease because you promised me you would pay for it."

"And I did!" she yelled. "You fucked up. Not me."

"I know, but I need you help me out," he said desperately. "Why are you being so selfish?"

"I can't believe you!" Erica garnered every bit of strength she had to not slap him in the face. "You spoiled brat. I didn't have to give you anything!"

"Are you serious?" he asked. "You're really gonna leave me hanging like this? I'm screwed, Erica! I won't be able to move in with Aubrey. You're ruining everything!"

"You just ruined everything for yourself!" She looked him up and down, showing her disgust. "You're just another person I can't trust anymore, you unappreciative leech. I can't even stand to look at you!"

"Erica!" he called after her as she turned and rushed away.

"Go to hell!" she yelled without looking back. "Go to hell, Nate!"

She rushed into her car and drove off just as Nate reached her, slamming his hand on her driver's side door. She sped off down the street and reached the end of the block. Stopping at the stop sign, she looked back to see if Nate was following her.

He wasn't, but when she turned back, she watched as the father and daughter she had seen before crossed the street in front of her. She watched as he eyed her cautiously, very careful to make sure that his daughter was safely in his arms as he made his way through the crosswalk. The little girl, her head nestled in her father's right shoulder, looked into Erica's car as they passed by.

She made eye contact with Erica and her head lifted a bit with concern. Erica imagined she must look as frazzled as she felt right now and the girl noticed it. Or maybe she was just curious. Erica could see her point in her direction and say something to her father, but her father didn't turn. He just nodded and kissed the little girl on her forehead as they reached the sidewalk.

Erica jumped in her seat as the car behind her honked loudly. After a second, she stepped on the gas and drove on, feeling angrier than ever. She felt at that moment as if she had no one at all. As if she had never had anyone.

Sherise and Billie both sat at the end of the bed in Sherise's bedroom. Sherise had her arms wrapped around Billie and Billie's head lay on her chest. She wasn't crying anymore. She didn't have enough moisture left for any more tears, and she didn't want to drink the tea Sherise had just made for her.

"You have to drink something," Sherise said. "At least some water."

Slowly, Billie leaned away and sat up. Her eyes red and swollen, her hair a mess, she looked at Sherise and nodded. "Water."

Sherise got up and reached for the water bottle she had brought earlier from off the dresser. She returned to the bed, handing it to Billie.

"It's hard enough to think straight as it is," Sherise said. "If you let yourself get dehydrated, things will just get more confusing."

"They aren't confusing at all." Billie's voice was hoarse from the crying and yelling.

She'd come straight to Sherise's house in Georgetown after leaving her apartment. Not knowing what else to do, she'd called Sherise, who offered to come get her. Instead, she took a cab. Billie did her best to hold herself together, as the cab driver was already concerned enough to ask if she wanted him to drive her to a hospital. She must have looked as much of a mess as she felt.

When she finally reached Sherise's, Billie allowed herself to fall apart. Justin stayed downstairs and Sherise and Billie went upstairs. Billie told her everything from the moment Porter exposed Darina's plot to the second she ran out of the apartment after seeing Michael in bed with her.

Sherise's first instinct was to find that woman and beat her into the ground, but after Billie repeated the situation, after calming down, Sherise was more suspicious than anything else.

"You know you can stay here," Sherise said. "I'll change the sheets in the guest bedroom. No one has been in there in a long time."

"Thank you," Billie managed to say. "You don't think the babies heard me? Was I too loud?"

"No," Sherise said, although they probably had heard her. "Justin took them out for a bite to eat. They won't be back for a little while. Don't worry about them."

"I'm sorry," Billie said. "I'm so, so sorry."

"What are you apologizing for?"

"For being a baby. For being a failure at everything!"

"You're being stupid now," Sherise admonished. "This isn't your fault. From everything you're telling me, this woman planned and plotted all of it. She factored you into this."

"But I should have seen it coming," Billie said.

"You did," Sherise told her. "Just not soon enough. You can't possibly say that you have some blame here."

"How can I not?" Billie said. "That woman was a threat to my relationship with Michael from day one and I just held my suspicions because I was too weak to stand up to . . ."

"To a man meeting his son for the first time?" Sherise asked. "Your hands were tied, Billie. You knew that supporting Michael in this traumatic situation was the most important thing at the time. Besides, you did stand up. Michael didn't listen."

"You're right," Billie agreed, slamming her fist on the bed. "I tried to tell him to be more cautious. He didn't want to hear it. I get that. . . . I get that he was thrown for a loop, but he should have listened to me!"

Sherise sat back down on the bed next to her. "If I tell Justin, he'll go over there. He'll go over there and handle this the way this kind of thing was handled where we grew up."

"No," Billie said. "I want to kill him myself, but I don't want anyone else getting involved."

"If you're worried about Justin," Sherise said, "Don't let that law degree fool you. He can roll."

Billie knew Sherise was trying to make her laugh, but she couldn't manage it. She could barely manage to speak. She was just aching inside and out.

"I took too long," Billie said. "I tried to be patient with him, let him figure out what she was up to. I shouldn't have done that."

"You can never trust a man to figure out what a woman is doing in enough time. Their minds just don't work that way."

"But Michael . . ." Billie threw her arms up before letting them fall flatly back to her sides. "But he was smarter than most men. I thought he was . . . I thought he was stronger."

"He did seem more principled than that," Sherise added. "Getting high and cheating. But all men are just men."

"How could this happen to me again?" she asked. "It was behind my back the first time, but right in front of my face this time. How?"

"Billie, it happens to all of us," Sherise said. "We're all . . ."

Just then, Billie's phone, which was sitting at the other edge of the bed, rang—again. It had been ringing nonstop. Sherise reached back to check, but she knew it was Michael again.

"Just put it on silent," Billie said. "He won't stop."

"Well, you do have to talk to him." Sherise grabbed the phone and put it on silent.

"I'm not ready to talk to him," Billie said. "I can barely form words anyway."

Sherise noticed the face of the phone showed she had twenty text messages. She offered the phone to Billie.

"You can at least read what the asshole has to say."

Billie grabbed the phone and noted the texts. She pressed the button and started from the top.

"Please call me," she said, reading the consecutive texts out loud. "Baby, please call me. Where are you? I didn't sleep with her. I swear I didn't. Please call me. Where are you? Will you come home? She—"

Billie tossed the phone away. "Oh God, he must think I'm a fool."

"What?" Sherise asked.

She pointed to the phone on the floor. "He's saying she drugged him! Drugged him? What is this, some TV soap opera? Does he think I'm so stupid I'll fall for that?"

"Drugged?" Sherise asked. "What kind of bullshit is that?"

"I should be grateful," Billie said sarcastically. "At least he didn't try and pull the you're-getting-paranoid bullshit Porter tried on me when I first started suspecting he was cheating on me."

"Stop comparing the two," Sherise ordered. "Porter and Michael are nothing alike and . . ."

"What?" Billie asked, looking at Sherise and noticing her confused expression. "They both cheated on me, so they're more alike than different."

Sherise was trying to get beyond her sympathetic anger and focus. "I was just thinking of what Porter told you. What she did. What she said to him about helping her break you two up."

"Proves she was planning something," Billie said. "Of course he takes his time in telling me. That could have been the proof I needed to open Michael's eyes before . . . ugh."

"I doubt Michael would take to heart anything Porter had to say," Sherise shared. "He'd probably think it was all a lie Porter created to drive a wedge between you."

"It doesn't even matter." Billie fell back on the bed with a heavy sigh. "If he wanted to sleep with her, he was going to do it. Obviously, he did."

Sherise scooted to the middle of the bed. "It's not your job to stop him from cheating on you, but listen to me. This bitch was going to great lengths to hide her intent from Michael, right?"

"I thought so," Billie said, "but obviously he was getting her signals or they wouldn't have . . ."

"Or did he?" Sherise asked. "I mean, if she was trying to re-cruit Porter obviously she realized she had a challenge on her hands. She risked exposing herself if Porter decided to be an ac-tual good guy for once in his life and warn you and Michael the second she asked him in on it."

Billie sat up and looked at her. "What are you getting at?"

"Porter turned her down," Sherise said. "She didn't have much left. It's possible . . . Do you think Michael's telling the truth?"

"Oh my God!" Billie couldn't believe it. "You're falling for that, aren't you?"

"It's a possibility," Sherise insisted. "If this woman is evil enough to try and get collaborators in on this, she's evil enough to drug someone. Did he seem drugged?"

"You know what he seemed?" Billie asked. "He seemed like a high-on-weed, naked-ass motherfucker in bed with his ex."

"I'm just saying it's possible something was in the weed," Sherise said. "You can't say it isn't in your frame of mind."

"I'm in a good enough frame of mind that I know not to fall for bullshit like I did last time. I think . . . I think that the paternity test results were due today. They were trying to get results before they had to go back home, but it wasn't going to work out. I was grateful for that. I thought I'd rather be with Michael when he got the results instead of her."

"But clearly she stayed behind," Sherise said. "She must have been confident the results would be positive and wanted to take advantage."

"And she did. When Michael found out, he was probably feeling attached to her at the moment. They have a history. That's how it happened. I just know it!"

"You don't know it," Sherise admonished. "You don't know for sure."

"Where the fuck is Erica?" Billie asked. "Because you've gone nuts. I need an adult!"

"Fuck Erica," Sherise said angrily. "No matter what bullshit is happening between us, she should be here for you. This is more important than any of her insecurity issues and petty shit."

"I guess it's better," Billie added, despite feeling very hurt by Erica. "If she's so caught up in herself right now, she probably couldn't help."

"It's no excuse," Sherise added. "None."

"Isn't it?" Billie asked. "I mean, really, if she got my texts and your messages, she knows that my life has just been devastated. For her not to be here means that she is really separating herself from us. After everything we've been through, could petty shit really do that?"

"It doesn't matter," Sherise said. "Petty shit, real shit. You need her. We need her and she's not here."

"I need both of you right now," Billie told her. "I swear I don't know where my left or right is. When Porter did this, if I didn't have both of you, I wouldn't have made it."

"I'll get her back," Sherise promised. "Don't worry about it. I'll get her back and she'll be here for you no matter what. Nothing is more important than the three of us. She knows that. I just need to remind her."

When Billie stepped out of her office building, the cold wind slapped her in the face. It was unusually cold for December in D.C., but she appreciated it. Her face was burning. It felt like it was always burning. After surviving her first day at work since finding Michael in bed with Darina just two days ago, she needed this cold air.

She didn't think she would make it during the day. She had to talk to Sherise at least three times just to keep the strength to be focused enough to get through her meetings. Michael was calling her at work, but she refused every call. He had the nerve to send her flowers with a note begging her to hear his side of the story.

She tossed the flowers in the garbage. Hear his side? She'd seen his side. His side was the right side of the bed that he was lying in naked. No words could speak louder than that.

Her last meeting with her boss ended at four p.m. and Billie felt as if she'd put forth a normal façade for as long as she could. She needed to get back to Sherise's house to drink wine and fall asleep. She was just so damn tired.

So tired that she didn't even notice Michael walking toward

her as she stepped out onto the sidewalk. She didn't notice until he was right in her face.

"Baby," was his first word as he held his hands out and touched her arms.

She was shocked at first, not expecting this at all. Her reflexes were slow due to fatigue, but the second it registered what was happening, she shifted into gear. She jerked her arms from his grip and pushed against him with all her might.

"Get away from me!" she yelled.

People walking by the busy sidewalk turned to look at them, but quickly turned back and kept walking.

"Baby, you have to talk to me," he pleaded.

She looked up at him and could only feel full of rage. She loved him so much and hated him so much. There was a part of her, a weak part that she hated right now, that wanted to feel sorry for him. He looked pitiful, haggard, and spent.

"How could you come here?" she asked, taking several steps backward toward the building entrance. "Where I work?"

"I need to speak with you." He sounded as desperate as he looked.

"How did you even know I'd be coming out right now?"

"I've been here all day, Billie," he said. "I was hoping you'd take one of my calls and come down and talk to me."

"I don't want this drama at my work!"

"I'm sorry," he said. "I didn't know where you were all weekend. I was so worried about you!"

"Worried about me?" She laughed. "What did you think, I'd kill myself? You think you're worth that? How arrogant of you, you cheating bastard. No, Michael, I would never hurt myself over a cheating asshole."

"Billie, you have to listen to me. I did not cheat on you. I—"

"Stop!" She held up her hand to stop him. "I saw you. Are you gonna try the whole *you gonna believe what I tell you or what you see what your own eyes* routine on me? Because I have the answer. My eyes, Michael. I know what I saw! I believe what I saw!"

"You didn't see everything!" Michael yelled. "You came in at the end of—"

"The end of you fucking her!"

Billie got a few more looks, and realizing that a coworker could come by at any minute, she walked over to the side of the entrance, away from prying eyes.

Michael was right behind her. "I didn't sleep with her. I would never cheat on you, Billie. I don't remember ever touching her!"

"Oh." She turned around to him. "So the story has already changed. You're stepping back from you didn't sleep with her to the you don't remember sleeping with her storyline."

"I remember her coming over with the paternity test," he said. "I was just about to go online and find out. I thought she was on a plane back home."

"One thing led to another," Billie said. "I don't need to hear the details."

"That's just it," Michael insisted. "That's all the details I have. We were talking about how I need to be in Duncan's life and . . . I was drugged. That has to be it!"

"I don't need to hear any more." Billie would not be made a fool of.

"I've been trying to get her to tell me, but she won't answer my calls."

"So the slut didn't stick around to hold on to her prize?" Billie asked. "Oh well, I guess she got what she wanted. Now Duncan can have his family together."

"Don't say that," Michael pleaded. "Duncan is my son, but she is not my family. I love you, Billie. Only you."

"You know for sure?" Billie asked, even though she felt it was redundant to even ask. "The tests came back?"

He nodded. "He's mine but, Billie, I don't want to talk about Duncan right now. I want to talk about us. I swear to you . . ."

"Don't swear," she ordered. "It just makes the lie worse."

"It's not a lie!" Michael's anger was increasing.

"Well, I guess you don't know," she said. "You say for sure you didn't sleep with her. Then you say you're not sure if you slept with her or not. Can't make up your mind which lie will serve you best?"

"I'm not trying to do that," Michael insisted. "I'm just trying to let you know that I love—"

"Stop!" Billie wasn't having this. "Don't ever say that to me again! Don't tell me you love me. The only words I want to hear are when you're moving out."

"I'm not moving out," Michael said. "You're going to come home and we're gonna work this out."

"I'm not moving out," she stated. "I'm not the cheating whore, Michael. You are. You have to find a new place. Not me."

"Where are you right now?" he asked.

"None of your fucking business," Billie responded. "So text me when you're gone. I don't want to run into you again. I never want to see your face again, Michael."

"Billie, do you really think I would let you go that easily?" he asked. "After everything that has happened between us. The love we share. The future we've planned. Do you think I would just walk away from that?"

"You did," she said. "The second you stuck your dick in her."

"I didn't—"

"Stop it!" Billie was crying now, unable to keep up the façade of being the strong woman in the face of pain. It was too hard being this close to him. Looking at him was too much of a reminder of what was lost.

"Please," she begged. "Please, Michael. Stop doing this. I don't want lies. I'm not a rookie at this. I've been through it all before. I'm not willing to go through it again."

"I'm not Porter," he said.

"And I'm not stupid," she said back. "I know about the lies and the pleading and the begging. It's bullshit. Cheaters are cheaters, and you only get one chance to cheat on me."

She brushed against him as she walked past, feeling pain just from the contact. She felt her heart stop and her breath catch as he gripped her arm, pulling her back to him.

"You can't do this!" he demanded. "You can't just walk away from this. If I had cheated on you, I'd deserve it, but I didn't."

"You mean you don't think you did." Billie tried to pull out of his grip. "You're not sure, right?"

"You're not listening to me," he said. "You've got to listen to me. We need to sit down and—"

"And give you a chance to fill my head with doubts," she said. "Let you say the exact right words to make me question what I saw with my own eyes. Not again."

"Stop comparing me to Porter!"

"You're not different," she said. "In fact, you're worse. Porter's affair happened after months of temptation. You fell off right away. I mean, I know you have history and that probably—"

"Stop it!" he demanded. "Stop mentioning Porter."

Billie could see she was angering him and she was glad. He deserved it. "I will never, ever trust you again."

In that instant, he grabbed her and pulled her to him. His mouth came to hers and he kissed her demandingly, angrily, and with all the strength he had. Billie was shocked at how quickly her body reacted to this. Despite all she knew and all she felt, her physical reaction was almost immediate. The touch of him, the taste of him was so wonderful and perfect to her.

"If you won't trust me," he finally said after pulling away from her, "at least trust that."

"No!" Billie pushed away from him, stepping back. She hated herself for letting even a second's worth of love seep through for him. "Stay away from me, Michael!"

The look on Michael's face was stark disappointment and very real pain.

"How dare you?" she asked. "How dare you act like you've been wronged?"

"I thought you loved me more than this," he said. "I was certain you did."

"Don't you dare pull that shit on me," she warned. "Try to make me believe I'm the one lacking faith in us."

"You are," Michael said. "Billie, you won't even give me a chance to try and explain. Real love would at least give me that."

"Real love would have never put us in this situation in the first place."

He took a step back from her and, in that act, Billie felt more pain than she expected. She looked into his eyes and through her tears she could see him blink and look away.

This time, she made sure to keep her distance as she passed him to avoid any contact, but something told her it wasn't necessary. He made no attempt to reach out to her this time. She should be grateful for that. She wasn't sure if she could take him continuing to try and fool her back into his arms.

She couldn't take any of this. Her heart was beating out of her chest and tears were streaming down her cheeks. She had to get away. As she got onto the sidewalk, walking among the growing crowds, she didn't look back to see if he was following her. She didn't want him to, but was not sure she could stand the pain of what she suspected; that he wasn't trying to follow her at all.

The emotion was overwhelming. Anger, sadness, hate, love, desire, confusion . . . all of it was swirling around Billie's head and her heart right now. How could she possibly be considering anything he'd said? She'd been through this. That was the whole point. You learn from your lessons. She knew what she'd seen. She couldn't doubt herself, especially not based on one kiss.

But she was. Despite what her own eyes had witnessed, there was a little voice that reminded her of the look of pain and desperation in his eyes and the suffering in his voice. He didn't look like Porter when Porter had tried to make her believe he wasn't cheating on her. Porter looked like a guilty man trying to appear wronged.

Or maybe that was the gullible fool inside her that Billie thought she'd conquered. The Billie who continued to sleep with Porter, even after he could no longer deny his cheating. No, she wasn't going to be that woman again. She'd lost years of her life because of being a fool for a cheating man.

Never again.

15

"You're going to have to make it quick," Jerry said the exact moment Sherise entered his office at headquarters. "I've got a meeting with the Joint Chiefs of Staff at the Pentagon in an hour. The car is—"

"I'll be as brief as I can," Sherise said.

She took a seat in the leather chair across from his desk. He was tapping on his tablet furiously while gnawing on a pen. When he looked up at her, he stopped, noticing the expression on her face.

"What's wrong?" he asked. "It's one week from Christmas, for Christ's sake. What happened?"

"This isn't about the transition." Sherise noticed him calm down a bit. "Well, maybe it is a little bit. Maybe a lot."

At the sight of his impatience, Sherise decided it was time to go ahead with this. No second-guessing it. She had planned it as well as she could. She needed Jerry to make it work, and if he was as principled a man as she once thought he was, this was no sure bet.

"I know," she said. "Stephen told me everything."

"I don't know what you're talking about," he said, flatly.

"I know why Maurice has my job," she said. "No point in

pretending anymore. I know about Stephen's drinking problem and how Maurice found him in jail and used that to—"

"Stop!" Jerry shot up from his chair, his expression harsh and angry. "What the fuck do you think you're doing, Sherise?"

She gestured for him to calm down. "Just take it easy, Jerry. I'm not trying to do anything to you. In fact, I'm looking to protect you from that leech."

"Do you think I need you to protect me?" Jerry asked. "I'm the president-elect of the United States."

"Yes, but if you really used the power that your impending office had, none of this would be the problem. You could have erased Maurice from the face of the planet if you wanted to."

"Don't you think I considered that?" he asked.

"You could have done it and saved us all the shit we're going through."

Jerry shook his head as he walked away from the desk toward the window, looking out. His back was to Sherise but she could see how heavily this was all weighing on him.

"I know what I could have done to him, Sherise. I thought of the hundreds of things I could have done to that creep for blackmailing me. I don't want to be that person. I've never wanted to be that person."

"I understand that," Sherise said, even though she really didn't. It wasn't as if he was doing this drunk on the power he had. "But he threatened your son, Jerry. It would be your right to—"

"Then what?" he asked, turning back to her. "I felt bad enough having his record erased every time this happened."

"You weren't doing him any favors with that, but that isn't the point right now. The point is, I get that you don't want to cross a line your power allots you. I do."

"This is my family and my—"

Sherise slammed her fist on the arm of the chair. "My career that I've worked my life for. Do you remember everything I've done for your campaign? The fires I've put out? The wheels I've greased?"

"I understand."

"No," she insisted. "I don't think you do. But your problems with Maurice are bigger than mine, so I can understand that. I have a plan to get Maurice Blair out of your life and mine while keeping Stephen's . . . problems secret and not ruining his life."

"What's your plan?" Jerry asked.

"That's the thing." She leaned forward in her chair, looking at him with earnest. "I can't tell you."

He rolled his eyes. "You're planning to break the law."

"Not exactly," she said, even though in a way, she was. "But I'm planning on . . . Like I said, I can't tell you."

"But you are telling me," Jerry said.

"That's because I need your help."

Jerry shook his head. "I'm not getting involved in anything illegal."

"What I'm asking you to do isn't illegal, but it is a big deal."

Jerry returned to his seat behind his desk.

Corey must have seen her coming because the second Erica reached the floor where his garden apartment was, the door opened. He didn't step outside, just waited inside the door for Erica to approach. She found that odd, expecting him to be more excited to see her, but as soon as she reached his apartment, she could tell from the look on his face that he wasn't.

"Hey!" She reached out, touching his shoulder.

She leaned in for a kiss, but he didn't meet her halfway. When she pressed her lips against his, he only pressed his lips together.

Erica leaned back, confused. "You don't seem happy to see me."

"I wasn't expecting you," Corey said.

"You don't mind a surprise, do you?" she asked, wrapping her arms around him. "I have something to show you."

"What is it?" he asked, not budging from the doorway.

"You have to come with me," Erica said. "Let's go!"

She grabbed his hand and pulled at him, but he didn't budge. When Erica looked back at him, she could see that he wasn't planning on moving and he wasn't happy.

"Serious?" she asked. "You're mad that I dropped by unannounced? I thought you'd be happy to see me."

"Why?" he asked. "Because we had sex and then I don't see you for a week? Because you haven't returned any of my calls, emails, or texts? What the fuck, Erica?"

She sighed, her hands falling to her sides. "Look, I know. I know I've been hard to reach recently, but . . ."

"Hard to reach?" He rolled his eyes. "You've been impossible to reach. I come over to your place and we have sex, you telling me that everything is good between us and you trust me. Then, crickets. For a week!"

"I can explain," she said.

"Then you just drop by unannounced and want to play sweetheart?" He shook his head. "You must think I'm some kind of joke, Erica."

"I don't," she answered, placing her hands on his chest. "I got into this big fight with Nate and it just messed me up inside."

"And instead of coming to me," he moved her hands off his chest, "you avoid me."

"I was avoiding everyone," Erica said. "You don't understand, Corey. It goes back to a lifetime of supporting Nate, making sacrifices for him and . . ." Erica sighed, and feeling a sense of dread coming over her just at the thought of her last encounter with him, fought it off.

"It doesn't matter," she said. "I don't give a shit anymore. I didn't come over here to complain. I want to show you my new condo! It's a two-bedroom and everything is brand new. I've even got a doorman."

Corey had no reaction to her news and it annoyed her. Was he really going to be sensitive about this? Was he going to try and ruin her moment?

"Corey, I'm sorry, okay? I didn't return your calls. Let's not make a big deal out of this, please. I just closed on a great new place and you're the first person I'm telling!"

"So I'm supposed to feel privileged?" he asked. "That you're gracing me with this news? What would have happened if you hadn't closed on your place until next week, Erica? Would I not have heard from you until then?"

Annoyed now, Erica placed her hands on her hips. "Maybe not, especially with this attitude. I just needed some time away from everyone and everything, Corey."

"We all need that from time to time," he said. "But we tell the people we claim to care about before that, so they don't spend that time hurting or worrying."

"You want to talk to me about hurting?" Erica asked. "I'm the one who has been hurting. You don't know what I've been through, Corey."

"How could I when you ignore me and won't talk to me?" he yelled.

"I said I'm sorry! Can we please get past this?"

Corey shook his head with an amused smile. "You know what, Erica? I think . . . we need to slow things down a bit."

"What?" Erica was not expecting this at all.

"I don't want to go see your new condo," he said. "I don't really want to see you right now."

"If you didn't want to see me, then why have you been try-ing to contact me all week?"

He looked at her incredulously. "Are you fucking kidding

me? You don't even see what you've . . . I think you should go, Erica."

She was in shock. "What do you mean? Are you trying to break up with me?"

"You're erratic and angry and selfish," he said. "You're not who I thought you were. That's my fault, but . . ."

"Selfish?" she asked. "How many things have I offered to buy you and—"

"I'm not talking about financially!" He gritted his teeth in frustration. "I mean emotionally. You're selfish and inconsiderate. I tried to be a part of helping you, but I can't."

"Helping me?" she asked, enraged. "So you're on the help poor little Erica bandwagon too, huh? I need help?"

"Clearly you do," he said. "I tried to understand what you're going through, but you keep fucking it up and I'm done."

"How dare you?" she asked, seething with anger. "You asked me to tell you what was going on and I did!"

"Then you just disappeared," he said. "And that wasn't the first time. Before that, you were ignoring me. I can't deal with that shit, Erica. I won't deal with that shit."

"No one is forcing you to do anything!" she yelled.

"Good," he said. "Then I wish you luck."

Looking in his eyes, Erica felt a sting of pain that cut to the core of her. He really meant this. How could he do this to her?

"I don't need luck," she said. "I've never had it and I'm doing just fine."

With that, she turned and ran away. Her heart wanted her to run away, but her dignity wanted her to walk with pride. The tears that started streaming down her cheeks forced her to walk as fast as possible. She wasn't going to give him the satisfaction of seeing her hurt.

She didn't need him. She was better off without someone who was so needy and looked at her as a poor project in need of his help. She deserved a real man who could handle a woman like her. She deserved much better than Corey James.

"I told you not to worry about Erica," Sherise said, speaking into the microphone attached to her headphones. "I'll handle her."

"I needed the distraction." Billie was sitting on the bed in the guest room of Sherise's town house after coming home from work. "Michael is all I could think about. Our last encounter."

"Maybe you should have stayed and listened?" Sherise asked. "That's what you're thinking, right?"

"I'm angry because I feel guilty now. Why should I feel guilty?"

"You shouldn't, Billie. You haven't done anything wrong."

"But I feel like I did," she said. "The way he looked at me. And then him sending me a text today saying he's moving out tonight so I can come back home tomorrow."

"You wanted him out," Sherise reminded her. "The cheater is the one who should have to find a new place."

"It was just that there was nothing more to the message," Billie lamented. "No hoping we can talk again. No sentiment at all. No even wishing we can talk again one day."

"That's what you wanted," Sherise reminded her. "Or what you thought you wanted until you got it."

"Am I a bitch for having doubts now?" Billie asked.

"No," Sherise said. "This has taken a huge toll on you, but it sounds like you need to talk to him again. What does your heart say? You should trust your heart."

"I can't trust my heart," Billie said. "It's broken. But I do think I need some closure."

"I think you need to talk to him again," Sherise recommended. "Even if only to get that closure."

Billie sighed. "If he'll even agree to talk to me after the way I've shut him out."

"You're being too much of a softy, Billie. Remember how

this thing got started. All the wrong is on his side. He's got no right to be angry about anything."

"You're right." Billie sat up on the bed. "I think I'm going to call him, but we need to go see Erica too. This has gone on too long."

"Okay," Sherise said. "But just let me figure that out."

"When are you coming home?" Billie asked. "You said you had to run out at nine. It's almost ten thirty."

"In a little bit," Sherise answered. "I've got some business to take care of. Talk to you later."

Sherise hung up, turning to Beth Martin, who was sitting in the driver's seat. Her longtime P.I. was an attractive Asian woman in her late thirties who always undersold her good looks.

"It's taking too long," Sherise told her. "It didn't work. He probably thought she looked too young and . . ."

Beth cleared her throat and nodded forward.

Sherise turned and looked down the street. "Is that him?"

"Look," Beth ordered.

Sherise reached for the miniature binoculars on her lap and brought them to her eyes. She got excited at the sight of Maurice and the young woman Beth had found and paid to enact their plan walking up the steps of the District Hotel.

"You can trust her?" Sherise asked. "She's a prostitute."

"She's worked with me on some other projects," Beth answered. "We've paid her well. She thought it was funny."

"She got him to pick her out of all the women on H Street," Sherise said. "So she has to be good."

"I paid a few of those women to hit the road for the night," Beth said. "I made sure she was the freshest, youngest-looking one there. That was the easy part."

It was the easy part, Sherise thought. Now was the hard part. In many ways, their plan was ridiculous, but it had to work, so Sherise threw that thought from her mind. As she watched the door close behind her mark and his friend for the night,

Sherise did something she'd never done when enacting her plans.

She crossed her fingers.

The second Billie walked into her apartment, her heart felt like it had been stabbed. Nothing was different, but everything was. This was the first time she'd been there since running out after catching Michael with Darina. She didn't expect it to be easy and she was right.

Her eyes went straight to the counter that separated the kitchen from the living area where she'd last seen Michael's turned-off phone. He'd turned off his phone. Michael was addicted to his phone. The only times she'd seen him turn it off were when he was trying to seduce her and didn't want any distractions.

He wanted to be alone with Darina.

She walked over to the counter and placed her hand on it. She thought of the times Michael had propped her up on there and made mad, passionate love to her. She felt her body heat up just at the memory.

Or maybe Darina had turned off his phone and he didn't even know it.

These competing voices in her mind had been gaining steam after her encounter with Michael and then her last conversation with Sherise. It was impossible to separate her heart from her head in this, but she was trying as hard as she could to separate her past from her present.

"Michael?" She called out his name although she knew he wasn't there.

She had made sure he was out of the apartment before showing up, but didn't put it past him to lie to her and end up being there so he could get her alone and try to lie to her some more.

Or maybe explain the truth.

These conflicting thoughts were killing Billie. She couldn't determine the difference of what her common sense and experience told her to believe from what her heart wanted to believe in order to stop hurting.

Slowly she walked toward the bedroom feeling nausea begin to creep in. She reached the doorway and looked in at the scene of the crime. She felt an intense sadness, as if this pain would never go away. She was silly to demand Michael find a new place to live. Standing there, looking at the bed they once shared, the bed he defiled, Billie knew she couldn't live there anymore. She'd left the home she shared with Porter for Tara's sake, wanting to keep as much the same for the little girl as possible.

But no, she knew now that she couldn't stay here. It would be hard enough getting over Michael's betrayal if she started anew. But what if . . .

"Stop it," she told herself. "You stood right here, Billie. You saw him lying in bed with her half-naked and . . ."

But they weren't lying in bed. He was sitting on the edge. Darina wasn't in the bed next to him. She was standing near the bed, getting dressed. Billie hadn't actually seen them in bed together.

She turned away from the bedroom, heading for the kitchen, hoping there was a bottle of wine in the refrigerator.

The only reason she hadn't seen them in bed together was because Darina obviously heard her come home and call out Michael's name. She had gotten out of bed and was trying to get dressed before it all went down.

But why wasn't Michael doing the same? When Billie entered the bedroom, Michael was slow, confused. She'd thought it was sleep at first, then possibly the marijuana she smelled. But what if . . .

Alarmed at this realization, Billie rushed back to the bedroom. Standing inside, she fought the emotional wave that clouded her mind and tried to remember, actually remember what happened.

Michael had been groggy, slow to get out of bed. He wasn't trying to defend himself. He was asking her to give him a moment to think. He was trying to understand what was happening.

"Oh my God!"

For the first time, in a real way, Billie felt she had reason to doubt. She wasn't willing to doubt what she'd seen with her own eyes, but now she had realized that she wasn't going by what she'd seen with her own eyes. She was going by what she thought she was seeing with her own eyes, by what her heart and life experience told her she'd seen.

"Don't be a fool," she told herself. "Don't lie to yourself about what you saw."

She had to make sure she wasn't changing the facts to rationalize what her heart wanted. It wanted Michael to be telling the truth. It wanted him to hold her in his arms and make the pain go away. Was she willing to trick her mind into believing what it needed to in order to justify taking him back; to justify believing his ridiculous claim?

A story she hadn't fully listened to, after all. He deserved that at least.

Before Billie could think further, the doorbell rang and her heart leapt out of her chest.

"Michael!" She called out his name before she reached the door.

When she finally reached it, she grabbed the knob and swung the door open. Her heart was open, ready to listen to him, hoping he could explain this. Hoping he was telling the truth. But it wasn't Michael that she faced when the door opened, and the person she saw made her gasp.

"What are you doing here?" Billie asked.

"Hello, Billie," she said kindly. "Can I come in?"

"Michael isn't here," Billie said sharply after getting over her disappointment that it wasn't him.

"I know," she said. "I came here to see you."

After a long hesitation, Billie stepped aside and let Dee Dee enter the apartment, closing the door behind her. She watched as Dee Dee silently stood in the foyer, looking around the apartment.

"This is nice," she said. "I liked Michael's old place better, but this is very classy. It's more . . . you."

She turned to Billie with a smile, but Billie didn't have the patience to pretend to give a damn.

"What do you want?" Billie asked in a cold, curt tone.

Dee Dee smiled in a way that hinted for a second that she was nervous, uncomfortable being there.

"Can I sit?" she asked, gesturing toward the living room.

Billie shrugged and slowly followed Dee Dee into the living room. The last thing she needed in this world was to deal with this woman, and as she sat in the chair on the opposite side of the coffee table from her, Billie grew suspicious as to why she was even there.

"I'm sorry about you and Michael," Dee Dee finally said.

"Yeah, I'll bet you are," Billie responded. "So sorry that the second you heard about it, you jumped on a plane and came out here to comfort him and let him know it's for the best."

"I deserve that," Dee Dee said. "But it's not the truth."

"I'm busy, Dee Dee." Billie crossed her legs and sat back in the chair. "Can you please speed this up?"

"I know you must hate me," she said. "I haven't been at all kind to you."

"I don't hate you, Dee Dee. I just don't know why you're here if not to gloat."

"I'm not here to gloat," she said. "I'm here to apologize."

"For what?" Billie asked. "For doing everything in your power to make me feel like I didn't belong? For making

Michael feel like I'm not the right girl for him? You love Darina. I'm sure you're happy as hell that Duncan brought them
closer."

"I didn't think you were right for Michael," Dee Dee admitted. "I was certain you weren't. That was until . . ."

Billie leaned forward in her chair. "Until what?"

"Until I went to his hotel room and saw him today." Dee Dee
lowered her head as she focused on her hands lying on her lap. "I
flew in this morning and went to him first thing. He wasn't expecting me either, but after I talked to him on the phone a few
days ago, I had to see my baby boy."

"Did he send you here to plead his case?" Billie asked. "He
had to know better than to think you'd do it."

"He doesn't know I'm here." Dee Dee looked up and faced
Billie with a pleading expression. "He's a mess. I've never seen
him like this. I've seen him in pain. I've seen him heartbroken.
I've never, ever seen him in anguish and so . . . hopeless like
this."

"Look, Dee Dee, Michael can tell you what he wants, but
I'm not going to discuss our relationship with you. You're wasting your time."

"When Darina's relationship with the man she'd been pass-
ing off as Duncan's father fell apart, she came to me."

Stunned, Billie was certain she'd heard wrong. She suddenly
remembered what Dee Dee had said earlier.

"You came here to apologize," Billie said, growing immediately agitated. "You . . . you knew what Darina was up to! You
were a part of it!"

Dee Dee held her hand up in an attempt to calm Billie. "I
didn't expect it to go as far as it did. You have to believe me."

"I don't have to believe anything," Billie said. "But I shouldn't
be surprised. You helped her plan to seduce Michael and break
us up."

"When I found out that Duncan was Michael's, I wanted them to be a family. She wanted Michael and promised, if I helped her, she would bring Duncan to Atlanta and get Michael to move back too."

Billie shot up from the chair and pointed accusingly at her. "You're the one who told her about Porter! You're the one who told her everything about me!"

Dee Dee nodded, looking very ashamed. "I told her it wasn't likely that she could seduce Michael. I told her that Michael was loyal, but I could help her convince him to come back to Atlanta and that would be enough to cause a wedge between you two."

"And she could take it from there," Billie said, her voice fully displaying her disgust. "What kind of a woman are you?"

"I'm the kind who wanted her son back!" Dee Dee stood up from the sofa. "I'm not excusing my choices, but—"

"You just did excuse your choices!" Billie said. "You just tried to, at least. There is no excuse!"

"I'm getting old!" Dee Dee insisted. "I want my only grandchild in my life. And I need support. I need help. You were going to take my son away from me. You and your bougie lifestyle here in D.C. Darina would bring him home, bring him and my grandson to me."

"You're a selfish, vile woman!" Billie told her. "How can you live with yourself?"

"I didn't think this would happen," Dee Dee explained. "I thought she could draw a wedge between you two, and eventually Darina, Duncan, and I could all convince him you weren't the one. That you didn't belong. It would be less painful for him that way."

"Do you hear yourself?" Billie asked. "You were plotting and planning to manipulate your own son just for your own comfort. You didn't care how hurt he was. You knew what she was going to do and you helped her!"

"I would have never agreed to drug my son!" Dee Dee shouted. "I would never, ever agree to that. I would have never gone that far!"

"Are you saying," Billie asked, "she did drug him?"

Dee Dee nodded, her sorrow seeming more genuine now. "When Michael told me over the phone that he knew he'd been drugged, I couldn't believe it. I called her and she denied it at first, but I promised to help Michael make her pay."

"Make her pay?"

Dee Dee began to pace a little, her hand to her stomach as if to calm her agitation. "Michael has been threatening to call the cops on her. He was threatening to fight for custody based on what she did. I promised to help him and she confessed to me."

Billie's mouth opened but no words came out.

He was telling the truth! She was struck with such pain that she had to sit back down in her chair. She didn't know what to do with herself. She couldn't even think straight. Michael had been telling her the truth all along and she'd refused to believe him, even give him a chance!

"Michael has never loved anyone as much as he loves you," Dee Dee said. "Please, give him another chance."

Billie could only wonder, after having doubted him so completely and cutting him off so easily, if he would be willing to give her another chance.

16

Erica had just placed three empty boxes next to each other on her sofa. She had the newspaper wrapper on the table next to all her dishes and was ready to get started. She grabbed the first glass and slipped up a piece of newspaper. She started wrapping it around the glass when the doorbell rang.

She immediately hoped it was Corey. Still reeling from his decision to dump her, she had too much pride to ask him to give her another chance, but she wasn't fooling herself when she said she didn't want him back. She also didn't have the energy for it all. She just wanted him to show up and let it go at that. She would ignore that hiccup if he would.

But when Erica reached the front door, looking through the peephole, she realized she wasn't going to get her wish. The immediate sight of Sherise and Billie on the other side of the door made her happy . . . or want to be happy. It seemed like such a long time since she'd seen them, and the lonely, frustrated part of her wanted them around so badly.

But that only lasted seconds before reality sank in. Reality was, she knew what they were there for. They were there to give her a hard time . . . again. She didn't need this shit, and for a second, she considered not opening the door. When she heard

Sherise make a loud grumbling sound and press the doorbell even harder, Erica knew they wouldn't go away.

She opened the door, intending to ask them why they would come, but she didn't get the chance.

"What the fuck is wrong with you?" Sherise asked.

"Sherise." Billie rolled her eyes. They had discussed this. They were going to try and be civil.

"Nothing is wrong with me," Erica answered. "What the fuck is wrong with you?"

"Something is clearly wrong with you," Sherise countered, taking a step forward.

She stopped when she realized that Erica wasn't moving and gave her a look that said she didn't intend to.

"We're coming in," Sherise said. "So you can fuck off with this act."

"I see Sherise is being a lady, as usual." Erica stepped aside and they came in.

"We really need to talk to you," Billie said.

Billie stepped inside and closed the door behind her. She watched as Erica walked right by her and over to the sofa where she resumed packing. It hurt Billie that she didn't even want to hug her. It seemed like forever since they'd seen her.

"What's wrong with you?" Sherise asked. "You've just disappeared."

"I've been right here all along," Erica said. "Right where I've always been."

"Not emotionally you haven't," Billie said. "Emotionally, you've been . . . Wait, you're moving?"

Erica nodded as she placed the glass in the first box.

"Where?" Sherise removed one of the boxes and sat down on the sofa.

Billie sat in the chair next to the table. "Where, Erica?"

Erica sighed. "Why are you two here? Just to chew me out?"

"You'd deserve it," Sherise said. "Do you have any idea what Billie has been going through?"

Erica looked up at Billie and could see the strain in her expression. "Yeah, I'm sorry about that."

Billie smiled. "Things are not as bad—"

"You're sorry about that?" Sherise asked. "You hear that the man your sister, whom you are supposed to love, is going to marry cheated on her and you're just sorry."

"Don't tell me how I should react," Erica said. "How I'm supposed to feel."

"So you don't love her?" Sherise asked, accusingly.

"Dammit!" Erica slammed a glass she'd just wrapped on the coffee table. "Sherise, I don't need this."

"You don't need this," Sherise said. "You don't need anything or anyone!"

"That's right!" Erica yelled at her. "Especially not you and your damn mouth."

Sherise smiled with an arched brow. "You get my mouth whether you want it or not. That's part of our deal."

"What deal?" Erica asked. "The one where you two dump on me every time I act in a way you don't like or didn't tell me to? Every time I assert myself or don't follow your lead? I don't want that deal. Not anymore."

"What do you want?" Billie asked. "We came here to ask you that, Erica."

Erica looked up at Billie and saw that familiar compassion that always softened her.

"I wanted to be there for you, Billie," she said. "I swear to God, I did. I've been thinking about you a lot and how you must feel. Especially after everything Porter did to you. It's just, I . . . I can't deal with it."

"You can't deal with Billie getting cheated on?" Sherise asked, not feeling a lot of sympathy coming from Erica. "It was about you?"

"No!" Erica snapped. "It was just . . . I can't keep explaining myself. Look, Billie, are you okay?"

"I don't think Michael cheated on me," Billie said. "I really think there's a chance we can get back together."

"What do you mean you don't think?" Erica asked. "What do you know?"

"So now you're full of questions," Sherise said.

"I know he didn't intend to cheat on me." Billie sighed. "Look, I don't want to get into that now."

"Why not?" Sherise asked. "Now is the perfect time, Billie. Erica is temporarily interested in someone other than herself."

Billie groaned as Erica and Sherise stared each other down.

"We came to apologize," Billie said. "Sherise and I."

"Apologize?" Erica was surprised.

"Well," Sherise mumbled. "Sort of. Meaning that I don't believe that we've treated you as badly as you claim we did."

"Sherise!" Billie chastised.

"But," Sherise continued, "if you feel like we have, then it's valid and we're sorry. No matter what, none of us wants to hurt each other or make anyone in our circle feel like they're less important than anyone else."

"I think it's possible we've treated you like the little sister because you're the youngest," Billie said. "You've taken that as us treating you like someone who can't take care of herself or make the right choices. It wasn't on purpose."

Erica didn't know what to say. She didn't at all expect an apology or whatever it was that Sherise was trying to say.

"It just seems like everything I say and do is always questioned," Erica said. "Judged as less than what either of you says or does."

"Really?" Sherise asked.

"You especially," Erica said.

"Well . . ." Sherise rolled her eyes. "I treat everyone like that, though. Not you in particular."

"We're sorry for that," Billie said.

Erica nodded in acceptance. "Okay, you were right earlier. I am moving. I bought a new condo and I'm moving in next week."

Billie pressed her lips together trying with everything to not speak out. She was livid that Erica didn't at least show her the mortgage contract or allow her to refer a trusted real estate lawyer. She knew several.

Erica could see this was killing Billie and it made her smile. She appreciated that Billie was trying. Billie smiled in response and suddenly, the two of them burst into laughter. For a few seconds, Erica felt so much stress and frustration wash away as she doubled over in laughter.

"What's so damn funny?" Sherise asked.

"It's killing her." Erica pointed at Billie.

Billie leaned back on her chair, her hand against her stomach. She hadn't laughed in a long time. "It is. It truly is."

"Well, excuse me if I don't find any of this funny." Sherise got up from the sofa and walked over to the kitchen. "Where's the wine?"

"I know what you want to know," Erica said. "What neighborhood? What building? How much? Did you haggle down?"

"We want to know because we care." Sherise finally found the wine and brought it back to the girls. "Not because we look down on you."

She reached for one of the glasses that Erica had lined up on the table, but Erica blocked her.

"I'm packing these," she said.

"Fine." Sherise screwed off the top and drank straight from the bottle.

"Why are you packing alone?" Billie asked.

"Well, I couldn't very well ask you two," Erica answered.

"What about Nate?" Sherise asked.

Erica just shook her head.

"What?" Sherise asked again.

"We're not . . . talking right now," Erica said.

"What about Corey?" Billie asked. "Are you two still seeing each other?"

"Yeah," Sherise added. "What is the deal with him? When do we meet him?"

Erica was embarrassed now. "It doesn't matter."

Billie noticed the change in her expression. "When you say it doesn't matter like that, it means it matters. You see, we do know you."

Erica stopped wrapping the glass in her hand. "We're not talking right now either."

Sherise put the wine bottle down. "What happened?"

"It's just a . . ." Erica placed the glass on the table. She didn't want to, but she started crying right away.

She tried to wipe the tears from her face, but it was too late. Both Billie and Sherise rushed over to her, sitting on the floor beside her, and wrapped their arms around her. Erica let herself give into a rare show of deep emotion as she rested her head on Billie's shoulder and gripped Sherise's hand.

"I wish I had my phone," Sherise said. "I want to get a picture of Erica, the tough girl, crying."

"Stop it." Erica nudged her with her elbow. "It's not funny."

"I'm just doing what I do," Sherise said, with a smile.

"Tell us, sweetie," Billie urged her. "What's wrong?"

"He dumped me!" Erica finally admitted. "Corey dumped me! Nate betrayed me! I have no one."

"You have us," Sherise said. "You always have us."

"I don't know why this is happening to me," Erica exclaimed.

"I think you do, baby," Billie said.

"You're going to go on about Jonah again, aren't you?" Erica asked.

"I won't if you don't want to hear it," Billie answered.

"Since when did we care what any of us wanted to hear?" Sherise asked. "Of course it's Jonah. You're grasping for distractions to avoid dealing with your pain."

Erica rolled her eyes. "Just stop."

"It won't stop," Billie said. "It will only get worse unless you stop it."

Erica wrenched free of their grip and stood up, taking a step back. "If you guys are gonna go on about this, you can just leave. Just go."

"No," Sherise said adamantly as she stood up.

"We won't leave," Billie added, standing up too. "We will never leave no matter what."

"You always have us," Sherise said. "Whether you want us or not. But you'll lose everything else if you stay on this path. I'll have Justin and Cady and Aiden. Billie will have Tara and, well fuck, who knows what's going on with her and Michael. But you'll have no one."

"But us," Billie said. "Is that enough?"

When Maurice walked into his office that morning, his expression quickly changed from surprise to anger at the sight of Sherise sitting at his desk.

"What are you doing?" he asked, rushing over to the desk and placing his briefcase on top of it.

"Careful," Sherise warned. "You'll knock this box over, and it's full of your more delicate stuff."

Maurice looked in the box and then around the office. Seeing Sherise at his desk had kept him from noticing what the real deal was. Most of his office had already been packed in boxes.

"I helped you out a bit," Sherise said. "Gave you a little head start on getting out of here."

He pointed at her angrily. "Sherise, you're fucking with me again. I thought you understood that I wasn't going to put up with this shit anymore."

"You won't have to," she said. "You're going to offer Jerry your resignation letter today and get the fuck out of here."

"You're the one who's—" Maurice stopped mid-sentence as he saw Sherise turn the tablet that was in her lap around so he could see it.

The first picture was of him with the young prostitute laughing on the bed. She was fully naked. He was only half so. Sherise slid her fingers across the screen. The second picture was of him snorting coke off her small breasts. The third was of his mounting her from behind, grabbing on to her blond hair.

"What the fuck is this?" Maurice reached for the tablet, but Sherise held it away.

"Snorting coke is so eighties," she said. "But I hear it's coming back. Now this is more modern day."

She slid the screen, showing him the next picture of him dropping an ecstasy pill in a glass of a brown substance while he licked her neck.

"How did you get those?" he asked, agitated. "You were . . . spying on me?"

"You're a creature of habit," Sherise said. "Which is surprising considering you're such a lover of blackmail. You know habits make it sooo easy . . ."

"You've gone too far this time," Maurice warned.

"No, sweetie pie. You went too far this time." She slid to a picture of the prostitute. "Her name is Dana, by the way. Did you bother to ask? She probably told you her name was Kitty. Which is appropriate."

"Why do you say that?" he asked.

"Because she's just a little kitten," Sherise answered. "You see, Dana is unfortunately not the age she claims to be."

Sherise smiled as she saw Maurice's eyes widen. No, of course Dana wasn't really under-aged. Even as desperate as she was, Sherise would have never been a part of something that disgusting. But she wasn't above letting Maurice think he had.

"She's only fifteen," Sherise said. "One year under the legal age in D.C. So you've moved up, Maurice. Usually, when you pick up your H Street whores, you're only breaking one law. You broke two laws last night."

"She was . . ." Maurice was shaking his head. "Bullshit."

"So," Sherise surmised, "while you might not go to jail over law one, you'll definitely do some time for law two."

"I won't," Maurice said confidently. "I have connections that—"

"No one is going to touch this," Sherise asserted. "And no one is going to touch you when they hear of this."

"But no one is going to hear of this," Maurice said. "Jerry won't let this get out. You have no idea what you're dealing with."

"You said that to me before," Sherise began, "and it was true then. But not anymore. I know everything now, Maurice, and you should be ashamed of yourself."

"I don't believe in shame," he answered.

"You blackmailed Jerry over exposing Stephen's DUI hit-and-run to get this job." Sherise said it all as if it was a boring aside, but relished the look on Maurice's face.

"Jerry told you?"

She shook her head. "Stephen told me. How else do you think I found out about your whore habit? You weren't at that jail helping out a friend. You were arrested picking up . . . Diamond."

Maurice cleared his throat and gathered himself together for a moment. He looked at the ground and shook his head. When he looked up again, he eyed Sherise with contempt.

"If you know everything, then you know that I can't be fired."

"Why would you think that?" she asked. "You've got nothing to back you up. There are no records of Stephen ever being arrested or in the hospital. You made sure of that."

He laughed as if amused by her naïveté. "But I know they—"

"You know they existed?" she finished for him. "How well will that be taken from a statutory rapist with no evidence?"

"It won't just be me," Maurice claimed. "I have a high-ranking police department contact and the chief of staff at Vision Hospital to back me up. They're the ones who helped me get rid of the evidence. They're friends of mine and—"

"Not anymore," Sherise said. "Nathan O'Brien, the D.C. chief of police, has been tapped by Jerry to be deputy secretary at Homeland Security and former COS of Vision Hospital Joshua Bush as the new deputy sec of the Department of Health and Human Services. They're on his side now."

Maurice swallowed hard.

Sherise stood up looking him intently in the eye. "They don't even recall your name anymore."

Through gritted teeth, he said, "I can make things an awful mess for all of you."

Sherise just shook her head. "Do you have any idea all of the horrible things Jerry could have done to you when you first blackmailed him? He didn't use his immense power because he didn't want to make things worse. But now that he knows he can use them to make things better, I'll make sure he does."

"Jerry won't play dirty," Maurice assured her. "That's his weakness."

"No," Sherise corrected. "Stephen is his weakness, but Stephen is safe now and I promise you I will make sure that he plays as dirty as he has to if you make any trouble for him."

Maurice opened his mouth and pointed his finger at Sherise as if he wanted to pull his ace card, but quickly realized he didn't have one.

"It's over," she said, placing both hands on her hips and smiling wryly. "You need to save all that energy for figuring out what to do next. We can make this easy for you or hard. Your choice."

When Billie stepped inside Belga Café in the Barracks Row neighborhood, her heart felt like it was beating a thousand times a minute. She looked around and saw Michael sitting at a table in the back against the dark red wall looking . . . well, looking awful. Pain shot through every single inch of her at the sight of him.

This was the first time she'd seen him since their encounter outside her office building where she'd left him doubting that she ever loved him at all. Since her realization that he might have been telling the truth and Dee Dee's confession, Billie had come to terms with how much worse she had made an awful situation.

After she'd walked away from him, Michael stopped calling her. It had only been a couple of days, but Billie had gotten the distinct feeling he'd given up. After being in the apartment and remembering more clearly what she'd seen, or more importantly, what she hadn't seen, Billie knew she needed to talk to Michael. Then Dee Dee's surprise appearance and confession that Darina had been planning to seduce Michael all along made the situation more urgent.

When she called Michael asking if they could get together and talk, he didn't pick up. She left a message, but he didn't call her back until two days later. It felt like two weeks and as every hour passed, Billie was certain that her refusal to give Michael even a chance had ruined any chance for them to clear the air, let alone fix this problem.

She'd missed his call and had played his message agreeing to meet her at Belga Café today over and over again. It was emotionless, almost conciliatory. Billie wasn't hopeful, but allowed herself to be distracted by dealing with Erica for one day.

He looked up and saw her when she was halfway to the table. Billie didn't know what to do. Without thinking, she smiled at him, although noting that he looked miserable. Was that a good sign or a bad sign? Was he miserable without her and eager to be with her again? Was he miserable at the thought of having to talk to her after their last ugly encounter?

Michael didn't smile back. He sort of looked to the side and then back down. Billie felt her heart thud, having hoped he at least would pretend to be happy to see her. When she reached the table, he stood up because he was a gentleman.

It was terribly awkward standing only a foot or so away from the man she had intended to spend the rest of her life with and not being able to touch him. Or could she? No, it wasn't the right time.

"Hi, Michael," she said softly.

"Hi." He sat down as she sat down.

They looked at each other, their eyes focused, but not connecting. Billie was scared to death. She wanted to know the truth, but she wanted to be smart and not let her heart tell her mind what was real.

"Thank you for meeting with me," she said, her voice cracking a bit.

"This isn't what I wanted," Michael finally said. "I was hoping you would agree to see me for me."

"That's why I'm here," she said.

He shook his head. "You're here because my mother told you what she and Darina planned for me."

"Michael, please . . ."

"No, Billie." He held up his hand to stop her. "Please excuse me if I'm not happy about that. I just found out that my own mother plotted to destroy my relationship with the woman I loved out of selfishness and greed. That was bad enough."

"I'm so sorry, but . . ."

"But to find out that you're only willing to talk to me after she talked to you . . . I have to say that hurts even more."

"But you're wrong, Michael. That's not the case." She tried to hold his gaze, knowing that he was reluctant. "I mean, yes, having her confess to what she did made a difference, but I was already doubting before that."

He shook his head as if he didn't believe her. "The last time I saw you, your mind was made up. You didn't want to hear a damn thing I wanted to say."

"I was wrong," she admitted. "But, Michael, you have to cut me some slack."

"Do I?" he asked. "You didn't cut me any."

Billie was concerned by the change in his expression. He'd seemed nervous in the beginning, but now he was just angry.

"Michael, I believed you'd been unfaithful to me. You know what I've been through."

"So I'm supposed to accept that I have to pay for the sins of the man before me?"

"This was about what you did to me," she said. "I mean, what I was certain you'd done to me, not Porter. But yes, I was using my prior experience. It was to protect myself."

"Protect yourself," he repeated her, shaking his head. "From me. Never thought I'd hear that."

"Neither did I." She lowered her head, looking at the table.

The waitress approached them, but Michael waved her off.

"I've tried," Michael said. "I've tried to understand what you must have been going through. Exactly what Darina wanted you to. Exactly what my mother wanted you to."

Billie was overcome with compassion for him as she watched the pain on his face as he mentioned Dee Dee. She wanted to reach across the table and touch him, comfort him. She had to stay focused.

"But even with all of that," Michael continued. "For you to just cut me out of your life without even a chance, a word. You can't imagine how much that hurt me."

"Please don't say you thought I loved you more than that," Billie pleaded.

"Then what do you want me to say?" he asked. "Billie, I begged. I pleaded with you. Everything that we had, everything that we were, and you still didn't even allow me a chance to talk to you."

"It's because of everything we had and everything we were," she explained. "It's because I love you so much that I couldn't bear to hear you out. I was wrong to use Porter against you, but all I could think of was how I allowed my heart to make a fool of me. So much pain and so much time lost. I couldn't bear it again."

"So you were willing to just give up on us?" he asked. "Instead of risking a chance that it wasn't what you thought."

"Be honest, Michael. You know what I saw. That, plus the buildup of everything Darina had been doing and my history. All of it made me jump to a conclusion."

He shook his head as if he didn't want to agree, but couldn't resist doing so.

Billie saw him place his hand on the table and she didn't waste a second. She reached out and grabbed it with her own, squeezing tight. He looked at the action and then looked up at her.

"Now I'm begging," she said. "I'm begging that you believe

me. I know I have a lot of nerve because I didn't give you the same courtesy, but I swear to God, Michael, I was going to reach out to you before Dee Dee came over."

"Billie, you said—"

"I went home," she continued. "I went back to our home and it came rushing back to me. Everything was so suspicious. I couldn't see it the first time because of the shock, but I saw it then. I was going to reach out to you. Then Dee Dee came and . . ."

"So you believed me?" he asked. "You believed me when I said I didn't cheat."

"I believed you when you said you would never purposefully do that to me. I know she set this up. I was just so angry."

"I made it easy," he said. He placed his free hand on top of hers. "I'm guilty of that."

"You wanted to believe that she was being honest for Duncan's sake."

"Even at the end," he said. "When she came over with the paternity test. She was supposed to have been on a plane, but there she was trying to get cozy with a bottle of wine and a joint. It was how we used to celebrate big things. I just ignored it."

Billie shook her head. "She took advantage of the extreme emotional vulnerability you had, just learning that Duncan was really yours."

Michael slammed his fist on the table, garnering a few stares. Billie could see that he was still so angry over this. He had every right to be. Even more so than her.

"My abandoning you only made things worse," she said. "Michael, I'm so sorry."

"I'm sorry too," he said. "You warned me. But, Billie, it's most important that you know I didn't sleep with her. I know that now that I've spoken to her."

"You finally got in touch with her?" Billie asked.

He nodded. "I threatened her with everything I had. I threatened to take Duncan away from her. I have rights. She kept him from me. If she's arrested for drugging me, I have a very good chance of getting him away."

"That must have scared the shit out of her," Billie said.

"It did," he said, disgusted. "The only reason I haven't already is because of Duncan."

"He's already been thrown for a loop," Billie said. "As much as I wish all legal hell would rain down on her, he would suffer the most."

He looked at Billie, his hand squeezing tighter. "I was thinking about . . . I mean, what if I did that? Would you . . ."

"Oh my God, yes," Billie quickly proclaimed. "I would support you in every way I could. Emotionally, financially, and legally. I would move to Atlanta if you needed to in order to make this work. Michael, I love you with all my heart and I would stand by my husband. Whatever you—"

"Your husband?" he asked, his eyes widening. "Are you saying that you still want us to get married?"

"I do," she answered, without hesitation. "If you still want to marry me."

He laughed. "Do you really need to ask me that?"

"I abandoned you when we were tested," she said. "So yes, I do."

"It was a pretty big fucking test," Michael stated. "I think I can give you this one free pass. We both made some very big mistakes here."

"We'll make more," Billie said. "All I know is that I'll handle it better next time. I promise."

"I'll do a better job of listening to you next time," he promised.

Billie got up from her chair and came around the table, still holding his hand. She sat down on his lap and touched his cheek with her free hand. Neither of them cared that people were starting to look at them. Just being this close to him, touching him like this, washed away so much pain, suffering, anxiety, and fear.

When their lips touched, Billie felt so much pain and anguish wash away. She felt comforted and refreshed. His lips, so tender and pleading, brought her love and forgiveness. The warmth and ease with which her body responded quelled her fears.

When they separated, Billie looked down at him and smiled. "You know we're going to have to be on top of our game every day if we're dealing with Darina."

"We've got her number," Michael said. "This craziness she just pulled will always be in our back pocket if she ever gets out of hand. She won't have Mom on her side anymore. We can handle her."

"Together," Billie said, "We can handle anything."

Arlington Cemetery, located in Arlington, Virginia, sits along the Potomac River, near the Lincoln Memorial. More than 400,000 people are buried at the cemetery, mostly war veterans, but also nurses, spouses of decorated veterans, and prominent civilians.

The only time Erica had been there was with her mother when she was a young girl to visit the graves of President John F. Kennedy and civil rights activist Medgar Evers. Her mother had impressed upon her the sacrifice that the men and women buried there had made, but all Erica could remember was the morbid feeling of seeing so many white headstones.

It was her mother's words that helped Erica make her way through the massive cemetery to the place she needed to be. She had to remind herself that although Jonah Nolan had been an awful person in a lot of ways, he had served his country in two Gulf Wars.

She'd intended to come here anyway. After being with the girls, Erica knew they were right. Things were a mess and they were only going to get worse until she made peace with the man who made her.

"Finally," she said as she approached the headstone.

It wasn't elaborate at all. As opposed to the private section in the cemetery where families paid to have their loved ones buried, Jonah was buried in the public section, per his request in his will. Here, all graves had simple white marble headstones.

It was a Saturday and there were a lot of people in the cemetery. Erica saw them gather at headstones, many of them crying, touching the headstone, or taking a picture of it. Some were sitting next to the headstone, talking to it or offering it flowers. Erica wasn't doing any of that.

The headstone had his name, his title in the Air Force, and the dates of his life. Lastly, it noted LOVING HUSBAND AND FATHER.

Erica laughed quickly. "If they only knew."

She looked around, noticing that no one was near enough to her to hear what she had to say, so she decided to speak to him out loud.

"So, I'm here," she said. "I'm here to tell you that I pretty much hated you and everything about you. But you're dead now, so there's no point to that."

She took a deep breath, preparing to hear her own feelings. "All my life I wished that my father wanted me and loved me. But he didn't, so I got over it. Then I found out that he wasn't my father. That you were, and there was a part of me that thought maybe I could have a father who wanted me and loved me."

Erica felt the emotion that she wanted to fight off taking over and swallowed hard. "That's what I wanted. For you to be so happy you found me and want to make up for all those years we'd missed with each other. When I realized all you wanted was a secret daughter, I downplayed how much it hurt me."

She wiped a single tear from her right cheek. "I consoled myself with your attempts to have me in your life and the little bits of affection you showed as your way of loving me. But you didn't love me, not really."

Erica tried to compose herself as two elderly women walked by her, both carrying flowers in their hands. She waited as they got far enough away not to hear her.

"I wanted real love. I didn't get it, and no amount of money can make up for that. I was jealous of your daughter, who I thought you loved too, but now I doubt you loved her either.

"I wanted to make you pay for not wanting to be a real father to me with every purchase I made, but it only made me angrier because I knew it was all for nothing. But I didn't want to face up to that, so I blamed everyone else for why I was so unhappy and so constantly unsatisfied."

Erica caught her breath for a moment and stood still as if she was waiting for him to respond . . . to feel a response from him. There was nothing.

"Of course you have nothing to say," she continued. "Dead or alive, you're just not that person. I understand that now. You're not the person who can love and care and think about anyone above themselves. I don't think you've ever loved anyone in a real way."

She reached out and touched the top of the headstone. "But you did what you could. You loved as much as you were capable of. It wasn't enough and it wasn't the right kind, but it's okay. I let myself believe that your love was what I needed to be happy, but it's not.

"I was happy before I met you because I had, I still have, the love of my girls, my brother. I have friends and hopefully I have a boyfriend. If not him, I'll have one someday. But I really want it to be him."

She sighed heavily. "My point is I forgive you. I forgive you for not loving me and not doing right by me when you found out who I was. I don't hate you anymore. I can't afford it and I don't want to."

Erica slowly let her hand slip from the curved edge of the top of the tombstone. "I won't be coming back. I'm letting you go because every memory I have of you only reminds me of how it wasn't enough. So this is good-bye, Dad. Maybe in the next life, we can be a real father and daughter."

"Baby." Justin sat back in his chair at the head of the dining room table and placed his hand on his full belly. "That was the best Christmas dinner, ever."

At the other end of the table, Sherise was pleased. She had put a lot into it. After all, it was a special Christmas. She had decided to skip the traditional ham and go instead with a prime rib and lobster combo with a side of Brussels sprouts sautéed in garlic and bacon. Billie's homemade bread, her mother's recipe, was the perfect added touch. They were all so full, but made room for Erica's peach cobbler and vanilla ice cream. Everyone was about to burst.

Looking around the table, Sherise was extremely pleased to see everyone full and happy. Some of them, particularly Erica's boyfriend, Corey, looked like they were about to pass out. That meant it was a good meal.

She smiled proudly. "I thought a surf-and-turf Christmas would be something new for a change."

"This was amazing," Michael said. He leaned to his right, his arm around the back of Billie's chair, and kissed her on the cheek. "Especially the bread."

Billie smiled and rubbed her face against his arm, loving the smell of him. Their eyes connected and Billie saw something in them that she had feared she would never see again; complete devotion. It warmed her through her soul.

"Well," Sherise said. "We three girls spent the whole day

cooking while you boys watched basketball. It's time to clear the table. Guess who gets to do that?"

Justin groaned as he stood up. "Okay, boys, let's get to it."

"Hey!" Nate put his fork down, looking around. "Since when do the guys have to—"

"Watch it," Corey quickly warned. "You're about to say something you'll regret."

"Ice cream!" Cady, sitting to the right of her father, yelled out as she waved her spoon in the air. Her face was covered in peach juice and ice cream.

Everyone laughed and the tiny little girl couldn't have been more thrilled.

"It's a new tradition," Erica told her brother, who was sitting to her left. "Deal with it."

The women watched, their bellies full, as the men got up and started clearing the table.

As Corey grabbed her plate, Erica looked up at him and winked. He bent down.

"Did I do okay?" he asked with a whisper.

"You did great," she answered and kissed him on the lips.

With all the men gone, Sherise and Billie focused on Erica. She smiled, shaking her head. This was the first time they'd met him, and with all the fuss getting the meal together, they hadn't really had any time to talk about it.

"Go ahead," Erica encouraged. "Give it to me."

"I like him," Billie said. "He's . . ."

"He's a fit for you," Sherise added.

"What is that supposed to mean?" Erica asked, suspiciously.

"Don't get defensive," Sherise warned. "I mean he looks like he can handle you. You're nuts, and you need a certain type of man who can put up with that."

Erica turned to Billie. "Was that a compliment?"

Billie laughed and nodded. "As much as can be expected."

Erica sighed. "I'm just happy he's here."

"Come on." Sherise stood up, gripping a sleeping Aiden, who had been sitting on her lap, tightly. "Of course he'd take you back."

"I wasn't so sure about that," Erica said. "I . . ."

She quieted quickly as Justin and Michael rushed back into the room to grab some more plates.

"Let's go into the den," Sherise instructed. "I'm sure there's a game on we can be watching."

"Rub it in," Justin said.

The women laughed as they made their way to the den, Sherise carrying Aiden and Erica holding on to Cady. Inside, the television was still on and they all sat on the sofa, letting the babies play on the floor.

"It wasn't pretty," Erica said. "I basically begged. My ego took a bruising."

"Well deserved," Billie said. "Don't you think?"

Erica nodded. Billie was right. She'd been a mess and had sent so many mixed signals to Corey, it was no surprise that he didn't want to hear her apology at first. Erica didn't give up. She cared about Corey and really believed she had a future with him, now that things were much clearer. She wasn't willing to let it go and wore him down.

Unlike in the past, Erica had said nothing. She just listened to what Corey had to say, what had confused him, angered him, and worried him. When he was done, she tried to explain herself, which wasn't easy because she was still trying to figure it all out.

"Eventually," she continued, "he came around and offered to give me one last chance. I have a lot of hope. I'm glad you two like him."

"You'd still be with him if we didn't," Sherise said.

Erica nodded. "Well, I really like him."

"I can see that he really likes you," Billie said. "Everything is gonna be fine. He's forgiven you."

"And you two have too?" she asked, sheepishly.

Billie reached over and placed her hand on Erica's knee. "There is no need for forgiveness with family."

Erica smiled. "I'm keeping the condo, though. No matter what!"

"It was actually a good deal," Billie said. "After looking at everything. You did good."

"Of course I did," Erica said. "Told you I would. I wrote the check to the hospital too. Delivering it tomorrow."

After leaving Jonah's grave, Erica had an epiphany, an idea that seemed so clear and right to her. Of the money she had left, she was going to put half of it away for investment and retirement savings. The other half, some she was keeping, but most she was donating to the hospital where her mother had worked her entire life. The hospital where she was treated with love and care by her former coworkers when she'd gotten sick.

"You're lucky Justin took you back," Sherise reminded.

"I know," Erica said. "If he . . . Oh, look you're on TV."

All three women turned to the television as the newsbreak had a picture of Sherise. The newscaster noted the shake-up in the incoming Northman administration, with Sherise Robinson as press secretary, replacing Maurice Blair, who had declined the position.

"You really expect us to believe that he wanted to return to the DGA?" Billie asked. "What did he say? There were too many Democrat governors in difficult races in the next couple of years and he felt he had to go back to help them?"

Sherise shrugged. "He's right. Jerry himself said that he was willing to make the sacrifice considering how important the DGA would be over the next couple of years."

"Bullshit," Erica said. "You made this happen. You're really not gonna tell us?"

"It's not one of our secrets," Sherise said regretfully. "This shit involves the president–elect. It would be like Billie, a lawyer, divulging a secret of one of her clients."

She couldn't tell them that Stephen was in a secret rehab and that Jerry had offered cabinet posts to two people in exchange for their loyalty and secrecy. It wasn't the greatest start to get off to, but Sherise was back where she needed to be. She was in one of the most powerful positions in American politics and life felt under control again.

"So what if after the elections, he wants back in?" Billie asked.

"He won't," Sherise assured her. "Trust me."

"You're not worried?" Erica asked.

Sherise shook her head. "I'm going to be too busy to be worried about that loser."

"Not too busy, I hope," Billie said.

"Why?" Sherise asked.

Billie smiled excitedly. "We set a date! We're getting married in six months!"

Both Sherise and Erica screamed and reached out, hugging Billie tightly. Cady and Aiden were staring at them both, confused as to what this sudden delight was about.

"Why so early?" Sherise gasped. "Oh my God, are you . . ."

"No," Billie said. "I'm not pregnant. But we didn't want to wait any longer than we had to. We want to start our marriage, our family, and our lives as soon as possible."

"Here in D.C., right?" Erica asked.

"Right here in D.C.," Billie assured her.

They had discussed it all over the past week and decided against moving to Atlanta. There was still a relationship with his mother that Michael had to work on repairing, and his plans for being a major part of Duncan's life, but for now, Michael was the one who suggested their life together, their future together belonged in D.C.

"I thought the three of us were going to be split apart for a while," Billie said. "I thought we were going to break."

"No," Sherise assured her. "Nothing and no one can break our bond. Ever."

With all of the craziness that had and would forever surround their lives, this was the one thing that all three knew to be true.

POWER, SEDUCTION & SCANDAL

Angela Winters

About this Guide

The suggested questions that follow are included
to enhance your group's reading of this book.

DISCUSSION QUESTIONS

1. Was Sherise justified in her initial attempts to undermine Maurice Blair (before you knew what he'd done)? Was she entitled to that position or should she have put the administration first and waited her turn?

2. Was Billie wrong to want to resist moving to Atlanta, in the beginning, for the sake of her friends? She was clearly reluctant to leave Sherise, Erica, and Tara and openly showed that to Michael. Should she have only thought of Michael and their marriage/future? Or was Michael wrong in springing this on her, especially knowing how his family treated Billie?

3. What did you think of Erica's reaction to Jonah's death? Was it believable that she would be so affected by the death of a man who she only knew a few years and disliked most of that time?

4. Sherise's final plan could have jeopardized Northman's incoming administration. Did she have a right to risk it all for others, not just herself?

5. Billie was eventually proven right about Darina, but in the beginning, was she justified in being so suspicious and distrustful without proof? Was she being selfish about wanting to keep Michael from Duncan before the blood tests came back?

6. Erica was clearly hurting, but did she have a point about Sherise and Billie always treating her like a child or charity case? Based on the previous three novels in this series, is there truth to this?

7. What did you think of Billie's initial reaction to finding Michael "in bed" with Darina? Was she justified, or should she have calmed down and tried to figure it out more?

8. Was Erica's spending spree really as bad as Sherise, Billie and Corey made it seem? Was she really shopping through her pain, or was she a woman who, for once in her life, was able to live it up and get things she'd always wanted?

9. Was Billie justified in using her history with Porter in her initial decision to ignore Michael and not give him a chance to "sweet talk" his way out of this? Can someone just ignore that they were hurt before in such a situation?

10. Should Michael have accepted Billie back as easily as he did? Should he have made it harder for her considering her initial lack of trust in him?

11. At the end of the book, Sherise and Justin were stronger than ever, Michael and Billie were back on their path to marriage, and Erica had Corey, who had forgiven her for the way she treated him. Do you think all three of these ladies will have a happy romantic ending? Who do you think has the best chance at forever: Sherise, Billie or Erica?

Don't miss Grace Octavia's latest book in the
Southern Scandal series,

His Last Wife

On sale now!

1

"**P**ut more of that cheese on my plate." This directive murmur that edged on the possibility of a growl came from the cigarette-blackened lips of a woman in an orange jail jumpsuit, whose stereotypical back-braided cornrows and decidedly mean mug announced that not only had she been incarcerated for a very long time, but that this was likely not her first incarceration and it wouldn't be her last.

Six feet tall with a wide back and muscular arms, she was standing toward the middle of a rowdy line at a metal food-service counter in the gray-walled cafeteria at the Fulton County Jail. All around was a mess of loud, trash-talking female inmates in various stages of eating dinner and wide-eyed guards with their hands on their guns.

"I can't do that!" This uneasy response that was dipped in fear came from the Vaseline-coated lips of a woman whose orange jumpsuit was hidden beneath a white apron. However, this inmate's stylish two-strand twists that only had three inches of gray at the roots made it clear that not only had she just gotten to jail, but also that she didn't plan on staying and still wasn't clear about how life had led her to that place. Indeed, like half of the women in the jail, Kerry Ann Jackson had maintained that she was no criminal. But that didn't stop officers from putting her in handcuffs and placing her behind bars for allegedly tossing her ex-husband off the roof of a downtown Atlanta skyscraper.

"You better put more of that cheese on my plate, bitch!" The murmur coming from the black lips was definitely now a growl.

"But I already gave you the serving. One scoop. That's it," Kerry tried to rationalize, pointing to the soggy pasta shells on the growler's plate. Kerry was standing behind the service counter, holding a one-cup serving spoon over the pan of pasta shells and processed cheese that was supposed to be macaroni and cheese. The kitchen manager had given her one instruction: "One serving spoon per inmate. You fuck that up and you're back on the toilets."

"You think I'm simple, bitch? I know what the fucking serving is, but ain't no cheese on mine." She slammed the tray on the counter in a way that made the soggy noodles shake in the soupy yellow cheese sauce on her plate, and all eyes to the front and back of the line looked over at the spectacle. Guards chatting nearby craned their necks to get a look.

Kerry was ready to disappear. If the pan of artificial macaroni-and-cheese surprise was big enough, she would've jumped right in and swam to the bottom to escape. Drowned herself in the yellow paste just to avoid what could happen next. And it could be anything. Anything. She'd been in holding at the jail for three months and in that time she'd seen women spat on for less. One woman got stabbed in her right tit for chatting up one of the female guards who'd been sleeping with another inmate.

"Problem, Ms. Thompson?" a youngish white male guard with tattoos up both arms posed, approaching the confrontation from the back of the line.

Cornrows looked at him through the corner of her eye and spat, "Nah—none at all."

The guard looked at Kerry. "You okay?" he asked rather politely. He'd been working at the jail for over five years and in that time he'd seen Thompson and her cornrows come and go and stir up trouble in the jail each time. Kerry was new to him.

"I'm fine," Kerry lied nervously.

"Move it along then, Thompson." The guard nudged Thompson in the back with his index finger.

After taking two steps, she looked back at Kerry and mouthed, "*You mine.*"

Fear shot through Kerry's veins like electricity and she would've tried to run right out of that cafeteria had it not been for a whisper in her ear from the inmate serving green beans beside her.

"Girl, don't mind Thompson. She all talk. She'll set shit off, but if you buck up at her, she'll back off," she said, dumping green beans onto another inmate's plate. She was Angelina Garcia-Bell, a Latina with a short black buzz cut and beautiful long eyelashes that looked out of place on her mannish face. She was one of the two friends Kerry had made since she'd been locked up—the other was the inmate who'd gotten stabbed in the tit. "I told you that you can't let these chicks see you all scared. Bitches feed on that shit in here."

"How am I supposed to seem like I'm not scared when I *am* scared?" Kerry whispered, watching Thompson continue to peek back at her as the guard forced her down the line. "I'll just be glad when this is all over and I can get away from these people. When I can go home. See my family—my little boy."

"Won't we all be glad when that day comes?" Garcia-Bell agreed, scooping out another serving of green beans. "Won't we all?"

Most evenings after dinner, Kerry didn't go into the recreational common area to watch soap opera reruns on the outdated projection television with the other inmates. Instead, she'd head to the library, pick up a book, and sit at one of the tables in the back of the room where volunteers taught GED prep classes. There, she could read and think and pretend none of this was happening to her.

But Kerry didn't do that after the incident in the cafeteria with the macaroni and cheese. To avoid a confrontation with Thompson, she went straight to her cell and climbed into her bunk, vowing to stay there until the lights went out and later the sun came up. Maybe tomorrow would be different. Maybe Thompson would've forgotten their spat in the cafeteria. Maybe Kerry would wake up and be away from this place altogether. Tomorrow, she'd be sitting on the back deck of the Tudor off Cascade drinking margaritas with Marcy. Tomorrow, she'd be driving up I-85 in the old Range Rover with the windows down and the air-conditioning on. Music blasting, open road in front of her. Going to wherever she wanted. Tomorrow, she'd see Tyrian. Jamison. Home.

Kerry laid back in her bottom bunk and looked up at the picture she'd tucked into the spring beneath the top mattress. Two faces smiled down at her. A man and a boy with the same brown skin, dark eyes, and pug noses. They were standing beside a large wooden sign that read CHARLIE YATES GOLF COURSE AT EAST LAKE. The boy, who was a little taller than the man's waist, held a golf club in his hand. The man's right arm was draped around the boy. Both looked proud.

A tear left Kerry's eye and rolled back toward the pillow beneath her head. She closed her eyes tightly and tried to go back to the day she'd taken that photo. It was Tyrian's first golf demonstration, about nine months earlier. She and Jamison were already divorced by then, but that day was peaceful. Agreeable. Tyrian woke up that morning so nervous, anxious, and excited that he wouldn't stop asking his mother questions.

"What if I lose? What if it rains? What if it snows? What if I faint? What if my coach faints? What if no one comes? What if too many people come?" he listed so intensely Kerry wondered how a six-year-old could come up with so many worries. But he'd always been very smart. Advanced. Precocious. Like his father.

"And what if everything is perfect? Just perfect?" she'd said, placing his clothes on his bed. "Have you thought about that, my little worrywart? What if everything is wonderful and everyone has a great time?"

Climbing from beneath his bedsheets, Tyrian looked off to consider this like he was much older and wiser. "Okay," he said after a long pause. "It could be perfect. You're right, Mama."

Kerry winked at Tyrian, kissed his cheek, and said, "I'm always right."

And she was right. While her ex-husband was usually late to Tyrian's practices at the golf course and had gotten into the habit of using his recent victory in a tight race for mayor of Atlanta as an excuse to be absent to most of Tyrian's scheduled events, he was waiting outside the golf course, right by the sign, when Kerry and Tyrian arrived. Sitting in the backseat of his mother's truck, Tyrian squealed with the delight of a six-year-old son when he saw his father standing beside the sign.

"Daddy's here! Daddy's here already! He really came!" Tyrian cheered, tearing off his booster-seat seat belt before his mother could pull into her parking space and turn off the engine.

She was about to tell him to wait for her before he hopped out of the truck and bolted right to the person who'd become his favorite as of late—but she decided to let it slide that morning. All of the other little golfers unloading from their parents' cars had both mother and father in tow. She knew Tyrian wanted that too—for his parents to be together like everyone else's. And at that moment, he was just ecstatic that his life would look like all of the other kids' lives that day.

"My big boy!" Jamison said, gathering his son into his arms. "Man, you're getting heavy. I'm not going to be able to pick you up much longer!" Jamison laughed. The phone in his pocket was already vibrating with other things he needed to do, but he didn't reach for it. He promised himself he wouldn't. Today was about Tyrian.

"Hi." Kerry's greeting was flat and uninspired when she walked up carrying the golf bag Tyrian had left behind for her to caddy.

Jamison looked over at his first wife. "Good morning," he offered, smiling civilly.

"Good morning," she added to her greeting.

A few parents walked past with their little golfers straggling behind, waving at Tyrian. The whole time, just seconds really— but to the exes it felt much longer—Jamison and Kerry eyed each other for signs of anything new. Kerry had recently cut off her long, black permed hair and was wearing a short, natural do that Jamison thought made her look younger and thinner. Maybe she'd lost weight too. Jamison was wearing a new, expensive watch. He had the collar on his old gold fraternity golf shirt popped up to hide a hickey on his neck, but even with the carefully planned disguise and brown skin, and two feet of distance, his first wife could see it.

"Think we need to get to the clubhouse. I'm sure they're starting the demonstration on time," Kerry said drily.

"Of course. Of course," Jamison agreed and then added, "Hey, can you take a picture of Tyrian and me?" He pulled his phone from his pocket and stretched to hand it to Kerry.

"Guess so," she said, taking the phone.

"Cool!" Tyrian cheered, standing beside his dad.

The three organized the perfect photo shot in front of the

club sign and just before Kerry was about to take the picture, Jamison added one of Tyrian's golf clubs from his bag.

Kerry held up the phone and took a few shots. In the background, a new spring had the grass emerald green.

Once all were satisfied that the moment had been captured, Kerry was about to hand Jamison the phone when it rang and a familiar name came up on the screen: Val—Jamison's sultry assistant, who was making it pretty clear she was sleeping with her boss.

"Here," Kerry said, rushing to return the phone to Jamison.

"Wait, Mama! You get in the picture!" Tyrian posed with a big smile. He was becoming quite the diplomat. "We can take one with all of us."

Kerry and Jamison looked at each other like they were heads of nations always on the brink of war. The phone was still ringing with Val's name on the screen.

"Oh, we can't do that," Kerry said, handing the phone to Jamison. "There's no one to take the picture."

"I'll take it!" A fourth voice cut into the negotiations suddenly.

Behind Kerry was a young man in a Morehouse College golf shirt, holding what was clearly an expensive camera in his hand. An overstuffed camera bag with *Fox Five News* stitched into the top flap was hanging over his shoulder.

"It would be an honor to take a picture of our new mayor and his family," the man remarked.

"Thanks, brother," Jamison said, flashing his practiced public smile. "We'd appreciate that. Hey, what's your name? I love meeting my Morehouse brothers, you know?" he continued, reaching out to shake the young man's hand.

"I'm Dax Thomas—a reporter with Fox Five News Atlanta," he said. "Good to meet you, Mayor Taylor. You're doing us Morehouse men proud."

"At your service," Jamison said and the men chuckled at some inside joke.

Kerry reluctantly got into the picture, standing behind Tyrian's shoulder opposite Jamison.

In minutes, the image would be featured on Fox News's main Web site. The caption: *An awkward moment at East Lake Golf Course this morning, when Mayor Taylor takes a picture with his ex-wife, Atlanta socialite Kerry Ann Jackson, and six-year-old son, Tyrian.*

The bottom bunk where Kerry lay remembering her past rattled with a thud. She quickly opened her eyes, ready to react and jumped up, hitting the top of her head on the bottom of the upper bunk.

"Owww!" she let out, looking at a boot on the floor beside her bed that was no doubt the source of the rattling. Her eyes left the boot and nervously forged a path up the orange jumpsuit to the face of the kicker she was certain had come to pummel her.

"Damn! Calm down, boo! It's just me!" Garcia-Bell held out her hands innocently as she laughed at Kerry's head bump and fearful eyes. "What? You thought I was Thompson coming to kick your ass?"

Kerry rolled her eyes and looked out of the cell past Garcia-Bell. "Where is she?" She sat up, rubbing her head.

"Probably somewhere starting more shit with someone else. You in here hiding out?"

"Basically."

"Well, what was you gonna do if I was her? This ain't some dorm room. She can see your skinny ass right through them bars," Garcia-Bell said, pointing to the open cell door as she took a seat beside Kerry on the bottom bunk.

The mattress above them was bare. Kerry's first cell mate, a white woman who'd stabbed her boyfriend five times in the head, had bonded out.

"Guess I don't care," Kerry said. "If I'm going to get beat up, what does it matter if she does it in here or out there? I'm still getting beat up."

"It would be worse in here. No one around. It'll take a while for the guards to get here," Garcia-Bell explained. "Plus, Thompson got a lot of enemies. You never know if someone might want to sneak some licks in if she starts something with you on the yard."

Kerry looked off and laughed a little to herself.

"What? What's so funny?" Garcia-Bell asked.

Kerry's mind switched from inside the walls of the prison to outside, where her world was so different. A simple word like *yard* could mean so many other things; however, none of them included a tiny outside space with nothing but dry, depleted dirt and female prisoners fighting fiercely over turns to use deflated basketballs and rusting gym equipment.

"That word—*yard*—it reminds me of where I went to college," Kerry replied, not knowing if she should mention her alma mater, Spelman College, if Garcia-Bell would've heard of the historically black college or knew what the term meant there. In 1998, Kerry's time on the yard included watching her best friend Marcy step with her sorority sisters, sitting on the steps in front of Manley Hall, chatting with her Spelman sisters and professors about images of black women in the media, the future of the black woman in politics and, of course, black love. There she was a third-generation Spelman girl, was called "Black Barbie," and had dozens of Morehouse brothers from the college across the street chasing after her. There she met Jamison.

"You gonna have to let that shit go—all that shit from outside—who you were, who you thought you were—if you gonna make it in here," Garcia-Bell cautioned. "Ain't no tea and crumpets behind these here bars. In order to survive, you gonna have to knuckle up."

"Knuckle up?"

"Fight, Kerry. You gonna have to fight. Ain't nobody ever taught you how to fight?"

"You mean, like actual fisticuffs?" Kerry said, watching a group of prisoners who always stuck together walk by her cell.

"Don't ever say that word again, but, yes, that's what I mean," Garcia–Bell confirmed, laughing.

"No—no one taught me how to fight. Who would? Who taught you?"

"*Mi madre,*" Garcia–Bell said, as if it should've been obvious.

"Your mother? Please. The closest Thirjane Jackson came to teaching me to fight was how to keep the mean girls in Jack and Jill from talking about me behind my back," Kerry said.

"Jack and Jill? Like that nursery rhyme?"

"Yes. It was a social club my mother made me join when I was young," Kerry explained. "Had to be her perfect little girl in Jack and Jill."

"Well, you far from that now. And thinking about that out there ain't gonna do nothing but get you caught up in here."

"That's the thing: I don't plan on getting caught up in here. I'm not staying here." Kerry had convinced herself of this. After days and weeks and months of not seeing the sun rise and set, and missing the joy of witnessing the summer season shift to a muggy Georgia fall while enjoying a walk through Piedmont Park, she promised herself she'd be home by the holiday season. She'd be with her family. Dress Tyrian as a pirate for Halloween. Help make Thanksgiving dinner. Trim the tree for Christmas without complaining. Dreams of those simple things kept her hopeful.

"Hmm. You keep saying you're getting out by this and that time, but then I keep seeing you here in the morning."

Kerry had already told Garcia–Bell all about her case—about

how when she ran up to the rooftop of the Westin to find her ex-husband that gray morning, she knew something was wrong, knew something was going to happen. There was a woman up there. The woman was the one who threw Jamison over the edge to his death. Not Kerry. Kerry still loved Jamison. In the hotel room where they'd been cuddling just hours before, they'd talked about getting remarried. Kerry would be his third wife—after he divorced his second wife, Val.

Garcia-Bell already knew the whole story. Like everyone else in Atlanta, rich and poor, young and old, black and white, criminals and noncriminals, she wanted to know how in the world the city's fourth black mayor—who'd come from nothing and promised the people everything—ended up split wide open with his heart and everything hanging out and his face crushed beyond recognition in the middle of Peachtree Street during morning rush-hour traffic. She'd even heard this very version of events from Kerry's mother when Thirjane Jackson had been interviewed by a reporter with Fox Five News. But she let Kerry retell it all a few times anyway. She felt Kerry needed to.

"Well, one day you're going to come looking for me and I'm not going to be here. I've got people in my corner rooting for me. It's going to work out. I believe that," Kerry said.

"People?" Garcia-Bell struggled not to sound cynical, but it was too hard. "By that you mean your ex-husband's widow? The one who's supposedly going to bust you out of here and help you find the killer?"

"Yes. I do," Kerry replied resolutely. "I told you, she knows I didn't do this and she has proof. It's taking her a little time, but she's helping my lawyer build my case and soon, everyone will know the truth. I'm innocent."

"Sure's taking her a long time."

"These things take time. You know that yourself."

Garcia-Bell had shared the particulars of her case with Kerry too.

GRACE OCTAVIA

"Well, there's long and then there's *loooonnnng*," Garcia-Bell pointed out.

"What's that mean?"

"Nothing." Garcia-Bell stood up, ready to leave. She didn't want to hurt her friend's feelings. Since she was a teenager, she'd been locked up for some reason or another and she knew the worst thing in the world was knowing the one person on the outside who could do anything about her case was doing absolutely nothing. She didn't want to put that on Kerry.

"Come on, spit it out," Kerry pushed.

"It's nothing. It's like I said—it's taking a long fucking time."

"But you know the situation. You know Val can't just bust me out of here," Kerry pleaded in a way that sounded like she was actually coaching herself.

Garcia-Bell pointed to the top bunk. "White girl stabbed her old man in the fucking head five times and she bonded out. Ain't got no kids. Ain't have no job. They got a fucking confession out of her. She home." She pointed to Kerry. "Ain't nobody see you throw your husband from the roof. You got a child. A career and you say you innocent. And you rich. You mean to tell me that woman and that lawyer she hired to get you out of jail can't even get you out on bond? Come on, girl. You ain't stupid. I know that."

"It's not that simple," Kerry tried.

"To me it is. You said it yourself: Y'all hated each other. Then your ex-husband threw her ass out on the street after she had a miscarriage and you and the broad got all chummy just because you gave her a couple of dollars so she could get a hotel room. Then your ex-husband ends up dead while she's still married to him and she's got all his money and is living up in his house and running the business you partially own. But you think she rushing to get you out of jail? You believe that?" Garcia-Bell paused and looked at Kerry with a friend's concern in her eyes. "Please say you don't. I mean, maybe you want to believe it because she the only card you got to play, but *wanting* to believe it and *actually* believing it—that's got to be different things."

Tears returned to Kerry's eyes. A lump in her throat obstructed any response to Garcia-Bell's damning assessment.

Garcia-Bell sighed and cursed herself inside for opening her mouth. "I'm sorry," she said, bending down to look at Kerry. "Look, don't stay in this cell. Get out until lights-out and if you need anything, you holler for me." She looked into Kerry's eyes and kissed her on the lips quickly before walking out.

Save the guards and guns and jumpsuits and poorly selected paint, visiting day at the women's jail in Fulton County might look like it was a family reunion or big birthday party. Children and grandparents were everywhere. Babies being burped over the shoulders of mothers who were strangers, husbands sneaking in kisses. Aging parents begging their daughters to do it right the next time she got out. Sons and daughters, silent but hopeful, some still young enough to think Mommy was away studying at college and led to believe this place with cinder-block walls and bars was a dormitory and not a jail. And it could look like that. It was a women's jail, so the guards kind of pushed back when the families came to visit. With too many limitations the women could become bothered and act up later unnecessarily, so the warden—whose mother had been locked up for writing bad checks when she was just seven years old—told the guards to keep a close eye, but not pry. The women were prisoners. Not their families.

The day after the incident in the cafeteria, Kerry was actually surprised when one of the guards showed up at her cell to announce that she had visitors waiting. She hadn't seen anyone in three weeks. She kept calling Val, but there was no answer. Even her lawyer seemed extra busy whenever Kerry got through. After her divorce, her best friend Marcy had been in Haiti working with Nurses Without Borders for months. While she promised to be at her Spelman sister's side as soon as her contract was up and she was stateside, the village where Marcy was assigned had few working phones and the mail system was spotty at best. And Kerry's mother? Well, Thirjane was no jail-house regular—even with her daughter there. That's why Kerry was surprised a second time when she got to the visitation room and found Thirjane sitting in there on a bench. Tyrian was beside her, looking down at his feet. Thirjane placed her hand on his knee when she saw Kerry walking toward them with her hand over her mouth, like she was already holding back a cry.

Tyrian looked up and bolted for his mother like she was run-ning in the other direction and he needed to catch up.

While this wasn't an uncommon scene in the visitation room, where over fifty inmates were sitting with their families, most everyone paused to get a look at the reunion. This wasn't just any seven-year-old son greeting his mother. It was the dead mayor's fatherless child wrapping his arms around the murderous ex-wife, who half of them believed was a woman scorned—and . . . well . . . *hell hath no fury* . . .

Kerry got down on her knees and let her only baby smash right into her with his arms open. He nearly knocked her over and certainly knocked the wind out of her, but she was grateful for the intensity of the greeting. She'd need to hold on to that feeling for as long as she could.

"I love you," she whispered into Tyrian's ear once she wrapped her arms around him. "I love you so much." Saying she missed him always sounded like a given when she was coming up with something to say to Tyrian, during the few times her mother had brought the boy to the jail. She decided she'd go with the one thing she wanted him to think of when he was away from her: that she loved him.

She backed up and looked him over. Saw how much he'd grown. Those front teeth were almost back in place now and he was so much taller, had long arms and legs. Kerry touched them like maybe they were fake. She thought of Jamison. How he'd feel seeing Tyrian looking like this, becoming a little man-child. The tears she'd promised she wouldn't let loose were rolling down her cheeks.

"What's wrong, Mama?" Tyrian asked like he'd done something wrong.

"Nothing, baby. You're just all grown up. Getting so big and tall," Kerry said as they walked to the bench and table where Thirjane was waiting.

"You always say that, Mama. But I ain't taller. I'm the same," Tyrian said.

"No, you're growing. You just can't tell because you don't see yourself all the time. It's perspective," Kerry said.

"Perspective?" he asked.

"It means point of view—like how you see something or someone is based on your point of view," Kerry replied, stopping in front of her mother.

Thirjane stayed seated in her red St. John's suit. Her quilted Chanel purse was on her lap, her hands clasped over the top. She snapped, "It's not *ain't*, Tyrian. That's not proper English. I told you to stop using that slang."

"Sorry, Nana," Tyrian mumbled, sitting down beside her.

"Hello to you too, Mama," Kerry said, bending down to kiss her mother. Through thirty-five years of trial and error, she knew better than to be upset that Thirjane didn't run toward her with open arms, saying how much she'd missed her daughter in the month since she'd been to see her. This was Thirjane Jackson. All old black money, blue-vein Atlanta. She was the kind of Southern belle who likely had a silk handkerchief with her initials stitched into it in her purse. She was the kind of Southern belle who took pride in openly revealing that she had no idea on God's green Earth where a motel, crackhouse or jailhouse might be located. Now, here she was, visiting her only child in a jailhouse, and everybody knew it.

Kerry kissed her on the cheek and she pretended to do the

same, but really only kissed the air. She'd begged her daughter not to marry that Jamison Taylor boy. He wasn't even a real Morehouse man like Kerry's father had been—not with having only gone to the school because he lucked up on a full scholarship. That wasn't good breeding. That was a handout—a hand down. Who were his people? She never forgave Kerry for marrying him and the current situation seemed like punishment for both of them for that one betrayal.

Kerry sat down and went through all of her motherly questions with Tyrian. She asked about his schoolwork and his golf game. Listened to more stories about his new teeth and new friends. The girl in his class who was so pretty none of the other boys would speak to her. But he always did. He always sat right next to her and said something nice.

Nana Thirjane was on hand to correct each of his poorly selected words—both those with bad grammar and weak diction. Kerry smiled and listened intently, but as the judging went on, she couldn't help but to remember when her mother would carry on like that whenever she tried to get a sentence out.

"Sounds like you have a crush," Kerry joked with Tyrian.

"I like her," Tyrian admitted, poking out his chest a little, "but I'm keeping my options open."

"Options?" Kerry repeated, looking over at her mother and laughing at how adult he sounded. "Boy, what do you know about options?"

"My daddy told me it's not enough for a woman to be beautiful. She has to be smarter than she is beautiful. And nice. Be really nice to me, always. Nice to everyone." Tyrian looked proud to remember his father's advice, but also sad. As could be expected, he'd taken the sudden death very hard.

Kerry reached over the table to touch Tyrian's hand. "Your daddy gave you some good advice," she said softly. "Very good."

After a while, Thirjane sent Tyrian off to play with some other children who were putting a massive puzzle together on the floor in the center of the room as the adults took time to chat.

"So how are you doing?" Thirjane asked.

"How do I look like I'm doing?"

"Well, your hair is growing out. Maybe you could perm it again. It's so nappy." Thirjane reached over the table to finger Kerry's gray roots. "Could definitely use some hair dye."

"I'm in jail and you're worried about my naps and grays?" Kerry snapped. "There's no one in here to impress, Mama. Not your sorors or their stuffy sons." She flicked her mother's hand away like she was thirteen again and being forced to wear her hair up in a bun to attend one of those Jack and Jill balls she so hated.

"That has nothing to do with anything. What did you go bringing that up for?"

"Why haven't you been here to visit me in a month?"

"I was just here three weeks ago."

"You promised you'd bring Tyrian every week. You said you'd do it."

"So you want me to bring my grandson to a jailhouse every week to see his mother?" Thirjane leaned toward Kerry and whispered through her coffee-stained dentures, "You know that boy is urinating in the bed almost every night? And that's on the nights when I can actually get him to sleep without crying his eyes out about missing you and his father. How's seeing you in jail going to help him?"

"His therapist said—" Kerry tried, but Thirjane cut her off.

"That therapist doesn't know a thing about raising a black boy!" Thirjane said so directly Kerry knew to leave the matter alone. "Got me bringing my grandbaby to a jail to see his mama. Then when he's sixteen and ends up here on his own, everybody's going to wonder why. The less he's here, the better."

"Fine. Just once a month then, Mama. Please." Kerry sounded like a teenager negotiating curfew.

Thirjane cut her eyes hard on Kerry. "I know. It's only been three weeks. And have you thought about me? About me coming here? What people are saying?"

"Yes. I have. Because this is all about *you*. Right?" Kerry pointed out sarcastically. Every time her mother visited, it went this way—it would somehow go from being all about Tyrian to all about Thirjane; Kerry was always last. And it was interesting too, because as ashamed as Thirjane claimed she was, aside from her onetime interview on the news, she was hardly involved in Kerry's case. She cried and promised to avenge her child when Kerry had gotten arrested, but as soon as the cameras turned on her and one detective suggested that maybe she'd had something to do with the murder too, Thirjane quickly disappeared. She wouldn't even talk to Kerry's lawyer. She'd hired her own and said she needed to protect herself and her "interests."

"Don't be flip with me, Kerry Ann. You're not the only one suffering here. That's all I was saying," Thirjane said. "And what's going on with your case, anyway? I thought that Memphis girl and that Jewish lawyer you two hired were getting you out on bail, at least until the trial starts, anyway."

"Under the direction of District Attorney Brown, the judge agreed that due to the nature of the crime, I'm a threat to society." Kerry waved at Tyrian, who'd held up two pieces of the puzzle he'd fit together.

"A threat? That imposter of a DA, Chuck Brown, is the real threat to this city—sleeping with any woman who'll open her legs. And to think, he's a Morehouse man." Thirjane put her nose in the air after that comment.

"Well, Chuck Brown also cited your connections and my money and Jamison's money—adding that I'm a flight risk."

"That's a sack of manure—pardon my choice of words. But I don't believe that for one minute. Seems that lawyer and Val could do something about it. Listen to me, girl: that whore means to keep you in here. Meanwhile, she's out in the world living it up like her kind never knew how. You know she moved her mama into Jamison's house? In Cascade? Driving his cars. Using his club memberships." Thirjane clutched her purse and whispered, "I saw her at the country club."

Kerry looked down.

"Hmm . . . She's living high on the hog and you're living here." Thirjane looked around at the prisoners and guards, the walls and discreetly placed bars.

"Well, if you really feel bad about it, you can always help with my case. It's not like I have a whole lot of people in my corner right now. I just know Val has my back and she was the only one who stood up when I needed her" Kerry said, looking into her mother's eyes.

"What am I supposed to do? Put my house up to bust you out of here?" Thirjane whispered angrily.

"You know I have money. It's not about that."

"I'm an old woman. I'm not cut out for this. I have Tyrian and he's already a handful. Between his grades and acting up in school, I'm just holding on here." Thirjane's voice weakened like she was about to cry.

"Right. Sure." Kerry was getting tired and she refused to placate her mother.

The buzzer sounded over the loudspeaker in the room, letting the inmates and visitors know visiting time was over.

As the guards started walking through the room to facilitate the proper good-bye procedures, Thirjane reached out and held Kerry's hand.

"I'm really sorry about this," she said with her wrinkled, diamond ring–clad fingers shaking a little under early symptoms of palsy. "More sorry than you'll ever know."

Tyrian appeared and hugged his mother with his arms around her neck. He was already crying. He knew what the buzzer meant.

"I want to stay here with you," Tyrian mumbled in his mother's ear. "I promise I won't pee in the bed."

Kerry kissed him on the cheek. "It's not about that, baby. You just can't stay here. That's not how it works."

"But you didn't kill my daddy. You shouldn't have to stay here," Tyrian said a little louder.

"What?" Kerry backed up and looked at him hard. "Where did you hear that?" She looked at her mother, who shrugged.

"In school. Matthew Warrenstein said you did it—said you killed my father, but I know it's not true, Mama. I know you didn't do that."

"No. I didn't." Kerry's hand was wet from wiping away both her and Tyrian's tears. "And you don't believe that. You don't listen to those boys at that school. You understand?"

"Yes."

The room was clearing out and a guard walked past to give Kerry a sharp stare before she came back to inform her that it was absolutely time for her guests to depart.

"I'll see you next time." Kerry tried to loosen Tyrian's arms from around her neck, but he wouldn't let go.

"No! Mama! No!"

"Don't do this," she said, feeling his heartbeat quickening against hers. "Please."

"No!"

Thirjane stood and put her purse over her shoulder before reaching for Tyrian. Once she touched him, the boy started hollering and tightening his hold around his mother's neck.

"No, Mama! No! Don't make me go! I can stay. I'll be good. I won't pee in the bed!"

His tears were coming too quickly for Kerry to wipe them, so she started the heartbreaking task of peeling her son's powerless, pencil-thin arms from around her neck.

"No, Mama! Don't!"

She closed her eyes to escape the scene.

The boy's hollering turned to something like funeral wailing. It went deep down to his gut and sprang out with so much register the guards knew there was no way his grandmother would be able to get him out of that room by herself.

"No! No! No!" Kerry cried when two guards stepped in to pull Tyrian away. "Please don't. Please!"

"Mama! No!" Tyrian hollered furiously with the guards, who were nice enough, calling him "son" and such, physically lifting him off of the ground and carrying him away from his mother, kicking and screaming.

Kerry left the catastrophic farewell a wreck. She was crying so hard, the other inmates just moved out of her way as she headed back to her cell. They'd heard Tyrian's screams. It was a mother's pain too many of them knew. They made a little pathway for Kerry to walk along, undisturbed. Some showed support by patting her shoulder knowingly as she passed. Others called out, "It'll be okay" and "Be strong." It was one of those moments when being a woman or being a mother superseded all other circumstances and surroundings for these inmates in a jailhouse.

But Kerry couldn't really see or hear or feel any of this. Though she was moving along, every part of her being was with her child, hurting and aching, mourning the reality of separation. The only thing that kept her putting one foot in front of the other to get to her cell was knowing his little face was waiting there in the picture above her bed. She could lie down there. Let her pain fall back into the mattress. Close her eyes and be with him again that morning in his bedroom before they took the picture. She would tell him everything was going to be okay. It would be perfect. He would say, "It could be perfect. You're right, Mama." She'd wink at him and kiss his cheek.

But all of that would have to wait. Because only a few steps from the cell, someone blocked Kerry's pathway.

"What? You thought I forgot about your ass-whipping?"

Thompson was standing there, cracking the knuckles on her fat fingers.

"I'm not in the mood for this," Kerry said, sounding more tired than fearful. "I just saw my little boy and—"

Thompson cut her off. "I don't give a fuck about that."

"Thompson, I just said I'm not in the mood for this," Kerry said solemnly. "I can't deal with you and whatever pathology you're demonstrating right now. I just want to—"

"Path—what? What you call me?" Thompson poked Kerry's shoulder enough to push her back a few steps.

Some of the women gathering in a tight fight circle started telling Thompson to back off and leave Kerry alone, but all still stayed to see what would happen.

"I didn't call you anything," Kerry said. "I'm just letting you know I'm not trying to fight you. I'm upset about my son—"

"Fuck your son!" Thompson spat, stepping in so closely to Kerry's face a spray of saliva dotted the bridge of Kerry's nose.

"What did you say?" Kerry asked, feeling some switch of anger flicked on within the mix of sadness, loneliness, and now humiliation. "What did you say about my son?" Kerry didn't know it, but she was stepping up higher, up on her toes a little bit, so she could be eye to eye with Thompson. She was also balling up her fists and tightening her jaw.

"I said: fuck your—"

This time Kerry cut Thompson off—but not with words, with a tight fist to the mouth. Kerry flung her closed hand up high and came down on Thompson's mouth so hard it sounded like a bag of sand hitting the earth.

Every mouth in the spectators' circle was hanging wide open with surprise. Even Thompson seemed unprepared for the blow to her face.

"What the fuck?" she shouted loud enough to get some of the guards' attention. "You hit me!"

Before Thompson could cock her fist back to get a lick in, some rush of blood to Kerry's already heavy heart pushed her into a hysterical rage.

She just attacked.

Started clawing at Thompson's face with her arms flying in an uncontrollable pinwheel that made everyone around her back up and left Thompson taking hits and trying to figure out where and when she could get some in.

Kerry pounded and pounded as tears shook loose from her eyes. She was crying like she was the one being beat on.

With all of the fists landing on her, Thompson found herself backing up to a wall. And Kerry followed. Swinging and kicking. Cursing, even. "Fuck my son? Fuck my son? No! Fuck you! Fuck you!"

Thompson cowered into something that looked like a ball or a porcupine trying to hide herself away. But Kerry kept coming for her.

By the time security pushed through the circle (and it was only just minutes into the battle), they had to pull Kerry off Thompson the same way they'd peeled Tyrian from Kerry less than an hour ago.

Even when they got her loose and Thompson jumped up from her cocoon like she was ready to do something, Kerry looked like she'd been possessed, with her extremities flailing and obscenities of every language she could remember coming from her mouth—Latin in junior high, Spanish in high school, French in college—she cursed Thompson out in every language.

As guards dragged her away, the other inmates looked at Thompson with serious scrutiny.

"Guess you showed her," someone shouted from the back of the crowd and they all laughed.

"Bougie bitch beat your ass!" someone else added, giggling.

"She snuck me!" Thompson defended herself. "Y'all saw that! The fight wasn't fair!"

As the other guards started yelling for the inmates to clear the floor, some replied, "Bet you won't be looking for a rematch!"

She wouldn't.

GREAT BOOKS, GREAT SAVINGS!

When You Visit Our Website:
www.kensingtonbooks.com
You Can Save Money Off The Retail Price
Of Any Book You Purchase!

- All Your Favorite Kensington Authors
- New Releases & Timeless Classics
- Overnight Shipping Available
- eBooks Available For Many Titles
- All Major Credit Cards Accepted

Visit Us Today To Start Saving!
www.kensingtonbooks.com

All Orders Are Subject To Availability.
Shipping and Handling Charges Apply.
Offers and Prices Subject To Change Without Notice.